A TALE OF PIERROT
and other stories

BOOKS BY GEORGE DENNISON

The Lives of Children
Oilers and Sweepers and Other Stories
Shawno, a novella
Luisa Domic, a novel

And Then a Harvest Feast (FOR CHILDREN)

George Dennison

A Tale of PIERROT
and other stories

PERENNIAL LIBRARY

HARPER & ROW, PUBLISHERS
New York
Cambridge, Philadelphia, San Francisco, Washington
London, Mexico City, São Paulo
Singapore, Sydney

A TALE OF PIERROT AND OTHER STORIES. Copyright © 1987 by George Dennison. All rights reserved. Printed in the United States of America. No part of this book may be used or reproduced in any manner whatsoever without written permission except in the case of brief quotations embodied in critical articles and reviews. For information address Harper & Row, Publishers, Inc., 10 East 53rd Street, New York, N.Y. 10022. Published simultaneously in Canada by Fitzhenry & Whiteside Limited, Toronto.

FIRST EDITION

Designed by Ruth Bornschlegel

Copy edited by Margaret Cheney

Library of Congress Cataloging-in-Publication Data
Dennison, George, 1925–
    A tale of Pierrot and other stories.
    I. Title.
PS3554.E55T35 1987   813'.54   86-46056
ISBN 0-06-055079-1   87 88 89 90 91 MPC 8 7 6 5 4 3 2 1
ISBN 0-06-096169-4 (pbk.)   87 88 89 90 91 MPC 8 7 6 5 4 3 2 1

To my family, as always

CONTENTS

The author gratefully acknowledges
the generous support
of the Yaddo Corporation.

A TALE OF PIERROT
and other stories

ON BEING A SON
A Story of the Fifties

Sunlight was pouring into the room. A breeze from the open window eddied across the bed and touched the naked shoulders of a dark-haired young man who lay sleeping there. He lifted his head, and a look of joy came to his face. He had heard his mother in the garden talking with his friends. Eagerly, as if in love, he threw back the sheet and drew a breath to call to them . . . and a moment later was sitting on the bed, panting and depressed. The voices were ringing in his ears. The realness of the dream frightened him. Most disturbing of all was the lingering vivid sense of something delicious, some quality of life. . . .

He dressed himself and staggered to the kitchen, where he ate a piece of toast, fried some eggs, and brewed coffee. As his body revived, his chronic anger revived also, and he resumed the harsh ruminations that filled his days with images of the middle-class life he had rejected. He sat a long while smoking cigarettes and drinking coffee. He was making his living as a laborer, working as the need arose with pick and shovel, sledge hammer, and pneumatic drill; but he had just been paid, he had cleared the back rent and had put twenty-three dollars in his pocket. He would not be obliged to work again for several days.

Beyond the sunny windows, where he had imagined lilacs, grass, and tall trees, lay the streets of New York's Lower East Side. The tenement he lived in was a small one. His rooms were one flight up and cost him only twenty dollars a month.

He had picked up castaway furniture on the streets at night, and had bought some faded lawn chairs at the Salvation Army. Orange crates, up-ended and stacked against the walls, held his books. For a while the place had had a certain charm; classmates would come down with gallon jugs of wine, share potluck suppers, and sit around drumming on bongos and cans. He had been popular at school, where his intelligence and athletic good looks had counted for a great deal, but something had gone wrong, he had dropped his graduate work, he had not become a writer or a scholar. The apartment that once had been pleasant was dirty and bleak. It was like the club-houses that children make for themselves, in which the tables and chairs do actually function but are also symbols of tables and chairs. That he should be living this way at the age of twenty-eight mortified him and distressed the few friends left to him, who were adjusting to marriages, careers, and children.

He sat drinking coffee at the picnic table in the kitchen. He was excitable and appetitive, and now that he had eaten he began to ache with sexual longing, and he thought of Ellen Roth, who was available to him. He had known her for several months, but their love-making had been so disappointing that he had decided not to see her again. She never warmed, never got beyond the shepherding of her mind. She seemed to be covered with a pelt of numbness, and he took that numbness as a form of rejection. She had said to him, "I'm probably attracted to you because you're Irish and I'm Jewish" (his name was O'Brien, though on his mother's side he was French), and he had said to her, "Yeah, I guess," thinking to himself, "Oh God—she's not *attracted* to me at all." She was the only woman to have come to his apartment in many months. He had done a lot of listening that first night in bed, but she had quizzed him, too. She was in psychotherapy, and her questions, which at first had seemed mere babbling, had surprised him by their continuity. She had learned a great deal about him, and had hit on something that amounted to an open wound in his life. "You're not from New York, are you?" she said. He came from a small town near the city of Pittsburgh, but it wasn't like the suburbs of the East. He said, "No. How'd you know that?" "Your accent, mostly. But it's more than that. A different rhythm. You're not as quick on the uptake as New Yorkers are. And you sort of seem . . . I don't know . . . surprised by too many things. Do you have brothers and sisters?" He grunted in the dark. "I knew I was right about that," she went on. "You definitely have the character of an only child. There's something funny about you and your father, isn't there? I mean, I can hardly picture you with a father, and yet you don't seem to be a father-hating type."

"My father died when I was ten years old," he said.

"Oh, really?" said Ellen.

O'Brien's father had killed himself. Among his many painful feelings was a feeling of shame, and the shame was compounded by the fact that he hadn't known the truth for years, and finally had been told it by a stranger.

"Was he young?" Ellen asked. "What did he die of?"

"Yes, he died young," O'Brien said. "He had a stroke."

—and, as always when he spoke those evasive words, the scene of discovery came to mind. It had not been a stranger at all, though he thought of it that way, but his girlfriend at the time. They had been out in his mother's car at night, making love. She had asked him directly—clearly assuming that he knew—why his father had killed himself. The chill of that moment still lurked inside him.

Ellen hadn't sensed the lie. She had gone on with her investigation of his character, asking, "Do you have a stepfather?" to which he had answered "No," with a little laugh.

He finished his fifth cup of coffee, and his fourth cigarette. He hadn't moved, yet he had been glancing at the window continually. The sunlight excited him and drew him, and deepened his sadness terribly.

He had needed an hour to reach his characteristic condition of anger, impatience, resentment, yearning, sorrow, and incipient despair—a condition so overheated and abrasive that few people found him tolerable, and yet those few were drawn to him.

He jumped up from the table quite abruptly and ran down the stairs. But when he emerged from the building into the sunlight and the noisy, broad day, every impulse died and he stood there on the sidewalk bewildered.

He was dressed in a white shirt open at the neck and with the cuffs turned back on his forearms. He wore moccasin shoes and khaki pants. He thrust his hands into his pockets, lowered his head, and strode away furiously, he didn't know where.

1.

In New York in the early fifties a community of artists, no longer small, was scattered through the neighborhood around Tenth Street and Third Avenue. Its principal figures were a few young poets and a larger number of abstract painters, both middle-aged and young. The work of the painters was radically new and bold, and was internationalist in spirit, in all of which ways it differed profoundly from the conformist temper of the country as a whole. The new art, to O'Brien, was like a language, and at times it seemed to be the only one addressed to him in his uncertainties. He had become acquainted with a number of painters, attended their galleries, and occasionally visited their studios.

When he left his apartment that morning, therefore, at a loss for something to do, he set out in the direction of the midtown galleries, though many, he knew, would be closed. He had gone only a couple of blocks, however, when his feeling of aloneness in the huge city and his sexual longing combined abruptly into an agony of need. He went to a pay phone and for several moments stood motionless in the booth thinking of Ellen's legs and belly, her toneless, intelligent voice, her small apartment, in which there were too many fabrics. . . . Perhaps they could listen to music, some Verdi or Beethoven, something powerful that would keep his spirits from sinking. He began to dial her number. She lay unmoving beneath him and said in a neutral voice, "You're a great lover, O'Brien." He clicked off and dialed instead the number of Malcolm Dudley, with whom he often drank. Dudley was seven years older than O'Brien and was fond of him, though at times impatient.

O'Brien said, "Hi, Mal, what are you up to? Are you hard at work?"

"I haven't even had breakfast yet."

"Did I wake you up?" He hated the guilty, supplicating notes that hovered in his voice.

"I was up already."

"Are you doing galleries today?" Dudley was well established as a critic and historian of contemporary art. O'Brien occasionally went with him on his rounds and had begun to wonder if he might not try his hand at reviews. He asked this question, however, not because he thought that Dudley would be making rounds—he rather doubted it; August was dead—but because he was unwilling to admit that he was calling out of loneliness.

"No," said Dudley. He cleared his throat. When he spoke again, O'Brien could hear both hesitation and eagerness in his voice. "Actually," said Dudley, "that interview with Brockmeyer came through. I'm going over today."

"Today? To his studio?"

"Yes."

"That's wonderful, Mal." O'Brien paused, gritting his teeth and closing his eyes.

Dudley paused too, and then said, "I guess you could come if you wanted to."

"God yes," said O'Brien.

He emerged from the phone booth quite transformed, and so excited that he forgave himself for having begged to be taken along. Brockmeyer long ago had achieved the status of a modern classic, and was one of the people O'Brien idolized, though they had never met. As had other European artists, he had fled the Nazis, coming via Holland, but unlike the others he hadn't gone back.

It was twelve-thirty. Now that he had a destination and only an hour and a half to kill, O'Brien lifted his head and walked with a buoyancy that drew attention.

He went up Hester Street to Orchard, and passed between the pushcarts and the tiny stores, glancing on both sides at racks of dresses, suits, coats, big wooden trays of shoes, purses, hats, shirts, sweaters. Watchful hucksters dressed in drab suits stood in their doorways and on the curb looking at everyone—so it seemed to O'Brien—with suspicion and contempt. He went on to Allen Street and passed the public baths. Ahead of him a blue-uniformed cop was bending over an unconscious figure sprawled across some tenement steps. The cop swung his club against the man's feet and prodded his ribs. As O'Brien passed, the cop swung again, saying "You! You! Get up! Get the hell up!" The cop hit his feet again. The wino groaned and lifted his head. He was dressed in a filthy gray suit. He muttered something, but seemed unable to organize his legs. O'Brien looked back. The cop was hitting him again. The sound of the club set O'Brien's teeth on edge. He turned and went toward the two, alarmed at what he was doing and at what might happen if the wrong voice came out of him. He disliked the police. At times he hated them.

The cop looked up. He had seen O'Brien stop, and now with narrowing eyes he straightened, hefting the club and looking at O'Brien's shoulders.

O'Brien winked at him and with a toss of his head said, "I'll get him off your beat; I know the guy." The cop didn't answer. He was young and tough, but had a look of intelligence in his eyes. At last he said, "Awright, take 'im," and walked away, looking back.

O'Brien lifted the man and ducked his head under one arm. The drunk was emaciated and stank dreadfully. They went along slowly. The drunk revived somewhat and muttered, "God bless you. God bless you," and O'Brien said harshly, "Shut up! You stink!" "Where are we?" said the drunk. "Whatta you care?" said O'Brien. "You're in heaven. Who gives a shit?" "God bless you," said the drunk. "You stink," said O'Brien. He set the man down in a warehouse doorway just east of the Bowery, on a large piece of cardboard that obviously had been slept on. The man seemed to be in pain. His grimy, sweaty face was genteel, but was fixed in an expression of self-loathing. It was a face of suicide, of a man who regarded himself as a victim and perhaps could not imagine that there were some who might see him as a murderer. O'Brien despised him, yet when the man asked for a cigarette O'Brien gave him the rest of his Camels, and inserted a folder of matches under the cellophane. He walked away, glad to be out of the stink and pleased with himself, especially for that inspired address to the cop, the wink, and that well-tuned voice.

He went to Washington Square Park, thinking he might sit for a while on the big circular rim of the fountain, but when he came within the orbit of the bongo drums and passed through to the orbit of the guitars and throaty voices, he thought of the people he would find there, whom for years he had been encountering and avoiding at the same old bars, and he turned north without stopping. On Eighth Street he lingered at a bookstore window. Standing upright in a semicircle were twenty copies of a new book by one of the fashionable young poets of New York, homosexual, urbane, intelligent, gifted. The books alternately exhibited the title on the front and the photograph on the back. O'Brien felt crushed by envy, first of the work, but even more of the way of life to which it belonged, the interlocking circles of successful people, the worldly, intelligent pleasures of their gatherings, and the clearly marked stages in the futures of careers. He stood there in a reverie of self-abasement . . . into which there came the toneless voice and damaging, accurate questions of Ellen Roth: "How can you stand it, O'Brien? Idleness must be more painful than anything. You're like a man in jail. And you're like the jail."

O'Brien shuddered and left the window. He drank one beer at the Cedar Bar and then went to Broadway and Twelfth, where he saw Malcolm Dudley waiting for him, wearing a neat short-sleeved white shirt, open at the throat.

Dudley's dark eyes behind his horn-rimmed glasses were shining and his fleshy lips were stretched in what seemed to be a helpless grin. The hesitation O'Brien had heard on the phone was gone.

"Do you realize," said Dudley, shaking O'Brien's arm, "that Brockmeyer has given only one interview since he came here in forty-seven, and that was to *Time* magazine? Do you realize it?"

O'Brien did realize it. Dudley had mentioned it previously three or four times.

Their relationship was odd. Each condescended to the other with affectionate superiority, yet each found important things to admire. On O'Brien's part it was Dudley's learning, which O'Brien had come to see was no mere hoarding of information but a moral fact, an authentic virtue; most of all he admired his friend's intense engagement in his work. Dudley's idea of small talk was to raise some question of aesthetics, or some point of biography or social history. O'Brien's reaction to this was more than just admiring: he doted on it and clung to it—it was the very thing that was missing in himself. Dudley was aware of this and was touched by it, and as teachers often feel of certain pupils, he felt that O'Brien's intelligence was superior to his own. He admired the structural unity of O'-Brien's thought, and the fact that it was permeated by feeling. O'Brien's comments on particular paintings were trenchant and fertile, and on several occasions Dudley had made use of his actual words, asking permission at first, but O'Brien had laughed, saying, "Take it, Mal," and Dudley discovered that he was so little aware of himself that he didn't recognize his own thought when he saw it in print. Once, reading *Art News* at Dudley's apartment and coming in total forgetfulness on a brief analysis of his own, O'Brien had read the words aloud in a praising voice, and had added, looking up from the magazine, "Damn good, Mal!"

They rang a buzzer at a wide door set back from the sidewalk without steps, spoke into an intercom, and climbed the broad stairway of a massive loft building there on Broadway. They climbed to the very top and rang a bell beside a metal door painted white. The door was opened by a dark-haired, strikingly handsome, sullen boy of fourteen, who didn't speak to them, or even close the door behind them (O'Brien did that), and who preceded them across the room as if they weren't there.

O'Brien gasped as he entered the huge space. He walked forward as if on tiptoe, his eyes darting this way and that. He heard Dudley beside him say, "My God!" It was as if music had begun to play, and as if the air and light were not the dull presences of the grimy city outside, but the luminous medium of childhood. Everywhere he looked his eye encountered the saturated colors and the powerful, simplified forms of Brockmeyer's paintings. They leaned edge to edge all around the room, and against tables and chairs, and even against the paintings of other artists that decorated the living area.

Brockmeyer was fifty-eight years old. He was erect and tall, with a broad, bony ribcage and bony shoulders. O'Brien could not imagine that he ever really relaxed, or was ever passive, confused, or dull. His skull was large and looked even more massive because of the thickness and coarseness of his graying blond hair. His gray eyes were extraordinarily aggressive. He wore a navy polo shirt, seersucker pants, leather sandals, and a dark-banded expensive watch. There was nothing in him whatever of the American boy that O'Brien, without realizing it, invariably looked for in other men. Brockmeyer's fame had come early in life, and this was another of the things that to O'Brien seemed awesome, not simply for the fact of accomplishment but for the qualities it implied: self-knowledge at an early age; amenability to instruction; the calm required to stay indoors; the self-possession required to be alone. . . .

But there was still another source of O'Brien's charmed amazement on entering that marvelous space, and this was the woman who, in an attitude of familiar intimacy, her head tilted back, stood talking to Brockmeyer amidst the large potted plants of the living area. She was beautiful. She was entirely and without any qualification desirable, and was so exactly O'Brien's type that his mouth went dry and his knees trembled. He felt pangs of yearning, as for love already lost, because her life was so remote from his, and she seemed so much the very prize of fame and achievement. He felt invisible in his longing, or like a dog who might wind among their feet, or lie in a corner and look upward toward their faces. But she glanced at him and smiled. He became visible. Her smile was an almost maternal, sympathetic smile, and yet it was playful and girlish. Her smile teased him because he stood there abjectly in love with her—and it commiserated with him tenderly, precisely because he stood there so forlornly in love with her. He saw at once that she had had many lovers.

Her hair was a glossy black, short, wavy, and fluffy. Her eyes were a deep brown almost black. She was small but full-bodied, and her well-set hips flexed gracefully when she walked. Something about that walking enchanted O'Brien, the way her torso rode along above her hips, so lightly at rest, and the way she set each foot so firmly and lightly just the right distance from her body. She wore a sleeveless beige dress of silky jersey gathered in folds by a narrow belt. Her tanned arms were shapely and smooth. She seemed to be in her early thirties and was apparently the mother of the sullen boy, who now sat crosswise on one of the easy chairs, legs dangling, reading a magazine.

Brockmeyer came to Dudley and O'Brien. The woman sat on a sofa and picked up a large book from the coffee table. She kicked off her shoes and curled her feet under her with the book on her lap.

Dudley said, "I hope you've had a chance to read the material I sent you. I'd like to do a piece similar to the one on Rothko." Dudley had written these words in a letter to Brockmeyer, and then had said them on the phone, and now, because he was flustered, was saying them still again.

Brockmeyer said, "Yes, yes . . ." but later O'Brien saw the unopened manila envelope on a table with other mail.

The painter was not the least bit affable, but he was so immediate in all that he did, was so wholly himself and so observantly aware of his visitors that a lively informal manner became possible to them all. He shook O'Brien's hand and looked into his face with an uninhibited, unmoderated scrutiny that made O'Brien blink and clear his throat.

"Go look around," Brockmeyer said. "We can talk in a few minutes." Both Dudley and O'Brien had been glancing aside at the paintings. "These are all from the last three years," he said, as they started across the room. "The older things are at Moeller's now, most of them. Some are at Moon's." His pronunciation of English words was slightly Germanic; the accent was British, not American.

O'Brien and Dudley began a tour of the paintings. Dudley took out a notebook. Three galleries were coordinating a retrospective exhibition that would open in six weeks. This recent work had not been apportioned yet among the dealers.

O'Brien glanced from time to time at the woman on the sofa. Twice their eyes met and they exchanged a smile.

Nobody in the city was painting like Brockmeyer. Certain critics wanted to condemn him for his imagery, but this wasn't easy to do, and Brockmeyer's case was helped by the fact that imagery had appeared recently in the work of de Kooning. Justin Solomon had written, "It's late in the day for this unreconstructed German Expressionism, and for literary references of the kind that abound in this work"—but evidently it wasn't late at all: Brockmeyer's work was more than ever talked about, and even the abstract painters liked it.

O'Brien had admired it for several years. He went excitedly from one painting to the next, wondering how the simplified, sometimes crude figures achieved their power and avoided awkwardness and triviality. He was taken especially by a series of smaller paintings leaning against the larger ones. He studied them the first time around, and later went back to them while Dudley and Brockmeyer talked. These told the story of Perseus, Pegasus, and Medusa—or rather, worked variations on those themes. In one, Perseus, wearing the winged sandals of Hermes and a billowing cloak, otherwise naked, tumbled warmly and as it seemed rapturously among the stars high above the ocean, tumbled as one might sprawl on the grass on a summer night. It was like a dream, a strangely erotic dream, both grandiose and intimate. It was as if the youth had been depicted in the flush of returning blood after the moment of orgasm. Far below, in the corner of the painting, and not yet in Perseus's sight lay the tiny rock and tiny naked figure of the chained Andromeda. In another of the paintings the two monstrous Gorgons, and Medusa, their coldly beautiful mortal sister, lay sleeping before their island cave. Scattered near them on the beach like pieces of sculpture lay the intruders who had been turned to stone by the Gorgons' glare. In another Perseus was walking backward like a dreamer in a film by Cocteau. He was staring at Medusa's image in his shield, and the crooked sword had begun the backward arc that would take off her head. Finally, in a group of three paintings that ended the series, the winged horse sprang upward in jets of blood from Medusa's neck.

Brockmeyer introduced the woman, whose name was Claudia. She made drinks for everyone, and spoke to her son, who grunted something negative without lifting his head.

They sat together in the living area. It was set off from the studio by a line of low bookcases and a luxuriant tangle of greenery. Brockmeyer and Claudia sat on one sofa, Dudley and O'Brien on the other. Again she kicked off her shoes and tucked her feet under her. She smiled at O'Brien as she did this. He was watching her raptly, and was no more aware of himself than a child might be. Brockmeyer, however, was entirely aware, and so was Dudley, who was surprised to see that Brockmeyer didn't mind his mistress's flirtation but seemed bemused and was even regarding O'Brien in what seemed to be a kindly way. In any event, he was studying him with a very active curiosity.

They talked of the forthcoming three-part exhibition. Both Dudley and O'Brien expressed their admiration of the paintings there in the room.

Dudley said, "I'd like to run through the biographical chronology with you, and if anything occurs to you at the different dates, anything to fill out the reader's sense of your life—friends and colleagues at different dates, family events—I'd like to reach some kind of balance between . . ."

Claudia said, "I liked your piece on Rothko. It was really nice that way."

Dudley turned to Brockmeyer with an inquiring look. He had written the first seriously detailed study of Rothko and had won praise for it. Brockmeyer said, "Good. Good. There are two chronologies . . ."

"I have them both," said Dudley.

"There are errors in both," said Brockmeyer. "We can correct them now." He was ready for another drink. No one else was. He crossed the room to the liquor cabinet. He was drinking scotch on ice.

Claudia said to Dudley, "There's going to be a little show of Karl's graphics at Levine's. It's sort of a prologue to the big show—just a few things, but it's definitely worth seeing. They're cataloguing it tomorrow. I'm going there right after lunch and lend a hand. You could see it then if you wanted to." She turned her head and rested her eyes on O'Brien's. Dudley glanced across at him. Brockmeyer was aware of all this, and later, after the dealers had come, O'Brien saw him in the doorway of the small kitchen reach out and take Claudia by the lobe of one ear and pull her slowly toward him. He pulled her close, smiling, and said something. O'Brien felt that Brockmeyer was talking about him. Claudia too was smiling. She moved even closer, looking at the painter almost sleepily, arching her throat and lifting her breasts. But whatever she said was of a different order from her movements. Brockmeyer let go of her ear; his smile faded, and a rueful, bemused, ironic expression came in its place.

They discussed the paintings. Dudley said to Brockmeyer, "There's a quality of ritual, or ritual enactment, in your work. The situations are more like moments in drama than like narratives—"

"They're like dreams that have gotten away from the dreamer," said O'Brien. He spoke in an outburst and then abruptly stopped talking. He wanted to say more, but ideas were multiplying so rapidly in his mind that he couldn't cope with them. He felt tongue-tied and inadequate, and he was angry at himself for having contradicted Dudley, but there was no way to apologize or take it back.

This idea was not new to Brockmeyer, but the phrasing of it excited him. He leaned toward O'Brien, saying, "Very good! That's an excellent way to put it. The dream gets away from the dreamer. The dream survives the dreamer." He leaned back, and said, "*Ja* . . . the dreamer wakes up, and the dream goes running away down the street like the gingerbread man." He laughed delightedly, then looked with interest at O'Brien—who once again felt himself quailing in that uninhibited scrutiny.

"What do you *do?*" said Brockmeyer. "What is your work? Do you have work? You seem without a reason to live."

O'Brien pulled back, a look of alarm on his face. "Oh no . . . no . . ." he stammered, "I don't need a *reason* to live"— and that was true, true at least in the company of other people, but in fact—and he knew it well—he had been asking himself that very question in his unhappy, unstable solitudes.

Claudia said angrily, "That's an awful way to talk, Brock. You don't know anything about him."

And Dudley said, with a finesse of consideration that

O'Brien valued, "You have to admit you're without an occupation, anyway. I've told you this before, but you ought to try writing. You should try criticism and poetry both. Seriously, Ted."

O'Brien was flustered. He looked down at the floor with a silly smile, frowning at the same time. He raised his eyes to Brockmeyer's and said, "Thank you . . . for . . . for . . . but I really don't need so much . . . I mean, I know it's well intended . . ."

Brockmeyer nodded. "I'm sorry to be so extreme," he said. "I am not speaking in criticism." He crossed the room and poured himself another drink. O'Brien was astonished at the size of those drinks. They seemed to have no effect, except that the painter's eyes were brighter and his voice more intense.

The door buzzer sounded and Claudia answered it, throwing a glance at Brockmeyer and shrugging impatiently.

Brockmeyer said to Dudley, "My dealers are here. There was no way I could avoid this."

They agreed to meet again, and Brockmeyer promised him more time. Three well-dressed middle-aged men came in, and after a brief social mingling went over to the paintings.

Claudia pressed O'Brien's hand when she said goodbye to him. "Don't let Brock upset you," she said, still holding his hand. "He means well."

Brockmeyer said, "Be quiet, Claudia."

Claudia reached up with her other hand, pulled O'Brien's head down and kissed his cheek. "Goodbye," she said, and went to join the men who were looking at the paintings.

Dudley was waiting in the hall. Brockmeyer, who was somewhat larger than O'Brien, put one hand on O'Brien's shoulder and shook it, pressing firmly with his thumb. He was holding a drink in the other hand.

"Look at me," he said quietly. "Without my painting I would be a dead man years ago. If you were European I would not have to tell you this, but you are American, so listen to me.

You will not *necessarily* survive. It is not written in the stars.

"You are like a tightrope walker who is beginning to fall," he added. "You must catch your balance. *You.*" He shook him. *"You."*

He said to Dudley, "Come back then on Monday. Come at three." He said goodbye to O'Brien without inviting him back.

Dudley, too—so O'Brien guessed—resolved to go alone on his next visit to Brockmeyer's studio. He said to O'Brien, with an uneasy smile, as they walked down Broadway, "Are you going to see her tomorrow?"

"What?"

"She invited you to meet her at Levine's."

"Maybe she did. I don't know." O'Brien felt that if she had invited him she had changed her mind by the time she kissed him. He felt tremulous, almost about to faint. Dudley was unaware of it. He invited O'Brien to join him at the Cedar Bar to talk about the paintings, but O'Brien begged off and walked south by himself, toward Washington Square Park.

He found a bench near the chess players and sat there with his head bowed, chewing the inside of his mouth. He could scarcely see the people around him in the bright sunlight. He tried to organize his thinking so as to understand what had been said to him, but he was panicky and rushed to the most fearful interpretation: that Brockmeyer had seen the suicidal aspect of his character and had warned him that death was near. But his fear itself was like a voice saying, *No, no . . . I don't want to die.* He thought of his father and remembered again the scene in the car when his girlfriend had said to him, "Why did your father kill himself?" A confused image came to his mind of his father lying on the floor. His father had come home drunk one night and had fallen at the foot of the stairs. And he remembered, but briefly and without images, a censorious babble of women's voices.

The most frightening thought was that he had inherited his father's suicidal tendencies. He felt helpless and desperate.

But he was disbelieving, too. He could feel the vitality of his strong and still youthful body. Moreover, the world was too beautiful! He lifted his head and looked around him at the marvelous old trees, and at the blue sky shimmering between their leaves, and at the strolling people, and at a shouting, laughing infant and its young parents running back and forth on the grass with a German shepherd puppy near the KEEP OFF sign. Near him the chess players were bending over their games, watched by aficionados standing around them. He sighed deeply. It was absurd to feel such fears. Ellen Roth's flat voice spoke inside him, "You have a beautiful body, O'Brien." He laughed and shook his head, as if clearing away a bad dream.

He thought of Claudia. He had been so staggered by her beauty that he hadn't even caught her last name. Had she really invited him to meet her? Had she rescinded the invitation? Had Brockmeyer meant to shame him before her, or was it simply that he was unconcerned with other people's self-esteem, as O'Brien suspected? Brockmeyer's life seemed to him wondrous. To live on such a scale without sacrifice of pride! And that a man should be so powerfully placed in the world and so hugely competent in that place was mysterious to O'Brien. Brockmeyer's words came back to him: "You are like a tightrope walker who is beginning to fall." He began to feel panicky. He stood up and walked away in the direction of his own neighborhood. There were many books he wanted to read. Why was he not reading them? In order to read a book, one had to sit down somewhere, probably at home, and let go of the craving for love, and let the sunlight finally pale at the window. And wouldn't it be better to be writing something, anything at all, trying and failing, than to go on doing nothing?

He walked back to the Lower East Side via Houston, where he bought a knish at a crowded little shop. He finished it before he reached Delancey, and bought a steamed hot dog from a pushcart, with sauerkraut, mustard, and large flakes of red pepper. That was gone before he reached his own building. A distressing argument, a wordless yammering and screaming, arose within him as he looked at the sidewalk entrance. Trembling, he walked on past it. He went to a dingy little bar that he liked. It was near the Manhattan Bridge, was cool, dark, uncrowded, sour-smelling. He drank three beers and went back out into the sunlight and stood there blinking at the decrepit tenements with their zigzag black iron fire escapes on which people were sitting. He looked up and down the street at the bizarre assortments of people—the usual extraordinary scene. Some kids were playing stickball, and second base was the motionless body of a drunk. A ten-year-old boy stood beside the drunk with his foot resting nonchalantly on his rump, shouting encouragement to his friend at bat. A Chinese pimp went by with a Jewish prostitute. Both faces had the glazed, concentrated, moist, thin-skinned look of addiction. On the corner a gigantic black man held his balance and howled a lugubrious song, drawing deep breaths. He was looking intently down before him, where two small children stood, a boy and a girl, and the girl was conducting him in a sprightly fashion, as if he were an orchestra. Two grimy, vigorous Dalmatians, a familiar sight, crossed the street at a trot.

O'Brien walked to the door of his building, but again, as he stood before it, he quailed. The thought of entering his apartment—the thought, especially, of closing the door behind him—was more than he could bear. He went to the little candy store near the *Daily Forward* building, and this time dialed almost all of Ellen's number. But once again he replaced the receiver. He had become frantic, yet his face felt wooden and his mind cloudy. He walked north again, and west to the park, where he sat on the same bench he had sat on before. He had begun to think of his father. Other images came to mind. The process was involuntary. He could see his mother in many characteristic actions, and his mother's mother, whose money had sustained the house. Of his father, however, there were no images, only questions and wonderments. Why had his father killed himself? Why? Not because

ιy were unhappy and did not kill them-
nd then he saw that this question, in kind,
ιestions that might be asked of his own
ιe bear to be alone? Why doesn't he have
't he develop his interests?
the bench, where he had been sitting
..s in ... pockets. It was almost seven o'clock. He
went to a phone booth and called Ellen Roth.

She had expected him to call several days before, and she
spoke to him coldly, then began to upbraid him. "Why do you
think you can call me just any old time?" she said. "Do you
think I'm just sitting here waiting to put myself at your dis-
posal?"

Anyone else, asking those questions, would have spoken
them angrily, but Ellen asked them earnestly, as questions.
She seemed to be trying to make him turn his own power of
reasoning against himself, as certain adults do with children.
On the one hand it made O'Brien laugh at her; on the other
it annoyed him exceedingly. He said, "Ellen, I'm going to the
movies. Do you want to come?"

She was silent for a moment, and then she said, "Tonight's my group session. You ought to know that by now."

"What day is it?" said O'Brien.

"How do you know what's at the movies if you don't
know what day it is?"

O'Brien said nothing.

"It's Wednesday," said Ellen. And then she said, "O'-
Brien"—she was the only one who called him by his last
name, and he rather liked it—"why don't you come and sit
in on the group. See what it's like. Even if it hurts you, you'll
recover."

She was being clever—*even if it hurts you* . . . She had
invited him many times. He knew that she wanted him to see
her among the people who honored her perceptions and
preoccupations, and wanted him to see the psychotherapist

within whose awareness the evolution of her new
taking place.

"I have to go now," she said. "I don't want to be .
She gave him the address, adding, "It's up to you."

"It was up to me before you said that," he said. He paused
—and hung up—and wondered abruptly if in saying those
words he had actually committed himself to going.

He went to a lunch counter and had a hamburger and a
cup of coffee and then a piece of cherry pie.

Yes, he did need advice. And if some clarity were to
come into his life, some meaningful insight . . .

The address Ellen had given him was on the Upper West
Side. He went to Sheridan Square and took the subway.

David Kahn's wife answered O'Brien's ring and let him
in. She was a tall, dark-haired, patrician-looking woman, who
was not ungracious but who looked him up and down as if she
were searching for his hidden defects: was he homosexual,
alcoholic, agoraphobic, impotent, hypochondriacal, depres-
sive? She peered into his eyes with an unsympathetic look, yet
there was a stifled and subservient air about her.

Kahn was known at that time in New York not in the
journals of the profession, to which, technically, he didn't belong, but, more glamorously, in the literary magazines, in
which several chapters of his ongoing synthesis of classical
philosophy and psychotherapy had appeared. His work drew
openly and very heavily on that of Wilhelm Reich. He had
taught philosophy at Columbia for more than a decade, but
was one of the youngest members of the department. Of all
he was perhaps the best known. He was forty-one but looked
thirty.

A silence fell as O'Brien entered the room, and Kahn
took the occasion to relight his pipe. He was dressed infor-
mally, but his clothing, like that of his wife, was expensive. He
wore a light-blue cotton cardigan and a white shirt open at the
neck, but there was something polished and formal about him,

as if in reality he were wearing a suit and tie and vest. The apartment was bare, severe, and expensive. There were several geometrical abstractions on the walls, museum quality, almost. To O'Brien Kahn had the look of an only child, a mother's darling. His thick black hair was neatly trimmed at the ears and neck, but rumpled on top. He had slender, soft, nervous fingers, nervous lips, and the air of controlled impatience, of carefully hidden arrogance and disguised aggression that O'Brien had noticed in certain of the chess players in the park. O'Brien disliked him at once, and distrusted him.

Kahn smiled at O'Brien, or rather, so it seemed, smiled at O'Brien's discomfiture standing there in the analytical gaze of his four patients. Ellen, who was the only woman present, was also smiling, and O'Brien thought that there was something triumphant in her smile. She said, "Well, so you came at last," and introduced him to Kahn and the others. Kahn indicated a chair by the wall, the same kind that his four patients were sitting in: straight-backed with a gleaming steel frame and black leather seat. "Bring it over," he said, but O'Brien didn't move to take it.

The most striking of the participants was a burly, balding man O'Brien's age, who greeted him curtly in a brusque New York voice. O'Brien apologized for interrupting them, and said, "I'd like just to get an idea . . ." He looked around, hoping that Kahn's wife might support him as a nonparticipating observer, but she had left the room.

Kahn shook his head. "If you're going to be here," he said, "we want you to take part."

"You can't look through the bars of the cage," said the burly one. He wasn't smiling.

O'Brien felt somewhat alarmed. He hadn't anticipated taking part. It was precisely that that he wasn't sure about.

"Why did you come here?" said Kahn.

"To see what you do," said O'Brien. "Ellen talks about it."

Kahn lit his pipe, puffing at it protractedly.

"Why?" said the burly one.

"Why *did* you come?" said Ellen.

O'Brien balked. One of the other men, whose name was Bernie, and whom O'Brien judged to be homosexual, sat looking at him steadily with a sympathetic smirk. His eyes kept blinking and twinkling, and the smirk was so wide it amounted to a grin. The fourth member, a good-looking, solemn, sandy-haired man in his early thirties, who seemed to be blushing continually, said to O'Brien, "Why don't you take one of those chairs and join us?" They were facing one another in a small circle. Kahn was in the circle, but where the others sat up straight, he leaned back comfortably in a Mies van der Rohe chair.

Kahn said, "There are three ground rules: one, you don't have to answer any question you don't want to; two, if you do answer, answer truthfully; and three, any question at all can be asked. There are no sacred cows."

O'Brien moved into the circle between Ellen and Kahn. They all were looking at him. In any other context it would have been extremely aggressive, extremely rude.

Kahn smiled, and then chuckled and said, "Is your left hand afraid of what your right hand might do?"

"What?"

O'Brien looked down at his hands. His left was grasping the right by the wrist. He smiled and said, "Oh . . . yeah . . . yeah . . . we have to watch out for him." He opened the fingers of his left hand, and the right hand sprang away as if it had a life of its own. It drifted uncertainly into the air, then moved toward O'Brien's head. He pulled back. The hand moved away, paused, and as O'Brien watched it with alarm it sprang at him . . . and scratched the side of his head. O'Brien smiled and, with a mocking glance at Kahn, heaved a sigh of relief. His right hand drifted slowly down into his lap, where his left hand gripped it again by the wrist.

Bernie was grinning at him. Ellen folded her arms and looked at him dryly. Kahn held a match to his pipe. He never seemed to smoke the pipe, but was continually lighting it.

"Why did you come here?" said the burly man.

The sandy-haired man intervened. His voice seemed about to break into stammering, and yet he spoke with confidence. "You must be discontented in some way," he said, "or feel you could do things better. We all come for reasons like that."

"If we take your performance with the hands literally," said Kahn, "we'd have to say, first, that you fear something unforeseen might happen unless you keep a grip on yourself. And second, that you don't know whether that unforeseen thing will be turned against you hurtfully or beneficently . . . or turned outward."

"It says something else, too," said the burly man. "It says, 'I don't respect you' and 'I don't have problems the way you do, I don't need help the way you do.' It was arrogant and smart-ass."

"It was a self-conceited thing," said Ellen.

"Jesus Christ!" said O'Brien. "Haul off, will you! I just got here!"

"We're ganging up on you," said Kahn. A somewhat gentle note had come into his voice. "That can't be helped, it's just structural. There are five of us, and we're all looking at you."

"But you have techniques," said O'Brien, "you have theories . . ."

"Did you expect to hear a lecture?" said Kahn. "Sometimes we talk theory," he said, "mostly what we do is simply pay attention. One thing leads to another."

"What's your response to what Marty just said to you?" said Ellen. Marty was the burly man.

"Look," said Kahn to O'Brien, "try this. It's something we all do, we've all been through it. Go around the circle. Start with me. Say the thing uppermost in your mind, even if it seems cruel."

O'Brien could see the others settling in their chairs. He didn't start with Kahn but with Bernie, who sat to Kahn's left.

He said, "Are you queer?" He asked it almost gently, not out of sympathy, but to avoid the appearance of censure.

"As a nine-dollar bill," said Bernie.

"Was that uppermost in your mind?" said Kahn.

"Maybe not at the very top," said O'Brien.

"What's at the very top?" said Ellen.

"At the very top?" O'Brien turned back to Bernie and studied him, though he knew very well what the answer was. He said, "Why do you keep smiling? You smile all the time." As soon as he said this he wondered why he had passed over Kahn, and why nobody was calling him on it.

Bernie's eyes twinkled and his smile grew larger. Then he understood that O'Brien was seriously questioning him, and he stopped smiling. O'Brien saw at once that he was a man of real intelligence and that he cared nothing about that intelligence. Bernie's clownlike face looked pinched, frightened, and despairing. He said, "I can stop smiling, but only if I drop my eyes like this. If I raise my eyes to yours, I'll start smiling again. It's like a tic. I can't help it. I mean, I'm *doing* it, and I know I'm doing it . . . but . . . I mean, that's sort of the *me* I can meet the world with . . . it keeps me out of trouble."

Ellen said, "Well you did a real brave thing, Bernie, quitting that job. I'm proud of you. I mean it." Evidently they had been discussing this before O'Brien had arrived.

Bernie looked up at her, and instantly his eyes twinkled and his lips curled high at the corners in a peculiar smirk. "Thanks, Ellen," he said.

Kahn said to O'Brien, "What are you thinking?"

"Lots of things."

"Like what? Rattle them off, any order, go fast, go ahead."

"Everybody seems so smart," said O'Brien, "so alert. I don't know what I expected. And you're really experienced in each other. Anything I might say you've said already a dozen times."

"Not necessarily," said Kahn. "What else?"

O'Brien shrugged.

"You're balking at something," said Marty, the burly one.

O'Brien knew that he was indeed balking at certain things—at some because they frightened him, and at others because they seemed churlish and rude.

"Don't you wonder what we think of you?" said Ellen.

"It doesn't matter that much," said O'Brien. "I mean . . . I don't know you . . . except for you, Ellen."

"But that doesn't answer the question," said the sandy-haired man, whose name was Alvah. "Are you frightened?" he added.

O'Brien made a gesture with his hands.

"You're holding back from something," said Kahn.

O'Brien was almost trembling. He was remembering how easily Brockmeyer had seen the despair in him, and how vulnerable he had been to that insight, though it had presented nothing new, nothing he hadn't known for years.

O'Brien gestured with both hands in a way not characteristic of him. "Go ahead," he said. He addressed those words to Ellen, and was painfully aware that he preferred not to look at the others.

"They know all about us," said Ellen. "I mean . . . it's just that I know things from before this. I think of you as . . . I mean . . . you're kind of wonderful, O'Brien, but . . ." She sighed and said, "You're really screwed up."

"What does that mean?" said Kahn. "Spell it out, Ellen."

"Well . . . you know . . . tangled up, all mixed up. I think of you," she said, turning back to O'Brien, "as being really lost . . . really suffering . . . because in some ways you're so damn healthy."

There was a long silence. Alvah said quietly, "Do you want my comments too?"

Alvah was gazing at him with the rapt earnestness of a rural seer. His face was flushed darkly and his eyes were intent. "You seem . . . you seem . . . guarded," he said, "—against others and against yourself . . . and you seem . . . confused, puzzled . . . and yet you seem capable of spontaneity . . . but you're afraid of that, too . . . you're afraid of exploding . . . but above all you are simply confused, deeply, deeply confused. Something is missing.

"What's your relationship with your father?" he added abruptly. "You seem like a man who has grown up without parents . . . and yet you don't have the . . . the . . . something about an orphan . . . you're not like that."

"Yes," said Kahn, "you have a warmth to you, a kind of glow that's often missing in orphans. Tell us about your father. Is he alive?" Something had come into Kahn's voice that touched O'Brien.

"My father's dead," he said.

"When did he die?" said Kahn.

"I was ten. . . ."

"What did he die of?"

"A stroke," said O'Brien. He was aware that he had begun to sweat, but he was not aware that he was breathing shallowly, was jiggling one foot, and was blushing deeply.

Broad-shouldered Marty, whose shirt cuffs were turned back on very hairy arms, and who was leaning forward aggressively, as if ready to pounce, said, "Can you say what's on your mind right now?"

O'Brien didn't answer for a while; and then he said, "I'd rather not." He saw the front porch of his house, the door, the stairway, his mother's bedroom door, his mother sitting up in bed, the strong, domineering figure of his grandmother in a dark red woolen bathrobe.

"If you don't want to, don't," said Kahn, "but try to say what would happen if you did. For example, what would Ellen think about it? What would I think about it?"

O'Brien sensed a maneuver on Kahn's part; it seemed to him almost like a trick. And when he imagined acquiescing he didn't like the feel of it.

"I don't want to look at myself from your point of view," he said hesitantly. And then he blurted out, "I don't like you,

Kahn! You make a big display of your secret thoughts. I don't trust you."

"But you came here," said Ellen. "What does liking have to do with it?"

"You're arrogant," O'Brien went on, looking at Kahn. "You feel so superior to your poor screwed-up patients, and you don't hide it as well as you think."

"How the hell would you know?" shouted Marty.

"You have no modesty, O'Brien," said Ellen. "Maybe he *is* superior to his poor screwed-up patients. Maybe he deserves our deference. Maybe we're deferring to wisdom and learning . . . both of which you stand in need of, O'Brien."

Kahn sat in the leather chair with his head bowed. He had lifted his glasses and was rubbing his eyes. Bernie sat up straight, like a good little boy at school. He smiled continually and seemed mesmerized by O'Brien.

"I hate looking at myself from somebody else's point of view," muttered O'Brien, "and I hate taking myself as some damned object of scrutiny."

To his astonishment, Marty, who had been leaning forward and glaring at him, leaned back in his chair, relaxed, and smiled at him—smiled a remarkable and most attractive smile, his face alight with intelligence and good humor. "Now at last you've said something real," he said, "and I have the feeling, unfortunately, that you mean it."

"I'm going," said O'Brien, standing up.

"That's what I mean," said Marty. "I'd rather you stayed —but if you have to go, come again."

O'Brien nodded, not agreeing to come again, but acknowledging Marty's sudden friendliness. He glanced across at Kahn, who was lighting his pipe and was watching him. And in that glance O'Brien saw that Kahn understood everything: that his outburst had been defensive, that they had touched on something important and that he had lied about it. As for being accused of arrogance—that had happened to Kahn a thousand times and meant nothing to him.

Alvah was saying earnestly to O'Brien, "We all hate it; you're no different. What you've just described is nothing but 'the disease of psychology.' That's what Rank calls it. Once you have it there's no way around it; you have to plow right through."

This didn't register on O'Brien, but when their eyes met he said, really involuntarily, "Thanks, Alvah."

He nodded to Bernie, and to Ellen said simply, "So long, Ellen."

"Gee, O'Brien," she said, "what a shame! We're off to a *great* start! You ought to stay."

"No," said O'Brien, and he left the apartment.

He felt that he had done the right thing, yet he knew that he had been false and that somehow everything was wrong. He sat on the swaying, jiggling subway train with his head bowed and his hands in his pockets, unaware of the people around him. He couldn't collect his thoughts. From time to time a terrible hollow of anxiety opened within him and his head trembled. He felt guilty without knowing why, and felt that he had narrowed his options damagingly.

Much unlike himself, he went straight home. The thought of the voices and faces he would encounter in the bars was repugnant to him. He wanted to lie on his back in bed and smoke and think. He didn't want to *respond* to anyone, and didn't want anyone looking at him.

As he climbed the stairs to his apartment he heard the telephone ringing. He thought, *They'll hang up just as I open the door.*

But that didn't happen—the phone kept ringing.

2.

O'Brien recognized his mother's voice before she had finished even her first word. He knew at once that something was wrong.

She said, "Oh, Teddy, Teddy . . . I've been calling all day." Her voice went through him to all the little fibers that once were infant joy.

He said, "What is it, mom?"

She paused and said, "Teddy . . ." He could hear mixtures of tenderness, self-pity, self-conscious bravery, and sheer weariness in her voice. He was exasperated and compassionately alarmed at the same time.

"Mother passed away," she said. "She's gone, Teddy."

"Grandmother?" he said, astonished.

"Yes, dear." She breathed quietly for a moment. "I went in to see if she was awake this morning. . . ."

"Gertrude is dead?"

"You knew she'd been ill, Teddy, but I never told you how really bad it was. She had pernicious anemia. She came back from the hospital just three days ago."

"Are you alone there?"

"I think she came home to die, I honestly do. Mrs. Frank has been here," she said, "and the O'Neills came over. I'm alone right now. The funeral is tomorrow." She paused and said urgently, "Honey, I want you to be with me."

O'Brien said, "Yes, of course, mom. I'll be there."

"Can you get a haircut?" she said.

"There won't be time for that."

"She would have been eighty-two on Friday, Teddy. Now the birthday flowers . . ." She began to cry.

They talked a while longer. There was a midnight bus he could take.

He said goodnight to her and ran to the mirror over the kitchen sink. His abundant black hair probably did need cutting, but he was afraid to try it. He shaved rapidly and ran to the phone. He didn't own a suit or even a necktie, and hadn't for years. He called Dudley and said, "Mal . . . Mal, there's been a death in the family." That phrase seemed odd and dishonest to him: *the* family. He had never thought of it that way, as a social entity. His mother was almost an internal presence; he was scarcely aware that she had a life away from him. And his grandmother, his matriarchal, broad-backed, unbending, man-hating grandmother, the Lady of Iron, had been more of an enemy than family. He had avoided her, had had scarcely any contact with her for years. And yet he felt real urgency in the present event. He wanted to do the right thing—he was not yet aware how very much.

He changed his clothes at Dudley's well-kept, well-furnished little apartment, putting on a dark tweed coat that almost fit him, and a white shirt and tie. He borrowed twenty dollars, and an hour later was sitting on the Greyhound bus traveling westward through the night. He smoked continually and looked out the window and thought of the past, dumbfounded by the mystery of change and the fact of death.

Was she really dead?

"My grandmother?"

Had all those years really, really gone?

He dozed occasionally on the bus and kept waking up and peering into the night. Red lights, yellow lights moved this way and that; power lines plunged and lifted; there were fields of corn; cars and trucks and occasional buses passed him going the other way. He saw dark wooded hills with darkened houses; grimy, deserted streets; a small iron bridge on which a black man with a dog shuffled along looking over at the water.

He kept trying to organize his thoughts so as to grasp the fact of his grandmother's death, but the images from the past shifted continually and slipped away.

He had seen his grandmother four years ago, but her face and his mother's, too, appeared in images from the more distant past. Of his father he could remember only the framed photograph on the mantel in his mother's bedroom, a nice-looking tall man holding a mandolin and leaning on a window seat before some stained-glass windows. He wore pointed white shoes, a straw boater, a striped jacket. O'Brien had looked at that photograph many times trying to find his father's death in the set of the mouth or the expression of the eyes. The man seemed eager to please, and hopeful. He had been a wonderful dancer—so his mother had said. She too had been a dancer. There were photographs of a young woman in gowns, extremely pretty in a sensitive-looking way, with large eyes and a remarkably straight and elegant nose. She had thought seriously of a career on the stage, but her mother had objected, and she herself had said to O'Brien, "I didn't have the temperament for it. I could never have survived in that milieu." His father had run an insurance agency, which soon enough had failed. Then came the reign of the Lady of Iron —and his mother had become a little girl again.

He found it impossible to *remember* purposefully. Images of his high school sweethearts came to mind, images especially of Carole Bucholz, and it was not the terrible moment in the car that he remembered, but the feel of her, the softness of her shoulders, the girth of her hips, her way of kissing, the rounded, dusky little columns of her nipples, the delicious odors of her body making love. Had she married? Might she be living in the town? The thought that he might see her shook him awake . . . and it was then that he remembered the pale windows of his car and the glowing radio dial. He had parked at night on a road in the woods. He was seventeen. They had made love in the back seat and had climbed into the front to smoke. It was warm. The windows were pale with steam. He turned on the radio, and Carole slid cozily downward, twisting toward him on one elbow. The amber light from the glowing dial fell across her lips and eyes. Her forehead moved with some fleeting thought and she said something about the distant past. They had been neighbors for many years. And then she said, "Mother says you're not like your father at all. Do you think about him much? Why did he kill himself, Ted?"

Even as he sat there on the bus remembering it, O'Brien felt himself shrinking and gasping as he had done that night.

He had almost fainted. The music had dwindled to a pinpoint of silence and his vision had darkened. A dreadful, anxious sadness had sped through him, and then a flush of shame. He had heard his mother say to relatives that his father had died of a stroke. She had told him to ignore the malicious gossip of people who enjoyed thinking badly of others. He had done that on more than one occasion—but this was different.

"How do you know he killed himself?" he said. His mouth was dry.

"My mother was there," she said, "don't you remember?"

He remembered nothing of that event. He was appalled at what she said.

"What did your mother say?" he said. "What do you mean she was there?"

From that conversation O'Brien had learned how his father had died. When he got home that night he went straight to his mother's bedroom, snapped on the light, and shook her awake.

"What's the matter?" she gasped. "What is it, honey?"

"Is it true that my father killed himself?" he said.

"Oh!" she cried. She put one hand to her face, and with the other pulled up the blanket to cover her bosom. "I've told you before," she said, "—who have you been talking to? You know how he died. Hand me my bathrobe."

O'Brien lifted the lace-trimmed light-blue robe from the chair and gave it to her.

"He hanged himself in the cellar," he said.

"Oh!" she cried. "Where did you hear this?" She pointed to her slippers and he moved them under her dangling white feet.

"Is it true or not?" he said.

She looked at him like a stricken little girl and cried in a voice that was suddenly imploring, "Oh, Sonny! Sonny!" Instead of standing, she turned and fell on the bed, sobbing violently. O'Brien stretched out his hand to comfort her, but the notes of self-pity in her voice made him pause. At that moment her mother, adjusting the belt of her red woolen bathrobe, came bustling into the room.

"What are you crying about, Nancy?" she said. "My goodness, what a scene! What's it all about, Sonny?"

"How did my father die?" he said to her.

She narrowed her eyes and tensed her jaw. "Your father died of a cerebral hemorrhage." Those were her words, but the expression on her face made them mean, *Don't speak to me of that man.*

O'Brien had avoided them both for weeks and couldn't face Carole again at all. They had driven his father from corner to corner of that immaculate house, and then, by telling lies, had erased even the desperate assertion of his final act. O'Brien made up his mind to leave home. It would mean not finishing school, not joining the Naval Officers' Training Program, for which he had already qualified. He would enlist, instead, in the army. The war was underway. On a Thursday night, Lottery Night at the movies, which his mother and grandmother both attended, he sat at the little desk in his bedroom and composed a letter—or tried to. He wrote that his loyalty and love lay with the man they had defeated . . . and he wanted to say that he was leaving home in order to construct in some way a relationship with his absent father. But he couldn't imagine what that relationship might be—and in fact couldn't summon up a single image of his father. He sat there with the unmoving pencil in his hand trying to recall some least little glimpse of his father's face . . . but there came instead a wave of confused emotions and memories, delicious, guilty, and suffused with the perfumes of his mother's robes and gowns. He dropped the pencil. He could see the big three-part mirror of her dressing table, the lacquered container that held tissues, the array of phials, decanters, and enameled boxes. The aroma of those things was transporting. She herself was not present in the vision, and yet she permeated everything: an aura of care, an enchanting touch that was cool and yet warm, a bent arm, a cloud of hair. O'Brien walked unsteadily to the door. On the other side of his bedroom wall stood the very table that had loomed so vividly in his mind. He turned on the light, and with short steps walked into his mother's bedroom. He stood before the triple mirror and looked at his three images unseeingly. There behind him were the two beds, his mother's and his dead father's. He touched each of them and looked this way and that. He was breathing in little sighs. Something from the past was coming near; it grew larger and closer, assumed clarity . . . and with a moan of submission he gave way to it and fell full length on his mother's bed, not yet twelve years old, ill and feverish. She had brought him into her room and was using the other bed herself. It was time to sleep. She had served him a bowl of broth and sat for a while on the bed singing to him in a voice that unraveled the years and blew every defense away, away . . . and then she had danced, still singing, turning and looking back at him, so gracefully, so beautifully, and not a cell of his body had held back its love. . . .

These memories flooded O'Brien as he sat there in the minutely jolting, continually vibrating darkness of the bus. His life seemed hopelessly divided, hopelessly compromised. The events of the day—Brockmeyer's words and the remarks of the people at Kahn's—were present in his thoughts, the voices almost echoing in his ears, and yet everything seemed far away and irreconcilable with his past at home. Yet how could he live at all if he couldn't put the two together? He dozed repeatedly and awakened each time to the same dull torment of confusion and yearning. And then abruptly, with a sensation of bursting pressure, of something *giving way,* there occurred to him a thought that never had occurred before, a life-saving thought, namely, that *he could meet their demands, could do all that was expected of him.* It wasn't necessary *to believe,* but only to fulfill the forms, to live and let live!

To live and let live!

Oh my God, he thought, *I can do it! Of course! Of course!*

And he *knew* that he could, and knew that he did in fact want to be of value to others, to be of service where possible, to be held in esteem, and to enjoy once again the pleasures, securities, and occasional triumphs of his high school days, when, taken in the round, he had done more or less the expected thing. He sighed with relief, almost with happiness, and the terrible stress of confusion dissolved and drifted out of him. He could be a son to his mother; he could show her the kindness she needed; and he could live independently in the world, following values of his own.

He smiled and fell asleep in the darkness of the bus. He slept deeply. The bus arrived at his stop, and still he slept. The bus started again and went on.

3.

It was day, bright and well-advanced in sunlight, and the bus was tilting as it sped around a corner between buildings O'-Brien didn't recognize. He sat up in alarm. The ship of salvation had left without him! He ran gasping down the aisle and pleaded with the driver, who obligingly stopped and let him out. Two motorists heeded his trustworthy face and desperately waving arms. The second let him out a mere taxi drive from home . . . and O'Brien sat in a speeding cab looking at familiar things and drastic changes. An extensive woods in which he had built shacks had become a housing project. He saw new businesses and stores side by side in a garish yet drab and spiritless succession. But he recognized, high on a hillside, the tree-surrounded basin of the old stone quarry with its sheer straight planes of fractured rock, and he remembered the caves he had played in with his friends. And then he came to the borough park, the swimming pool and ballfield, and his breathing quickened and he could feel the beating of his heart. He leaned forward and gave directions to the driver— it was too late to go home—and shortly afterward, with his satchel in his hand, he stood before a one-story, red-roofed, stone-and-brick edifice on the main street, the decorous white sign of which, affixed to the side of the building near the doorway, read: HAMMERSCHMIDT FUNERAL PARLOR.

The institutional appearance of the place was softened by white trim and white shutters folded back at the windows, but the cropped evergreens against the building, the privet hedge, the close-cut unused lawn—there was something about these things very sobering to O'Brien. To the left of the building the mourners' parking lot was almost filled with cars; to the right a driveway sloped around back to the basement. He could see two hearses and two limousines parked back there, and several cars besides.

He stepped up onto the threshold apprehensively. He shook himself and breathed deeply, then opened the door and entered . . . and his feet landed soundlessly on well-padded beige carpeting.

The scent of flowers was almost stifling. Another odor, a chemical odor, was woven through that scent. There was a murmur of restrained voices. A number of people were standing in the lobby near an alcove in which he could see a rack of flowers and the foot of a casket.

The murmuring stopped abruptly. Everyone, without exception, turned and looked at O'Brien. Some whispered to others, as if in perturbation. Most were elderly; a few were middle-aged.

O'Brien stood there nervously looking back at them. Why this scrutiny? He didn't recognize a soul, nor did he see his mother. A totally bald elderly man in a dark blue suit came toward him, reaching with one hand and cupping the other at his waist. As the man drew near the counterfeit sympathy deepened on his face, and he laid his head to one side. The skin of his face and hands was a powdery white. The deference of his gestures and the contortion of his face seemed to set him apart in a hushed, almost priestly remoteness, but his eyes contradicted all that. They were vulgar, avid, piercing eyes of a dark and brilliant blue. Seeing those eyes, O'Brien understood something he might never have inferred from the décor of the place, namely, that in the rooms downstairs the dead were cut open, scooped out, drained, sewed up, and pumped full of chemicals. He stepped back as the old man drew near him.

"We've been waiting for you," the old gentleman said quietly, yet with an odd urgency. "Would you please come with me just for a moment?" He indicated a little room to the right of the entrance.

O'Brien looked over his head, trying to find his mother, and this apparently disturbed the old man, who spoke to him anxiously. There was a whispering and a certain agitation among the people across the foyer. O'Brien was puzzled, and he too became anxious. A question was coming to his lips, but the old gentleman took him by the elbow and with astonishing rudeness turned him toward the little room. O'Brien pulled free and looked sharply at the man, but followed him without speaking.

The old gentleman closed the office door, saying, "Your uncle had hoped to meet you here . . . and he *will* be joining you later at your home."

O'Brien's father had had one brother, but it was not conceivable that he would be coming to this funeral. Was there some error? What was going on?

The old man's voice was confidential and calming. His eyes, however, were not calming at all.

"Perhaps all of the details of this tragedy didn't reach you," he said. "We feel it would be best if you knew . . . beforehand . . ." At that word he moved his head in a way that clearly indicated the body in the alcove. ". . . the accident," he said, "was extremely severe . . ."

O'Brien's vision darkened and a current of cold air passed across his face. Was this man telling him that his mother had been killed? He stammered, "What do you mean? What are you saying?" He felt that he was about to fall, but at that very moment there came the sound of women's voices near the door, and a brisk, mild knocking. One voice said, "I'm sure it is, Nancy," and the other voice: "Teddy? Teddy, is that you in there?"

"Yes, mother, I'm here," cried O'Brien.

The door swung open, and a graying woman, whose features, though handsome, were haggard and oddly slack, hurried toward him. She fixed her eyes on his with a yearning, pleading look that made him stiffen and draw back. She wore a small hat with a delicate black veil, which she lifted, pursing and moving her lips in preparation for his kiss. A terrible sorrow passed through him.

He embraced his mother and kissed her cheek, and held her with one arm when at last she released him.

"Ah, Mrs. O'Brien . . ." said the old gentleman, who was beginning to see his error.

She introduced them, and O'Brien shook the dry, soft hand, marveling at the obsequiousness of the man's apologies and the extreme distaste shining in his eyes. They went out into the foyer. There the woman who had accompanied his mother greeted him, glancing at his hair. Two funerals were in progress. The mourners in the nearer alcove were now in full view. They had resumed their muted conversations. But once again all conversation stopped . . . and this time their expectations were fulfilled.

The front door had opened. A very large, wide-hipped young man stood stiffly in the doorway, his soft, large face puckered in a dignified, censorious look. With short, awkward steps he came into the foyer, forgetting to close the door. He wore a dark suit, a dark tie, a white shirt with a curved English collar.

"That's him! That's him!" O'Brien's mother said, taking his arm. She was trying not to be overheard, and produced a hissing sound that made him shudder. "That's the Giles boy," she whispered.

The old gentleman rushed forward, clearing his throat. Someone closed the door. The mourners in the alcove and foyer were watching fixedly. A stout woman with glasses whom O'Brien hadn't seen before hurried across the foyer. "Wallace," she said, "before you come in I want to talk with you." She put her hand on the young man's arm, looking up into his face.

The young man patted her hand reassuringly, then abruptly bent down and said in a quaking voice, "Is she . . .?"

The old gentleman took the young man's arm and repeated the very words he had said to O'Brien: "Would you please come with me, sir, just for a moment . . .?" but the young man stood there immovably.

O'Brien began to notice certain signs: that deep flush was probably chronic, not momentary; his hands were trembling, and his eyes, which were badly inflamed, were twitching uncontrollably.

The young man looked around with panicky birdlike movements, and stepped falteringly toward the casket in the alcove. The stout lady tugged at his sleeve, and the old gentleman went along beside him, holding his arm, clearing his throat and saying, "Sir . . . sir . . ."

"Wallace, please get hold of yourself," said the stout lady. "She would want you to get through this . . . listen to me, Wallace . . ."

He had begun to walk on tiptoe, not as an adult might walk for quietness, but as certain children when excited break into a tiptoe gait. The ladies in the alcove moved out of his way. At the coffin he seemed to lose his balance. He regained it, bent forward and put his face close to the body. He straightened again, shaking his head and rubbing one cheek rapidly. He turned with an anguished face as if looking for help, and then he peered at the body again and stretched out one hand. The old man said hoarsely and with overt exasperation, "Please, Mr. Giles, don't make a scene!" —having said which he leaped aside. The young man's legs buckled beneath him, he pivoted with a moaning, retching sound, and fell face down on the floor, heaving violently. The smell of putrified whiskey and half-digested coffee filled the air.

There was a muted outcry among the women. O'Brien darted across the room. He moved the young man's face out of the mess, and knelt beside him, holding his forehead and shoulder. "Don't try to get up," he said. "There may be more coming." The young man's face, which had been flushed, was gray, and his wide-open eyes were unfocused. O'Brien's words hadn't registered.

A blur of white flashed past him. Two towels landed on the floor. A boy of fourteen, responding to orders, ran around O'Brien and knelt on the other side of the groaning man. The boy wore a necktie but no coat. A well-dressed heavy-set man pushed in beside O'Brien, knocking him off balance. He seemed to O'Brien not merely heedless, but officious and arrogant. "Come with me," said the well-dressed man to the recumbent one. "Get on your feet now . . . come lie down."

The boy was mopping up the mess with the towels. Two more towels fell to the floor. The bald old gentleman had returned. He held a chrome-plated canister of deodorizing spray and he whisked it over the towels, over the carpet, and released a blast into the air.

O'Brien wondered why they were cleaning the carpet but weren't cleaning the man's face. And why did they think it so important to get him out of sight?

These questions did not *engage* O'Brien, but flitted coldly through his consciousness. The fact was, he had crossed some line or zone of conscious restraint, or perhaps of intention, and no longer knew what he was going to do. With an odd gesture, as if he intended no more than to catch the well-dressed man's attention, he dug his elbow forcibly into his ribs, saying with a smile that was merely a baring of the teeth, "He *is* lying down."

He was alarmed by what he had done. He heard his mother saying, "Teddy! Teddy!" and heard the voices of several women and a couple of men. He jumped up and with a feeling of remorse extended a helping hand to the man he had just knocked over, and whom he now realized to be—actually now recognized—Hammerschmidt himself.

But the old gentleman with the spray and the coatless young boy helped him to his feet. He looked steadily at O'-Brien, who felt he had never seen so sustained and pure a look of hatred. *He must be hell to work for,* thought O'Brien. This observation, again, merely hovered in his mind and did not engage him. He wanted to apologize, but somehow he couldn't bear to. Many voices were speaking at the same time. "Teddy! Teddy!" his mother said, pulling him by the arm, trying to make him face her. "We mustn't interfere." The stout lady with glasses confronted him, saying, "Who are you! You have a strange way of helping! Have you no respect?"

"I know who you are, Mr. O'Brien," said Hammerschmidt, "but perhaps you don't know who I am"—he waited for O'Brien to acknowledge his authority or admit to his own inexcusable ignorance, and he glanced at O'Brien's hair, at his ill-fitting jacket, at the shoes that never once had been polished, and at the trousers that had been slept in on the bus.

O'Brien turned his head and scanned the little crowd. Their faces were puzzled, alarmed, and hostile. His mother was speaking to him and tugging at his arm. The old gentleman with the spray and the young boy in the white shirt were struggling with Giles, who was sitting up.

What was it about those faces? They seemed odd to O'-Brien, peculiar. They were subdued, restrained, worn down by a lifetime of orders-from-above. Some seemed to hate him, and seemed to wish they could inflict pain on him for not living as they lived and enduring the sufferings that they endured. O'Brien pursed his lips and looked over their heads toward the alcove . . . and seeing the casket flanked by racks of flowers, he wondered what "the Giles boy" had seen, and he stepped through the crowd and went up to the coffin.

Hammerschmidt came after him, saying grimly under his breath, "This has gone far enough, Mr. O'Brien." The stout lady and his mother came too. At the bier they all stopped talking and watched him.

What O'Brien felt, however, was in no way indicated by the reverent posture of looking down into the coffin. The crudely painted, daintily gowned figure was partly a corpse and partly an effigy of wax. Under the stronger feelings of anger and disgust he felt a stirring of childhood horror.

Why had they chosen to exhibit the remains at all? Why? since they had known, obviously, that the sight would be distressing to the son?

The answer to that question was spoken inside him by a voice he was to hear again that morning. "For money, O'-Brien. For money," said the voice.

It was Ellen Roth. She spoke condescendingly, as if surprised by his incredible naïveté, and that tone seemed to him more important than the words.

O'Brien turned and looked at the faces in the crowd. His head was trembling and his hands felt cold. Why were they going through with this travesty of a ceremony? Why didn't they see what was plain to be seen? In the confused wheel of his feelings there occurred still another: he feared them.

An elderly man stepped up to the coffin and crossed himself. Hammerschmidt said to O'Brien, with polite hatred, "Make way, please." And O'Brien's mother took his arm again, saying, "Honey, honey . . . we're due at church. Come . . . pay your respects." She adjusted her veil and brushed something from the lapel of his jacket. Her face was strained and anxious and her eyes were pleading with him. The bald old gentleman and the young boy were supporting Giles, one on either side.

O'Brien was panting and was unaware of it. He went beside his mother over the soundless carpet. Several mourners were waiting for them in the other alcove. He saw the outside door open and saw two more come in.

O'Brien's mother said, "Teddy, mother talked about you

the day before she died. She *did* care about you, dear."

Something in her voice cut him. The tender note implied forgiveness on his grandmother's part, or a change of heart, but she had been inflexible in her hatred even of the memory of his father, and he believed that if indeed she had spoken of him she would have said her usual things: *When will he straighten out? When will he get a decent job? When will he get a haircut?*

They came to a polished walnut stand supporting an incongruous little announcement plaque: movable white plastic letters on a black ground, identical with those to be seen on the menu boards of luncheonettes. The topmost name was *Mrs. Gertrude Ouelette Barker;* below it: *Mrs. Nancy Barker O'Brien and family.*

O'Brien paused before the sign. His mother said, "What is it, Teddy? What's the matter? You seem so troubled."

He shook his head. He was panting and couldn't catch his breath. He wanted to shout something, anything, just to clear his lungs and come back to life. He felt that he was vanishing, simply evaporating.

Here again the scent of flowers was overwhelming. He recognized several of the people but didn't know their names. All were elderly. There were two couples. The rest were women except for a fleshy, very handsome man in the early years of old age. He had thick white hair, wavy and luxuriant, and had the manner of a retired professor. When they shook hands, O'Brien felt that this man looked at him with a special significance.

O'Brien's mother stepped up to the bier, crossed herself, and made room for O'Brien. He stood beside her and looked down into the satin-lined coffin.

What lay there, wearing a maroon brocaded gown that he recognized, a brooch and pearls that he recognized, eyeglasses on a ribbon that he recognized, its fingers crossed over an orchid, was a painted, waxen, crudely-made effigy just like the one in the other coffin.

O'Brien's mother murmured, "She looks so peaceful."

Was there skin beneath that dreadful, powdered, greasy paint? He bent closer. The perfume was dense and harsh.

Two new arrivals joined them, a card-playing friend of his grandmother's and her son. These were the Benickes, who lived nearby. O'Brien nodded to them both. He didn't trust his voice. William Benicke was ten years older than he, and had been held up to him many times as a model son, a model businessman, a model citizen. The small mother and her large son looked down at the painted figure.

"She had a full life," said Mrs. Benicke.

"Yes, she did," said her son.

"She?" said O'Brien loudly; and he added, thinking that he was muttering, but in fact he was speaking the words quite clearly, "Oh God, I hate it! I hate it! I hate it!"

All three looked at him, his mother with great alarm.

The expressions on their faces filled him with rage. He screamed at them, "I wouldn't know who it was if I hadn't seen the name on that goddamn menu!"

And having said this much, he let go completely. "Curse you! Curse you!" he shrieked. His voice rose like a siren. He turned and reached into the coffin and struck the dead face with the flat of his hand, screaming, "Are you under there, you wretch? Where are you?" Harshly and violently he rubbed away the paint on the side of her face, clamping her head with the other hand. He had forgotten that she had worn a wig, a "transformation." It moved. And some sort of filler moved beneath her cheek.

There was a terrible outcry. Several people seized his arms and waist. He could hear his mother, and could hear William Benicke, who was trying to hold him, saying, "Good God! What are you doing? Are you mad?" The bald old assistant ran up and ran away, calling, "Mr. Hammerschmidt! Mr. Hammerschmidt!"

The opposition of all those people caused a change in O'Brien. He fought with them and his rage didn't lessen, but a separate consciousness began to work inside him, offering justifications and speaking at times with a cold, cold levity.

When Benicke seized him, O'Brien swung backward with his elbows and connected. "Where is the body?" he screamed. "Hammerschmidt! You can't bury her if she's not dead!" He reached into the coffin again, carefully pushing aside a solemn, frail old man who had come to Benicke's assistance and who very bravely stood before O'Brien blocking his path. With both hands O'Brien seized and ripped apart the lacy neckband of the brocaded gown, breaking the chain of the locket and scattering the pearls of the necklace. Gray skin came into view, sagging against her collarbones and her wasted, pathetic ribs. He heard gasps of horror and cries of outrage and disgust. Several men took hold of him, and he staggered and fell to the floor under a mass of bodies. He could hear the ripping of his coat and shirt. "The real truth is down in the cellar," said the voice of Ellen Roth inside him, and he screamed, "Down! Down to the gutbin!" He saw that this would not take place, and he shouted, "Bring up the guts, Hammerschmidt! Save us the garbage!" He broke free again. Someone jumped in front of him and jumped away. But other defenders massed together and blocked him off from the casket. He saw the stout woman with glasses standing there with her fists raised above her head. He swerved aside and picked up a rack of flowers and threw it against the wall, shouting, "No flowers! No flowers!" Ellen Roth was laughing. He doubled back and laid both hands on the end of the casket and tried to heave it off the stand, but the opposition rushed in to support it, and others pressed him down again to the floor. He saw that Hammerschmidt himself was one of the wrestlers now. Soon O'Brien could scarcely move. That cold, uncontrollable levity was all that was left to him. He shouted, "Hammer-SCHMIDT! Hammer-SCHMIDT!" as if turning the name into a birdcall. "Habeas CORP-us, Hammer-SCHMIDT! Produce the BODY, Hammer-SCHMIDT!" He laughed loudly and gleefully. And then he noticed that two of his assailants wore uniforms of blue. He was lifted horizontally into the air, and the walls and floor slid by him bumpily.

4.

O'Brien was neither arrested nor taken to the hospital. He was subdued by one man and was driven to his home.

The man was the younger of the two policemen. He had been a classmate of O'Brien's in high school, had played football on the second team, and had looked up admiringly, almost worshipfully to O'Brien, who in those days had easily pinned him in wrestling and outrun him on the field.

He set O'Brien on his feet in the bright daylight of the parking lot. O'Brien was still struggling, but Clatty, with one arm, immobilized both of O'Brien's arms. The massiveness of muscle astonished O'Brien; it was as if he had been anchored to a granite wall. Clatty snapped handcuffs on O'Brien's wrists and held his two arms easily with one hand. He put his other hand over O'Brien's mouth, out of which curses, laughter, and obscenities were streaming, and pressed with excruciating power on both sides of the jaw, saying calmly enough, "No more of that, Ted."

"Don't hurt him!" cried O'Brien's mother.

"He'll be all right, Mrs. O'Brien."

Clatty looked at O'Brien with earnest scrutiny and said, "Can I let you go, Ted?"

O'Brien didn't know what to do. His eyes jerked this way and that. Many people had come outside. He realized of a sudden that he wanted to be stopped, wanted to be immobilized. He sighed and dropped his head. All the energy had gone out of him. Clatty repeated his question. O'Brien raised his eyes to Clatty's and nodded.

"We'll take him home," said Clatty to O'Brien's mother, "but I won't release him unless a doctor says so."

"Are you coming out of it, Ted?" he asked.

O'Brien said quietly, "Hi, Clatty." He was light-headed,

confused, and very tired. Clatty removed the handcuffs.

In the car, sitting beside Clatty, who had asked his mother to sit up front, O'Brien said, "How've you been, Clatty?" His eyes were closing.

The doctor was portly and balding, but O'Brien recognized the urbane, wryly witty young Dr. Stewart who had tended him in his childhood. He had brought a nurse. He questioned O'Brien, obviously wanting to know if he was rational. "You'd better lie down, kid," he said. "I'm going to give you a shot. It'll help you sleep."

The shot was administered in O'Brien's old bedroom upstairs. His mother loosened his shoes and took them off, and slipped off his torn jacket.

Clatty rested his hand on O'Brien's shoulder where he lay on the bed. "I'm sorry about the cuffs, Ted," he said quietly. O'Brien pressed his hand and said, "That's okay, Clatty." He let out a long sigh and felt his neck and shoulders relaxing. "I always liked you, Clatty," he added.

His mother was bending over him. He wanted to say something to her, but he was so amazed that she was there, that she had come to him in his hurt . . . He lifted both arms to her and said, "Mom . . . do you know . . ." He forgot what he wanted to say. Then he noticed tears in her eyes and this filled him with gladness. He smiled at her. A massive softening and spreading had happened inside him, irresistibly large, irresistibly gentle, and his consciousness followed it and joined it peacefully.

It was evening when O'Brien woke up. The light was fading at the windows. He heard a telephone ringing and could hear a woman's voice saying, ". . . thank you . . . yes . . . he's sleeping . . . the doctor has been here. He's coming out of it. Thank you very much."

When he realized where he was, he remembered the events of the morning and he sat up in bed quaking with guilt and anxiety. The jacket he had borrowed in New York, now torn and dirty, lay on a chair beside the bed. He found a crumpled pack of cigarettes.

He couldn't remember the moment in which he had passed from compliance to violence, though he remembered many things. He felt terribly at fault toward his mother—but of all the actions of that morning's outburst, there was not a single one he wished he could take back.

Two sets of memories came to dominate the others. He could see again the brave frail old man who had stepped so resolutely into his path. He wished he could explain to that man why he had tried to tear things up. He wanted him to know that it was a principled violence, not a mere aberration; and he wanted him to know that there were many many institutions of American life that he would gladly destroy, destroy utterly and permanently. He found it difficult, even in imagination, to complete this explanation without setting his teeth in rage. Each time he did this the face of the old man faded away.

The other dominating memories were of Clatty. They had not been close friends in high school, but they had been friendly, and they had trained together for a month before their final football season. He remembered Clatty's joyous early-morning greetings on the empty field, and he remembered his hopeful, encouraging, openly admiring ways. There had been a gladness in Clatty, a lovingness that had been hurt many times in that adolescent world.

The telephone rang again. O'Brien heard his mother's voice, apparently answering the identical questions she had answered before. . . .

Daylight was waning. The white brick grade school had faded in the distance, but rich, darkened greens still glowed near the house: the sycamore tree at the side, the poplars and elms of the adjacent yard, the huge butternuts, the maples, the big cherry at the end of his own large yard, the catalpa across the alley, and the ivy on the house beside it.

O'Brien's face and neck were scratched. He was bruised

in many places. His jaw was sore where Clatty had squeezed it.

He heard the telephone again, and once again listened to his mother's gracious, musical voice. That voice, for the first time, was sounding in the house unopposed, was simply on its own.

He wondered if the burial had taken place. But it must have. That was why the nurse had come—to sit with him during his mother's absence.

His mother came to the door and knocked softly, saying quietly, "Teddy? Are you awake, honey?" He put out his cigarette and didn't answer. When he heard her footsteps on the stairs he took another cigarette from the crumpled pack.

He thought of Brockmeyer, and of the beautiful woman he had seen at the studio; and of Malcolm Dudley; and of Ellen Roth, and David Kahn. It was incredible that he had seen them just yesterday; they seemed years and years away. He thought of them at length. He remembered Ellen saying, "You live the moment with great vitality, O'Brien—but you live the years with something like despair." He had known immediately that that was true, but he had turned her words aside. She had said them in an odd way. Those phrases—*live the moment . . . great vitality . . . something like despair*—were not the kind she ordinarily spoke, and he had said to her, "You're imitating your therapist, aren't you? You're speaking in his voice." "So?" she had said. "That's okay. It's part of the process of assimilation. I mean, all kids imitate their parents, don't they? And whatever else I'm doing, I'm growing up." "Yes," he had said, "that's a good point"—and they had dropped the subject of his despair.

His mother came to the door again and knocked. She opened the door very quietly, but didn't enter or speak. O'-Brien wondered if she smelled the cigarette. She closed the door and went away. A moment later the doorbell rang, and then he heard voices in the living room.

He found a piece of paper and wrote a note saying, *I'll*

see you at breakfast. I'm trying to think. He slipped this note under the door, and locked the door from the inside. Moving quietly and swiftly he raised the window, removed the sliding screen, put a chair into place . . . and stepped out onto the back-porch roof.

The sudden openness of sky and night was like a sigh of relief. The night was so wide, so filled with trees and stars, so high, so extraordinarily beautiful! It seemed to be pulsing. The moon was a thin crescent, the stars were numerous and bright, and there was only the mildest, softest movement of summer air. Everything was familiar: the large trees, the scattered yellow rectangles of lighted windows, the regularly spaced houses following the slopes of the hills, the dark expanse of grass in the yard, the flagstone walk, the flower beds. . . . He breathed deeply and looked up at the moon, and then, staying close to the wall, stepping only on the overlapping joints of the roof slates so as not to break them, he made his way to the edge of the roof. He kept one hand on the rainspout and one on the ivy-covered trellis and stepped down to the ground, as he had done so many times in his boyhood and youth, unsuspected by his sheltered mother or his self-assured grandmother.

He went around to the front of the house, just far enough to glance into the living-room windows. One of the visitors was Mrs. Benicke; the other was a woman he didn't know. He went around back again, walked up the flagstone path between the beds of flowers, descended the steps by the double garage, and set off down the alley.

The town was still magnetized by the erotism of his youth. Certain streets seemed to glow and draw him. He passed the house in which handsome, erotic, chaste Angelina had lived, whose breasts were the marvel of the school. In the very next house lived, or had lived, another Italian family, also known for its daughters, but especially for Donna, whose singing could be heard from the kitchen window or the darkened porch in the evening. She had married and moved away when O'Brien was twelve. He went to the corner, where there had been once a weedy tract with short, steep slopes on which two willow trees had grown, and where with his eight- and nine-year-old pals he had thrown himself into the sports and games of the Great Depression, in winter sliding on barrel-stave skis, in summer swinging from the end of a strong rope. The hollow had been filled. Three houses stood on the tract, each with a yard. The house on the corner was fenced both ways.

He turned to the left, following the route he had taken to grade school, along which they had played endless games of marbles. Here again were magnetic houses in which girls had lived who had matured before his own puberty: Lillian, who was slim and dark-haired, on the left; and on the right, on a high bank, Ramona, who was shy and guilty-looking, with a frightened voice, a pretty face, brown hair, a full, soft body.

There were no houses beyond the grade school, only fields, and in the distance a highway. O'Brien passed the school at a pensive gait and turned up a leafy alley toward the center of town. He could hear radios and voices from time to time, and the sounds of cars. Soon, half expecting to see a sixteen-year-old girl come to the window and lean out, he stood behind the small redbrick house to which Carole Bucholz had moved in her teens. A plump middle-aged woman passed in and out of the kitchen. It was not Carole's mother. He went on, crossing the main street of the town and plunging into another quarter, this one magnetized by three girls, but especially by Wanda French, who had initiated him sexually when he was fifteen. She had been three years older than he. He had probably loved her, but had been so giddy with lust and gratification that that had never occurred to him. Her fiancé had finished college and come home, and she had broken with O'Brien, who had been her secret. He looked at her house with fascination. He could see an elderly man and woman reading newspapers in stuffed chairs, and they were indeed Wanda's parents. He had seen them many times, but never once had they seen him. They were close to death, those two. He walked on, circling gradually to the left, and in fifteen minutes entered a little park that he had used to love and of which, in recent years, he had dreamed. Enormous elms, maples, sycamores, and poplars were scattered on terraces down a long hill, at the foot of which lay the borough swimming pool. Midway on the hill, on the broadest terrace, there was a playground for children, and facing it across an open space with a drinking fountain was a large octagonal pavilion with a bandstand. Its roof was of asphalt shingles; its wooden posts and latticework sides were a freshly painted white. He had attended dances there for years, looking on as an excited boy, and finally dancing himself. The usual music had been a juke box, but on special occasions a band had played. He heard voices as he walked, voices softened by the foliage of the trees, and he encountered strolling couples, their arms round each other's waists, or holding hands. A gang of excited boys hurried past him. He went up the terraces on small dirt paths he knew by heart, up a flight of wooden steps, through the open gate of a hurricane fence . . . and there lay the hard-packed, grassless football field, with simple bleachers on both sides and a black cinder track encircling it, and the redbrick high school just fifty yards away. The faces of teammates came back to him and he remembered the arduous routines he and Clatty had gone through in their training. He remembered the Friday-night dances at roadhouses, victory cigars, and the late sweet hours in the car when Carole had made love with abandon. He walked the full length of the field, savoring the sky and the mellow night. Evidently there had been a baseball game that evening; groups of friends and family groups had remained in the bleachers and were talking. Several young boys, ten and eleven years old, awake, one would think, long past their bedtime, were running short sprints in the darkness on the cinder track, their heads down and their arms pumping. Two mongrel dogs chased each other among the boys.

O'Brien went on. He came to the main drag again and crossed it, and went down a dirt road that passed between two cemeteries, a small one with graves from the Revolutionary

War and a large one with extensive tracts of undisturbed grass. Both cemeteries had served as playgrounds and as lovers' walks.

Not a single thought had crossed O'Brien's mind all this time, though he had had no other intention than to think.

The dirt road had descended a long hill and now was climbing a hill of the same pitch and height. At the top O'-Brien saw a tree that he remembered and that aroused a pang of confused longing. Several times that night he had recognized particular trees with an affection that bordered on joy. This one was a large maple with heavy, widely branching limbs. It stood just inside the white picket fence of the cemetery on the very crest of the hill. He and his friends had built a platform in its branches when he had been thirteen. They had stolen cigarettes and had smoked them in this leafy hideaway. Often he had gone there alone and had lain on the platform looking out at two tiny white steeples, set among trees and rooftops, near the bend of a river. Hundreds of tiny white houses in curving rows stepped up the wooded slopes that rose from the river. Before the town lay some large fields, on which cattle could be seen. The fields were bordered by a curving white road. He had loved to look at that town and dream the romance of the future—adventure, love, and achievement, all cloudy and enticing. He looked up at the dark tree. It was one of the few things that seemed larger than he remembered. The platform was gone. He climbed the fence and hoisted himself into the branches, glancing at the stars as he climbed. The Milky Way was rich and dense. He found a comfortable perch, lit a cigarette, and looked out. Insects ticked and pulsed. All around him was the broad, quiet feel of a settled summer night, somewhat cooler now than before. He could see a few lighted windows, and here and there on rooftops a dull gleam of starlight. A car passed below him. He wanted to collect and organize his thoughts and he had expected that here, especially, he would be able to do that, but nothing purposive came to mind, only more images of the past: going away to war in the navy, and the dull misery of enforced studies that meant nothing to him but temporary advantage—a bad choice. And then the years of alienation in New York, the discovery of social injustice and of radical politics. . . . He finished his cigarette, climbed back down, and walked home. Before he reached the house, he knew that he would go back to New York the next day. It would distress his mother, and for that he was sorry.

Almost all of the houses were dark now; his own was entirely dark. Forgetting that he had locked his room, he crossed the porch and tried to open the front door, which proved to be locked. In the instant that he tugged on the handle he remembered that his father had come home late one night, as late as this, too drunk to climb the stairs, and had fallen and passed out cold on the foyer rug.

He went around back and climbed the trellis, crept stealthily over the roof slates and looked cautiously into his mother's bedroom. He could scarcely see her. She lay on her side, facing away from him. Her outline under the summer blanket was simply a female shape, broad at the hips. She slept neatly, decorously, as she did all things. She had been good to him when he was a child, and had failed his manhood terribly, counseling at every turn cowardice, expediency, and money. He sighed, and wondered how she would fare now that her mother was dead.

He stepped inside the open window of his room, inserted the screen, and went to bed.

5.

In the morning, in the first moments of consciousness, the enormity of what he had done sped through him in a wave of guilt and anxiety, but this time he saw things as they must have appeared in the eyes of others, and he understood that he had indeed lost all control. Even so, there was nothing he would willingly take back. Why did he feel guilt, then? He was puzzled, because feel it he did.

At breakfast he said to his mother that he would be leaving later that day. A small panic appeared in her face, but she was too aggrieved to argue with him.

He said to her, "I want to come back in a couple of months and spend some time with you, but I can't stay now, mom. I just can't."

She answered quietly, studying his face, "I understand, dear."

He borrowed enough money from her to pay back Malcolm Dudley and buy him a new coat, though she mended the torn one very skillfully. While she worked on it, he walked to the florist's shop on the main street, where he bought a wreath. Later, driving his mother's car, he went with her to his grandmother's grave, which wasn't far from the tree he had climbed during the night. He was surprised to see that his grandmother was buried beside the grave that held his father's ashes. He placed his wreath on the newly-mounded earth. He wished that he could pray or give some sign that he did actually honor her death, though he felt no sorrow at all. He stood there with a bowed head. He put his arm around his mother's shoulders and kissed her temple, glancing aside at his father's small headstone. His mother watched him cautiously. Several times she seemed about to speak. She said at last, "Let's go home now, Teddy. I'm glad we came, dear; very glad."

That afternoon he went to the attic with her and she opened one of a number of cedar chests and took out some shirts, an expensive woolen sweater, two pairs of pants. She knelt by the box while he held these things against his body. The pants were only a trifle short. The other things were all right.

He said to her hesitantly while she knelt there, "Were you in love . . . with dad when you married him?"

She looked away and said quietly, "No . . ."

He hesitated, and she said, "This is not a good time, Teddy."

She offered to drive him downtown—the bus would be leaving just before dark—but her night vision was poor, and so he declined and walked to the trolley, wearing Dudley's mended jacket and carrying a suitcase that had belonged to his grandmother. When night fell the bus had passed beyond the city. He sat by a window not even looking out. He wanted to sleep but couldn't. He remembered coming home after the war, eager to read the books he had had to put aside, and wanting to try his hand at stories, but his grandmother had upbraided him endlessly: for not shaving every day, for letting his hair get long, for lounging around with a book in his hand, for not finding a job, for keeping late hours, for seeing girls she didn't approve of. He heard his mother's voice speaking in the girlish tones that had charmed his friends. "It's such a rough game, Teddy—it looks as if you're knocking him down"—over a picture in the paper of O'Brien tackling a runner; and his two friends had laughed and one had said, "You have to admit, Ted, it does look that way." He shook his head. Her naïveté had made them feel like seasoned, worldly men—as only raw, raw youths can feel. A face appeared among these memories that alarmed him. He didn't recognize it and yet some powerful emotion was attached to it. And then he remembered: it was the solemn, brave, frail old man who had stepped before him so resolutely up at Hammerschmidt's. . . . O'Brien gasped and put both hands to his face. He slid down in his seat, his ears buzzing and his face and hands as cold as ice. He could see his grandmother's body in the casket, could see himself striking it, shaking it roughly, and ripping the brocaded dress. Something in his mind had blocked those memories, had held them away totally, but now he could hear again the cries of horror, and could see again, where he had torn her dress, her bloodless skin sagging against the bones. . . .

This rush of memory didn't end, but like an anchor emerging from the ocean brought with it strange relics, *relics of the present:* he remembered the day his father died. He had seen it all, had seen the body lying on the basement floor, had seen the policemen going into the house. Their car was across the street; neighbors had gathered around it. It was not only his mother and grandmother who had kept those things from him, but he himself. Now all those events came back to him.

It was late in February, a Saturday morning. He was ten years old. He had rushed out after breakfast, mackinaw open because the winter was breaking, and had gone toward the grade school, where his friends often gathered. Once out of the house, however, he had begun to dawdle. In one pocket of his mackinaw he carried an orange, and in the other a small polished block of wood on which he had cut the outline of a bull's head with an electric stylus. He had made one just like it for his friend Sammy. As he walked along, he turned it in his pocket, stroking it and tracing the outline with his fingertip. He called on Sammy, but there was no response. He went to the garage around back, where Sammy's father often used a lathe and table saw, but no one was there. He walked on through their yard, across the alley, and through another yard to the old cemetery. There was no caretaker. Several times, in an empty corner near the houses, he and his friends had built fires and roasted potatoes. But no one was in sight. He hadn't been there since the snow had receded, and he found the horseshoe they had lost in the thick grass of autumn. He hung it prominently on the bare bushes. Then he went back to the street and made his way toward the school. Down the street, on the opposite sidewalk, three of his friends were hurrying toward him, skipping from the gutter to the pavement. Two older boys were striding ahead, not looking back. Before he could wave or shout he realized that they had seen him. They looked away and broke into a run, the younger boys pushing the elder in their hurry. A pang went through him. What were they guilty of? Or what had he done? At the end of the block the father of another boy played water from the garden hose over the driveway, washing the cinders out. He was talking to a neighbor who stood on the front porch in his shirtsleeves. Both men stopped talking as he passed them, and both looked at him in a peculiar way. He was puzzled and worried, and ran home, keeping to the alleys.

A police car was parked across the street. A large number of neighbors, some without coats or sweaters, stood talking around it. He was afraid to go in. He ran around back, and there, crouching on his hands and knees at a window not much bigger than his head, he looked at the strangers who crowded the cellar, and he caught glimpses, as they moved, of the body of his father on the floor.

He had wandered the streets all day, afraid to go home, sick with sadness, confusion, guilt, and shame. He threw his orange furtively into a sewer, and with a strange, perplexed anxiety threw his polished block of wood over a house down into a stand of trees.

These scenes came back to O'Brien as he sat there on the bus, his face in his hands. They came back with a power both of recognition and estrangement. What a secret he had planted in his life! He had lied to himself for years, exactly as had his mother!

He took his suitcase and tottered down to the front of the bus, where he prevailed upon the driver to let him out. He called his mother from a gas station, and then stood near the pumps and questioned likely drivers and soon was given a ride to the city, from which he took the trolley to his own small town.

As he walked from the trolley stop down to his home he wondered what the neighbors might be thinking who just three hours ago had seen him leaving town.

6.

O'Brien drank tea with his mother in the kitchen. She had been crying and was very tired. He knew that she was hoping he would stay with her. He didn't want to encourage those hopes and hurt her again, and so he began by saying that he would leave in the morning. She watched him silently. She wore a blue robe with a white lace collar. Her face looked older than it had before.

"Mom," he said, "the reason I came back . . . I want you to know . . . all these years . . . I thought because you lied to me about dad . . . but on the bus . . ."

He told her what had happened.

"It was me, not you," he said, "and I want you to know . . ."

"We were afraid you would be ashamed," she said.

"Well, I want you to know how sorry I am . . . I'm sorry for the things I've done all these years. I've been a rotten son."

"You haven't done bad things, Teddy. And you haven't been a rotten son. You got off the track somewhere, that's all."

"I don't know exactly what I'll do," he said, "but I want to be of help in some way . . . and . . . I don't know, mom . . . just be better."

She reached across the table and rested her hand on his. "I know you do, darling," she said. "It was dear of you to come back and tell me."

He leaned over and kissed her forehead; but when her eyes met his, they were merely tired, there was no spark in them of special acknowledgment. And when his eyes met hers they were only observant, somewhat remotely observant, though he had meant every word he had said.

She came down with him early in the morning, dressed in her robe, intending to go back to bed, and they embraced and parted at the door.

The day was beautiful, bright and clear. As he went up the street carrying his suitcase he imagined that the neighbors who had seen him leaving and arriving yesterday were watching him leaving now, and he giggled, imagining them saying, "Oh yes . . . that's O'Brien."

But he had been scoured by emotion so many times that after that moment of humor a convalescent, constricted mood settled down on him and he walked along with his eyes on the ground.

He took his seat on the trolley. There were only a few passengers, several women, one with a little girl, one elderly man. No one seemed to recognize him. He sat alone at a window on one of the double seats, slouching and bracing one knee against the seat in front. In the distance he could see the tops of the large trees in the park by the high school. Every house by the tracks was familiar to him, and the red-and-white trolley itself was as familiar as the furniture of his own home. He listened to the dense, firm sound of the steel wheels on the steel rails, and the whispering and clicking of the contact arm sliding along the wires overhead, and he felt the vibration of the firm woven straw seat beneath him, the same vibration that during the hot years of puberty and adolescence had given him erections. He remembered how difficult it had been to control that, and he thought of the girls of high school, the great study unmentioned in the curriculum, the older ones about to leave when he arrived, the younger ones arriving just before he left, with their budding, sensitive breasts and their exciting infatuation with the great mystery. He thought of the kinds of hips, and the kinds of buttocks, and the motions in which they were displayed; and of the many kinds of breasts; and of the long-legged girls, and the long-waisted ones; and of shoulder-length hair in this color and that; and of eyes and the use of eyes, playful eyes, bedroom eyes, eyes that promised to share the guilt, to create a secret and keep it; and of kissable moist lips. . . .

This phantasmagoria passed as it were just inside the threshold of consciousness, without special energy and without altering the stasis of convalescence. The trolley rolled along at the ends of the dead-end streets: backyard, house, frontyard, street, frontyard, house, backyard, alley, trees everywhere, now over a high trestle, and now houses and yards again . . . white sheets were swaying on a line, bellying and rippling in the mild breeze . . . and there crossed his inner vision, in one swift flow of images, the events of the winter and spring of his eighth year. The backyard had filled with snow that year, and one day, after a fresh snowfall, an apparition of such beauty had appeared that he had caught his breath at the window and had clapped his hands with delight. It was a red-and-white collie dog, trotting to and fro, its elegant paws tossing the white powder and its plumed tail sweeping the drifts. He ran out to it immediately. The dog was friendly and high-spirited; it came to the porch to be fed, allowed itself to be petted, and romped with him in the snowy yard. All winter the dog played in the neighborhood, eating at several houses and sleeping outdoors, and then, before spring, it vanished.

O'Brien was not yet aware that in remembering these scenes he was gazing at the face of his young mother. He had argued with her and had pleaded, and finally she had relented and bought him a puppy. He named the pup Rennie, and took care of it himself, feeding and bathing it, housebreaking it and training it to keep off the furniture. It slept in a box by his bed, but often he would lift it up quietly and place it against his pillow and fall asleep talking to it. In midspring the pup caught a cold. The cold worsened rapidly. His breathing became a horrible gurgling and his eyes a filmy gel. He was unable even to lift his head. O'Brien's mother brought some paregoric from the medicine chest and gave a large dose of it to the puppy. "You have to understand, honey," she said, "Rennie can never get well. He's going to go to sleep now, but instead of waking up he'll just keep sleeping." She took his hand and went with him out of the room, closing the door behind them. Two hours later she carried the dog's box down into the cellar. The man from next door came over and the boy heard the side door opening and saw the man crossing the yard with a bundle under his arm and a spade in his hand. He ran out after him. His mother called to him to come back, but the man waved to her that it would be all right.

While he dug the hole he talked to the boy. The dog would become part of the earth again. Everything belonged to the earth and returned to the earth; it was like going home. "You'll see grass and flowers here in the summer," he said, "and then you'll know what I mean."

The boy didn't speak, but kept looking at the checkered oilcloth in which his dog was wrapped. He couldn't tell which end was his head and which his tail, there was so much wrapping. The man dug two feet down and laid the bundle in the hole very gently. He handed the spade to the boy and watched while he threw in a covering of earth, and then he took back the spade and filled the grave to the top.

The boy's father didn't come home for supper that night. He and his mother ate alone. He could scarcely swallow. He was embarrassed about not eating and didn't want to draw attention to himself, but later that night, after he had been in bed for an hour, he lost his self-control. A strong wind had come up. It had begun to rain fitfully. He thought he could hear the dog whimpering. It seemed possible that the medicine had worn off, the dog had awakened and was buried alive. He knew very well that the chances were against it, but he kept listening at the window. He opened the window and put his head out in the rain and tried to penetrate the darkness to where the dog was buried. The whimpering sounded again, clearly and unmistakably. He ran to the head of the stairs and called down to his mother that Rennie was crying. He heard his father's voice. They were whispering loudly, and he could tell by his mother's tone that his father had been drinking. The two of them came upstairs.

His mother saw the open window. She closed it and said to him gently, "Go back to bed now, dear, and try to sleep." He said, "Rennie's crying, mom," and began to sob violently. She sat beside him on the edge of the bed and put her arm around him and stroked his cheek, explaining to him that what he had heard was the wind, that Rennie was fast asleep and would never wake up. She held the covers for him and with her other hand insisted that he get back in bed. She leaned over him and kissed his forehead, saying, "Try to sleep now, darling." She left the room, but stopped in the doorway.

His father, all this while, had been watching him.

"Edward, let him sleep now."

But his father sat on the bed. The boy felt himself shrinking. They wouldn't raise their voices but they were fighting all the same, and there was something deadly in it.

His father said thickly, "I'm sorry Rennie's dead." The boy didn't answer. "He was such a nice pup," his father said. There was a far-off quality to his voice that the boy was familiar with but didn't understand.

The only light in the room came from the hall.

"I think I can hear him," said the boy.

For a few moments neither the boy nor his father spoke. Suddenly, in the silence, the understanding passed between them that they both were listening. In the moaning of the wind there seemed to be another sound like a dog whimpering.

Again they looked at each other.

"Come," his father said. "Get dressed. We'll go and see."

While the boy put his clothes on he could hear his parents' voices downstairs. They were having a real argument now.

At the foot of the stairs his father was holding out the boy's rubber raincoat. His father was wearing his own, a gray gabardine.

It was late April. The night was chilly. There was a turbulence in the yard; the shrubs with their new buds were thrashing and bending in the wind and flickering erect again between the gusts. The rain wasn't heavy, but it was driven by the wind and lightly stung his face. The ground was soggy. They went up the flagstone walk. The back-porch light threw a hazy glow that grew dim at the end of the yard. His father walked behind him with one hand on his shoulder. "Did you help bury him?" he asked.

They stood looking down at the torn, slightly mounded sods. His father's trouser cuffs and pointed shoes, a light tan, were wet and a little muddy. He put one foot on the blade of the spade and pushed it in. Soon the checkered oilcloth came into view and the rain crackled on it, flashing where the drops washed the dirt away.

His father knelt and lifted the bundle out of the hole. He laid it on the grass and lifted away the swaddling of rags. The dog's feet could be seen, and then his back . . . and there he lay, in profile against the rags and the oilcloth and the wet grass. His eyes were open, his pointed ears were stiff; his mouth was open, showing his small teeth; his lips were black and ragged. The boy knelt and put his hands under the dog and picked him up. He heard a wrenching, gasping sob behind him, and then he dropped his head to the wet shoulder of the dog and crouched there crying violently. At length his father picked him up and carried him back to the house, and evidently he had fallen asleep before they reached it.

O'Brien was crying on the trolley. He sat slouched in the seat, his chin on his chest and one hand over his face. He tried to cry silently but there was nothing he could do about the heaving of his chest.

He saw again and again certain expressions on his father's face, certain movements of his hands and eyes, and saw the boy lifting his head to look at his father—and O'Brien's crying broke out afresh each time. After years of nothingness he was seeing the face of his father, and it was this, not the memory of the dog or the boy, that moved him so powerfully, the suffering of the tormented man, who at the time of those events was only twenty-eight years old, O'Brien's age in the present. He thought of his father's strange, distracted look, with its immediacy and odd, yearning sweetness, and its other presence that was watching with a sickened cold smile and that must have been the one who killed him two years later. He thought of the alcohol he had smelled on his father's breath that night, and of the handsome, well-kept hands that had held him, not—so he thought—consolingly, but desperately, and needing something to cling to. He remembered the inert legs on the cellar floor, and he murmured, *Poor man, poor, poor man.* They must have felt like outsize children, those two, desperately trying to raise a child of their own, unable to comfort or sustain each other, and really adrift in life.

He sat there on the trolley not looking up, unwilling to put an end to those thoughts, unwilling to get up and leave.

And the trolley, in the meantime, with its grinding, rolling vibrations, and the openings and closings of its doors, passed through the whole of its downtown loop, and carried him back to the suburbs.

He laughed aloud as he went down his street again, suitcase in hand, imagining the neighbors who had seen him leave and then promptly arrive, now having seen him leave again and even more speedily arrive, saying, as they lifted their heads, "Ah . . . there's O'Brien."

As he drew near the house he saw his mother on the porch talking to the mailman. She stood there after the mailman went on, sorting letters.

O'Brien called to her and she looked up in surprise, and seeing him waving and grinning, she came alight for a moment with the girlish charm he remembered from his youth. "Why, Teddy," she said, as he stepped up on the porch, "how nice to see you!"

7.

O'Brien stayed with her for a week. He helped her bring down boxes from the attic, not only her mother's things but her own as well, dresses, shoes, and hats she seemed willing to part with now. She sorted everything into piles, some to be given to friends, some to be held for the church bazaar, and some for the Salvation Army. They cleaned out closets in the bedrooms and shelves in the cellar.

She introduced him one night to a caller. It was the handsome gentleman with the luxuriant hair, whom he had met at Hammerschmidt's, and who turned out to have been, as O'Brien had guessed, a professor of English literature, at least briefly, and then for many years an administrator at a small college in the city. They sat in the living room with tea and cake. O'Brien saw that the man was not a scholar, had no intellectual interests of any kind, had run out of steam long ago, and was left with nothing now but attitudes and genteel pretensions. O'Brien saw, however, that these very things meant much to his mother, to whom they promised companionship, stability, and peace.

The suitor's name was Oscar Parsons. He stared at O'-Brien with desperate, antagonistic, cautious eyes, and said, "I have the leisure now to go back to a study that I pursued for many years with considerable interest . . ." and so forth, and described in brief an idea by no means negligible, but he spoke every syllable with agonized deliberation, knowing that O'-Brien, who sat there nodding encouragingly, took it all to be utterly empty. As for O'Brien—he had noticed that Parsons's ankles hurt him when he walked; he could hear the whispering of Parsons's dentures; and he judged by the way Parsons held his wide, fleshy body on the edge of the easy chair that several ailments were in progress, perhaps severe ones.

Yet both men were aware that O'Brien's mother was pleased, and both glanced at her deferentially as they talked. Three months later she wrote to O'Brien saying that she would be marrying Mr. Parsons, but this letter was followed a mere two weeks later by another telling the grievous news that her husband-to-be was dead of a massive coronary thrombosis. When O'Brien saw his mother next he was shocked by her appearance, and he asked himself, "Has she really given up the hope of love? Even of companionship? Is she resigning herself simply to living in that house alone?"

During the week that he stayed with her, and while her hopes were still high, he planned what he would do when he returned to New York. He would locate the woman named Claudia, whom he had met at Brockmeyer's studio. He would try his hand at gallery notes and articles . . . and he wondered if that would bring him into friendly competition with Dudley; there was something he relished in that thought. He decided, also, to go back to school. He could take one course at a time, more if possible, and finish the classwork for his doctorate. He would move to a new apartment. He would apply for an instructorship, though he didn't believe that he was cut out for teaching. And he would eliminate the sex from his relationship with Ellen Roth. Perhaps after all they were friends; certainly they were not lovers.

Over all these thoughts, which perhaps were not quite plans, and yet were more than mere wishes, there hovered the figure of Brockmeyer, the painter. The things O'Brien admired in him, and envied so painfully: his extraordinary security in the world, his *place* in human life, and the powerful gift that sustained it—these things were not to be dreamed of for himself; yet it was clear, in spite of that, that he had taken Brockmeyer as a personal ideal, he did not know why, or in what way he could emulate a man so superior to himself.

Of the changes in his relations with his mother he was most aware of this one: that where before he had thought complainingly, *She doesn't know me, we are almost like strangers,* he now observed objectively, and with a willingness to improve the situation, that they were indeed, in important ways, really like strangers.

Like strangers—except that her voice, at times, could irradiate his being from some stronghold within him; and when she broke into song, as she did one afternoon working alone in the kitchen, he felt a love and sorrow that he dared not attempt to express.

She came out of the kitchen and sat in her chair in the bay window over the flower beds. She had left a stack of papers on the window seat, bills and unanswered letters, and she placed some on the little table before her and bent over them and began to write. O'Brien was removing slipcovers from the furniture in the living room and he glanced at her without speaking. The light was hazy in her reddish-brown gray hair. Beneath her chin there sagged the second chin of settled middle age. She had put on her glasses. The flesh of her arms was too full, too soft. Her skin was blemished in many places, arms and face both. He looked in amazement at her fingers, at the gentle hump at the top of her spine, at her rounded shoulders, at the square-heeled, plain, strong shoes she wore, and at her thickened ankles. All was change and death; and yet he saw a schoolgirl in her posture at the little table. She looked up and saw that he had been watching her, and smiled. O'-Brien felt a catch at his heart, and then he blushed guiltily, as if in seeing her in this mortal dissolution into dust he had robbed her of filial love.

By so much was he still unweaned.

A TALE OF PIERROT

We are an industrial city, but the old hillside town of stone houses and cobblestone streets still exists. One can still look down into the park of the ancient square and see the huge, carefully tended trees, and the tawny openings that are the bumpy, dusty lanes for *boules*. One can see the diminutive bandstand, and on the far side of the park, not vastly changed from former years, the two restaurants and two cafés. It was here, near the promenade, that half a lifetime ago there appeared a spectacular canopy of white and orange stripes, an irresistible sight, especially from a distance at night, glowing among the trees. Beneath it a company of young Parisians guided our Provençal townsfolk in the making of banners and lanterns, papier-mâché figures, masks and emblems. And it was here, in this park, on the night of the carnival itself, that Minot Larbaud, my mother's youngest brother, my own much-loved uncle, discovered the sublime, ridiculous gift that changed his life.

1. MINOT'S MASK

Minot was thirty-two; I was twenty. We were devotees of *la pétanque* and bowled in the park almost every evening, often with his fiancée, Estelle, and her youngest sister, who became my wife; and then we'd take a table at Flam's, or—after the canopy went up—join our acquaintances at the long tables under the striped canvas. Masks and banners dangled among the lights. Placards with red lettering and green borders, yellow-and-blue shields, cardboard hats, unfinished masks lay on the tables among jars of paint with long-handled brushes. Sedate housewives and some few husbands kneaded mounds of clay and plunged handfuls of shredded paper into buckets of watery paste. The canopy was open on four sides. Waiters hurried in to us from across the promenade, and in the shadowy park masked children leaped from behind trees with their hands in the air. The discreet, yet insistent dense clicking of the steel balls of *la pétanque* sounded continually.

Among the theater folk who were instructing us was a slender young woman who was a dancer and mime. She fell in love with Minot and watched him for days in a trance of adoration. Finally, in a halting, whispering voice, she spoke to him. She was shy beyond belief. One could imagine that her true speech consisted entirely of ecstasy and despair, and that she had become a mime for sheer lack of ordinary words. A few days later we noticed that she had begun to imitate the intonations of his voice.

Such things were frequent with Minot. People stared when he passed. We said at home that he was Nature's boast. He was not tall, but was like a mighty Percheron, broad, immensely powerful, yet buoyant and lively in his bearing. His eyes were as brilliant and black as eyes can be, and his close-cropped hair was black. His skull was massive, his face broad at the cheekbones and chin.

All this was magnetic, but the infinitely attractive thing about him was something else, something rare and truly wondrous. It was his kindness. One would have thought it would take a patriarchal form, but in fact it was almost childlike, quick and sweet, and with a quality of unconscious faith. In other respects he was the image of ordinary civil life. He was a businessman, a supremely brilliant one, but he had gone into business early (our family's winery, of which he was the virtual manager) and had known little else but work.

This, then, was the man our young mime had come to adore. One night, in her stammering way, she asked permission to make a casting of his face. I realized, watching Minot's response, that he had been aware of her infatuation from the beginning. He spoke to her gently. She was a convalescent in the world.

A little crowd stood by and watched. He sat in a chair and she put a sheet around him. She dipped into a jar of petroleum jelly and slicked his eyebrows and the line of his hair. Even the waiters paused, some with trays of drinks balanced shoulder high. The kindliness one found so attractive in Minot resided chiefly in his eyes, and now that his eyes were closed one saw the massiveness of his features, and their calm, indifferent power.

He climbed onto a table she had prepared for him and lay flat. She placed straws in his nostrils and wedged them with bits of cotton, then stretched a towel over his hair and pinned it beneath his chin. Pat by pat she covered his face with plaster. She stepped back. He lay still. He looked like some chalky effigy dug from the ground.

Several nights later he and I were playing *boules*. As we finished our game we saw that three monsters had been observing us. One of them cried gruffly, "Good throw, Larbaud!" A moment later we heard the voice of the mime: "Monsieur Larbaud!" She came running, pressing a cardboard box against her stomach. She opened it and took out a casting of his face. The monsters lifted their masks and crowded beside us.

The casting was fine. One could see even the lashes of his closed eyes. She held it so that it caught the light.

"It's excellent work," he said.

She was rapturous. "I want to make you one," she said. She put it away almost reverently, and took out something else. "I tried this, too. It came out well, I think. Would you want it?"

It was a papier-mâché duplicate, trimmed like a mask

and painted white. Minot held it at arm's length. He smiled and expressed his thanks . . . but really, there was something about this mask he didn't like at all.

2. CARNIVAL

After two centuries without it, we were reviving our ancient carnival, though in a secular form, and at the harvest of the grapes rather than at Lent.

Cars had been banned from the old city. Strings of colored lanterns swayed like necklaces over the darkened streets. Excited youths were striding everywhere, and one could hear shouts and bursts of music.

Just at nightfall our doorbell rang. There came a knock at the inner door, and a massive Pierrot strode in.

My mother laughed. "How odd, Minot!"

He was wearing the mask of his own face. He had cut holes in the eyes and had painted the eyebrows black.

"But you look fine," she said. "Let me see you."

He posed for her, turning slowly to show off the loose tunic and pantaloons, all white, trimmed at the sleeves, the throat, and the tunic's edge in paper lace. He bowed to her, sweeping the floor with his conical hat.

I was dressed in a turban and cape. People were singing outside. My mother pushed us toward the door, promising to meet us in the park.

Balls of fire—torches—were flowing and bobbing downhill. Tiny goblins and princesses darted this way and that, and hastened back to striding groups to clutch the hands of kings and witches, houris, bandits. Our more sedentary neighbors leaned from their windows and called down to us gaily. The sky was black and filled with stars.

Minot and I joined our committee at the ancient town hall. The courtyard was noisy. Several bears, holding wrenches and screwdrivers, were tightening the slats of a four-wheeled cart. A stout monk stood on a chair and addressed the gathering in the voice of our socialist mayor. And then spoke a bear who was obviously our fire chief. Now the cart was ready, and the musicians climbed into it. We handed them their flutes and trumpets, a violin, a wineskin. We had arranged for a horse to pull this bulky contraption, and our monk emerged from the shadows leading it, but before he could reach the cart a startling laugh issued from the mask of Minot. He leaped between the shafts and seized them with his hands. Someone called "Pierrot!" There was a roar of approval. Minot strained. The cart began to roll. Several of us ducked between the shafts and got behind him. Our mayor abandoned the horse and scampered out front with his big bass drum. We emerged into the square and were met by delighted cheering, upon which our musicians struck up heartily. Our carnival was underway.

Of the many entertainments of that extraordinary night, now so far in the past, let me mention one, since it affected Minot (or so I believe), and contributed to his own fateful performance.

We had stopped our music cart at a corner near the crowded square. A fire truck was waiting for us, clanging its bell. Our horde of followers fanned out. Searchlights played over a building, and settled on a window two stories above the street, the shutters of which promptly opened. A lovelorn maiden leaned out. She held a paper rose, and while our horns and violins sighed for her lugubriously, she threw up her arms to the moon. Suddenly a handsome prince, a miraculous emanation from the shadows, ascended into the air, pedaling rapidly with his feet. He rose almost to a level with the maiden, and then dropped out of sight. In a moment, to her great joy, and to the joy of the crowd, he reappeared and they held out their arms to each other. . . . But I shall say no more of these aerial lovers, except that the prince's flights were powered by twenty bears in the darkness down below, catching and throwing him in a canvas rescue net.

Late that night, after other entertainments and the consumption of surely several tons of pastries, our town was contentedly falling asleep—except that fifty or sixty couples were still dancing in the park. Elsewhere the festive lights had been extinguished, but here, before the little band pavilion, the festooned lanterns glowed red and yellow and blue above the dancers' heads and against the still, black, starry sky.

Estelle and Minot had quarreled. That is, Minot was acting strangely and Estelle had quarreled with him. I had escorted the women home and had returned to the park. The musicians were playing a waltz. I found Minot gliding and pirouetting among the dancers by himself. Estelle had said that he was drunk, that she had never seen him this way, that he had refused to listen to her, etc.

He still wore his mask. His movements were so graceful, so extraordinarily balanced that I couldn't believe he was intoxicated. He seemed to float. His eyes were visible at the cut-out eyes of the mask, and I could see that from time to time, and for long moments at a time, his eyes were closed. The other dancers had removed their masks, as had I. We had removed them all together, hours ago, under the striped canopy where the refreshments had been served. Not that we meant to return yet to our lives of calendars and clocks! The musicians gave no sign of wanting to stop. There were bottles, cups, and glasses on the bandstand at their feet, and a clutter of paper in which pastries and sandwiches had been wrapped.

I spoke with Minot. The dark eyes that peered from his mask looked directly into mine, but without reciprocity.

I said, "I took them home," and he echoed my last word: "Home."

I was disconcerted and said, "Well, our carnival has been a great success." The massive head nodded, and the voice said, "Success."

I said, "Do you suppose there's more wine?"

Pierrot nodded again and said, "More wine." And then he laughed, laughed so winningly and deliciously, and with such prolonged abandon, that I too began to laugh, as did several couples nearby, who picked up his echo: "More wine! More wine!"

Hands thrust a wineskin toward me. Dancing couples stopped to chat, and little groups of talkers danced as they talked, trios and quartets gliding this way and that with their arms round each other's waists. We made up names of songs and requested them; and the musicians invented songs and filled our requests. The night air was as tasty as the wine. Above the gaily colored lanterns and the shadowy, massed leaves of our trees, a pointed moon could be seen. I heard laughter. Someone cried, "Larbaud!" I turned to see who was calling, but could not tell and could not see Minot. Then with comic abruptness the conical hat and masked face of Pierrot rose above the dancers. He held a wineglass. Several voices cried, "Larbaud!" He dropped out of sight. A moment later he emerged again, and there was laughter and a flourish of trumpets. Many voices called, "Larbaud!" He pretended to sip from his glass. This gesture, and his elevation in the air, made the grave face of his mask seem hilarious. He soared upward again —to a surprising height. The band greeted him with a crescendo, and we dancers, all of us, without ceasing to dance, cried, "Larbaud!" We were no longer a mere social group. We were the dancers of the dance called The Leaps of Pierrot. We whirled and laughed and shouted, "Larbaud!" And our glee brimmed over into joy, confused, disoriented joy, for he performed what one would have thought to be impossible.

The nearest strings of lanterns were not high, but they were higher than our heads. He rose into the air. He seemed to move like a seal in water. His head and shoulders reached the height of the lanterns. He raised one arm and turned his back to them, as if baring his belly to the stars. He passed over the lanterns and came to earth lightly on the other side.

We could not believe what we had seen. Rather, some believed and some did not. What a hubbub there was! The band was simply blaring. We were shouting all kinds of things. Perhaps we were singing. Pierrot threw up his arms and ran off into the night.

I went after him, calling first, "Larbaud!" and then, "Minot!"

He was trotting up the hill. He stopped and waited for me. We went through the narrow streets and came out on the hilltop, where there were trees. He was singing and reciting verses. I was laughing and talking volubly. I kept falling behind and then running to catch up. I was talking about some exploit, some marvelous event that made me laugh. Was it only a leap? The framework of the universe—that is to say, the structure of my thought—kept coming apart. One moment I was anxious, the next moment giddy and free. What song was he singing? I overtook him and began singing too, at the top of my voice. And then I shouted, "Minot! What have you done? It's absurd, Minot!"—and I laughed and fell behind, and felt the universe hammer frighteningly at the framework of my thought. What was he shouting? That bulky Pierrot was striding away. I had to run to catch up. He had lost his hat. His mask rode the top of his head, observing the stars. He was singing again, was quite drunk, actually, yet looked like an ecstatic choirboy. I felt that I should reason with him—that is, I kept reasoning with him, but always ended by joining his song.

3. GAMES

There are men whose gifts surpass the ordinary more spectacularly than did Minot's, gifts of spirit, intellect, language, imagination. We are accustomed to the almost godlike superiority of a handful of men. And certainly there was superiority in Minot's gift. But there was also something primitive. Even his admirers, seeing him leap, could not suppress their smiles. Minot himself would shrug with amusement. On the other hand, he could not resist leaping. He was possessed. And his demon, alas, was a giddy little boy . . . or something worse.

As for me . . . I was elated by this power. I wanted to be close to it. And truly there were times when it was not ludicrous at all, but sublime. I would say this especially of the international competition that established his fame.

I carried a card that identified me as his trainer and gave me access to the grassy field bounded by the running track. I held his sweatsuit while he leaped. I carried his extra shoes and a hamper of food. Otherwise I lay on the grass and watched the games, indulging the sweet fancy that the long evenings of my boyhood had come again, our wrestling matches and games of soccer, but heightened in a public form and brought to the very edge of human capacity. The games were decorative. Here in this great arena was the physical splendor of the human race. And here were we others who admired and shouted praise. The athletes were our ornaments and we were theirs.

The air was clear and brisk. The national flags that crowned the ring of steep bleachers trembled continually and were occasionally lifted into full display. Beyond the flags one could see the tops of mountains, and above the mountains a pale bright sky with vivid clouds.

Early in the day Minot attracted attention. His massy, powerful body was matched by two or three others, but his bearing was unique. He could not divest himself of authority. It was in his posture, his level gaze, his composure, his courteous attention to everything around him. Young competitors attempted to cow one another. They made displays of confidence, or of contempt. Minot was benign, encouraging, personally indifferent. But then came the moment of leaping, and I myself, who loved him, felt a twinge of embarrassment. Where the other jumpers loped toward the bar and sprang into the air from one foot, Minot simply stood before the bar and looked up at it. His patriarchal grace would vanish. Here was a stout little boy bending his knees and swinging his arms, as if preparing to jump down from a chair, or the step of a porch, except that his eyes were raised. The other jumpers would gather by the pit, for the word had gone round, "Larbaud is up!" He would bend his knees deeply several times, and then with a great swing of both arms would launch himself upward, headfirst. His leaps were greeted by laughter, rather admiring than derisive, and by shouts of candid delight. *"Olé* Larbaud!" *"Viva* Larbaud!" *"Jawohl* Larbaud!" He would emerge from the sawdust pit with a smile and a massive shrug, as much as to say, "It can't be helped."

Later in the day the cheering ceased. Still later there were glances of hostility. But by now the crowd in the stands had discovered him. They called his name before he leaped, and cheered and stamped their feet after he had cleared the bar. They saw him, certainly, as an underdog, an outsider who nevertheless might win.

We ate on the field and rested.

All through the day there had been sprints and relays, javelin and discus. The slow mountain twilight deepened in the grass and drifted upward like a dye in clear water. The leisurely high jump entered its final rounds.

The stands were crowded at our end of the field. French athletes gathered at the jumping pit and feasted their eyes on this remarkable teammate, of whom they knew nothing but rumor. When Minot leaped now, our cheers expressed more than mere enthusiasm. Some deeply lodged hope, if hope is the right word, had been stirred into wakefulness.

A blaze of light, shocking in its suddenness, closed off the sky and drained the color from the grass.

Only three competitors were left: the tall black American, the muscular Russian, and Minot. A booming electrical voice announced that all three had surpassed the former record. Another voice succeeded the first, and then another, in the languages of the nations. The bar was set higher.

Minot won. There was prolonged, delighted cheering, and the French members of the combined international band released a salvo of the "Marseillaise."

The crackling voices spoke again, but in less official, more human tones, for they were obliged to inform us not only that Monsieur Minot Larbaud of France had established a new record of seven feet six inches, but also that he would attempt the unprecedented height of eight feet. In this event, as in the sprints, such an increment is vast; it represents the accumulated prowess of many decades. The other athletes understood this. They pressed together in great numbers round the jumping pit, but they were silent, or looked into each other's faces and spoke in consternated whispers. The shadowy thousands in the stands, however—or a great many of them—seemed released into glee. They stood on tiptoe and waved. They clambered on seats and called ecstatically, "Larbaud! Larbaud!" Photographers forced their way to the pit and knelt or threw themselves beside it.

Minot was bending his knees and swinging his arms. This style, which had seemed so comical earlier in the day, evoked a concentrated hush. His final gathering of force was accompanied by the assisting gasps of thousands, and he soared upward, reaching with both arms. At the peak of his rise he curled into a ball and rolled over the bar.

A sibilant great breath passed over the amphitheater, many-throated, yet soft and high. It was followed by silence. A young athlete beside me was sobbing violently. A few cursed, and I heard moans that were like moans of despair. Now came an explosion of voices that was positively frightening. The crowd was roaring.

Minot stood beside me, his blue cotton jersey draped across his back. His face was radiant. His eyes were opened wide and were shining and unfocused. Officials measured the bar. They measured the measuring tape itself; and each little group gave way to another, which repeated the procedure. They conferred with Minot, who said he would jump "one last time." This was accepted, although the tradition is to perform to the point of failure. He asked them to set the bar at nine feet. They stared at him uncomprehendingly, and said, "Of course. Yes." With the aid of boxes, the bar was set.

The roaring in the stands abated to a rumbling. The first crackling of the loudspeakers brought silence. A faltering voice announced that Monsieur Minot Larbaud of France—and this name, now, had become a universal property, it was no longer the name of a competitor, it was Monsieur Minot Larbaud of France—would jump "one last time." The announcer omitted to state the height. He could not bring himself to speak it. Nor could those who followed him. The silence that now fell endured for many minutes. A subterranean, a secret information sped outward from the jumping pit in whispers: *the bar is set at nine.*

Minot stood before the bar and gazed at it. If an unreasoning hope had been released among us—if, to put it fancifully, invisible doves in thousands fluttered above our heads—this image of Minot gazing upward to that impossible height stopped our throats with pathos: we stood in the darkness of the cosmos in a tiny point of light; how small man is! how limited! The stadium was silent and was utterly without motion. Even when he bent his knees in his final burst of force, there was no responding gasp.

His body arced upward in the glare of light, an arc like a motion of the mind, so pure it was, and so free of the restraints of our heavy earth. To the purity of this arc he added, as he soared outstretched across the bar, a gesture of grace, or joy, that swept us all into a delirium of pride: he lifted his head and spread his arms like wings.

We many thousands stood there singing—or so it seemed. There were, in actuality, complex emotions scattered through the mass. A voice cried, *"Mein Gott!"* Another: "He didn't do it!" There were shouts of rage and indignation. But the torrential jubilation swept everything away. The stands were a waterfall of human bodies pouring toward Minot. He was lifted on shoulders and hands, was carried about the field like a banner, was placed alone on the platform on which other victors had received their prizes. The band was playing thirty songs at once. The loudspeakers were mute. Minot stood there smiling, one arm raised. Someone handed him a glass of wine. He held it aloft and turned in all directions. The cheering never ceased. Fragments of the "Marseillaise" could be heard. Minot turned toward the music and, heels together, tossed off the wine. The cheering voices rose still higher. Hands and shoulders claimed him again, he was whirled about the field, and finally—followed by a capering, crazily shouting throng—was carried through the gates outward into the night, outward, that is to say, toward the lights of the nearby town.

The newspapers of the world were filled next day with images of Minot Larbaud. Larbaud crouched at the jumping pit. Larbaud in the air, arms outstretched like wings. Larbaud on the platform saluting his admirers with a glass of wine.

4. FAME/DEJECTION/THE EVERYDAY SURREAL

In the months after Minot's victory, no newspaper or magazine could go to press without his photograph, his quoted words, or words about him. One could not listen to the radio but one would hear Minot himself, or doctors, psychologists, politicians, film stars offering praises—and interpretations—of his extraordinary powers. The effect on our winery's sales was breathtaking. But Minot himself was vanishing. He was bewitched, vacant, elated—and apparently was unaware of the isolation that pursued him in the very thick of his public life. The world was ringing in his ears.

A well-known impresario organized a tour of exhibitions. I could not forgo taking part, though I came to dread the sight of Minot in short pants, barelegged, the number nine displayed on chest and back, saluting his audience with a glass of our own wine. Yet the leap itself—"the prodigious leap," as it had come to be called—was as dazzling as ever. We performed in every city of Western Europe and made two trips to England. Within five short months Minot was wealthy. An American tour was arranged.

But now a number of things happened, the first and most important of which was the dejection of Minot.

The spell was wearing off. Rather, it was intermitted by periods of clear-eyed restlessness and by moments of what seemed almost to be despair. His long romance with Estelle had ended, but it was not this that was troubling him.

One night, in a taxi carrying us back to the hotel from what had seemed to be a triumph (and he had been elated, but now was sitting in the corner with his head bowed and his arms folded on his chest), I urged him to put an end to this career. For I had come to believe that his talent was a meager thing compared to the rare intelligence he possessed; compared, too, to his character, which was perhaps the rarest thing of all. The words I spoke to him were these (I remember them clearly, for they rang very foolishly in my ears): "Take up your old life again. You were happy."

He was silent. I realized how dreadful those words must have sounded. "Take up your old life." As if anyone can do that!

At length he said—to my surprise—"I look forward to leaping."

The newspapers that week reported the proceedings of an international athletic conference. Minot's leap had had a depressing effect on the champions of other countries. There was talk of removing the high jump from future competitions, but this too had depressed them. Nothing had been resolved.

The very same papers that week carried an advertisement for a circus, the star of which was a clown who called himself M. Aussi-Larbaud . . . and there he was, in baggy pants and painted face, sailing through the air "ten feet high," a bottle of beer in one hand. Minot was delighted. He laughed with a gaiety I had not heard in many months. "Ah!" he said. "We must go!"

We did, and the clown was marvelous. He wore enormous springs on his feet, concealed by his trousers. He stood at least eight feet high and before jumping paraded around the arena with a gait that reduced us all to helpless laughter. He leaped a ten-foot bar with ease, swigging from his bottle as he crossed it. He would not stop leaping. He leaped over the ringmaster, who began to pursue him. He leaped over an elephant, over a horse, over a painted wagon. Soon dozens were pursuing him, and he eluded them all with great bounds, swigging from his bottle. But now five other clowns burst into the arena, all eight feet tall, all equipped with springs. They too chased him, and the whole procession bounded exuberantly out the exit.

Even after the lights came on, people remained at their seats chattering and laughing. We heard the following conversation:

"You see, my friend, there is nothing much to it."

"Eh? What? He's wearing springs!"

"Precisely."

"Larbaud jumps without springs. He jumps barelegged. Everyone can see."

"Exactly the ruse of a clever charlatan."

Minot was listening intently. When he saw that I was looking at him, he smiled paternally, somewhat sorrowfully, and shrugged.

He was subjected, in the next few weeks, to a perfect plague of comedians, the most noteworthy of whom was a nightclub entertainer who began appearing everywhere with an absurd explanation of the famous leap. Speaking in grandiose intellectual tones, he presented himself as an *ologist,* the world's leading *ologist;* and praised *ology* as the purest form of knowledge, much superior to the corrupted lesser *ologies:* soci, psych, physi, anthrop . . . and suchlike rant for five or ten minutes, coming at last to The Integral Theory of the Prodigious Leap, which was nothing but the bare assertion that there were in reality four Larbauds, each of whom jumped two and a quarter feet, adding up to nine.

The disturbing thing about this absurd performer was the hilarity he induced in his listeners. One did not know what to make of it. Minot too was taken aback. The worst, however, was yet to come.

The estimable magazine *European Sports* published the resolutions of a multinational committee of athletes, trainers, and athletic directors. With distressing unanimity they agreed that the high jump should be rigorously defined, and that such styles as Minot's (which was referred to by a variety of disparaging names: kangaroo hopping, cannonballing, etc.) be absolutely forbidden. Many suggested that his performance be stricken from the records. This was not agreed upon, although that memorable night was indeed reduced to a footnote.

There now appeared in one of our scandal-mongering newspapers an article by a pseudo-scientific oddity hawker, who speculated that Minot Larbaud—whom he called The Cat Man—was a mutant, a freak of nature whose prowess could be explained by the fact that he possessed the striated muscles of the cat family. The article was replete with charts and diagrams, and ended with the observation that, were Larbaud actually a cat, his leap would not be prodigious at all, but mediocre.

Minot's last performance was a disaster. It was in the south of France, in an indoor arena. The preliminary entertainments passed without incident. He made his entrance and saluted the audience. I stood near the improvised jumping pit. The house lights were darkened and a spot of light followed Minot. He removed his sweatsuit and handed it to me. He stood before the pit and gazed at the bar, and then began the rhythmic crouching that would end in the explosive leap. At the very moment of his deepest crouch a chorus of catcalls split the silence. Minot stood erect, listening. The greater part of the audience were loyal to him and shouted their indignation, but the catcalls broke out anew, louder than before. Minot came to me and took the sweatsuit from my hands, calmly donned it, and walked in measured strides from the arena. He never leaped again.

The local newspapers carried headlines: CAT MAN WALKS

OUT. Even the Paris papers questioned the authenticity of the prodigious leap.

The final blow was a radio symposium devoted to this very question. Among the disputants was an undersecretary of education. He seized attention by saying that he had been present that night at the international competition. And then with devastating, bland assurance, he remarked that a trampoline had been concealed at the jumping pit. It was evident that no one believed him. On the other hand, no one called his lie. The moderator said, "The allegation is serious. Are you quite certain?" And the secretary replied, "My dear fellow, I bounced on it."

What Minot felt at this time I am unable to say. I tried to reach him that very night. He was not at home. Worse, he did not return.

5. AWAY

My mother was distraught. It was unlike Minot to retreat like this, unlike him to reject us in his time of need. Yet, because of this rejection in the face of love, I came to see that when a man is struggling with his world even love is of the world.

For three months we waited anxiously. There came at last a letter from one M. Blanchard requesting that we meet him in Paris.

At the appointed time and place, Blanchard appeared; that is, Minot appeared.

He had gained a great deal of weight. He wore a beard. His hair was long and full. Both hair and beard were dyed a chestnut brown.

We were so glad to see him that I did not at first fully notice the quiet that had come into his speech and manner. He had digested a melancholy that must have been severe. I thought that I understood him. He had suffered injustice and a massive insult; his notoriety was painful. The events of later years taught me that I understood him very little, if at all.

He begged us to protect his new identity. He said that he wanted peace, and longed for obscurity. We ate and talked. He had made elaborate plans for a new life. We strolled by the Seine listening to his words of hope while our hearts sank.

My own life, and my mother's life, were much changed by the change in Minot's. I will not say that our lives became drab, for they did not, but they were grievously diminished.

I married the sweetheart of my youth. Four children were born to us. I did not leave the winery, although I often longed to do so.

Minot too eventually married. We visited him frequently, but visits are a poor substitute for daily life in common.

He had settled expensively, near Paris, and had established a factory of electronic equipment. He prospered, raised three sons, erected an extraordinary greenhouse in his garden, and divided his evenings and weekends between horticulture and literature. Novels, plays, books of poems filled the shelves of his study. There came a time when his letters slacked off. For several months they ceased altogether. Our telephone rang one night and my mother answered. I heard her greet Mathilde, Minot's wife . . . and then she cried out in alarm.

Minot had been taken to a psychiatric hospital. Mathilde could not say what the trouble was. He had become melancholy, had refused to leave his room, had refused to speak, and finally had lost so much weight that she had become terrified.

Late that night we were put through to his doctor, a young psychiatrist, who added nothing to Mathilde's description, yet managed somehow to calm us while at the same time imparting the information that we would not, as yet, be allowed to visit.

We met this young man several weeks later in the lobby of the hospital. He was thin and austere. He cautioned us not to demand a response from Minot, and he requested that we visit him singly. My mother went first.

I questioned him. No, he said, Minot was not deranged.

Nor was it quite correct to say that his extreme withdrawal was self-destructive, though certainly it was dangerous.

"My impression," he said, "is not that he has attacked the self, but that he has withdrawn volition from it. One might say that temporarily he is without self. He does not know what to do."

His face came alight. "He is vital," he said. "He is extraordinary. He is like a baffled animal who gathers himself within his fur and waits. My treatment—" Here he smiled in such a way as made me want to take his hands. It was a smile that told me much. It lit his face with an expression that men inherit from their mothers; and I understood that this austere young aristocrat had come from a working-class home; I even fancied that I could see his mother bending at her work, harassed, overburdened, vehement in opinion . . . and intellectually free.

"—my treatment," he said, "is to keep away. No drugs. No talk. He is curing himself. I know he is."

He nodded—it amounted to a bow—and went away.

The blank face of the elevator opened and my mother emerged. Her plump cheeks were wet and she was wiping her eyes.

"I cannot understand it," she said.

"Did you speak with him?"

"No . . . and yet I think he is all right. Ah . . ."

Minot lay motionless in bed, his arms at his sides on the unwrinkled blanket. His head was raised by a pillow. He had aged appallingly. For a moment his eyes touched mine, and I fancied that they greeted me. I was so swept by emotion that perhaps I did not act wisely. I wanted to embrace him and could not hold back, but before I reached the bed he had closed his eyes. I kissed his brow.

It was hard to believe that he had glanced at me a moment past. His breathing was so regular and calm, his eyelids and temples so relaxed in closure that he seemed to be asleep, more deeply asleep than sleep.

I sat in a chair by the bed.

His thick hair and beard were gray. It was this, chiefly, that had shocked me. And then I realized that he must have stopped dyeing them. Perhaps they had been gray for years. He was gaunt. Nevertheless, this massive skull, these broad cheekbones and wide, nervously modeled brow, seemed more than ever awesome. I was struck most of all by the play of thought upon this motionless face. His face was alive with thought, not such thoughts as begin in words, but the deep thoughts of the organs and limbs.

I sat there for thirty minutes. We spoke not a word, nor did he open his eyes. I listened to his breathing. Perhaps he listened to mine. We communed in silence. And I felt that— as I have heard happens in the meetings of certain sects—our silence was expressive and achieved a meaning.

My next two visits, a week apart, were the same. We communed in silence.

And then I found him sitting up in bed. He nodded to me when I came in. And while I stood there soaking up the past that once again appeared familiarly in his eyes, he said gravely, "Thank you, Jacques."

Words came tumbling out of me. I wanted him to be well. I wanted to cancel the interlude of sickness.

He shook his head. "Jacques," he said, "I've been resting from making sense."

Yet we did talk, and the following week talked more, and more still the week after that. At the conclusion of which visit he handed me a piece of paper bearing the title of a book, and asked me to buy it for him and send it at once by messenger.

It was a book on birds, large and handsomely illustrated. The following evening I was at home. The telephone rang. It was Minot.

"Where are you?" I cried.

"At the hospital," he said.

"Jacques," he went on, "I have finished the book. It was delightful. Will you do something?"

I was astonished. The book contained more than six hundred pages. Past events came back to me: prizes Minot had won at school, his brilliance in business, his phenomenal memory.

He dictated the titles of several books and asked that I bring them when I came.

All were on birds, their anatomy, the mechanics of flight, social organization, evolution.

I found him sprawled comfortably on the bed in a welter of books. He was cheerful. When I asked why he so admired birds, he laughed and said, "I don't. They are dreadfully bourgeois: territory, status, duties of the home. I except the very young. Best of all is the egg."

I too laughed. But I repeated my question. He shrugged it away and held out his hands for the new books.

A few days later I received the following letter:

Dearest brother,
     I shall be going home tomorrow.
     You and Berthe have been so patient! I have seen how often you have wanted to question me, yet refrained. I would like to explain to you now as much as I can, and then, if you will agree, never speak of these things again.
     You know how painful it was for me to leave you and Berthe. I won't dwell on this. But I doubt that you have guessed how painfully I have suffered the loss of the town itself. Apparently I was happy there. I mean that I must have experienced the one true happiness of life, the happiness one can possess only if one is unaware of it. Yet there is some solace in acknowledging that a wound of this kind never heals. I don't mean that I regret the past. It could not have been otherwise. I am not sure that you have understood this. I know that you thought me somewhat ridiculous in my exhibitionistic career. Well, Jacques, I did too. But I must tell you this: it was a joy to leap, a joy to give way utterly to my powers. I was glad to throw myself away. What is dignity compared to joy? What is selfhood, for that matter?
     Yet everything was wrong. I would have preferred that

such powers as mine were ordinary, as ordinary as dancing or skating; I should have had company, and might have shared my happiness and have partaken of the happiness of others. As it was, I suffered isolation without the relief of solitude; and then insult without any hope of correction.

Well, I am strong-willed. I willed away the past. In material ways, as you know, I prospered. My deliberate forgetting became a habit, as familiar as the habit of unhappiness. I am describing the formula for the passing of time: it flows right by; one can almost see it go.

But then something happened that I was powerless to control. All that I had banished from my waking life erupted in my dreams. I doubt that I can describe them to you. They were intolerably beautiful. I dreamed of leaping—not as I leaped at the international games, or later, but as I leaped that splendid night of our carnival. Except that my leaps became flight, sustained, effortless flight. Night after night I took to the sky, the sky of noon, always, drenched in sunlight. The settings of these flights were not exotic—nor were they the environs of the suburb in which I now live, but our town, Jacques, and my own home. Think of the things you know well . . . the olive trees in the garden (the one we mended so many years ago was thriving!), the chestnuts, the asparagus bed, the stone fountain. But imagine that when you look at them they respond, they receive. I cannot describe it. They were so dear to me. And there were the cobblestone streets of our hill, and the iron railings, and the houses. There was never a soul in sight, and yet I wasn't saddened or confused, rather I awaited their return, almost deliciously, as one awaits the resolution of a movement in music. How much green there is from the sky! How many shades! How well they go with the ochers of our bare earth, and our terracotta roofs!

One aspect of these flights I dare not dwell on even now. I saw things I had never seen before and could not have guessed existed. There is a bird's nest in Popil's English chimney. It is braced against the bricks where the lining is broken. Near the peak of Tabard's terracotta roof there is a whole line of glazed tile, deep blue. And do you know that the servants of our wealthy recluse, Boudaille, live in a wretched hut of galvanized metal at the end of the garden? I had thought it was a potting shed, but there is a television antenna on the roof. One of the metal sheets of that roof was formerly a sign of some sort. I could make out faded orange letters . . . AUD . . . FILS.

Do these things exist? God help me, perhaps they do! I would rather not know.

How much I could tell you about flight! We associate colors with sounds, though certainly we cannot see them. The currents of the air have a similar effect. The updrafts are like the sun; the downdrafts are cool and silvery, they are like waterfalls, but gentler. Can you imagine birds diving away beneath you? I could not identify them.

I am told that dreams are brief. These seemed to last entire nights. I would awaken with images of clouds in the corners of my eyes, and my lips still tingling from the wind. And alas! here was my heavy body. Here was my motionless bed. Here was my heavy clothing, my stonelike shoes, my heavy, heavy life. I could not bear the thought of *responding* to anyone. And then I could not bear the thought of speaking at all. And finally I did not even wish to move.

I know that you believe my collapse was due to unhappiness. But it was not that, Jacques. It was joy. Joy attacked me every night and beat me down.

Yet there was something providential in those dreams. My memories have been tamed, the real past subdued.

The books you searched for so patiently, and so kindly brought to me, were suggested by Henri, for whose presence here I thank my stars. He is a brilliant and compassionate man.

Perhaps, to anyone but me, his suggestion was obvious. I did not think of it, and would not have. Nor could I have said to myself, as he said to me, that my collapse was not the first stage of illness, but the second stage of a recovery that began in dream.

Some aura of those dreams does indeed seem to flicker through these pages. And the imagined space of my flights has become the real space through which these highly organized creatures make their way. I have seen, too, that the more specialized these texts become, the more general they really are. Which is only to say that nature is continuous. "From the evolutionary point of view, the bird is simply the method by which the egg perpetuates itself." I read this sentence with something like joy. And I experienced my only intuition of eternity—which, so it seems, has nothing to do with time, but with the imperishability of the boundary at which consciousness becomes aware of itself gazing at the inexplicable. To glimpse this boundary, or better (should one be so blessed) to stand at it, must be, surely, to attach oneself to the spirit that endures long after life has passed.

But I will call you soon and we can talk of this at length.

6. MINOT BLANCHARD

For years Minot had preserved a Mediterranean presence in the large garden of his home near Paris. That is to say, he had nurtured through all weathers two trees, an olive and a fig. They represented the South to him; I should say, rather, they were an actual piece of it. The large greenhouse turned an el in the garden and was constructed so that a sheltering dome, in the arms of the el, could be placed over the trees in winter.

It had always been a pleasure to step into this leaf- and flower-crowded space. The light of day was rich and variegated, and at night the recessed shadows of indented leaves were complex and attractive. When Minot returned from the hospital, this domesticated wilderness became his true home. He equipped the far end of the greenhouse with bookcases, worktables, and a sofa. He retired from business, and spent his waking hours in the softened light of this retreat.

Minot's three sons grew to strapping young manhood. The large house was their domain and their mother's. All were vigorous, endlessly active; yet when Minot emerged into the dining room for the evening meal, the house grew quiet. It was not that they feared him—on the contrary, he was kindly, and they seemed to adore him—but that an aura of solitude surrounded him, I would say *attended* him, like the retinue of a monarch.

He had grown stout. He seemed enormous. His steel-gray hair had become a mane, his beard luxuriant and of patriarchal length. He would pause in the doorway and remove his spectacles and rub his eyes while his vision adjusted to the indoor light. He was so centered, so gathered within himself, that one watched his simplest movements with fascination. When he peered through his glasses again, stepping with weighty ease into the room, his eyes were warm and his smile openly affectionate.

More equipment appeared in the greenhouse: a microscope, a cabinet for slides, dissecting tools, a balance scale. Pages of manuscript accumulated on the desk.

I did not know what to make of this work. But there was much that I did not know at this time. I did not know, for instance, that Minot had established a correspondence with scholars in several fields.

By custom, during our visits, it was I who went to fetch him for dinner. I would take him an apéritif, and we would sit and talk for a few minutes before going in. Often he would turn aside, suspending a phrase he had just begun, and would jot down a word or two, or a paragraph, or a whole page. And I would sit there and watch him write, knowing that even if I had wished to disturb him I would not have been able to. Green leaves cascaded around us. On a shelf near his bent head, the skeletons of three small birds were mounted as if in flight, one behind the other, like generations of the dead or the unborn. Minot would finish his notes, and would reach for his apéritif.

If he never spoke of the papers that grew so numerous on his desk, he spoke enchantingly of the lives of birds; and of problems of evolution and genetics; and of the ecology of the small islands on which some few species had become wingless; and of oddities of creaturely perception, the cameralike vision of the bird, with its wide arc of monocular vision and its narrow band of binocular vision straight ahead. He had become fascinated by the question of individual differences within a species.

The publication of Minot's first book was an occasion of delight. More than five years had passed since he had become a monk of study. We arrived one weekend and were greeted with suppressed excitement by Mathilde, who said only, "Go to the garden!"

Minot was striding up and down with his hands behind his back. He raised one arm in an exuberant greeting.

"What is it, Minot?" I said. "Why is everybody smiling?"

"Ah," he said softly, "I am smiling because I am pleased ..." and he held up beside him, on a level with his face, as if it were a companion he might throw one arm around, a large thick book with a glossy cover. A moment went by before we quite registered that beneath the title was printed the name Minot Blanchard.

His three strapping lads came running to join us. It was a delightful moment. His pleasure was so open that we were able to embrace him, pat his back, shake his hand, and fuss about him to our hearts' content.

Later, over pastries and champagne in the garden, he said, "We take our books for granted, but you know they really are magic. I don't mean their replication, though that's quite wonderful, and it's certainly true that my existence has been multiplied. No, I mean that spirit becomes matter, and matter again becomes spirit. Any primitive could tell you that an object capable of such a thing is magical."

Intellectuals who were not scientists admired the structure of Minot's book, and its style, but said that he had not added anything to existing knowledge. No doubt they were correct. Scientists, however, who knew better the immensity of human ignorance, praised the book warmly. Perhaps he was such a pupil as masters long for. But, more than that, he had brought several fields together not by stressing their common knowledge, but their common mysteries, which he had made visible not solely as intellectual questions, but as the delight and solitude of the questioner and the social bond that makes him write it out. It was a radiant book.

Paris was clamoring to see him. He never stirred from the study in the garden. It was at this time that I realized—

though I had known it all along—that for five years he had not ventured from the house. Our two families, and the young doctor who had remained his friend, were his entire acquaintance.

I believe that certain men know intuitively the master rhythms of their lives; they know the time of death quite accurately. Minot was husbanding time.

His second book was printed three years later. It too caused a stir, but in other quarters, for it was speculative and difficult. Its merits were debated in learned journals. I have not followed its fortunes and am not competent to do so. I have little motive at present. Within three months of the publication of the book, Minot was dead of a cerebral hemorrhage. He had entered his sixty-first year.

I was named executor of his literary remains. For three months I went daily to the desk in the greenhouse and studied his papers. His correspondence was large. There were letters from amateurs and scientists, and later, after his own book had become known, from poets and writers and members of the public. We must track down his replies, as he did not make copies. But there will be a volume of selected correspondence, and then perhaps (it is not in my hands) a volume of studies and notes.

The three small skeletons in flight that I saw so many times on the greenhouse desk are now on the desk in my study. Not a day goes by but that I gaze at them.

In his will, Minot requested cremation. The words were addressed to me. They were these:

> I entrust this to you more than to the others, as I know you will not be turned aside by sentiment or convention. I do wish earnestly for my body to be cremated, and I do not wish for my ashes to be buried, or for any stone or memorial to be erected. Scatter my ashes in the garden, or for that

matter anywhere. I mean that I am at home, Jacques. I know that you understand.

7. FOUR MEMORIES

1. During my sixteenth year I was ill for three weeks. A celebrated theater company was touring *Le Tartuffe*, but I was confined to my bed the night they played in our town and had to content myself with reading the text. Late that evening, I heard Minot's voice downstairs, and the voice of a woman I knew to be Estelle Drolet. A moment later they entered my room, followed by my mother.

The sight of them was almost tormenting. Their faces were glowing. Minot was dressed in black, with a dazzling white shirt and black tie. His close-cropped hair was black, his eyebrows black, his eyes black and brilliant. Estelle, though somewhat taller than he, gave the impression of looking up into his face. After every glance she seemed alight with gaiety. She wore long black gloves and a black dress that left her arms and throat bare. I had seen her often; why was I so bewildered? There was something mysterious in the way her hips curved and melted into her slender waist, and in how that waist passed so smoothly into her lower ribs. She wore a delicate silver necklace that glinted dully as she breathed.

Minot was talking volubly, something rare with him. His voice was not loud, but its timbre was very dense, compacted in that mighty chest. My mother brought chairs.

"Was it good?" I said. "I mean the actors. I mean was the production good? I mean did you enjoy yourselves?"

"It was excellent," said Minot. He threw up one arm and recited several lines, apparently in the accents of the leading actor. My mother laughed delightedly, and Estelle lowered her head and smiled at him. She turned to me and said, "Oh, it was crowded!"

I knew where they had sat: in a loge at one side, reserved in perpetuity for our family; for the theater itself had been given to the town by a later generation of the same ancestors —my father's side—whose château is now the winery. My mother's side goes back just as far: she and Minot are descended from the broad-backed laborers who had hauled the château's stones.

"A great lot of your chums were there," said Minot.

"Well, what . . . what—" I ended by saying, "Were the sets very fine?"

Minot was smiling at me. "When the curtain opened," he said—and he drew apart his powerful, short-fingered hands. . . .

He described the set. He described the entrances of the actors, and spoke their lines. He began to pace and to gesticulate and change his voice. Our smiles faded as we listened. He no longer glanced at us. His face was ablaze with energy, and yet was somnambulistic. I had never seen him look so happy.

"Good heavens!" whispered Estelle, as he rounded a couplet. "Exactly so!"

My mother was biting her lower lip. Minot moved about the room.

My mother came to the bed and sat beside me. "The book," she whispered, and pointed to the end table.

We opened the book and found our place. The text read:

> . . . Les hommes la plupart sont étrangement faits!
> Dans la juste nature on ne les voit jamais;
> La raison a pour eux des bornes trop petites;
> En chaque caractère ils passent ses limites. . . .

Minot raised one hand and shook his head. *"Les hommes la plupart sont étrangement faits!"* he said. *"Dans la juste nature on ne les voit jamais; la raison a pour eux des bornes trop petites; en chaque caractère ils passent ses limites. . . ."*

At the end of Act One he emerged from his reverie and smiled. "Intermission," he said.

"Minot," said my mother, "you are incredible!"

"How do you do it?" I cried. "How can you *remember* all that?"

He came over and sat on the bed. His great weight tilted the mattress so that my mother and I had to adjust our positions.

I thought that he was trying to phrase an answer to my question. But he smiled and pointed to the book and said, "Did I do it right?"

My mother nodded and said, "Perfectly, Minot."

"Good," he said, and stood up.

"Perhaps if you just started playing soccer," he said, "your body would decide to get well."

"Please, Minot," said my mother.

Before I fell asleep that night, I thought long about the differences between men. And something I had noticed but had not understood persisted in my mind as a question. This was the face of Estelle—for when Minot had finished his performance she had glanced at him almost with fear. Fear is too strong a word. Yet a serious disquiet had sped across her face.

2. By the time I was twelve years old I had come to savor the prestige of having Minot for an uncle. He seemed to know everyone. His local fame was greater and more enduring than that of our mayors, though—as far as I could tell then—it was based on nothing more than the pleasure of greeting him as he passed. He traveled everywhere on his bicycle. One would see him flitting among the cars of the morning and evening rush, waving almost continually, his briefcase flapping from the handlebars.

Late one afternoon my young chums and I were sprawled on the grass of our soccer field. We saw him speeding down the precipitous street above us. I leaped up and waved. I did not know that he was coming to our house for dinner, and I was not sure that he could see me. He jumped his bike over the gutter, glided down the grassy slope, and pulled up short in our very midst. My chums greeted him gleefully. He motioned for me to hop on the crossbar, which I did. We circled deep into the field, and then turned back toward the slope. He pedaled mightily, leaning as far as he could over my crouching figure. Our speed carried us to the top. He jumped the gutter and entered traffic. I glanced back at my chums. The looks on their faces filled me with joy.

3. He stands in the doorway of our house, both arms above his head, a bottle of wine in each hand. It is his sister's —my mother's—birthday. I hear my own voice crying shrilly, "Minot is here! Minot is here!" And then I run to fetch my mother.

I am nine years old. Minot is twenty-one.

4. Early in my fourth year, and not long after my father's death, Minot and my mother and I spent a week at the beach in St. Tropez. We preferred the little cove on the outskirts of the town. My mother read under an umbrella. Minot held me in the shallow water and showed me how to paddle with my arms and legs. I played near my mother then, and he searched the little tide pools for whatever might be found. His massive body had not yet grown hard. He was a patient, quiet boy. All afternoon he studied the sea moss and tiny life forms in a few feet of sand, rock, and water. From time to time, he came to us to show what he had found. He came once walking carefully, holding his hands before him like a bowl.

Kneeling in the sand, our heads bowed over his cupped hands, we saw a pool of water, slightly shaded, clear and cool, such as one might find in a cavern, near the entrance; and in the pool a tiny, almost transparent fish, the body of which, when it was still, drifted outward like a ghostly pennon from the anchor of its round black eye. It darted to and fro so unpredictably that one might think it bodiless, a mere neural impulse in some larger other body; and then it would be still, and the black speck of its eye would accumulate presence and begin to seem like a gathered intelligence.

THE CARBON PAPER POET

A scholar and essayist, forty-three years old, on sabbatical from his university, arrived one spring night at yet another party in his neighborhood on the Upper West Side. The animated drone of the voices was terribly familiar to him. So too was the look he saw on many of the faces, and could feel establishing itself on his own. It was a look that combined energy and distraction, as when some turn of opinion dear to the mind, or some display of knowledge or boast of career amounts actually to a division of the soul, so that an aura of discontent and needfulness plays about the face. Eyes dart continually toward the door, ears remain cocked, as if to catch some hoped-for voice, but that voice apparently never speaks. As he made his way toward the long table that served as a bar, he noticed a young couple in the process of leaving. They were relatives of the hostess. While they said their goodbyes, their year-old baby rolled on the floor at the feet of a prominent literary critic. The critic looked down from his great height. He moved one pointed black shoe and touched the baby's ribs, and the infant chortled and squirmed, and looked up at him, waiting for more. But the bespectacled man, having set this little motor in motion, was content to observe it. Then he turned his head, gazed into the other room, and sighed.

Our scholar saw at once that something unusual was happening. The eyes that ordinarily would have been darting toward the door were darting toward the other room, and the people standing near that room were smiling. At first he thought, *Ah, some celebrity is here,* but the smiles were oddly condescending. And then he saw that in spite of that condescension there was real fascination on many of those faces, and without further speculation he stepped into the room, which was far more crowded and far noisier than the first.

The spectacle that drew so many eyes was a woman—and he, too, stared at her, but he did not smile, or feel anything resembling condescension. She stood out among the other women as a daffodil stands out among blades of grass. And she was like a daffodil, luscious and fresh, and in every way extraordinarily vivid. Her hair was a soft, blond mass, very thick and abundant. She wore an outrageous sleeveless, clinging dress, of an expensive fabric but of a style almost laughably out of fashion, homely and small-townish, yet festive and extremely attractive. It was a polka-dot dress. The large dots were a purple almost black, their background a pale yellow close to ivory. There was scarcely a wrinkle to be seen it held her body so tightly, and this body was of a kind not often encountered, but very often symbolized: full hips and bosom, a rounded small belly, a narrow and yielding waist—all so rare and of their kind so perfect that the fascinated stares of men and women both were alight with curiosity, and with the pleasure of discovery, and were not by any means confined to the usual desires. Her skin was a healthy, glowing white; her arms and shoulders were shapely and smooth. To look at them was almost tantamount to stroking them.

But there was more to be seen in her than this. A quickness and sweetness of childhood hovered about her. She seemed unspoiled. Even her posture, erect and unself-conscious, was that of a child. Her face, too, which was so amazingly pretty as to be beautiful, would have resembled that of a child had it not reached its own fullness and completion. As it was, one could see in her still a prepubescent girl to whom the baffling accident of sexual ripeness had occurred quite suddenly, and from which accident she was looking out, as it were, with a lively, modest, somewhat bashful girlish look.

Several of the women present were strikingly handsome, and several others were appealing for reasons of character and spirit, yet none possessed her power of attraction. As for those who were vain of intelligence, and to whom opinion was both weaponry and adornment—they glanced at her with a disdain that was almost ferocious, and that carried over to the men, who could not take their eyes from her. Some few of the women present were obliged to confront once again the un-happy discoveries of early youth: that rejection would be a nagging fact of life, and that jealousy, envy, and sexual yearn-ing would be frequent and would require an effort of the spirit to surmount. Some watched her with a sorrowing yet un-grudging admiration.

In the women's responses there was little that was conde-scending. It was on the faces of certain of the men that the condescending smiles appeared—and our scholar noted it with displeasure. This embodiment of desire was after all the embodiment of male desire, and moreover was a gift from the blue. Who could *merit* such perfection? The proper responses, so it seemed to him, were simple gratitude and praise, cer-tainly not these condescending smiles.

A tall, willowy man, a colleague at the university, stood before the young woman in the graceful, utterly confident slouch with which, habitually, he confronted the students in his classroom. He was speaking to her, and from time to time, without taking his eyes from her, he sipped from his glass. A little smile of superiority lurked at the corners of his lips, and he gave the impression that he was entwining her in nets of subtlety and learning, and that soon, immobilized and help-less, she would cast up her eyes to him and surrender her will and her body along with her inferior opinions. And our scholar, seeing this, thought, *Yes, this is the identical conceit that drains the mind from that man's books, leaving mere cleverness and neutered information; yes, it is precisely this immodesty that allows him to treat the rare inventions of mankind as if they were mere increments of learning, or mere*

*extrusions of the historical context; and yes, it is this that
allows him to write of great men as if they were not great at
all, and allows him to condescend toward their errors as if
they were the errors of ordinary folk.*

—and seeing that the young woman stood there with her
head bowed, and seemed to be at a loss, he thought of the hero
of his own field, whom he almost worshiped for his great-
hearted fearlessness, and he said to himself, *Ah, if only Sam
Johnson were here he would set the matter straight!* and so
thinking, he strode across the room.

But, as he drew near, he made several discoveries. She
was not as young as he had supposed, though the perfections
that had amazed him at a distance were not diminished at
close quarters. The second discovery was that she was not by
any means overwhelmed or at a loss. She simply wasn't listening to the willowy professor. She held her glass with both
hands and sipped from it. And our scholar understood that she
was quite aware that she was being patronized, quite aware
that many in the room resented her, and certainly that many
others admired or desired her. She raised her head and sipped
from her glass, holding it with both hands. She looked calmly
this way and that, and bowed her head again.

Now our scholar came quite close to her. He nodded to
his colleague, invaded the space of the little cluster, smiled,
and inclined himself toward the young woman. It was at this
moment that he first inhaled her perfume. Pangs of memory
went whirling through him. She turned to him, not quite
straightening her bowed head, but tossing aside the massy
blond hair—and, really, it was like the sunrise, he simply stood
there agog. Her eyes were brown. She straightened her head.
She was smiling at him, was smiling fondly and happily. And
there raced through his consciousness a kind of stuttering and
stammering. *Why me? What can she see? Is such a thing
possible?* He had already formed a compliment in his mind,
but this compliment seemed of a sudden hopelessly general,
nor was there any need to put it into words, it was expressed

a hundredfold in the great pleasure that beamed from his face, which was as frank and happy as a boy's. Something in her gaze made him think of the gaze of a healthy infant, whose happiness does indeed require certain things, but is not caused by those things. He spoke to her, and she to him. Soon he noticed that she was blushing, and he saw that she was vulnerable to emotion yet did not defend herself against it—and her blushing appeared to him not only as a sensual fact, but a moral fact as well, an embodiment of bravery and generosity. She touched his arm as she spoke to him, and the oval of warmth beneath her fingers was like an island neither could bear to leave; and soon, quite naturally, their fingers were intertwined, and they stood there holding hands while they talked. And because this blaze of recognition had in it the power of coalition, and the sweet sufficiency of shared feeling, competing conversations melted away. The willowy professor shrugged and turned his back. Others left, too, but their places were filled immediately, and the newcomers did not smile at her condescendingly, but seemed to be warming themselves pleasurably, as at a domestic fire.

Our scholar and the young woman left quite soon, and walked to his apartment in a small building nearby. The spring night was mild and sweet. She took his arm as they walked, and he could feel the softness of her arm and bosom, and could feel the yielding, flexible motions of her waist as she strode along easily beside him, balancing without effort on her spike-heeled, putty-colored shoes. He felt incredibly at ease with her, cared for, and esteemed; and yet the amazement he had felt when first she had looked at him did not entirely leave him. Though he turned to her continually, and had no other thought but of her, he nevertheless, from time to time, raked her with a gaze as it were of verification, from the soft, abundant mass of blond hair, over the modulations of the polka-dot dress, down the sheer-stockinged full calves, to the trim ankles with their well-defined bones and tendons, to the strong, small feet in the high-heeled shoes. And even when everything, the feel of her and the sight of her, convinced him of her present-ness, he was still nonplused by the great gift of that presence, and he said to himself again, *Why me?* But now, with an excited, headlong laugh, he dismissed that question, and would gladly have dismissed selfhood itself just to attain her. He said to her, "What a glorious night!" and she smiled and agreed, and pressed his arm, unaware that his eyes were dart-ing surreptitiously and happily to every store window, and even to the windows and shining bodies of cars along which her blond and polka-dot apparition might pass, arm in arm with himself.

They made love with the same extraordinary combina-tion of ardor and companionability that had sprung into being at first glance. She was dazzlingly new, yet wonderfully famil-iar, and he tasted all the sweetness of bliss without the anxiety of unlikeness.

They rested and talked. She saw that he was giddy with excitement, and she stroked his face and spoke to him sooth-ingly, guessing easily enough that he had endured too much loneliness. And he, on his side, saw that there was indeed a friendly young girl looking out through her face, a kid sister, good-natured and generous, and he spoke to her with the gentle but lively interest that had endeared him to many stu-dents.

They went to the refrigerator. She wore his seersucker bathrobe. She looked over his shoulder, and said that it seemed lonely, this refrigerator. Many things had spoiled, and there wasn't much anyway.

They sat at the table and ate ice cream. He dressed rap-idly and went outside, and came back with groceries, and the Pepsi she had asked for. They ate again, and made love again —and finally she fell asleep late, late at night.

Our scholar, however, was much too excited to sleep. He put on his bathrobe and went to the kitchen. Before leaving the bedroom he turned in the doorway and stood there look-ing at her. She lay on her stomach, with her shoulders uncovered, and her elbows bent and spread like wings. Her hands were buried beneath the pillow. He could see her face in profile against the pillow, and could hear the smooth, regular sound of her breathing. The usual lights of New York came in at the window and transformed the darkness of the room into a lovely twilight. He stood there so long that he became aware that his own breathing had fallen into the rhythm of hers, and when he noticed this he smiled and lifted both arms.

In the kitchen he remembered that he had neither edited nor typed the book review he had just written. Fearful that he might wake her, he closed the bedroom door. He went through the kitchen into the living room of the small apartment and closed that door, and then went into his book-lined study and closed that door, too. . . .

We have reached the point in our narrative at which the event referred to in our title will occur. It is not the sort of thing that occurs in waking life, yet our scholar's reactions to it were of a kind familiar to everyone, a kind by no means confined to dream. Nor was he dreaming. . . .

He had closed three doors behind him, yet his study was transformed. The air was luminous, and the space itself seemed to be pulsing with the distant beating of her heart.

He sat down to his work weightlessly, and soon, without effort of will, the review was finished. He separated the pages and put the originals into a large manila envelope, already addressed. The carbon copies he stacked for his files. As he did this, however, he saw something on the last page that made him stiffen with amazement and alarm.

It was only a poem. But there hadn't been a poem in the text; he hadn't quoted one, hadn't written one. Moreover, it stirred something deep in him, a meaning profoundly his own, except that, for a brief while, it remained obscure.

He read:

> The heart of my heart
> is a child

who doesn't know
her own name
    or where she's going

or to whom joyously
she extends her left hand
    (one close at her side)

or her right sorrowfully
for no one is there.

If the meaning of the words did seem to be his own, the presence of the poem was uncanny—and fearing that he was plunged hopelessly in dream, he clutched the paper in one hand and staggered back through the rooms of his apartment as through the years of his past.

But no—she lay in the same position, sleeping soundly. He went close to her, and knelt beside the bed and looked at her face, and very lightly stroked her hair. She breathed easily and peacefully.

He went back to his desk, and sitting in the cone of lamplight read again:

The heart of my heart
is a child
who doesn't know
her own name
    or where she's going . . .

He had used carbon sets for typing. Each set consisted of a sheet of paper, a sheet of carbon, and a second sheet, all joined at the top on a perforated strip. He opened the large manila envelope and took out the originals. The poem was not to be seen. He knelt by the wastebasket and took out all the carbons, and on one of them found the poem. By holding the carbon sheet up to the light he was able to see, on its dull side, the text he had composed and typed, and on its black and glossy side, in mirror writing, the poem.

Abruptly, and with a pang of sorrow, he saw what it meant. It referred to the loneliness he had endured for so long —for six years since the death of his young wife in the first year of their marriage—loneliness, and the slow, slow death of love. He had so ardently wanted a child with her that that wanting had become an imagery almost physical, and then the imagery had become memory: he could remember walking hand in hand with his wife, and yes, the child had been a little girl— except that that had never happened. His wife had died in pregnancy.

Was that what the poem meant?

If it did mean that, it meant many other things as well.

He read it several times, kneeling there on the floor. And because he had begun to ponder its meaning, the uncanniness of its presence troubled him less. He was not its author, but no one else was, either. And, if it was a gift, the gift had been made to him.

He put a carbon set into the typewriter and typed some paragraphs, but without effect.

He read the poem again . . . and for the first time felt gratitude. It had come into the world. First it had not been, and now it was, and that was wonderful. The feeling of grati- tude calmed him. He said to himself, *With more evidence surely I'll come to understand the causes of which this poem is the effect*—and by these means, unaware, he entered a domain not of reason at all, nor even of reason deferred, but quite simply of faith and hope. And in the weeks ahead, during which time other poems appeared or were sent to him in the identical way, he found himself attuned not in the least to the advent of new evidence, or augmented reason, but solely and entirely to the spectacular gifts themselves.

He put out the light in his study and went back to the bedroom. The sight of her under the covers on the bed aston- ished him as much as had the poem. He lifted the blanket and sheet to climb in with her, and was overcome anew by her beauty. The heat of her body, her nakedness, his own nakedness—all these things astonished him. She turned to him sleepily, accepting his caresses . . . and once again they made love.

In the weeks that followed, she lived with him almost as a prisoner. No doubt he feared to lose her, but their little island was so vastly preferable to the outside world that he did everything he could to eliminate all contacts. Perhaps she understood his needs and fears, or perhaps she felt similar things herself. In any event, she shared his attitudes, and abetted him in every way.

It was astonishing to him that he, who was as talkative as his loquacious colleagues and was not without pride of opinion, should pass long hours with her quietly or even silently. They played cards, and listened to music, and talked of their lives. He realized that of his entire acquaintanceship she was the only untutored adult. She was not only untutored, however, but unspoiled. He played some Beethoven sonatas for her, in Schnabel's performance, without a word of preamble, and watched the amazement grip her face. She listened scarcely breathing, had never guessed that such power could be wrung from the piano. Of the pounding in opus 110, she said that it was like knocking on a door, to get out or in, but the door wouldn't open. Our scholar was moved to hear her speak like that, and was moved again to see that she did not distinguish between the composer and the performer, but responded like a child, as if it were all one thing.

Her high-heeled shoes were too tight across the toes. She let him reduce her calluses with gentle strokes of a pumice stone, kneeling before her holding first one foot and then the other, while she leaned back in the easy chair, tilting a glass of Pepsi to her lips. Often they talked about food, and at times their conversation was as simple as the menu of a modest restaurant—except that *egg rolls cooked just right* were infused with the redness, softness, and motility of her lips, with her healthy and attractive teeth, and with the homely motions of her jaws, just as the words *Chinese mustard* had in them the wrinkling of her nose and of his. Often he feared that she would want to go out for these treats, into the outside world, but she seemed content to have them delivered, or to wait while he brought them, and she seemed to enjoy eating them there at home, not always on the table in the alcove, but sometimes in bed, and sometimes on the coffee table, sitting cross-legged on the floor, and sometimes on the sofa, holding trays on their laps. There was something playful and childishly adventurous in all this, as if they didn't have a settled way of life, as indeed they did not, but were improvising continually. Occasionally, while they watched TV together, sitting on the floor after such a meal, he found himself remembering the amber glow of the radio dials in the cars and darkened rooms of his youth, and he remembered the songs that had accompanied his youthful loves.

During all these weeks the mysterious poems kept arriving, though never at his bidding. It was as if his typewriter, or rather, the most hidden of the papers held by its roller, were the terminus of a process originating in places far away and unknown to him, and the poems had come by conduits he could not control or even intuit. He never read these poems to her. He did not want to confess to her that the bliss she had brought to him was interrupted by bouts of sorrow. He did not want her to know that, when he went alone into his study and closed the door, he became vulnerable to feelings beyond his control, and beyond her own power to assuage. The poems were of loss and love, and this too he wanted to keep from her. Tears would flow down his cheeks when after writing paragraphs of his scholarly prose he would break apart the carbon sets and find those wondrous messages. He would read them and shake his head dumbly. And then he would go to her where she lay sleeping in bed, or lay napping on the sofa (and often he thought that she was dreaming), or sat curled in the big chair reading a magazine, or listening to music. Sometimes he would find her dancing by herself. Waves of gratitude would move through him, and a great joy of being. His days were strange compounds of sorrow and elation. As for the poems—he was at peace with the fact that he could not summon them, that they came at their will and not his own. Nor was he troubled when their meanings were obscure, or when they alluded to events he only partly recognized. He was warmed by the thought that other persons, too, would find their lives expressed in them, or might qualify as well as he, or better, to receive them, since they too had lost persons they had loved, had lost parents, had despaired of early hopes, had suffered loneliness, anxiety, and doubt, had passed many nights tormented by longing.

But, just as he kept these poems secret from her, she too, he soon learned, was keeping secret from him certain events of her past. There were things she did not want to talk about.

She had been the youngest child in a family so large that the children of her eldest sister were older than she. Three of her elder sisters had come back with their husbands and had raised their children in the enormous, unkempt, convivial house. There had always been dancing, games of cards, singing, a playing of piano or guitars, people listening to radio or watching baseball or soap operas on TV. There had been gallons of Pepsi in the refrigerator.

She had never told him her age. Occasionally, however, when she lay sleeping, or was occupied with some activity, he would look at her appraisingly—or would try to: his glance would melt into admiration, or desire, or a contemplative reverie he could scarcely bring himself to end.

He did ask her if she had been married, and she said that yes, she had been married, she had been married at the age of fifteen.

And had she had children? No, there had not been any children.

He saw that she was lying, but he said nothing . . . and because he paused, wondering what to do, he realized that she knew he knew . . . and then he saw that she was grateful that he did not pursue it.

But where was her husband now? He could not forbear asking this. She bowed her head and smiled, and he saw that her head was trembling slightly. He understood that he should not question her, and so he desisted.

She spoke to him one night of a large willow tree at the end of the paved road near her home. Opposite the tree stood the last lamppost of the street, and there were thousands of moths whirling around high in the cone of light. In one direction lay the darkness of an unpaved road, and in another a darkness in which could be heard the gentle purling of a shallow stream, to which a footpath led across a tiny field.

She stopped talking.

"Yes," he said, "what about the tree?"

All she could add was that they had played there.

He looked at her sharply, but no, she wasn't longing for the past. She wasn't longing for anything. There was no self-pity in her voice, or even nostalgia. It was something else. And he felt sure that this something else was something he shared with her, though perhaps, indeed, all people shared it.

They had just made love and still lay in bed. He said to her that nothing in the world was more mysterious than change. Our hearts invented permanence, but everything in fact was change. All things passed into other things, all states into other states. We were loath to see it. And because we were loath to see it, we did not see it. And because we did not see it, it took us always by surprise.

And he realized, but did not say, that in speaking of change he was speaking also of death.

She sat up brightly. He soon saw that she had thought at great length of these things, had applied herself earnestly to puzzle them out.

She knelt before him naked on the bed, her legs tucked under her, resting back on her calves and heels as easily as a child. Her back and head were erect. Her hands lay in her lap. The great blond mass of her hair was tousled, her white skin seemed almost luminescent in the twilight . . . and all that womanly, full-bodied presence had been forgotten utterly in her devotion to what she was saying. She looked so irresistibly beautiful that had he not been exhausted by love he would have embraced her. He was grateful that he could listen to her, and that these unaccustomed words were not swept away by desire.

She spoke of the changes in people, of how certain emotions could not be renewed and therefore occurred only once or twice in the whole of a life; and of how in some people an essence of character might endure through years of hardship, while in others there was no such endurance at all, but early collapse, followed by decades of wretchedness and fear.

For several nights these were the themes of their conversations.

Her earnest, truthful, untutored thought moved him deeply. He felt both chastened and inspired. Yet it was during these very conversations that the space she had warmed throughout the apartment, and had brought to such a golden glow, began to cool, and the hands of the clock to tremble, as if each minute were a blow.

There came a time when she talked no more in this style, but drifted off into long reveries, or perhaps into memories. He was afraid to interrupt her . . . and his fear and restraint tainted everything. He looked at her dully and longingly, ill with loss and hoping to be cured.

She said to him one day that she wanted to go shopping and needed money. A terrible anxiety sped through him. *Yes, of course,* he said, *it would be a pleasure,* and so forth, though in truth every word cost him a great effort of control.

She left the apartment. He leaned against the wall with a pounding heart and bowed his head, too weak to move. *She'll fall in love with someone else,* he thought. *She won't come back.*

She came back early in the evening, carrying an expensive-looking box. He spoke to her with affected ease about her expedition into the outside world, and said that he was eager to see what was in the box. She untied a bright red cord, removed a blue top, lifted away two large, pale green flaps of tissue paper—and there lay a dress identical with the one she was wearing, but glimmering and new.

He was appalled and angry. He cautioned himself: don't reproach her in any way, don't try to coerce feelings that must be given freely. And so he spoke to her lightly—or rather attempted to. The tension in his voice betrayed him; and in fact he was trembling.

She, in the meantime, pretended that she had not noticed these things. And so on both sides there were omissions and deferrals that were tantamount to pleas, accusations, and refusals. It was as if he were pleading, "Don't leave me!" and were also shouting, "How dare you not love me! How dare you torment me!" and she were answering with cool anger, "How dare you ask me to prefer your feelings to my own! How dare you try to control my comings and goings by the mere assertion of your wishes!"

It would be better, he thought, *to say exactly what I feel* —but sadness hollowed him out, and a chill of anxiety filled the emptiness. Their love was ended. There was nothing he could do. Love cannot be commanded.

He began to rage at her anyway. He said that he would hide her dresses, or destroy them, that he would boil her shoes and she would have nothing to walk in. And he said that certainly he would *not* give money to her for the sole purpose of destroying him.

She looked at him silently.

He shouted, "Yes! Who cares!"—as if she had said to him, "You're behaving like a fool."

She asked him if he thought he could lock her in.

"I do!" he cried. "I can! I will!"

And he did lock her in. He kept her prisoner for three days. He went about his work. She amused herself, as usual. But they didn't talk, and she spent her evenings on the sofa, and fell asleep with the TV muttering low.

On the fourth day he was obliged to mail a manuscript and keep a business date. He locked her in. Two hours later he returned. From the end of the block he could see her polka-dot dress and bright blond hair moving vividly in the sunlight against the dark brick wall of his building. She was staggering down the fire escape, holding her spike-heeled shoes in one hand. In the same hand she held something else. He saw that it was the box of chocolates he had bought her as a gift and then in his anger had hidden. She swayed awkwardly on the narrow iron steps, as if there were no suppleness in her body. Her blond hair bounced and swayed. She popped another chocolate into her mouth and hurled the empty box away from her. He began to run. Several workingmen and passersby were watching her. In fact, a small crowd had gathered. As she put her weight on the cantilevered section just above the ground, she slipped and fell, but caught herself on the iron railing. Her little shoes went clattering to the sidewalk, but two men ran to them instantly and retrieved them. Others steadied the fire escape as it touched the pavement. She put on her shoes, and with short, vigorous, staccato little steps ran to a taxi that was standing at the curb.

Our scholar was drawing near to her. He shouted desperately, but if she heard him she didn't turn her head. One of her shoes fell off as she leaped into the cab. For a moment he couldn't see her, but her white, shapely arm emerged from the still-open door, followed by her smooth shoulder in the sleeveless dress, and then the blond mass of her hair. Her extended fingers picked up the shoe. And now in reverse order there vanished first her head, then her shoulder, then her arm, then her hand holding the shoe. The door of the taxi closed, and the taxi drove away.

He went back to his apartment, which now was like the tomb of his life. Her after-image flickered everywhere. He could see her in the polka-dot dress moving about the kitchen, could see the mounds of her hips and shoulders as she lay on her side beneath the covers on the bed. He searched for the dress he knew she had abandoned, but couldn't find it, and it was like searching for the woman herself. Every room held traces of her: magazines and paperback novels, the *TV Guide*, empty Pepsi bottles in the pantry and full ones in the refrigerator, shampoo and toothpaste and hair conditioner. . . . Most painful of all was the scent of her perfume. He noticed it everywhere, and kept turning to see if perhaps, after all, she really was there with him.

When he laid his head on the pillow that night, the scent of her perfume on the very same pillow pierced him with grief. He held the pillow close, and pressed his face against it, and then he thrust his head beneath it, and pulling it tight against himself gave way to a wild sobbing, saying her name over and over, and saying, "Why did you leave me? Why did you go?"—unable to remember that he had asked the obverse question at the beginning of their love: "Why has she chosen me? Why *me?*" When he awakened in the morning he felt his grief descend like sickness into the first bright moments of consciousness, and it was not until noon that he realized that he had not eaten breakfast.

He wanted to talk of his grief to someone, but of each friend and acquaintance he said, "Not him . . . not her . . ." and gave up the hope. He went to his study to compose a letter now seriously overdue. The letter was actually an installment in a long correspondence with his former teacher and thesis advisor, who was elderly now and lived in London. Their correspondence was in good part professional and deliberate, and was intended for publication as a book. But now, as our scholar sat at the typewriter, he remembered this man's kindly, intelligent face, and remembered how often he had received encouragement during the labors of his doctorate. He abandoned the scholarly subject and poured out his heart, ending with the words *Please write me, please say something about all this.* When he had finished typing he pulled apart the carbon sets . . . and gasped. There were poems on two of the second sheets. This had happened many times before;

nevertheless, he was astonished. He read the poems avidly, as if he believed that perhaps they were messages from *her,* or from the man he had just written. He wanted solace, advice, some word of hope, or some counsel that would strengthen him for the task of endurance that lay ahead. None of these was to be found in the poems. There was something cruel in the poems, something indifferent to such suffering as he presently felt, a strange, impersonal violence, or if not violence nevertheless a tearing and stretching of the web of social life.

Yet one of the poems made him laugh—almost as if by a blow, so strange it was. And then he saw that the other poems were comic as well, not in such a way as to produce a forgiving or reconciling laughter, but in another way, a breaking-free of the earth, a breaking-free of possibility and limitation, perhaps of mortality itself, except that—so he came to see—this very sense of freedom from the earth was an earthly thing.

For more than a month these poems accumulated. He studied them earnestly, though he didn't like them. They were harsh. Yet he admired them, and came to value them. No one could afford such a freedom as they demonstrated; it was not a paradigm for life at all. Yet how dreadful it would be if the giddy attractiveness of that freedom were to vanish from the world!

The changes in his life were abrupt and many. He was not the man he had been, and he did not go back to the same old round. He found that midway in middle age he had acquired a certain style, evidently of romantic attractiveness, though he understood quite well that its worldly appeal was not based at all upon worldly things, but upon modesty, solitude, and the sobriety of endurance. His scholarship deepened, but his pleasures deepened, too. Eventually he married and raised a family, and became a younger man in his great love for his children. Those two brief, astonishing incursions of poetry into his life had long since become a book, but that book was not followed by another. He had come to love it deeply, but poetry was ended in his life.

Or so we believe. Perhaps actually that wonderful naming of the world, and that vigorous motion of mind that was more than personal and that yet had the quality of individual pride, and all those prior enchantments of the senses (which seemed timeless), and the stoppings and startings of the affections (most mortal of all)—perhaps all those things, with all their chimings and surprising sweet music, did actually come back again one day. That too is possible. Perhaps they did.

OILERS AND SWEEPERS

For Peter Schumann
and
The Bread and Puppet Theater

A MISTAKEN NOTION OF WHEN TO
BEGIN SINGING

The eight men of the maintenance gang, who come to work at midnight, stand in a row against a whitewashed wall of the factory. They glance at one another with frightened eyes. They are dressed in gray shirts, gray trousers, and gray caps like baseball caps. Only one—Bosun—is younger than sixty. He is fifty-nine, but is robust and has been placed in charge of the others. He stands at one end of the row. There is a small window just above his head.

Bosun leans forward and looks down the row. He clears his throat loudly. The men face front and clear their throats. They check their flies. They breathe deeply and hold the breath, waiting for a signal.

But no one signals.

They let out the breath.

The row breaks up.

The men stand in a group whispering.

PORTRAITS—I: MEN EATING
SANDWICHES

The men face one another on two benches in the basement locker room.

Bosun sits on a metal folding chair between the benches.

He removes a Thermos bottle from the concave lid of a black lunch box, and five of the men, who possess similar boxes, follow suit. All six unscrew the tops from the Thermos bottles and fill them with steaming coffee or tea.

Skilly and Fred, however, have brought their lunches in brown paper bags. They have pushed coins into the machine upstairs and now they place opened bottles of orange soda on the bench and proceed to unwrap their sandwiches.

For several minutes the chief movement is of hands holding white squares of bread.

The white squares, when not in motion, are held near the lap, or are placed on the waxed-paper wrappings that clutter the benches. And then a square is seized by a hand and is carried to a mouth, from which it is returned to its resting place, diminished in size.

If one were to click a camera at any given moment, there would be a good chance of catching at least one square on its way to a mouth. And occasionally, especially in the first few minutes of the lunch period, one might see all eight squares thrust at the same time into all eight mouths.

When lunch is ended, the faces of the men once again seem bored beyond hope. There are times when Fred, looking down at the large broom he is pushing, cannot think what it is called.

As for Bosun . . . friends have said to him, "No sweat, Bosun . . . easy." But he fears failure and strains his back over tasks a child might accomplish.

Bosun's eyes are small and dull. His bony jaw is thrust forward. One feels that he longs to smile and laugh, and there are times when the men of the gang do actually try to bring him along in that direction, though it must be said of the gang as a whole that they are stoic rather than light-hearted.

In the meantime, killing winds, fires, droughts, floods, quakes sweep the earth. Man-made wars combine all these, adding imprisonment and torture. Hunger and actual starvation cripple and kill hundreds of thousands. Even in the wealthy nations, grief and pain strike many, and uselessness and boredom drag down many thousands more.

MATER DOLOROSA—I

Perhaps all sufferers are victims, but victimization cannot create a figure of suffering, there must be some principle of transcendence—courage, persistence, endurance—for otherwise the sufferer has collapsed and does not represent suffering, but defeat.

Nor may compassion be extorted. It must be freely given.

Thus the eyes of a figure of suffering—it is a woman; she is sitting by a window in a straight-backed chair—the eyes are downcast. They are turned down in the modesty of suffering and the privacy of suffering.

She does not pity herself. Nor does she compare her pain to the pain of others. Nor does she upbraid others because she is in pain and they are not. Her relations in the world have been severely reduced, but they have not been trivialized or corrupted.

She is sitting in a straight-backed chair. Her eyes are cast down and her head is bowed, but her neck and back are erect. Her hands are lying one upon the other in her lap. There is a window in the wall behind her.

The window is of the same spiritual order as the unconscious pride expressed by her posture. Were she to collapse into self-pity the window would vanish. The window is the presence of the world. Perhaps it is her emblem, as the saints in medieval paintings were depicted with their emblems, which very often were their fates.

WINDOW

There is a noise of voices. The voices grow louder and several children come racing by the window. And then for a long time the window is empty; rather, it is filled with sunlight and the massed leaves of trees, which catch the air and shimmer like a stream.

Or—if it is winter—there passes a smiling man in a bright red cap carrying on his shoulder a small evergreen tree.

If the woman remains in this posture of bowed head and downcast eyes, it is not because she is ignoring the world that passes at her window. She would be glad enough to look if one were to touch her and say, "Look . . ."

The task to which she is attending has no need either of eyes or hands; therefore her eyes are cast down and her hands are lying one upon the other in her lap.

FRED—I: SITTING

Another attempt is being made to use Fred as a figure of suffering, for there has been much sorrow in his life and he has borne it well.

He sits in a straight-backed chair, places one hand upon the other in his lap, and bows his head according to instructions.

But now he must be told to stop jiggling his foot. He obeys immediately. But the fingers of one hand are drumming rapidly on the back of the other. Also he crosses his legs. When these errors have been corrected, he begins to cough, and every time he coughs, his hand flies up and covers his mouth. And then he crosses his legs again.

Fred is dismissed.

As he ambles awkwardly across the room—his feet are crippled—it is clear that he is not without dignity. He is tall and thin, but is kinked and bent in several directions. His mouth is twisted to one side. He seems to be laughing bitterly. One would not say that bitter assent and wry laughter were fixed upon his face, but rather that without cease he is nodding bitterly and laughing wryly.

He chats with Skilly during lunch; but in the coffee break he retires to a corner of the locker room. Here a canister of powdered soap rests upon a low metal table. He removes the canister and in its place spreads a copy of the *Daily News.*

He turns the pages of the newspaper slowly. His body is curved above it like half of an arch. His head is suspended like a lantern.

FRED—II: LISTENING

The workers in the plant know the notes and timbres not only of the machines but also of the steel stairs and bannisters, the doors and door frames, the floors and walls of the corridors, the windows and the mesh protectors in front of the windows, the porcelain stalls, bowls, and toilets, the metal lockers, the wooden benches, the casings of the time clocks, the beverage dispenser, the brick walls, the cyclone fence. The workers are not aware that they know these notes, but in fact they have stroked, scratched, scuffed, thumped, tapped almost everything, not only with fingers, knuckles, and hands but also with shoes, boots, umbrellas, coat buttons, keys, coins, can openers, lunch boxes, safety helmets, beer cans, glass bottles, Thermos bottles, rings, watchbands, tools of all kinds, pocket knives, nuts, bolts, and washers, small stones, and odd bits of wood. The characteristic resonance of every object in the plant is wholly known to them—and they are unaware that they know. In fact, they would be surprised if one were to point it out.

Fred is unique in knowing that he knows. He has experimented everywhere: stepladders are like xylophones, a steel bannister can be played with a wrench. He is especially attracted to the dense, terse vibrations of heavy iron and steel: the mountings of the lathes, the ponderous tables of the planers, the mighty casings of stationary engines with their massive bolts, the immovable sides of great boilers and furnaces.

Some of his rhythms are banal. Others are original. A few are strange, especially those he produces when he is listening closely to the sounds and is unaware of the patterns he is creating.

INTERLUDE: ESCAPE OF THE ANT, PERCUSSION

A child is sitting on the hard-packed earth behind a two-story, two-family house. He clutches an aluminum pot firmly in one hand and with it tries to strike an ant. But the pot hits the ground at a slight angle, and the ant rushes along as if in a tunnel, the roof of which unaccountably vanishes and returns.

The patience of the child is impressive. He does not give way to anger, but twists his body and crawls after the ant, pounding the ground energetically.

Fred is transfixed by the sounds and rhythms of the pot in the hand of this child. The vibrations of the pot are conventionally musical, but the hard-packed earth, with its vast inertia, produces a baffling, compelling sound that rounds off quickly into silence.

Fred is guiding the large broom around the bases of the machines. The child, the ant, the hard-packed earth behind the two-story, two-family house—all are vivid in his thoughts.

The truth is, the memory is obsessive.

The pot strikes the earth with irregular accent and loudness. The pattern is highly structured. Is it a pattern? Something in this duality of openness and structure thrills Fred and pains him. He wraps his house key in his handkerchief, and tapping quietly on the massive platform of a planer, accompanies his memories of the child with the pot.

He adds rhythms of his own, modeling them upon the surprising impulses of the child.

From time to time there scurries this way and that across his inner vision a shiny black body with black wire legs.

CHANGE—I

Overhanging banks of brush and sod collapse into the current and sink, and the brush, washed of stones and earth, comes to the surface downstream, spinning. The water is brown and thick. In certain reaches it is dimpled, in others covered with bubbles, in still others roiled, or adrift with scum, or frothy. There are places where it is white and turbulent. The current is strewn with debris. Uprooted trees have knocked down houses, barns, sheds, bridges. Whole meadows are drowned. After three days the rain ceases, but the violent runoff from the hills continues for another day. The flood peaks at night. By the following evening the river is moving less rapidly. Continuous barrows of muddy wreckage have appeared on both sides. Carcasses of animals are wedged against rocks and trees. Men in boots move awkwardly among heaps of debris. Next day women and children join the salvagers. Trucks and bulldozers can be seen. The river is no longer frightening, but is strong and cheerful. The sky is blue and the sun warm. Late in the day two boys in bathing suits drift by, stretched full-length on uprooted trees. Their faces are grave and euphoric. They feel no malice, yet they admire the devastation with an avidity that is close to enchantment. Perhaps others might admire it too, knowing better than the boys what boredom and pain had been fixed within those freshly broken things . . .

The men and women move stiffly, scraping at muddy mounds with shovels, and tugging on the handles of rakes. Occasionally, where the river narrows, the eyes of the boys and the eyes of the salvagers meet. Neither gaze will recognize the other, but the gazes hold until the river has pulled them apart.

WINDOW, AND FIRST SONG

The men are preparing to sing. They are standing in a row before a freshly painted white brick wall. The small window above Bosun's head is a pale, vivid silver, the silver of a sky bright with sun but obscured by haze. A bird appears, wings outstretched, and then is gone. By moving to one side, one can bring the leaves of a small tree into sight. The pulsing silver recedes beyond the white and yellow blossoms and the dark green leaves of the tree. And now because there is an object close, one can see the distance of the sky. Far, far in the distance the silver light continues to vibrate.

There is a chord of music followed by another chord.

Skilly, Fred, Bosun, and the rest are singing the song of Hardy's "During Wind and Rain," in the setting of Felix Arenas:

> They sing their dearest songs—
> He, she, all of them—yea,
> Treble and tenor and bass
> And one to play
> With the candles mooning each face . . .
> Ah, no; the years O!
> How the sick leaves reel down in throngs!

How do they come to know this song?

They sing:

> They clear the creeping moss—
> Elders and juniors—aye,
> Making the pathways neat
> And the garden gay;

126   A TALE OF PIERROT

And they build a shady seat . . .
Ah, no; the years, the years;
See, the white storm-birds wing across!

Skilly's tenor, though uncertain, surprises everyone. The others are not musical, yet this rough sound is music. The window frames the pale silver of the distance. Startlingly close, a bird appears, wings outstretched.

The men sing:

They are blithely breakfasting, all—
Men and maidens—yea,
Under the summer tree,
With a glimpse of the bay,
While pet fowl come to the knee . . .
Ah, no; the years O!
And the rotten rose is ript from the wall.

The blossoming tree is out of sight. Its small spear-shaped leaves were a dark, dark green. Its blossoms were cream-colored, and their centers were yellow like the butter of summer.

Skilly sings alone several lines, and the others join him.

They change to a high new house,
He, she, all of them—aye,
Clocks and carpets and chairs
On the lawn all day,
And brightest things that are theirs . . .
Ah, no; the years, the years;
Down their carved names the rain-drop ploughs.

Who has taught them this song? Who has rehearsed them?

Even in lives one knows well, there are influences and events of which one knows nothing. It cannot be otherwise.

Yet we hear of these things with pangs that are like the panic longings of those who have been abandoned.

MISCHANCE. FRED'S FEET

While the eight men sing they steal glances at one another's faces. Each wants to be an onlooker without ceasing to be a performer.

After the first verse, Fred stops singing. He lowers his eyes and pulls at one ear. In spite of his efforts to *keep up*, in spite of his glancing at his comrades' faces, and his preparatory muttering, he has been singing a different song entirely, the second instead of the first of the two songs the men have prepared. ("Fred," they say afterward, "you got two left ears.")

While he stands there hanging his head, he remembers other mortifying things, especially the mortifications of his feet.

His feet are crippled, the right in such a way that only a shoe meant for the left will fit him.

He remembers how the unworn shoes had accumulated in his closet, and how he had sat at the card table in his furnished room writing phrases and crossing them out until finally, with a curse, he had written: *Man with two left feet* ... "To hell with it!" he had cried. He had crumpled the paper and had hurled it to the floor. Soon, however, he had picked it up. . . .

Wanted, man with two right feet, to swap or purchase shoes.

Wanted, man with foot trouble to swap or purchase shoes —and more, until he had fancied he could see figures coming toward him as through a mist, some limping, others walking slowly with canes, still others swinging their bodies like pendulums between crutches.

For sale, eighty-five shoes, right foot only.

But the hobbling figures kept emerging from the mist.

"No, no!" he had cried, clinging to his solitude. He had torn the paper to bits. He had put the shoes in a box and had put the box beside the garbage can, saying to the world at large, "Take 'em! Take 'em!"

FIRE

Often—especially if in spirit he is "hurrying along," but in flesh is moving, as always, rather slowly—Fred looks down at his feet with contempt and exasperation.

He fears fire. He fears that in a race for the exit he will be trampled. Therefore he has apprised himself of the locations of all exits, even of windows and vents that might be used as exits. He rehearses obsessively and now possesses a repertory of escapes that covers the entire plant. When a voice inside him says, "I oughta show the boys," he shakes his head and mutters bitterly, "Let 'em figure it out."

After years of such brooding he hears a mighty ringing. Workers everywhere shout to one another, "What the hell is that?" and answer, "Who the fuck knows. Let's clear out!" Soon the word *fire* can be heard on all sides.

As Fred had feared, the younger workers rush violently toward the main entrance. In their violence they are like a force of nature. They are as terrifying to the older men as fire.

Fred's comrades have begun to collect themselves. And Fred, instead of fleeing, as so often he had imagined, stands rooted to the spot.

He calls to his comrades, "This way, boys! Skilly! Hey!"

In his fearful imaginings he had thought even of these older ones as members of a frightening multitude called *others*. Now as he directs their flight, observing with fascinated clarity their actual gaits, he sees that they are not a horde at all, nor frightening. Each seems to know his weakest link, the seam or joint or juncture box which if strained or jolted will spring apart and spill the ribs or vertebrae like blocks across the floor. They run glidingly, with sagging knees. One holds his sides, another his belly.

Fred stands there. His left arm is extended. It points toward safety. His right arm is bent and beckoning.

When the last man has passed him, he shuffles along. Later the men praise him and he is pleased, but as he follows unhurriedly in their wake he is saddened by his indifference to the fire.

WINDOW

One can close one's eyes and visualize the window that appeared above Bosun's head while the men were singing. And one can hear again, in memory, much of their song.

It is as a memory, a fading image, that the window frames visions nearest to delight, childish things that please the heart and perhaps mean nothing: a red castle with white battlements upon a steep, steep hill of green. Or perhaps the hill is of clanging glass, and many charging horses have slid back down. Near the castle is a pit in which an unknown prisoner stands proudly, his arms across his chest, holding at bay by the power of his eyes a rearing, raging bear.

Now the window is a field of red. The red is the red of Saint Valentine's heart.

Now the window is pulsing with the pulsing deep blue called *before daylight blue.*

MATER DOLOROSA—II

The woman is not young, her death is not unexpected, but she is dying of a devastating, swift disease, and is dying in pain, and therefore her death is shocking.

Her three children, who are themselves the parents of children, some grown, have come long distances to be with her.

For several weeks she has rested between bouts of pain. Now even with ameliorative drugs her pain is constant. She can no longer hold a glass or cup or a fork weighted with food.

A distant neighbor telephones to ask if she will canvass her parish for a well-known charity. Her husband conveys the message from the doorway of her room. The dying woman smiles and enunciates slowly, "Tell her . . . I'd . . . be delighted."

A wave of pain stiffens her and the admiring smiles vanish from her family's faces. She does not express the pain, but expresses her astonishment at its intensity, saying softly, out of her rural childhood, "Gee whillikers . . ."

Three weeks more must pass.

Two of her children leave to care for children of their own. They cannot bring themselves to put into words the finality of farewell. Their words are soothing and vague. First the man and then the woman lean over her bed to embrace her. She seems not to hear what they say, but looks into their eyes, which have filled with tears, and kisses each one hungrily.

Pain continues the work of prying her from the world.

She sleeps much. Her son reads to her. She talks briefly, dozes, talks.

From time to time she hallucinates. "Oh," she says, "this medicine makes me talk so silly." There is amusement in her voice. She begins to tell of a dream that seemed strange to her, but sighs and closes her eyes.

The guardrail of the rented bed must be put into place now, for she is not capable of preventing herself from falling. She cannot find a comfortable position for her hands. The bars of the little railing are cool and she puts her wrists on them, letting her fingers hang motionless outside the bed. Her fingers are swollen. The skin seems fragile and overheated. Her fingernails and skin are colored all the same pale ivory.

Her hands remain in this position while she dozes. She falls asleep facing her son and husband, and she does not withdraw her hands from the little railing. The room grows dark. Her hands are motionless.

Soon the disease has affected her speech, and soon thereafter she can only grunt.

The nurse washes her in bed, dries her gently, and daubs her skin with alcohol. The woman lifts one arm and strokes and pats the nurse on the back of her head. After the nurse leaves, the woman takes her son's hand in hers and laboriously draws it to her lips and kisses his fingers, looking at him gravely. He leans over the railing and kisses her.

Her coma begins soon after.

She must be turned in bed and washed of her urine. She opens her eyes fearfully. The two men speak soothingly, but it is impossible to know if she recognizes them. In a few moments she is asleep again.

For three days she breathes loudly and with difficulty. She has turned her face to the wall. Her hands lie on the blankets over her abdomen, and from time to time her fingers pick at the blankets. Her eyes remain closed. The father and son moisten her parched lips, and put water drop by drop into her mouth.

At breakfasttime her loud breathing abruptly ceases.

Her son leans over her and listens for her breath, her heart.

Her husband folds her hands on her bosom and places his crucifix between them.

Her son holds her motionless head in his arms. He is weeping. He kisses her forehead and cheeks. He wants to speak to his father, who is standing beside him, but he cannot find his voice.

WINDOW

The fronds of a palm tree and the leaves of a live oak almost fill the window, but there is a corner of well-trimmed lawn of a coarse, drought-resistant grass. The moans of mourning doves can be heard, and sometimes the birds can be seen. Two squirrels leap and run in the live oak tree, and perch alertly.

Daily the sun rises on their curiosity and pride, and sets on their readiness for sleep.

HOW SKILLY GOT HIRED (THE MEETING ROOM)

Fred and Skilly are members of a patriotic organization. Their meeting room is painted battleship gray and is floored with squares of dull linoleum patterned to resemble marble. The room is crowded with wooden folding chairs, a sofa, some easy chairs, a television set. There is a long, narrow table. At one end of the table, in a stand, is an American flag. At the other end, also in a stand, is the flag of the organization. The window behind the table is large and overlooks the street, one flight up. The window is covered by venetian blinds which have never been opened. The blinds are extremely dusty. The skeleton of a small tree of some sort rises out of a mound of cigar butts and gum wrappers in a large urn near the American flag. The butts and wrappers are fresh, but the tree has been dead for years, perhaps a decade.

The men play cards, smoke, watch television, drink beer. They have escaped from wives, children, grandchildren, crowded apartments, empty flats. They have these escapes in common, and they have in common that they belonged to the armed services in time of war.

The rhetoric of the organization expresses pride. It also expresses a desire for revenge, on whom and for what it is not clear. Some of the men are cowards in all possible ways, but many are brave and want to be called upon to risk their lives. They are willing to risk the lives of many millions to attain this. Some detest themselves. They yearn for praise. They want to die meaningfully and be praised in death. Most of the men are intelligent, some are extremely clever, very few are stupid. Almost all are ignorant, many are abysmally ignorant, and their ignorance is compounded by superstition. They live in a world of miracles and wonders—unfortunately rare—and of waste, confusion, and willful boredom, which are routine. Some of their faces are wild, as if for the millionth time they have just heard the insult whispered from the shadows. Several wars are represented. The men pretend that they are organized by their wars, but they are organized by age and economics, ailments and chronic passions: lower back, feet, skin; racism, horse betting, poker.

Much business is conducted here. When Bosun told Fred that he was enlarging the crew, and said, "I was wonderin' if you knew somebody," Fred said, "Yeah, I got just the guy." He didn't have anyone in mind, but he knew he could find someone at the meeting room. Sure enough, Skilly was at the meeting room and was out of work.

Skilly was watching baseball on TV with half a dozen others.

Fred leaned down and said near his ear, "I got sump'm I want to talk to you about after the game."

Skilly said, "Naw, the game's nuthin', it's just a game. . . ."

Fred explained the job to Skilly. Skilly said he would take the job. He also said that he wanted to think it over.

Fred said that the job was available, but that he didn't know anyone who could fill it.

Skilly asserted that such a job was a snap, but on the other hand was difficult. He asserted further that he was available for the work. He asserted further that he would take the job.

Fred said that it was not up to himself to do the hiring. He said he would put in a good word.

Skilly apologized for being assertive.

Fred apologized for seeming to be such a man as one must apologize to.

Skilly assured him that he did not seem to be that kind of man.

Fred said, "Yeah . . . well . . . I gotta go, Skilly. I'll put in a word tomorrow. Or maybe you oughta just come in, what the hell . . ."

Skilly said, "Wait up. I gotta clear out myself . . ."

They looked around the room to see if anyone was noticing their departure and required waving goodbye to. But nobody was noticing.

As they went down the stairs, Fred assured Skilly that he, Fred, was just an ordinary man, and was a regular guy, and did not need to be apologized to.

Skilly apologized again. He assured Fred that he too was an ordinary man, and that he knew very well that Fred was a regular guy.

They reached the sidewalk and stood there a moment in silence.

Fred apologized for existing.

Skilly apologized for existing, but added that everyone had to live.

Fred agreed with that.

Skilly agreed with Fred, as if Fred had said that everyone had to live.

Fred said, "Yeah . . . well . . . okay, Skilly . . ."

Skilly said, "Okay, Fred. I'll come in tomorrow. Just ask for Bosun."

Fred said, "Just go to the locker room in the basement. Ask for Bosun."

Skilly said, "Yeah. Well . . . Okay, Fred. See you at the plant."

As they turned from each other, Skilly said, "I guess it wouldn't hurt to come around a quarter of."

Fred said, "Never saw it hurt." He laughed, and Skilly followed suit and laughed.

Skilly said, "See you then."

Fred said, "Yeah. Okay. So long, Skilly."

They parted.

The distance between them grew by several strides.

Fred was overcome by uncertainty. He wondered whether the copy of the *Daily News* tucked under his arm was not somehow the copy of the *Daily News* he had seen tucked under Skilly's arm. He turned and called to him: "Hey! Skilly!"

Fred laboriously ambled toward him and Skilly, with his own peculiar gait, a stammering or stuttering gait that was nevertheless determined and purposive, came halfway.

They met and Fred said, "I was just wonderin' if you had your paper."

Skilly said, "Yeah . . ." and showed him his copy of the *Daily News.*

Fred showed Skilly his own copy of the *Daily News,* saying, "Yeah . . ." And then with one finger he lifted the cuff of his sleeve and looked at his wrist. "Say, it's not so late," he said. "Whatta you say we have a drink?"

Skilly said, "Yeah, it ain't late at all. I wouldn't mind a short one."

They went to the saloon on the corner, and Skilly held back so that Fred would enter first.

PORTRAITS—II: SKILLY NUDE

To see Skilly nude is to understand that mankind could not exist were it not for the world of man-made things. No creature so far from its species' norm could survive in the woods or fields. Nothing fits. Parts that should be stout are thin, that should be long are squat. His neck is a muffin caught between collarbone and chin. His arms are like pieces of garden hose, the more surprising in that they bend exactly where the elbows bend on other men. His chest is two nipples on the upper circumference of his belly. He has no groin. It is as if a huge basin with a spout were hanging from his neck. His legs are long, and like his arms are tubular and thin. His feet do not have arches. His toes lie there. abashed, as if discarded.

A child might look and without emotion see a little fat guy. But those separated from childhood by physical desire and the experience of longing will tend to be repelled by the sight of Skilly, or will laugh aloud.

They are laughing now. He's at boot camp thirty years ago, back from the showers with a towel round his gut. Here at the bunk are a crowd of sailors and the CPO who without success has drilled him for the last three weeks.

"Skilly, you freak, we're gonna find out what makes you not tick! Atten-HUT!"

The towel is yanked from his waist.

"Keep your hand at yer sides! Now Skilly, I'm gonna call cadence, and you get in step, you understand? For-WAD . . . HARCH! HUP! Two, three, four, HUP! Two, three, four . . ."

The cadence is marching away, eight strides in perfect time, and Skilly, alas, has taken only three. The barracks shakes with laughter. The chief is squatting. He is spraying beer out of his mouth.

"Skilly, you're hopeless. You're hopeless, Skilly. This way, goddamnit, keep moving, *hup, hup, hup . . .*"

He wants to watch up close the fall of Skilly's foot . . . and here now Skilly's heel touches the floor. He is striding with a will. He is working his knees. His foot rolls forward. It rises to the ball. . . .

"Aha!"

Skilly's arch collapses, his foot falls back, his heel is on the floor again.

"Skilly, I've seen a lot o' freaks. . . ."

The barracks shakes with laughter.

"How the hell can you keep the count?"

"No, sir."

"You're hopeless, Skilly. Get dressed."

Skilly puts on his uniform.

"Skilly, I appoint you company scribe. I hope to fuck you can write."

"Yessir."

Skilly cocks his gob's hat over one eye and sticks a big

cigar in the corner of his mouth.

He opens his beer with a flourish.

CHANGE—II: BY REPETITION, RAIN, FLOOD, ETC.

Overhanging banks of brush and sod collapse into the current and sink, and the brush comes to the surface downstream, spinning.

The water is brown and thick. There are places where it is white and turbulent. The current is strewn with debris. Uprooted trees have knocked down houses etc. After three days the rain ceases, but the violent runoff etc. By the following evening the river is moving less rapidly. Continuous barrows of muddy wreckage etc. Carcasses of animals are wedged etc. Men in boots move among heaps of debris. Next day women and children join the salvagers. Trucks and bulldozers can be seen. The river is no longer frightening. The sky is blue, the sun warm.

AN EXCEPTION

Many things in the plant are washed; some are stripped, cleaned, and reassembled; some are vacuum-cleaned; some are cleaned with solvents. The floors are swept and scrubbed. The locker room, the toilets, the decrepit upstairs lounge with the beverage dispenser . . . all are regularly cleaned. But the windows are never cleaned. They look like tinted glass. They are more like walls than windows.

Fred said to Bosun once, "Wouldn't you think we oughta clean them windas?"

Bosun shook his head. There were no standing orders regarding the windows, and he knew that the absence of instructions regarding the windows was tantamount to instructions regarding the windows. More than that, it constituted a tradition.

Fred repeated the question to Skilly. "Wouldn't you think we oughta clean them windas?"

Skilly raised his head with surprise. He looked first at one window and then at another. Finally he shook his head and said, "Nanh."

PREPARATIONS FOR THE SECOND SONG

The men are whispering. They are clustered in front of the white brick wall. There is no need yet to stand in a row, but the form of The Row is active in their minds. They are magnetized by the idea of The Row.

Copies of the text are passed among them as a favor to those who are not quite certain of the words.

Actually they are all quite certain of the words. But now two of them begin studying the text, and the others, seeing it, are assailed by doubt and begin studying the text.

WINDOW

The darkness at the window is blacker than night. It is as black as black velvet.

If the window were lower in the wall, Bosun's head and shoulders would be framed against black like a Gothic portrait. His gray baseball cap would appear as *costume*. His small eyes and heavy jaw, without ceasing to be Bosun, would become signs for the endurance and transience of mortal fact.

Now the window takes on hues of slate. The night sky can be seen. Here is Job's Coffin. Here is Orion. Here is the Bull.

Now the sky is displaced by a field of dark blue, symbolic of Night and Heaven. The stars are as large as a hand and are five-pointed. They are made of hammered silver, or perhaps only of foil stretched upon wooden forms with an elegant and playful crudeness.

The silver stars appear in a lower corner of the window, as if streaming across the sky in vast numbers. And then they move to the center. There are only seven. They are surrounded on all sides by darkness, like a band of wanderers. Now they dance out of sight diagonally upward, seeming again to be spangling a great field.

SECOND SONG

The men stand in a row against a whitewashed brick wall of the factory.

They are humming a sour, massive tone. Now clanging, strange chords emerge from the tone and wander this way and that. Skilly's voice lifts up alone.

> The silver Swan who living had no note,
> When death approached unlocked her silent throat.
> Leaning her breast against the reedy shore,
> Thus sang her first and last, and sang no more . . .

Voices like sprays of raindrops, or like pigeons hurled into sight above the roofs of houses, repeat isolated words, changing their acidity or sweetness. And then the voices hum again their strange wandering chords, while Skilly's voice, in this second setting of Arenas's, follows a line of its own:

> Farewell all joys, O death come close my eyes,
> Farewell all joys, O death come close my eyes.

After the words have ended, the sour, massive humming continues.

As the humming fades, the lights, too, fade into darkness.

And then the lights come back and the men stand there blinking.

PERSISTENCE OF SONG. PERSISTENCE OF SINGING

The songs are given without condition, the offer is absolute.

Little in life is given so freely.

Or perhaps much is given: all love, all art, many fruits of the mind. Nature itself persists by increase.

Once the songs have ended, it is clear that the singers are also listeners and the listeners singers. Satisfaction is indivisible. It is not personal.

ARRIVAL OF CANISTERS

A dozen canisters of powdered soap, ordered months ago, have been delivered to the loading platform. They must be moved indoors.

RESCUE OF THE NEW MAN

The new man, Mr. Simmonds, falls ill before the 2 A.M. break. His eyes bulge, he is hot to the touch, his skin is covered with fiery blotches.

No one notices.

He says, "I feel shaky, boys. Am I hot? Do I look okay?"

They look him up and down, and a couple press their hands against his forehead.

"You're okay."

By lunchtime (4 A.M.) he can no longer walk.

No one notices.

By the second break he has vomited and cannot stand up.

No one notices. They finish their coffee and go off to work on the floor above.

Mr. Simmonds calls, "Boys! Boys!" but they don't hear him. His fever has made him panicky. He stumbles along, trying to catch up. He gets to the top of the stairs, and calling, "Boys! Boys!" tumbles back down.

The men hear the noise and stop.

No one is willing to say, "Did you hear that?" for the sound has ceased. But in the silence, which is protracted, and without breaking the silence, they pass beyond the stage of "Did you hear that?" to the stage of having already agreed to take action.

Avoiding all jolts, they go rapidly ("run") to the stairway.

Mr. Simmonds lies at the bottom, unconscious, blood trickling from several cuts.

One lifts his head, and kneeling, holds it in his lap. Another wipes his face, carefully avoiding the cuts. A third loosens his collar and fans him with his cap. Bosun goes to the intercom a few steps away.

Fred: "Poor guy. He's hot as a poker."

Skilly: "He musta lost his balance."

Bosun: "Yeah. He lost his balance."

On the intercom: "Tell the doctor we got a guy here lost his balance. Yeah. We think it happened on the stairs."

A DEVOTION MISPLACED

Fred dreamt that Bosun shook his fist at the sun. Bosun spoke to the sun through a megaphone and commanded it to rise.

A FIGURE OF BEAUTY

A beautiful youth appears at the plant. He is unlike the other workers. His face is radiant, innocent, confident. He seems interested in everything and everyone. His hands are not callused, but are pink and shapely, yet they are strong and he works with a will. He must be told to slow down.

The word goes round that he is a student.

The men understand that he will soon leave them. They resent him. Yet his radiant, responsive face is irresistible. By lunchtime it is clear that some of the workers will harass him and others defend him.

Skilly, Fred, Bosun, Mr. Simmonds, and the rest see him only in passing. They are going home and he is arriving.

They are walking as they walk, and he comes by as if borne on air. He nods to them and smiles.

They do not quite stop, but almost stop. They bump each other. They turn and follow him with their eyes.

They face front again and without speaking continue on their way.

CHANGE—III

The fire burns on three fronts, consuming the stunted dry growth of thousands of acres. Little clumps of flame, which are foxes, rabbits, and raccoons, spurt from the advancing front and ignite other fires where they fall. Small planes circle the hills. A white powder spills from their bellies. As far away as fifteen miles, half the sky is dark. Four days later the wind shifts and the fire is turned back upon its ashes. Returning residents find trees blackened halfway and individual leaves divided into black and tan. The naked hills are powdery and gray.

Two weeks later the rain commences, ending a drought of twelve years. All day the rain is heavy and steady, and then it becomes violent. Homes that had escaped the fire are lifted by sliding mud and sent spinning and tumbling down the slopes.

KOLCHUK'S HAND

A great hand of molded fiberglass finds its way to the factory. One of the foremen, who is also the shop steward, uncrates it. He calls Skilly and Mr. Simmonds and says to them, "It's filthy.

It ain't been washed since they made it. Scrub it down good."

The hand is five feet high. It stands on a block of polished wood and is called "A Worker's Hand." After lunch the men gather round it in the upstairs lounge. One tells the story of Kolchuk's artistic daughter, and others, who knew Kolchuk, nod emphatically, as much as to say, "Yep, this is Kolchuk's hand."

But their solemnity is brief.

"Shit, no," says one. "That ain't Kolchuk's hand. He used to tape one finger. When he took the tape off it fell down like a wet noodle. It'd fall in his coffee if he didn't tape it; he had no control."

The men laugh. One of them says, "It's Robinson's hand," and the laughter grows harsh. Robinson's hand had been severed at the wrist. He worked in another plant now, as a watchman.

"Kolchuk was missing a joint on the middle finger."

Several men in the lounge are missing parts of fingers. They nod.

It wasn't Kolchuk's hand.

It wasn't anybody's hand. It wasn't tired enough, or strong enough, or crooked enough. Its veins weren't puffy enough. Its skin wasn't gray enough or loose enough. The men dinched their cigarettes on it and wedged dead cigars between its fingers.

The shop steward summoned Skilly and Mr. Simmonds and said, "Let's clear this thing the hell outa here."

They put it on a dolly and took it to a storage room in the basement. A few weeks later they threw it on a truck and it was hauled away with a load of scrap.

BOSUN'S SUNDAY

He dresses in a gray suit that doesn't fit him. He wears a tie that makes his neck puff out. With his broad, powerful wife, who is two years older than he, he walks sedately to church and then to the home of his eldest son, who lives nearby.

Bosun could afford to have his suit altered, but he does not wish to express discontent. He could make use also of the full-length mirror on the back of his wife's closet door, but it makes him uneasy to look at himself. He distrusts emotion and is under the impression that he never dreams. Even with friends he talks guardedly.

Yet Bosun's marriage is companionable. He has never been angry at his wife, has never upbraided her. After more than thirty years he still speaks to her with courteous formality. She cooks their food and serves it. He makes their coffee and serves it, and washes the dishes. When they leave their apartment of a Sunday morning, he crooks his arm for her and they fall in step.

By long custom he takes her his pay envelope unopened. One day his fingertips notice an unaccustomed something in the little brown packet. It seems to be a paper clip. He opens the envelope. A typewritten slip is pinned to the paymaster's slip. He unfolds it and reads:

> We regret to inform you that due to circumstances beyond our control your employment has been terminated. Please report to the office upon receiving this.

His ears are ringing. A terrible chill numbs his mind. He puts the slip back into the envelope. He licks the flap and seals it and puts the envelope into the pocket of his gray shirt. Twenty minutes later, in the privacy of the toilet he opens the envelope. Here again is the folded narrow piece of paper.

> We regret to inform you that due to circumstances beyond our control your employment has been terminated. Please report to the office . . .

Something like horror passes through him, leaving shame in its wake. He feels that he has been injured and that the injury must at all costs be concealed. He feels that he has been judged and that the judges are correct, he is guilty.

He does not speak to his comrades. He avoids their eyes and at quitting time leaves them with a nod.

He feels that he has failed her. As he nears his home he has begun to say to himself, "I have always failed her."

She, however, takes a different view. She says that his employers are "ignorant fools." She says that there are many jobs to be had and many places that will appreciate him. And she says it's about time he took a vacation, anyway.

MATER DOLOROSA—III

The older men and women, descendants of the region's settlers, would stop her in the street when she went to town, and inquire about her son and speak to her of bygone generations of her dead husband's kin. When the boy was eighteen she felt that her work in him was ended. She spoke to him of her yearning to bring back the farm. She said she was not sure it would be good for him, a farmer's life was difficult and would make poor use of his gifts for literature and music, though hadn't Robert Burns been a farmer? . . .

There was much else that she meant to say. She had thought it all out. But he patted her arm, and smiled. "I know, Mom, I know," he said.

And so they had repaired the barn, lifting the entire structure on house jacks and laying stout new sills on beddings of stone. They had poured cement for a milking parlor, and when all was ready had purchased twelve cows.

But now the youth has been killed by a drunkard on the road. His adolescent sisters fear they will lose their mother too. The skin of her face, which had been taut and girlish, hangs loose. Her eyes are glassy and her movements stiff. Yet, when the others arrive for the service, she does everything that needs to be done. They drive to the cemetery in six cars.

The sky is a soft blue. Small white clouds are scattered

across it, a sight so pretty it is almost painful to behold.

The rural cemetery is crowded with trees. The grass is the bronzed green of late summer. A mound of sand can be seen. The party approaches on foot.

Beside the sand a casket rests on two beams over a small, deep pit. Fresh flowers have been placed in a vase by the headstone of the father's grave. Friends and family sit on the grass near the casket. They bow their heads. A white-haired man holds a Bible.

For a long while all are silent. A young man begins to speak of the dead youth. The others lift their heads and look at him gently. He speaks briefly and bows his head again. A woman speaks. The two sisters are weeping and cannot talk. A young woman sitting with her own family is weeping also. Some speak of the childhood of the dead youth, others of his adolescence. All are silent awhile. The white-haired man reads several verses from the Bible. He asks if anyone would like to read and he hands the Bible across the circle. Verses are read also from the *Book of Common Prayer,* and the dead youth's aunt reads some poems that have been typed on white paper. There is a long silence. The white-haired man glances at the others and says softly, "We must go through with it now." He stands and waits, and the others, moving stiffly, get to their feet. Four men pick up the straps under the casket. Others remove the supporting beams. The men lower the casket into the grave and pull up the straps.

Those who are not laboring stand by the grave or move aimlessly, avoiding one another's eyes. The dead youth's sisters and young friends throw flowers into the grave. Several of the men are crying soundlessly, shielding their eyes. The elder sister kneels and drops gently into the grave the torn and mended sheets of the Beethoven sonata the youth had been studying. A moment later the first shovels of sand strike the casket hollowly, and the weeping grows louder. The younger sister falls to the ground.

The elder sister speaks to one of the men and he relinquishes his shovel. As she lifts her first bladeful of sand she glances across the open grave and sees her mother stretched face-downward on the grass. Her knees are drawn under her and are spread wide so that her abdomen touches the ground. The young woman remembers how in a shadowy corner of the barn, many years ago, their mortally wounded she-goat lay dying on a bed of straw, while its kneeling kid vigorously and playfully poked its udder with its nose.

Later, at the house, the mother organizes everything, serving first the repast and then the late supper for those who will be staying overnight.

As the night grows dark the voices in the parlor, though still muted, become livelier. Occasionally there is the sound of laughter, though never when she is in the room. She takes note of it without resentment.

WINDOW

The mother turns from the farmhouse stove to the table, a pot of coffee in her hand, and is startled by a sound at the open window. The leafy thicket at the window sways, the leaves part, and so gently as scarcely to be a presence at all the great presence of the cow appears, beautiful eyes in the shadows. Its gaze fills the room.

The mother steps outside, and standing on the small wooden porch whispers, "Go home, Polly! Go home!"

SAVANNAH. ARMS. SKILLY'S NIGHTMARE

In the darkness of the theater Skilly discovers that the African film is a documentary made by anthropologists. His disappointment is brief. These scenes of real life interest him far more than the lurid things promised by the ads. Muscular, well-formed men propel their great canoes down a mighty river. The men are not paddling only with their arms, but thrust powerfully with their backs, bending low with each stroke. They put ashore in time to hunt and make a simple camp. They butcher small animals and cook them. Something in the way they use their hands is enchanting to Skilly. Are they ambidextrous, all of them? Their fingers are strong, yet are sensitive, as if the fingertips were tingling. Muscular shoulders and arms emerge continually onto the screen. The canoes pursue their journey. In the great savannahs downriver there is a lion hunt. There are nighttime scenes in camp. The men work in groups. They sing as they work, and smile often. Muscular shoulders and arms emerge continually onto the screen. Skilly cannot bring himself to leave the theater. He sees the film three times.

When he falls asleep that morning (for he observes his working hours even on the weekends), he recalls many of the scenes from the film. A hunter receives the lion's charge on his shield and rolls with the impact. The handles of a dozen spears project from the lion's body, and the lion stands on two feet, twisted. There is a moment in camp in the morning: one of the men, hastening toward the river, moves a dozing dog out of his path with the handle of his spear. His movement is firm, masterful, even implacable, yet it is gentle, extremely gentle. The canoes are in white water. In the prow of each canoe, balanced on a tiny platform, a man with a long pole fends off the rocks. How proud he is, the one in the first canoe! His balance is like the balance of a bird in flight. He smiles and smiles. He is proud of everything, certainly of those shoulders, those sensitive and mighty arms.

Skilly sleeps. Hours later he awakens with a start. Something has frightened him. The blinds are drawn. Dim daylight fills the room. The usual noises come from the street, the usual noises from the building. It must have been a dream, a nightmare. He is sweating, his heart is pounding. He is sitting up in bed.

EATING

The men have come to work through heavy rain and wind.
Even indoors, on the first floor, the storm can be heard. Workers near the windows glance up in alarm. Gusts of wind throw
the rain so violently against the glass that the raindrops sound
like stones.

The storm is not audible in the basement. There is a
stillness, as of waiting. Occasionally the lights flicker. They
seem dimmer than usual.

Skilly, Fred, Mr. Simmonds, and the rest sit facing one
another on two benches. Some cross their legs. Some spread
their legs and slouch. They seem lost in thought. The white
squares of bread rise and fall. Bottles of soda, cups of coffee and
tea rise and fall. The men's jaws work slowly. The men swallow
gravely. Peristaltic waves carry the aliment warmly to the
secret heart.

INTERVIEW WITH
THE AUTHOR OF CARYATIDS
Excerpts from a Tape, 1972

The truth is, I'm an example of obsession. I write incessantly, and I write plays, nothing but plays. Given the needs and suffering of our world, I don't think it's very important. Your brother, too, by the way, is obsessed. He suffers a great deal in not knowing it. He trusts his talent too much, and talent's a cheap commodity. Well, you're lyricists, all of you. I suppose to be young is to be lyrical. But no, I was Andy's age when I wrote *Caryatids,* and that's not a lyrical play. Don't imagine, though, that I was lacking in fervor. I had it in abundance. And that outgoing, that *generous* arrogance of youth. And when they began stoning the actors . . . I must stop saying that. . . . Do you want to hear all this? It's nothing but reminiscence. When I say, by the way, that we are estranged from created nature, I'm not referring only to grass and trees. We too are created things. Yet our faces, for example, have become almost invisible. We see nothing but our relations with each other, psychological things, historical things, aspects of our culture. The mysterious *givenness* of creaturely existence quite escapes us. It was this that I was concerned with in *Caryatids.* I wanted to reveal it. I wanted, rather, to *recreate it in awareness.* And you misunderstand me if you imagine that I meant to shock. On the contrary, I have been astonished by my audiences' reactions. Many of my plays have been closed—closed, revived, celebrated, abused. *Caryatids* alone has produced outrage. It has never been done professionally. Nor ever in its entirety. Only three attempts have been made.

The first was in the basement of a church near Washington Square. I had just written the play. I was keyed-up. And I was anxious. But I was hopeful, too. And I felt . . . I don't know . . . a certain spirit of loving. . . . Perhaps what I really wanted was to be loved. I suppose I did. And when they began throwing things at the actors, why it seemed that a dreadful mistake had been made, a dreadful misunderstanding. I didn't hesitate a moment, I leaped onto the stage and threw up my arms and cried, "I am the author! Listen to me!" Ah, yes . . . "I am the author" . . . Doleful words! But at that time . . . well, there was a great deal I wanted to say to them. I felt that if I could . . . could *reorient* them in a few of their values, everything would fall into place. And I actually thought they'd stop throwing things, you know, and listen to me. But when I cried, "I am the author! Listen to me!" they shouted right back, or some few of them did, "He's the author! Get him!" and they began swarming onto the stage. I said to myself, "Good Lord! They're serious!" And really, you know, this moment . . . well, I must say, the meanings of my life have rarely come to me in the calm of reflection, but curled, as it were, in the fist of shock. They chased me right through the wings, on through the dressing rooms, and right out the back door. The moment I leaped into the street I learned something important, and I'll tell you what it was. I had assumed . . . that is, deep in my heart I had believed that our arena was the theater, and that we were free there and shared some few basic, reliable agreements. But when I leaped into the street I looked behind me, and good heavens! there they came! They looked so strange! I'm not sure they were angry at all . . . but they certainly wanted to punish me. They wanted to teach me a lesson. I suppose they were angry after all. . . . They were shaking their fists . . . so I ran . . . I was dodging pedestrians and flitting between cars, and they came right behind me, these people I had been pleased to think of as my audience, or worse, *the* audience, and I said to myself, not exactly in these words, but the thought was quite clear: *"The arena of art is life itself!"*

This was a large thought, not a small one. A great many other thoughts were attached to it. Yet, in spite of this mental activity . . . I find it odd, wondrous in a way . . . I mean to say, the outdoor scene was brilliantly alive. It was one of those mild, sweet evenings toward the middle of September. The sidewalks were crowded, traffic was jumbled and slow, and the horns of the taxis seemed to hover on the air. There was something festive about the scene, so rich and highly colored. How good it would have been to mingle with the others! A tourist bus discharged its passengers, and they leaped aside as I plunged across their path. I heard someone say, "He must be a thief." I, who had wanted to be loved! And what if they were right, quite right, all of them? I couldn't help but ask myself that question. And it did seem to me that yes, they were right, quite right, all of them. But this didn't mean that I was wrong. Far from it. I didn't in the least feel wrong. There loomed in my heart instead a strong and consoling insight, namely that the correct and proper thing for me and for my art was the conflict itself. As you see, I'm of short stature, and even then I was somewhat . . . well, not corpulent, and not stout, either . . . roly-poly. I have always been roly-poly. Yet I outdistanced them, left them in the dust. I was able at last to walk down the sidewalk at a dignified pace. I had arrived by now in what is perhaps the most rational quarter of New York: the heart of Chinatown. I turned in to a little restaurant and read the menu as fervently as if it had been a review of my play. I wanted to think, to puzzle things out, and I ordered half a dozen dishes so as to give myself time. But there was nothing to think about, nothing at all. It was odd. It was as if I were saying, somewhere deep in my being, words I didn't believe at all: "All's right with the world." And I did, in fact, breathe a little prayer.

I say, must I do all the drinking? You haven't touched your drinks. You know, when you appeared at my door I had quite forgotten my talk with Andy, but I thought, "How nice to receive a visit from such an attractive young couple!" You don't *like* alcohol, do you? Of course not. Your generation doesn't drink it. Shall I send down for some pot? I should imagine they'd have some at the desk. Room Service certainly has it. I mean the chap himself. I'll just ring.

It's impossible to say when I began. I was raised in the theater. My parents were actors. In a professional way they knew Yeats and Synge, O'Casey, Robinson, and the Fays. But they had settled in London before I was born. I was five years old when we came to the States, and here of course everything was different, they became teachers, dramatic coaches. I said that *Caryatids* was my first play. And it was, in the sense of mature work. Actually, I had written a dozen or so plays before it. The inspiration for *Caryatids,* by the way, wasn't literary. I went to call on a friend one day, and finding the door to his apartment unlocked, I walked right in. There on the sofa, stark naked and writhing like great pink snakes, were he and his girl. Of course I turned immediately and hurried out, but I carried within me a deep, perfectly quiet shock of discovery. I had seen their two bodies with unprepared eyes, and they were as mysterious as animals. By mysterious I mean beyond category, beyond mere conception, in an absolute sense quite strange, as all the shapes of the creation are strange, stranger than dreams—horns, hoofs, wings, beaks, the bark of trees, thin reeds, gills, fur. The creation of those enormous, smooth surfaces, which in the next instant I recognized as my friends, but saw first simply as flushed and glowing surfaces, almost red, sensitive, with segmented subdivisions here and there, and odd round, hairy ends—such a creation was awesome. I mean it really demands a certain awe—but we are so inured to it we don't see it at all.

I have seen many things with unprepared eyes. My talent, indeed, consists exclusively of this. I mean to say that I have no talent, no literary ability as such, only this tendency to be unprepared, and the willingness to say simply what I have seen. *Caryatids* was the beginning. I have followed its themes in almost all my plays. In *Tristan,* for instance, which was the first of my real successes, I wrote the romance, I should say the lust, the grand, insuperable lust of the spermatozoa and the egg. I had come to wonder less at our bizarre sexuality than at the fact that nature, evolution, say it how you will, finds a path through those crazy forests and brings together, unerringly, perfectly rational spermatozoa with perfectly rational eggs. I played off the one tendency against the other. The evolutionary vista released a laughter like the laughter of the gods, while the spectacle of our human errors, in all their dear fatality, released both sorrow and compassion. One night a man in front of me turned to the woman beside him and said, with a dazzling smile, "How sad!" to which she replied, with tears in her eyes, "But it's so funny!"

How I would love to hear such praise of *Caryatids!* The second production was not a bit more encouraging than the first. I rehearsed the actors myself, young friends and acquaintances here in New York. My parents were dead by then, but a friend of theirs from the days of the Abbey—a fine old chap, actually, a bit erratic, perhaps—was running the drama department at an elegant little college not far from the city, and invited me to use their facilities. I hardly knew him. He didn't know the play at all. God knows what he said to his people there. They gave us a royal welcome, and the theater that night was mobbed. Needless to say, I was apprehensive. Yet, seeing all those bright young faces, and the rumpled tweeds of the faculty—their magazine, by the way, has been excellent on the whole; I hope yours is as good—and that, too ... well, actually, you know, I began to feel hopeful. I watched from the audience, well toward the rear. The house lights dimmed. The anticipatory hush filled the space. The recorded overture burst forth—a novel effect at that time—and seemed to seize them exactly as I had hoped. The first of the nine scenes—which had aroused such anger before—passed almost uneventfully. I did hear a few voices, not many ... a kind of grumbling . . . skepticism, mostly . . . nothing important. The voices fell silent. The play proceeded. And I began to be . . . I began to feel . . . well, there was something extraordinary about the silence of the audience. I hardly know how to describe it. It wasn't simply the silence of attention. It was as if . . . as if a mystery were unfolding. Yes, I *can* describe it to you: *it was the silence of the sentinel who hears a noise and must identify it.*

My heart began to thump so loudly I thought it would be heard. I felt both joy and fear. You mustn't misunderstand me. It wasn't a question of mere egotism. I didn't feel that *I* was being accepted, or even that my play was. No, what I felt was that my meaning, *that* meaning, that truth was creating its space in the world, its pasture of souls. I felt like weeping, and like crying aloud in happiness. Someone giggled, a girl, I believe, in one of the front rows. I thought, "Of course! She too is overwrought." Someone else giggled, also a girl, and then several girls giggled together. I was trembling. I wanted to calm them, to urge them to be patient. But now some lads were giggling as well, then it came in clusters and flurries, and soon whole sections were joining in. I was baffled. The entire audience was giggling. Indeed, I giggled myself, I don't know why, it simply jumped right out of me. A moment later, with a loud, very musical effect, the giggling exploded into laughter, rocking, sweeping gales of laughter. And how extraordinarily it had changed! The first giggling had smacked a bit of empty superiority, but the later giggling was childlike, a simple response, as it were, to tickling; and finally the laughter . . . the laughter was glorious, it was free, undirected, angelically wild, and I thought, "Aha! They'll break through!"

But now the Cycle of Food—the third scene—was underway, and the laughter changed over quite abruptly to hiccups, and then to cries of disgust. Now indeed there were angry protests. The actors, God bless them, went right on. They couldn't have stopped anyway, since the end of that scene is on film. By now certain of the audience were truly enraged.

How strange! How sad, really. One would suppose that these rational careers, these ordered mores, were the merest cosmetic film over an actually cataclysmic disorder. The white-haired Irishman, my parents' friend from the Abbey, jumped to his feet and positively screamed at the actors, "Stop this disgusting travesty!" If it was only a travesty, why was he so enraged? If it was disgusting, why didn't he leave, or in any event simply vomit? I am afraid, alas, that he wanted my meaning *not to exist.* I was shocked by what he did. He clambered onto the stage and seized a young actor and hurled him against the projection screen. This from a figure of authority! It was like a signal. Everyone began to shout. I saw that in a moment a dreadful, a *gleeful* violence would break out. And I was appalled by this attack on the actors, who in any event were quite innocent.

I raced down the aisle, shouting as loudly as I could, "Stop! Stop!" I leaped onto the stage and threw up my arms and cried, "Listen to me! I am the author! Let me explain!" The old Irishman caught my arm and bellowed, "Are you saying, you dreadful renegade, are you saying there's an explanation for this vomitous . . . this vomitous . . ." Another voice supplied the word for him—"*Drek!*" Still another voice cried, "Let him talk!" I began to talk. And to my astonishment they listened. The old Irishman stalked away. And I really meant to *explain*—that is, to make clear to them the underlying meanings of *Caryatids.* I tried to formulate the philosophic abstractions that seemed to be required, but I found myself helplessly, quite helplessly, reverting to the play itself, and I actually began to describe it image by image. To make matters worse, I began at the beginning. I couldn't help it. It was as if a magnet were pulling me. I actually stammered, and apologized . . . and went back to the beginning, recapitulating everything they had already seen. Some began to howl with laughter. I persisted. I even acted some of the parts. Someone cried, "Get that madman off the stage!" Another: "He's putting us on!" Another: "No, man! It's part of the show!" I tried to explain that no, I wasn't putting them on. And no, it wasn't part of the show. This only made them angry. There were cries of "Clear out! Clear out!" followed by a chorus of obscenities. I saw a motion in the rear. A book came arcing toward me, badly aimed. I looked around. The actors had run away. I was alone on the stage. The next instant a perfect shower of books, shoes, candy bars, and goodness knows what else descended around me. That dreadful, gleeful violence I had feared had broken loose. I didn't stay a moment longer. I turned right around and sped through the wings, past the dressing rooms, and out the back door. I could hear them shouting behind me: "Get him! Get him!" And I could hear their footsteps across the stage.

Alas, here were no city crowds to hide among. Before me lay a grassy yard and the men's dormitory. I ran straight across. By the time I reached the upper hallway I could hear shouts and footsteps down below. But there were other voices, too, quieter, closer, girls' voices as well as boys', and as I ran down the hallway I received a lively impression of the advantages of an upper-class education. I saw an unoccupied room and threw myself on the bed. I pulled the covers over me and lay as if asleep. The shouts and footsteps drew near. They were opening doors and slamming them. I realized that my stratagem couldn't possibly succeed. The door next to mine was thrown open. A voice said, "Ooops! Sorry!" The door was closed. My own door was thrown open. I grunted and moaned and raised and lowered my body vigorously. A voice said, "Sorry, sorry." The door was closed. I had no sooner sighed with relief, however, than the door burst open again, and once again I had to grunt and moan and raise and lower my body. Good heavens! This went on for the next half hour. I was exhausted.

But I was impressed by the consideration the students showed one another. And I was puzzled. I had done nothing more in *Caryatids,* after all, than lay bare on the stage the anatomy, or perhaps I should say the skeleton, of the very pleasures that so delighted them. Why had they become aroused? I had plenty of time to think about this as I lay there lifting my body and groaning. I saw something I should have seen before, namely, that in revealing the invisible caryatids of life I had confronted my audience with perceptions they had long ago converted into conventions and shared beliefs. My play was like a hand that unravels complicated knitting. I saw that from the point of view of human culture, *Caryatids* was profoundly subversive. Consider it—the assumptions of romantic love, the conventions of friendship, the mythology of the family, the illusions of communication—all these, if only momentarily, had been dissolved and blown away by the powerful simplicities of *Caryatids*.

I wanted to pursue this line of reasoning still further, but the shouting had died down. I could hear them talking in the hall. "He's in the dorm, that's for sure." "All right, we'll wait him out. We'll put a watch on all four sides."

I examined the room. In the closet was one of those bulky white tennis sweaters with a gigantic B across the chest. I put it on. There was a little hat on the dresser, one of those plaid things with a tiny brim. I put that on, too. And then I picked up an armful of books, twisted my face into an innocent smile, walked down two flights of stairs, and emerged from the building with what I took to be an air of nonchalance.

Here was the wide, refreshing night. But here, too, were the hostile troops, lounging in little clusters across the lawn. They were drinking beer from cans and nibbling pretzels. There was a holiday spirit among them. I stood there for a moment. That is to say, I didn't want to move. Something quite amazing was happening. What I mean . . . well you see . . . I felt *exactly* as if they had greeted me with heartfelt applause. More than that, it was as if they had honored me in some way. And I really felt these things, though I knew very well that if they recognized me they'd capture me and do something awful. Now what could all this mean? What could it possibly mean?

The clue, so it seemed to me, lay in the fact that though they meant to punish me, their demeanor was not only guiltless but was positively happy. Usually when crowds of people are angry, they are not *merry* at the same time. I've never seen it. Have you? Angry crowds tend to be sullen; and the feeling of outrage, occurring in a crowd, passes over, usually, into angry action—but here it was passing over into celebration, a kind of holiday, and it was doing this without losing its purpose. What did it mean? What could it possibly mean?

Why, it meant that though the truths of *Caryatids* had been enormously arousing, the students had perceived them as being wholly *other*. It meant, in short, that my play had manifested a new order of consciousness, an order already deeply established within them, but as yet unrecognized. History was with me! Time was on my side! I stood there smiling happily, quite as if my play had been a triumph. And I feel sure that happiness was the best disguise I could possibly have had. A motorcyclist arrived with a case of beer strapped on back. He dismounted, and while he was passing out the cans, I hopped on the cycle and rolled away.

Soon I was gliding south beside the Hudson. I'm subject to euphoria, though I may not look it, and that ride . . . that ride . . . I don't quite know how to put it . . . I felt *illuminated* . . . joyous . . . and I kept *discovering* things about my play. I had composed *Caryatids* far more intuitively than I had realized, and now at last I was beginning to understand what I had done. I was shouting from time to time, and looking up at the moon and stars, and perhaps because of that I saw something that no doubt should have been obvious, namely, that our sense of eternity, or at least of time beyond human time, doesn't come to us from our perceptions of the physical universe, but from our awareness of our own very human consciousness, which has no boundaries, no beginning, no end. And I saw that this consciousness, this boundless field, is livable and tolerable only because we furnish it with ideal forms, human inventions that are like campfires on a plain at night.

Some of these forms are the work of millennia, others of mere centuries. The idea of *the human,* for example, surely had an origin somewhere in time; it came into existence as a result of human thought. And so did the idea of *the individual,* though much later. And the idea of work, and of family, and of vocation, and of love. These are grand, one would say *superhuman* ideas. They have organized our times and lives. But we are their victims, too, and they are veils. The uncanny silences of *Caryatids,* and its almost mindless imagery, had actually, I do believe, unraveled, if only briefly, some few of those veils, revealing, or I should say *invoking,* the unhuman chemistry of the universe, the mysteries of sentient matter, the isolation of individual feeling, the natural superfluity of entire species, the illusions of communication. In short, I had caused to flood across the stage the true pathos of the infinite, and also, by reaction, the homely, persuasive, and quite appalling prescience of individual death.

When I realized this, I couldn't help but murmur a prayer of gratitude. The three last scenes of *Caryatids*—which never yet have been performed—are devoted entirely to death. I can't tell you how thrilling it was to become aware like this of the intuitive correctness of the entire structure of my play. More than that, I understood that this very discovery was an increment of mastery, since it is precisely this leap of understanding, this claiming of wider and wider purviews as the domain of reason, that forces the unconscious to its most profound and rewarding tasks. It was thrilling to see this. I began to sing. I began near Poughkeepsie and I was still singing when I got to the George Washington Bridge.

I say, it's getting late! Why don't we order some food before they close the kitchen. There's a menu right there. Look through it and see what you'd like. I've been interviewed four times this week. This, the fifth, is the most enjoyable, partly because you are young, attractive, and sanguine, but also because you have allowed me to say my say without interruption. It's positively exhilarating. I have heard a lecture on Grotowski, a lecture on Artaud and Ritualism, a lecture on The Death of Language, and a lecture on Guerrilla Theater— all preceded by the words "What is your opinion?"

Well, yes . . . There are actors who want to liberate themselves and liberate their audiences, and of course these are the ones who quote Artaud. I don't know how I feel about their theater, but they do more good than harm surely. The problem is, they begin with the premise that they *are* actors or even artists, whereas serious liberation of the self can't accept such foregone conclusions. And it seems naïve to imagine that salvation can be achieved symbolically.

But I have seen two excellent new groups, and I feel more hopeful about American theater than I have in years. It was just a few months ago, during my last visit to New York. I chanced to overhear a quarrel on one of the side streets of the Lower East Side, a man and wife, both middle-aged, both rather large. He was waving his arms and shouting, and she was facing him rather grandly, her arms folded on her bosom. Five or six passersby had stopped to listen, all, like myself, devotees of this sort of drama, an ideal audience, actually, shyly attentive, awed by passion. "What I want," the man was shouting, "is a domestic life, not a communal life!" And our five or six faces reflected the thought *he wants a domestic life.* "I am tired of that horde of teddy bears!" he went on. "The only time I get a decent supper is when half a dozen are staying on as guests!" He had made a definite point, and we turned to the woman to discover her answer. "You can't tell me who to have as friends," she replied. "Very well," he said, and we turned back to him, "if I can't have a marriage, I'll get a suite at the Chelsea and have a harem!" This must have struck home to a number of the listeners. There was a definite eagerness for her reply. "Go ahead," she said, "it'll do you good." And here the drama ended, for she strode away.

Just then, on the corner, an extraordinary group appeared, twenty or so people dressed in ragged costumes and led by a bearded man beating a big bass drum. The large woman joined them. One of the marchers handed her a banner. Others thrust huge papier-mâché figures above their heads. The drum was augmented by trumpets and fiddles. How appealing they were! Like a band out of fairy tales! or medieval country fairs. I fell in behind them and we proceeded west. We had gone but a few blocks when it became apparent that some unusual event was underway. Traffic was jammed, horns were honking, people were hurrying along, almost all, it seemed, in the same direction. Yes, exactly . . . the antiwar demonstration in Washington Square, the one for which the *New York Times* gave the figure of four thousand, though I myself overheard the police, and the figure they gave to each other was fifteen. You couldn't see a blade of grass, they were sitting shoulder to shoulder, and when they shouted all together, it sent shivers up your spine. The entire park was barricaded. Police in uniforms ringed the barricades. We passed through, our bearded leader pounding the big drum as loudly as he could, but in the slow, arresting tempo of the dead march. There were welcoming cheers on all sides. I can't tell you how moving it was, this recognition and welcome, or how beautiful these young faces appeared to me, so intelligent and determined, so grave and yet elated. There is something to be said, you know, for a country that can produce such faces as these. They moved back, pressing against each other, and formed an arena, and our troupe began to enact a play. Masks were donned. The gigantic figures came to life. A narration was spoken through a megaphone. The trumpets and fiddles were heard again. I won't try to describe the play to you. It was a play of death, rather of the persistence of life in our imagination of death, and the resurgence of homely care in the aftermath of terror. I was astonished at its power and the sureness of its art. It was not a protest play at all, not political, except in the deepest sense; rather, it was an art of compassion and courage, a strength-giving art. The play was short, twenty-five minutes or so, and when it ended there was silence. We could not applaud. It had been like a prayer. Yet finally we did applaud, as there was no other way to break the spell. The actors took off their masks and sat down among the others, many of whom embraced and kissed them. I caught sight of the woman I had originally followed. She was standing alone and was smiling with a kind of fierce compassion. There, not far away, was her husband, who had evidently forgotten the Chelsea and his harem. There were tears in his eyes. They rushed to each other and embraced, and then patted each other's backs, the way married people do.

I have thought much about this group since then. They knew their audience and they sought it out. They were partisan in the flesh—but their art was free and universal. There was not a moment of mere rhetoric. Such art is rare today. Yes, alas . . . it is.

But let me tell you of the other group. It was midnight. I had stepped out of a bar in the theater district, and as I paused in the doorway a spectacular woman passed by . . . no, not a woman: a cloud of hair, an aura, a whirl of feathers, velvet, sequins, and lace. She was holding the arm of a short, gallant, scholarly-looking man, was flicking her boa back and forth, saying in a husky voice, "I'll take my curtain call tonight stark naked."

I watched them as they went down the street. Her head was erect and motionless, but she swayed her hips and flung out her arms in elaborate gestures. Needless to say, this woman was a man, a man who by no means wanted to be mistaken for a woman, and who yet wanted us to realize that he would be delighted to be mistaken for a woman. What strange sanity there was in this! And what obvious obsession! There occurred to me, abruptly, one of those insights one has long possessed, namely, that I was observing, at that very moment, an authentic, if limited, work of art. It seemed, moreover, that this authentic work of art was about to participate in a second work of art, apparently a play. They turned in to a doorway at the end of the block. I hurried after them. A placard proclaimed in outlandish letters that *Whores of the Apostles* would commence at twelve, starring Cynthia Gateleg, Mary Ann Moxie, Lamarr, Moonmaiden, Beetle, and among others an actor who had chosen to call himself Duc de Guermantes.

The little lobby was crowded. There was an air of excitement, of connivance, actually. The curtain was forty minutes late. People chatted. At last the lights were dimmed. The strains of "The Star-Spangled Banner" burst forth, mixed with a radio announcer's voice and heart-rending animal cries, as of cattle in a slaughterhouse. The curtain opened. But it would be a mistake to try to describe this play to you. My very memory of it is false to its clutter and grandiosity. Nor is there any way to convey to you the chaste effect of these actors' extreme licentiousness, or the childlike modesty of their headlong plunge into vulgarity. The first setting was of a charnel house. Some six or eight persons appeared in chains amidst skulls and bones, the victims, all, of Maldonado the Second. As for Maldonado the First, his skeleton was prominently, in fact blasphemously, displayed nailed to a cross, grinning evilly, distinguishable from all skeletons one has ever seen by a gigantic, segmented penile bone, erect. The dialogue was bombastic, elevated, decorated with lines from Elizabethan plays, from comic strips and films, homosexual bars, politicians' speeches. The spectacular woman I had seen on the street, her femininity reduced now to an enormous wig, did indeed take her curtain call stark naked, reciting a speech beginning with the words "Devour me!"

And what was it about, all this wildness and grotesque carnality? Why, so I believe, the same thing as that little performance I had seen in the street, the man dressed as a woman, for in fact his gestures belonged neither to the masculine world nor the feminine, but to the world of the imagination. More specifically, to the imagination captured by yearning. These actors were like children engaged in make-believe, who with a few gestures and rags of costumes sketch out a kind of spiritual diagram: the world of the possible—with this difference, of course, that our actors' diagram was of the impossible, one would say the *eternal impossible*. Their blasphemy, their outrageous egotism may have seemed demonic, but in fact they were priestly figures. They were acting out for us the wilderness of impossible desire, in rejecting which we experience our social cohesion. In the Biblical sense, they enacted the scapegoat. Their method, too, for all its wildness, was a spiritual method: be true to impulse and delight, be true to yearning. It leads to catastrophe, of course, but that was already behind them, for these were not ordinary people. Or put it another way: the catastrophe, already, is behind us all. It is the death of the heart to deny it. And since there is no other ground to dance upon, why, dance upon it!

Yes, I trusted them. I trusted their delight.

Fame is a convenience, a marvelous convenience. It transforms the chaos of cosmopolitan life into the simple order of a village. It surrounds one with courtesies and attentions. How I should have to fight for my opinions, and how dear they would be to me, if we had met in a bar and I were unknown to you! Your generosity allows me to take them lightly. They are only opinions.

There is no sustenance in fame, no more than in hope. I have said that I am obsessed, and no doubt I am. I am a driven person. But what sustains me is another matter. I am sustained by pleasure.

My greatest joy—nothing has matched it—was the composing of *Caryatids*. I had written a dozen plays before it, but the conception of *Caryatids* was a great leap into my own existence. For two entire months I lived in transport. It was spring. I sat by an open window eight stories up, on a side street near Riverside Park. I thought that I could feel the pulse of the universe, the great systole and diastole of being, thought that I could *hear* it in the ordinary sounds of the day, the motors and horns of cars, the music from radios, voices, the barking of dogs. I suppose I wasn't quite sane. Or perhaps I was then, and am not now. In any event, I have never since experienced such feelings. I have told you of the extravagant hostility aroused by this play, and of my own awakening to the realities of art. Yet when I say to you that the point of my art is to be anticultural, I say it without bitterness, just as I produce it without anger. Nor do I accuse myself if my work, in spite of my best intentions, has created new conventions and fashions. What is a man that the world should not devour him?

As for fame, such fame as I know, it is a small thing compared to the vast and quite correct indifference of the rest of the world.

This lesson was afforded me just a few years ago aboard a luxury liner bound for France. The captain, it developed, was a fan of mine, and kept inviting me to dinner. He was a widely read man, not talkative, but grave and attentive. Like many self-educated men, he overvalued literature, and treated me with a deference I found quite embarrassing. One night I mentioned that a company of young actors was traveling with us. He suggested that we invite them to perform a play of mine, or at least to give a reading, adding that he had several of my books in his cabin and would be happy to mimeograph the text. The other guests expressed great interest, and so I agreed, but I said that I would like to surprise them with something they could not have seen. They imagined, of course, that I was referring to a new play. What I had in mind, however, was *Caryatids*. The filmed sequences had been done again and were a great improvement over the original footage. But, more than that, I simply wanted to see it, this work of my youth. And I hoped that by careful preparation I might see it for once to its conclusion. So many years had passed! Times had changed. I thought, indeed, that I might make use of my fame. I would speak to the audience *before* the play. I would appear in my dinner jacket. I would fix in my lapel a rose from the captain's table. I would stand before them, in short, as one officially approved, indeed, favored, and how—

so I wondered—could this fail to temper the play's effects?

It came to pass exactly as I had planned—better than I had planned. The captain himself introduced me to our invited audience. I bowed. He left the stage. I began to speak. But my confidence somewhat wavered, for I noticed faces, *kinds* of faces I had never yet encountered at my plays, grave, enduring faces, eyes and mouths unsoftened by familiarity with ideas or aesthetic forms. I had intended to speak briefly of the antecedents of *Caryatids*, its philosophic kin, as it were, but my eyes returned to those enduring faces, and soon it was to them alone that I spoke. I spoke at great length—persuasively, I believe, and with simplicity. At last their eyes responded. Their lips and jaws relaxed. They nodded approvingly and settled back in their chairs. I signaled the light board, and as I stepped from the stage our little theater was plunged into darkness.

You may know that Felix Arenas composed the overture to *Caryatids*. It's a medley of recorded heartbeats and breathing under various conditions of excitement and calm. Mingled with these human sounds are electronic tones. To this extent the overture is formal, but it's open to chance in an interesting way. Small microphones scattered through the audience—suspended from the ceiling, actually—pick up what sounds they can, throat clearing, sighs, odd little groans, whispers. These are amplified, but are played back a split second later. The effect is startling. People do not recognize their voices, but the spontaneous quality is unmistakable; they listen alertly. A few, of course, become uneasy. As the overture ended I heard a woman say, "Is this what he was talking about?" Otherwise, there was silence. And I do believe, actually, that this was the most earnest, the most serious audience I have ever yet encountered.

As for the play—you must forgive me if I say that I was simply bewitched. The language, of course, is always enchanting. Less than a third of it is mine. The rest is quotation from our classic authors, the Bible, the *Book of Common Prayer,* the literature of psychoanalysis and of law, newspapers, encyclopedias, cookbooks, gardening manuals. Some of it is spoken as dialogue and belongs to the action. Most of it, however, is rather like background music in the films. The actors are masked. Their style is abstract and ceremonious. Some few of their scenes are recognizable—the murder of Abel, Christ before Pilate, and the freeing of Barabbas; but they enact eating and drinking and sleeping; they enact touching and taking leave and greeting; they enact calling by name, and they enact speaking. Occasionally, as I say, their gestures coincide with the language, and occasionally, too, they coincide with the filmed, full-color images on the projection screen. But often all three elements work contrapuntally, or independently, or in conflict.

The filmed images are chiefly of the human body and of events beneath the skin. One would say they were biological, but their effect is overwhelmingly spiritual. They are simply radiant with intelligence, the unearthly intelligence which is in fact the most ordinary property of earthly life. One sees, for example, the patient cilia of the oviduct brushing the ovum to the womb. One sees the salmonlike flight of the spermatozoa. All parts of the body appear. They are seen closely, and sometimes in magnified detail so that their action is not lost in one's conventional sense of process. Sometimes the motion is slowed, which makes visible the host of extraordinary movements we take for granted and actually do not know exist. The choreography of the tongue and lips, for example, in speaking; and of the tongue and teeth in chewing food; the ordered, peristaltic waves of the esophagus, voluptuous in their fullness; the minute vibrations of the eye; the opening and closing of the pupil, creating light; the mysterious gestures of the fine hairs of the belly, which appear sensitive, almost wondering, and are agitated periodically by the explosive pulse of the blood; the blind socket of the navel undulating like a flower on the sea; the luxuriant pubic forest in its amphitheater of belly and thighs; the bearded lips of the vagina, closed and yet open; the awesome levitation of the organ of the male. Flickering among these images, repeatedly but so swiftly as to be almost invisible—though the ending of the play develops this theme in its fullness—is the falling of a lifeless hand, which is in fact the hand of a cadaver.

In the meantime, other primal images appear. In the Cycle of Food one sees kaleidoscopic images of the slaughter of a calf, the disemboweling and dismembering of its body, the searing of its flesh, its further destructuring by teeth and tongue, the process ending in the action which of all actions best symbolizes man's continuity with nature, an action for which, however, we have no name not contaminated by attitudes and counter-attitudes, depicted here by a figure of undeterminable age squatting with the simplicity of an infant or a dog. The sequence is brief. It is repeated several times. I have never determined, all told, the number of distinct images. Many hundreds, certainly. And of some there are many variations, as for instance of smiles, and of tears, the tears of children *spurting* from their eyes, the tears of the aged slipping, as it were, quietly down their faces, hardly glimmering. One of the most affecting sequences is the birth of a child by the so-called natural method, in which the mother is not anesthetized but lends a wise volition to the spontaneous labor of her body. We see the head of the infant emerging, and then his shoulder, and then he is out and bawling and she is smiling and reaching for him. I am sure you will understand me if I say that I was enthralled. I had never seen so much of the play before, nor had I seen it in many years. For once I neglected to observe the audience. Not that I was unaware of them. I heard voices, certainly, mutterings of protest, the usual hiccups. But suddenly—the din was actually growing—I heard a sound that thrilled me, a sound that told me that my play, or some part of my play, truly had been perceived. It was the sound of quiet weeping.

But when I noticed this, I noticed also, alas, that many

people had become upset. Quite a few were standing. From nearby a woman sobbed hysterically, and another laughed in the same fashion, with overtones of bitterness and contempt. More of the men jumped to their feet, seeking, apparently, to protect their women. They shouted insults toward the stage, which was rapidly emptying. And then the shouting men looked around, evidently in search of me. I heard the words —and how oddly conservative they were, or not oddly at all, the inevitable conservatism of deep feeling—*cad, wretch, disgusting abomination.* That phrase, *disgusting abomination,* spread among them like a war cry. I heard, too, "deserves to be thrashed," and "deliberate insult," and "What does he think we are?" and again, on all sides, "disgusting abomination." A booming voice rose above it all, repeating the same phrase but altering it slightly, much to my disadvantage, for it cried—and it was the captain himself, and he was pointing straight at me— "Apprehend that disgusting abomination!" No one moved. They expected, I suppose, that the ship's officers would rush forward and seize me. But no ship's officers came forth. A sudden lurch of the ship sent us stumbling. This too they seemed to blame on me. The captain bellowed again, "Apprehend him!"—and there was a concerted rush of fifteen or twenty angry gentlemen in evening clothes. I stood there, doubting that such mature, responsible-looking souls would actually thrash me, but their faces—settled grimly into that expression with which by now I was familiar: determined, dogged anger, the desire to punish—their faces made clear that they did indeed intend to thrash me. I turned on my heel and sped from the room.

Memories of youth! And sad comparisons. For though I went down the passageway as rapidly as I could, I am not sure that my gait could be called running. I was gratified to see, however, as I looked back at my pursuers, that the nameless gait which encumbered my once-youthful limbs encumbered theirs no less. I was favored, too, by the narrowness of the corridor, for they were forced to pursue me single file, which afforded a striking perspective of bobbing faces and raised fists.

A turn of the corridor delivered me into the elegant little discothèque. The din was deafening. The dancers were flickering on and off. I ran right through, and my pursuers behind me, and no one noticed. I found myself in the service pantry of the bar. A French waiter sat reading a newspaper and smoking a Gauloise. He looked up and said calmly, "What would you like, monsieur?" I replied, "Nothing, monsieur, don't trouble yourself." "Au revoir, monsieur." Another step brought me to the bar and lounge, and here the serious drinkers, the Messiah-waiters, to a man turned their hopeful/hopeless eyes upon me. I sped to the indoor promenade, and then to the outdoor promenade, and as I turned I saw that not only had I not shaken my pursuers, but they had doubled or trebled in number. How hungry they are for excitement, I thought, and I am not hungry for it at all.

The night was cool and bright. How agreeable fog would have been! Where can one go on board a ship at sea? Where indeed but round and round? I saw a narrow stairway and clambered up it, and for a moment was tempted to stop there and hold them off, like Roland at the pass, but, I must confess, the temptation was not strong. The trouble, really, lay in my inability to feel enmity toward them. Stand them off? Pikestaff in hand? It would have amounted to nothing but an explanatory lecture, the same that I had given already with such unhappy results. Escape was preferable—though whether it was possible was another question.

I was now on the swimming deck, on the shuffleboard court, which afforded no hiding place whatsoever. But here was the swimming pool, entirely glassed-in this time of year. I opened the door and entered. It was dark and deserted. I felt a surge of hope—but I heard footsteps on the stairway I had climbed; and suddenly the lights flared on, and I understood that the indoor stairway, too, had now been breached. As always, the stress of crisis spurred my imagination. There were café curtains along the glass walls of the enclosure, mounted on long brass rods. I seized one of the rods and pulled it apart. Now that I recount these events to you, my desperation, even to me, seems extreme, especially in view of the actual outcome. At the time, however, I was determined to escape. Rod in hand, I descended the ladder of the swimming pool. By holding fast to the ladder I was able to overcome my buoyancy. The rod afforded me air. I had no sooner begun to breathe through it than the space above me echoed and boomed with voices, indistinct, distorted by the water. I could imagine well enough what they were saying. "He couldn't have vanished! Where did he go? Where?"—precisely as if they had awakened from a dream, and the dream had escaped them. I had become, in effect, the Unconscious of them all, submerged out of sight, yet troubling the world with my unseen presence.

I am not speaking fancifully. These were my thoughts at the very moment I am describing. And I felt peculiarly at peace, peculiarly right. I do not mean, of course, that I could have stayed there very long, I mean only that the situation itself had become metaphoric, or symbolic, and I was, as it were, at rest in the nature of things. And I felt . . . not pity, but compassionate sadness toward these mortals I had so distressed with the evidence of their mortality. Yet even these, I reflected, these outraged ones, would bear out, in the daily rounds of their lives, the truth and correctness of my play. For the rationality of fleshly life is reflected in the rationality of our homely cares, our drawing of water, our cooking of food, our tending of the sick, our raising of children. The true wonders of history are to be found not in our pyramids and flights to the moon, but in the fact that, thus far, we have managed to survive. When you consider that all governments and most great men must be counted among the hazards to human life, this survival appears remarkable indeed. And of what does it consist? Why, of nothing but reasonable, ordinary human kindness, mutual aid, work more or less honestly done, duties more or less honestly fulfilled. It is the only history susceptible of demonstration, yet it remains the unwritten history of the world. If only there were a poet great enough to forge an epic of this! And to attach to it the part I had but touched upon in *Caryatids,* the miraculous created matter which seeks its own good and multiplies its life, the blindest part of which is as discerning as an eye!

The exaltation of these thoughts was such that I did not, for a moment, respond to a little event which proved to be of considerable importance—though even after I had understood its importance there was nothing I could do, for one hand was occupied with the ladder, the other with my brass breathing tube. I am referring, of course, to the rose in my lapel. For it, too, was buoyant, more buoyant than I, and it seemed to be tugging, pulling itself free, bent upon ascending as high as it might. Red rose of art and fame! Pull loose it did, and before my unwilling, helpless eyes it ascended the short distance and bobbed freely on the well-lit surface of the pool. The hubbub of voices ceased. A voice said, "Look!" Another: "It's a rose!" The breathing tube was plucked from my hand, and I too had no choice but to ascend.

The room, to my astonishment, was quite crowded. And for a moment it was silent, as evidently my ascension from the depths had something about it of the awesome. I was the first to speak. I had gained a level with the others. Still touched by the inspiration of my thoughts, I blurted out, "My friends! No one is lost!"

"Seize him!"

It was the captain, of course, and this time two ship's officers did indeed step forward. Their grip upon my arms, however, transformed the matter from one that was primarily metaphysical to one that was preeminently legal. Now it was my turn, touched by the emotion of indignation, to speak in those oddly conservative accents. I did not say, "Take your hands off me" or "Let me alone." No. What I heard, issuing from my own throat, was the voice of a respectable Victorian gentleman. "Unhand me!" I cried. "You have no legal right . . ." "On board this ship," the captain interrupted, "I am the dispenser of legal rights. Lock him in his cabin and bring me the key!"

And that is exactly what happened. I was able to finish a play I had been working on, and to read a book of poems. They fed me, however, on bread and water, a truly spiteful thing to do, and a great pity, as the cuisine on that ship was excellent.

Good heavens! We've talked right through the night. I've deprived you of sleep—unless, indeed, you are night owls. Ah, good! Yes, I have always been a night owl, a *trasnochador* . . . at least since my twentieth year. *Trasnochador?* It's a lovely word, isn't it? I heard it in Mexico. It means night owl, people like us. I do love the peace of the night, the feeling of the city's sleep spread out around me. And this color in the window now, this deep before-daylight blue . . . see how it throbs! . . . it's almost a totem for me. Night after night it announces the end of my work.

Would you like some coffee? I can make us some . . . and then we must break this up. I'm due in Philadelphia by noon.

You see how brief that deep blue color is! The sky is lightening already. In a few minutes the eastern faces of the buildings will be bright, and the western faces still plunged in darkness. Just below there—you can't see the roof from here —lives an Italian family, restaurateurs, quite wealthy ones, actually, but they're country people at heart, and they keep a flock of pigeons on the roof. The old man comes up at day-break and lets them out. Some are tumblers. You'll see them hurtling up and wheeling, as if the pattern of a great wheel were tilted in the sky just above the rooftops. At the height of their rise the tumblers flip backward, like medieval acrobats doing somersaults in praise of God. So I fancy it. They'll be up in a minute now. When they first appear, it's as if a gust of wind has hurled some leaves into the air.

Philadelphia? Ah, well . . . they're doing a play of mine . . . a young group . . . I've been on the point of mentioning

it a dozen times. I'm rather excited. I feel . . . well, you see
. . . well, actually they are doing *Caryatids,* and I think . . . I
think a new spirit is in the air. I think they'll perform it right
to the end. I think it will be received. I think it will be understood. Yes. Truly, I believe it will.

THE SUFFICIENCY OF EVERYDAY LIFE:
Avenue A and Eleventh Street, 1963

I.

Early in the 1960s a group of New York poets built a diminutive theater in a Lower East Side settlement house and proceeded to produce their own plays. One Friday in spring an
opening-night party was in progress in a downstairs meeting
room. There had been gallon jugs of wine on a long table, a
wedge of cheese, and some pumpernickel bread, but none of
this had lasted long. The lights grew dim and the air smoky.
Here and there people still talked in little clusters, but almost
everyone was dancing, at first to the songs of Bessie Smith and
Ray Charles, but later to old Billie Holiday records, which
were played again and again. The odor of marijuana was
strong.

The play that night had been unusually good. All through
the evening friends and acquaintances had spoken apprecia-
tively to the author. He was a tall, awkwardly graceful man of
forty-two. Ordinarily there were lines of suffering in his face,
but on this occasion he was so openly and completely happy
that simply to look at him had made many people smile. An
attractive, brown-haired young woman hovered near him all
evening, not so much speaking with him as listening to him
speak with others. Then they had begun to dance, and hadn't
stopped. She looked up into his face repeatedly. He understood that she had made up her mind to sleep with him, and

he was pleased, yet it was not until the room was almost empty that he was willing to go.

The night air was delicious after the hours of dancing. It was past three. They walked to his tenement apartment, twenty minutes to the north, and went to bed companionably. She was shapely and smooth-skinned, a delight to touch and hold—or would have been had she not been so passive. Her compliance troubled him, and after they had made love he found himself gazing at the ceiling, dwelling yearningly on images of his young wife of long ago. They had used to love until weariness had ended it, and often had fallen asleep in each other's arms.

His mood of elation returned. The windows had become a vivid silver. He leaped out of bed, raised the sash, and thrust his naked torso into the daylight and the morning air, breathing deeply and noisily. The city was still sleeping. He stayed there for a moment, looking at it. How could one love such a crumbling sprawl? Yet at that moment he did love it, and could easily have thrown out his arms to it.

Karla was sitting up in bed, studying his strange apartment. "Gee," she said, "what a neat place, Taggart!"

She meant it. He was pleased. He scarcely thought of it as a place at all. Books were everywhere, even above the windows, and where there weren't books there were paintings, the work of friends. He sat on the bed beside her and they talked. She spoke with a Texas drawl, as did another of his friends, and it charmed him. It seemed innocent and affectionate, and there was a savoring in it of ordinary things that one didn't hear in northern speech.

He put on his shorts, and she her slip, and they went to the kitchen, where she watched him make an omelet. While they were eating she said, "People come to you for advice, don't they, Taggart?"

He looked at her sharply. "Do they?" he said.

"You know they do," she said. "I was talking with Morris

about my problems, and he said, Why don't you talk with Taggart?"

She didn't tell him that she had watched him one night through the window of a restaurant in which he had been sitting with a friend. The other man had seemed troubled. Taggart had been leaning forward over the table listening to him, and that patient, highly charged attentiveness had moved her strangely. She had gone across the street and for ten minutes had lingered in the shadows, watching him.

"What kind of problem?" he said guardedly.

"It's not psychological, so stop worryin'! I have a spiritual problem, or a problem of destiny."

She leaned forward abruptly and said, "My main problem is, I don't know what to do with my *life*. I thought I wanted to be a teacher, and then I thought I wanted to be a social worker and do some good in this world. And you know I worked *hard* for those foolish degrees! And now I've been a social worker for a whole year, and it's worse than teachin' school!

"Taggart, there's nothing more disgusting than a bureaucracy! It's supposed to be impersonal and fair, all those rules and regulations. Well, do you know, those rules are *spiteful*. . . . Oh, but it's not even that, it's just the misery these people live in. I thought I'd be helping them, but it's pathetic. I end up lying to them. I just go home sick at heart every blessed day."

He had known other social workers, other teachers, street-gang workers, psychologists at city hospitals, psychologists at family court. There was nothing to say.

She was leaning back, sipping from her cup. Her face was angry, but it was thoughtful too.

"You're giving me good advice," she said wryly. She laughed and said, "I guess I really mean it. You're the only one who hasn't lied to me. And I know what I'm going to do, I'm going to quit that job. My folks'll be upset. Aren't you *tired*, Taggart? I'm just collapsin'. But I think I'll go home. I have a date at five."

In the instant that she said this, he realized that he would have liked for her to stay. He asked her whom she was seeing.

"He came to your play," she said, "but he didn't come to the party. Did you notice an enormous young man in a T-shirt, with curly black hair and glasses? He's built like Hercules, but he's the gentlest thing. Well, I'll introduce you sometime, only don't tell him we slept together."

He went to bed after she left, and fell asleep thinking of Naomi. As he lapsed from consciousness her image became bright, and the pain of the past took on sweetness. She stood above him on the stairs, was coming down slowly, smiling, transfixed like a child on the one beam of their eyes.

On Monday Taggart spent an hour with the young painter who had designed his sets. Before leaving he stopped to see Morris Pasloff, the director of the settlement house. He had remembered a story—bizarre, if true—that linked Karla with Tilson Morgan, the spectacularly handsome black who ran the drug and street programs.

Morris thought that Taggart already knew.

"Didn't you hear about the wedding?" he said. "You know Tilson got married about five months ago. . . ."

By way of telling the story Morris acted the parts. He paced back and forth, changing his voice and gesturing dramatically. He was good at it, and Taggart remembered the delight with which he had spoken of the old Yiddish theater on Second Avenue, the stars and plays he had seen as a child, and those he had seen later as a young man: Maurice Schwartz and Jacob Ben-Ami, Joseph Buloff and the impoverished radicals of the Artef group, with whom his sister had performed. Morris was in his sixties. He was still muscular and walked with the truculent, rolling gait of his Bedford-

Stuyvesant boyhood, though in fact he was endlessly good-humored.

Taggart knew the church in which the wedding had been held.

"It was packed," said Morris, "it was an event. I would say half the crowd were old girlfriends of Tilson's. Well, so it went along . . . then the minister comes to those fatal lines—*'If anybody here knows why these two should not be joined'*—up stands Karla. Oy! Taggart! What a jolt! I was sitting right beside her. Actually I was there for a reason. We knew something might happen . . . but not this. And you know something? She was fabulous. *'I love Tilson Morgan, and by rights I should be up there marrying him, not Marcia Libkin.'* Isn't that something? And she says, *'Now, you admit it, Tilson, or else tell me right here in front of everybody that you stopped loving me, because you never said it to me.'*"

Both their faces were alight with admiration. Taggart said, "Jesus . . ." and then, "What did Tilson say?"

"Ah, well . . . he's really something, you know. *'I have put aside all other women and I will CLEAVE to this one!'* Ha! Yeah! The worst thing was, she had a knife in her purse."

"A knife?" said Taggart.

"Don't repeat this . . ." and Morris told him the following story:

Tilson had come home with Marcia one night and had found Karla sitting on the bed. She took a switchblade from her purse and pressed the button, saying to Marcia, "I'm going to cut you up." Tilson had gotten between them and had sent Marcia into the corridor. Karla had said, "Don't touch me, Tilson; I'll cut you too," and so Tilson had gone away with Marcia, and Karla had slashed the bedclothes and the mattress, the chairbacks and the drapes . . .

Karla telephoned Taggart early that evening, and he invited her to supper. She brought wine. They lingered at the table after they had eaten. A dusky, softened light came in over the roofs.

He asked her about the incident in the church, and she laid her head back and let her eyelids droop. He saw an image of pure southern orneriness. "You don't have to worry," she said. Her voice was as flat and steady as her gaze.

"I wasn't," he said sharply.

"Do you think I was wrong? Well, I did a lot worse than that . . ." and she told him of the encounter at Tilson's apartment, which had been more destructive than Morris had said.

Taggart was puzzled. "He could have hit you with a chair," he said.

"Sure he could've. He's *strong*. He can pick me up with one hand. But you have no idea how sweet that man is. He's just a stud, that's all. He can't help himself.

"Anyway," she said, "I had more right to him than she did. She didn't love him. It was just sex."

"Would you have used the knife?"

"Did you think I'd just crawl off and cry?" she said. "I just hate the way you do things up here. You never face off and have things out. You're always so *reasonable* you end up bein' crazy! Do you know, the most romantic thing to me was back home when two black women fought over a man, and I mean they used knives. The one who lost was lucky. She was stabbed and cut, but she was still the lucky one, 'cause that stud went off with another woman anyway, and the girl who won killed him and went to jail. Up here you'd go talk to a psychiatrist, wouldn't you?"

He understood that she would not have used the knife.

She told him she had quit her job. He asked her what she was going to do, and she tossed her head angrily and said, "Think!"

The kitchen was almost dark. They had enjoyed the fading of the light, had actually collaborated in that enjoyment, though neither was aware of it.

They left without clearing the table. There was a reading at the Eiffel Express and Taggart wanted to attend it.

In the heyday of the Beats the Eiffel had been a social center and forum, and almost a hostel. The poets were scattered now, but their communal impulse was by no means ended.

Karla had passed the coffeehouse often, but with its bulletin board, to which letters and notes were always pinned, its display of book jackets, its racks of newspapers, its air of quiet and self-absorption, it had always seemed like a private club, and she had never gone in.

It was spacious and pleasantly shabby. Motionless figures at oaken tables were reading books and magazines. Some with rounded backs gave shelter to small notebooks in which they wrote rapidly. At the counter in the rear, a bearded man in a blue shirt flipped the levers of an espresso machine.

Karla saw at once that Taggart was known and admired here. A number of people waved to him, and several came over, smiling, and praised his play. Someone mentioned the review in the *Post* and pointed toward the bulletin board. And in fact the bearded man at the counter was waving to Taggart and pointing to the bulletin board. Taggart took Karla's arm and they went across the room.

A new critic at the *Post* had described the play extensively. The clipping was pinned amidst a profusion of notes, many of which asked for rides to California. There was a photograph of the actors.

"My God," breathed Taggart. He read on silently. Something more than pleasure had appeared on his face, and Karla saw it. The world had opened for him, as if miraculously.

People kept arriving. Karla heard of poets she didn't know, whose well-being and whereabouts seemed to be of vital concern to everyone. This one was in San Francisco, that one in India, another in Japan, another cutting wood in Washington State, another on the Cape. The voices were animated and had grown loud. She saw two of her former professors from NYU. They were dressed in blue jeans and wrinkled shirts.

She and Taggart sat at a large round table, already crowded, and ordered cappuccinos. The man in the blue shirt spoke a word of introduction, and in a shower of friendly, welcoming applause, a slight, abundantly bearded man walked to a clearing at the end of the room and sat on a chair near the piano. He placed his briefcase near his feet, and opened a manila folder on his lap. He looked up at the audience. He seemed shy. He stroked his long, thick hair away from his eyes, and stroked his spreading beard downward. There was an air about him of the quiet of a hermetic life, druidic and musical, but he spoke ironically and with great aplomb. He said a few words about his method, cleared his throat, and proceeded to read from a work in progress composed by laws of chance. From time to time he reached to the side and struck a single note on the piano.

The room was quiet except for the poet's voice. Two waitresses with broad hips, corduroy skirts, and long black hair veered with heavy grace among the tables.

The performance was flawless. The poet was nimbly engaged, dryly detached. Admirers occasionally called out, "Good, Jackson! Bravo!"

Taggart thought it interesting that these lines composed by chance should be so elegant. The method had eliminated the heat and broken edges of individual life.

Achilles Spina was in the audience and began to interrupt. "Jackson!" he called. "Hey! Jackson!"

"Yes, Achilles?"

"You're not a midget."

"Thank you, Achilles." The poet proceeded with his poem.

"I always thought you were a midget. Hey, Jackson!"

"Just a minute, Achilles." He struck a note on the piano.

Karla had become restive. She had felt warmed by the sight of so much friendliness, so many people who knew one another. She had glimpsed a way of life unlike any she had ever known, and she was eager to share it. But now, try as she might, she couldn't understand the poetry! It was baffling. She couldn't even make out sentences. It was baffling to the point of perversity! The vistas that had opened for her closed abruptly, and she was angry.

The heckling of the scowling fellow in the back had caused some laughter. Karla turned to Taggart and whispered, *"Do you really like this stuff?"* She began to say something, but he glared at her and told her to be quiet.

There was a great deal of talking afterward. Taggart and Karla went with a group to the Cedar Bar. She saw that Taggart himself, who had chastised her, was actually bored. Soon they left. They began arguing immediately.

It was a warm night. The sidewalks were crowded. From First Avenue to Avenue A, voices arguing in Spanish occasionally harmonized with theirs and then rose higher. They had passed the Jewish stores and the enclave of the Italians, and now the shops, bars, and little grocery stores were Slavic, with here and there a *bodega* or storefront Pentecostal temple. Farther east the Puerto Ricans were dominant, and farther still the blacks.

Taggart was annoyed with her. The Eiffel was a place of communion. He had read there several times himself and was scheduled to read again soon. He said something about poetry, and she said sullenly, "I didn't know you wrote poems."

"I write plays, poems, and essays," he said.

"Well, you seem like a writer, but you don't seem like a poet."

"What's a poet?"

"How do I know? Those jerks with beards!"

"Listen, Karla, why do you think you're entitled to just breeze in and have it all your own way? It's poetry, not a bus schedule. People give their lives to it. Spend one week, just one week reading poetry, any poet, and then we'll talk about it."

He was still annoyed that she had said he didn't look like a poet. "There are poets who dress like stockbrokers," he muttered.

He was wearing a blue work shirt and wrinkled khaki pants. She didn't know what he meant.

Their mood wasn't right for going to bed. They hesitated at the entrance to his building, and then went back to Second Avenue and bought ice-cream cones.

It was past midnight. Thin, swift youths hastened this way and that, or drifted upright, scarcely noticing one another. Young men and women—though there were far more men than women—stood in clusters, glancing this way and that, not speaking, or sat in small groups on the steps of tenements and watched the car-jammed street with vacant intensity. They had come from towns and cities in New Jersey, Connecticut, and Long Island. Taggart never failed to be astonished by their numbers. In the days of his own distressful youth he had been a loner, lucky to find a friend. There had never been populations like this, or mass entertainment, or such rafts of money floating free. . . .

They walked east again, and he was quiet, but he did not feel estranged from her. He sneezed, and high above them a voice called, "Gesundheit!" and a black-haired boy with the features of a gypsy waved down to them cheerfully.

Karla stayed with him that night. Their quarreling had brought them closer, but still there was no moment in which she quickened with excitement.

The lights from the street and the adjacent building made a luminous twilight in the bedroom. She lay on her back with one arm flung over her head. Her abundant brown hair almost covered the glowing oblong of the pillow. Taggart leaned on both elbows and looked at her. As often, he wished that he were a painter, these things were so beautiful: slender, rounded arms, the shadows of the throat, closed eyes, lashes.

He asked her about her friend, the young Hercules named Marshall.

She opened her eyes. "Ohhh," she sighed, "I don't know. That poor boy is sufferin'.

"Taggart, you won't let on I told you these things, will you?" She turned and faced him, leaning on one elbow. "Well, he doesn't look it at all, he's the most handsome, manly-lookin' Adonis, but you know he's sufferin' something awful because he's homosexual."

"No," said Taggart, who that afternoon had seen him at the settlement, "he actually does look it."

"*Really?* How can you tell? That just baffles me."

He didn't answer immediately. He could see the youth quite clearly, yet it was difficult to say what the signs were. He carried his deep chest and broad shoulders like an image on a placard, and seemed himself to be spellbound by the image, as if he had become his own fetish. And, though he tried to appear stern, the sweet, needful face of a three-year-old boy peered out through his features.

"Would you rather go to sleep, Taggart?"

"No, no," he said. "There are lots of things that tell you he's homosexual, but none of them has anything to do with sex. He has a special relationship with other men, and I suppose it shows. Maybe the thing that really counts is aversion to women."

"Yes," she said, and there was a silence. "We tried to make love last Saturday. We could kiss all right, that was nice, but there wasn't anything I could do to get him ready. Oh, it was awful, Taggart. He cried and cried. He feels such shame, and I believe he truly wants a wife and children. And to think of all this in Greenwich Village! Why, this place is full of homosexuals! They don't hide a thing, and they're as happy as larks."

She paused and said, "He'd be better off like that, wouldn't he?"

"Why doesn't he go to a therapist?"

"Oh, Taggart, he's had two whole years of that foolishness!"

"Really?"

"You can't turn around in this town without bumpin' into a psycho-this or a psycho-that! I had 'em at school, and then I had 'em at work, and then I had 'em at school again, and I never heard such a lot of pompous foolishness in all my life. They were the worst people I ever met."

"It's a disgusting field," said Taggart.

"Then why in the name of all that's reasonable are you asking me to send that poor boy . . ."

"Karla! There are *wonderful* people in that field. It's a *high* calling. It's much too difficult for most people who go into it. It needs wisdom and honesty. It's a *spiritual* task."

The questioning wrinkles vanished from her forehead, and her cheeks became smooth again.

They lay on their sides in identical postures, heads propped on hands.

"I have a friend who's worked a lot with homosexuals," said Taggart. "Let Marshall go talk with him."

"Does he actually cure people?"

"Ah . . . no . . . I don't know if that happens. He works with the shame, the guilt, the unhappiness. I know people he's helped. He's good."

"Is he homosexual himself? I bet he is. He'll just seduce Marshall, he's so gorgeous."

"He's queer, but he won't seduce him." He kissed her and rolled away.

"Taggart, don't go to sleep yet." She shook his shoulder. "Taggart, did you ever make love with a man?"

"Yes," he said.

"Well, aren't you the easiest person! I thought you did. I don't know why, but I just thought you did. Did you like it?"

"Yes . . . no . . . it was complicated."

From the beginning of this conversation Taggart had

wanted to say something reassuring, specifically that sex was a natural expression of affection, but now he remembered that this was exactly what Julian had said to him years ago, and in that instance it hadn't been true. Julian had been compulsive and ritualistic, almost bodiless, and the sex had not expressed Taggart at all. He felt a stirring of revulsion that had destroyed the friendship.

"It was somebody I was close to," he said, "one of my teachers in graduate school."

Karla was listening.

"I still don't understand him," said Taggart. "Sex was some kind of magic for him . . . and revenge. Maybe what he wanted was to be a boy again. I don't know. But there were wonderful things about him. It was wonderful to walk around with him. He was so interested in things! And he knew so much! He was a dazzling talker."

Certain aspects of Julian's character made Taggart melt again with admiration. He remembered the high spirits and hopefulness of the early months of their friendship, and he felt sorrowful to have lost all that.

"What happened?" said Karla. Taggart's praise of Julian had made her feel lonely.

"I don't know," he said. He said it with a sigh and a stab of pain. "It was impossible to breathe around him. He was strange, my God . . ."

"Do you still see him?"

"Oh, no, Karla, he died years ago."

"How old was he?" she said.

"Not old—fifty-one. He really drank himself to death. He was so bloated you couldn't recognize him."

"I used to think it was so sick for men to do that with each other," she said. "Tilson told me everybody did in prison, including him. Tell me something, Taggart—were you worried? Did you think you were homosexual?"

"No, Karla. Maybe if I had been younger."

She was frowning pensively, looking at the ceiling.

"We really do make too much of these things," he said. "It's incredible how narrow and cold our conventions are."

She said, "Yes."

"Were you ever in love, Karla? I mean before Tilson. Back in Texas."

"Oh, yes," she said. She turned to him and smiled. "You'd think he was the squarest thing. He works for the telephone company, and he's president of the Kiwanis. But oh my, he's a handsome man."

Taggart waited.

"I guess he didn't love me, that's all. He has four children now. But we were sweethearts in high school . . . and we made love too."

She laid her head on the pillow.

Images of summer nights came into Taggart's mind, alleys and the backs of houses, his little gang of boys. They were running. They were looking into windows and clambering over roofs. He had been thirty-two when he had met Naomi, but it was in this ambience of tenderness and lust that she had seemed to belong.

Karla didn't telephone for several days. Taggart called her. He called repeatedly for three days. And then a letter came from Texas.

She had given Marshall the psychotherapist's number. She had visited Duane, the former sweetheart with four children. She was staying with her parents, who weren't angry after all.

I've decided what I'm going to do, she wrote. *I'll tell you when I get back.*

Taggart went downstairs into the noonday heat. He had made a date with white-haired, idealistic Everett Wilder, of whom he was fond to the point of adoration.

Everett was wearing huaraches, seersucker pants, a short-sleeved white shirt. He held Taggart close by the arm as they walked. They might have been father and son, they looked so much alike.

Everett was in his seventies. He lived at the eastern end of Taggart's block with a Puerto Rican woman who had had three children and had borne him two. He had fathered four others in Texas, and five more in Mexico, where for a decade after the Revolution he had worked as a surveyor and village teacher. Ever since Taggart had known him he had been mailing off sums of money in different directions. He spoke of the tenants' association he had worked with for a decade. A rent strike was coming up. Then he spoke of a neighborhood boy who was thirteen and couldn't read.

"Taggart," he said, "do you know the Spanish-speaking population is about seven hundred thousand now. Wouldn't you think there'd be a few teachers who could speak the language?"

He stopped walking and stood facing Taggart. They were in front of the park. The pigeons that had flown away came waddling back. "Why couldn't we open our own reading clinic?" he said. "It wouldn't be hard. We could get space in a church, or a storefront if we could find the rent. Only I don't mean a *clinic* at all, more of a clubhouse where the kids could hang around. Now, don't you know some o' them would start reading comic books? Sure they would. And then it's only a little hop to the racing forms . . ." He laughed childishly and said, "Yeah, that's the way we'd do it." His rural accent was delightful.

He took Taggart's arm again, saying, "Seriously, Taggart, ask around about space. Would you do that?"

They began threading the traffic of the avenue. At their previous meeting he had told Taggart of a Puerto Rican youth who had been arrested on serious charges. He was a figure in the neighborhood, had been a warlord and had dealt drugs, but he had started a new life, had actually become political, and now had revealed stunning gifts

as a writer. Everett was arranging for him to be tutored—
he was certain to be imprisoned—and Taggart had agreed
to help.

Everett shuffled straight ahead in his open shoes that
looked like slippers, seeming not to notice the trucks and
cars that came hurtling by. When they had crossed he said
quietly, "Taggart, I'm grateful to you." And a moment later,
"I've known Luis since the day he was born, literally. He was
a wonderful child. And he never did go wrong. It's so easy to
get into drugs down here. But he really did quit, anybody in
the neighborhood can tell you that. Somebody planted junk
in his car. He thinks the cops did. Maybe they did. You question him yourself, Taggart. You have to form your own impression."

Everett opened the door of the Ukrainian restaurant and
motioned Taggart ahead, saying in a quiet voice, "We have to
rally round, that's all. It's his time of need."

The restaurant was plain and clean, with many dull-
white surfaces and squared corners. They drank coffee while
they waited. From the crowded counter came laughter and
shrill voices.

". . . forty-six, forty-eight . . ."

"No! No! No!"

"Yes!"

A gorgeous young couple, both blond and dressed identi-
cally in blue jeans and blue T-shirts leaned over the counter,
their tousled heads touching.

"Forty-four!" the youth shouted. He was laughing.
"Forty-six!"

"That's what I said!" the young woman screamed. Their
voices shimmered with speed and pot. Two inches of golden
skin glowed like neon between the girl's jeans and her shirt.
A wizened, fierce-eyed Ukrainian leaned back to look at it. He
studied her face, and looked at the coins that were strewn over
the counter. At length a large waiter gestured for quiet, and

with authoritative deftness swept the coins two by two into his open hand.

Taggart was impressed by Luis, as Everett had said he would be. And the lawyer, Lester Cohen, turned out to be a man he had seen often near the Upward Bound office with a young Puerto Rican woman. It turned out, too, that Cohen had handled the CO case of a friend of Taggart's during the Korean War.

Luis was twenty-two, tall and extremely good-looking. He was observant and grave. There was great pride in his manner, and the hint of an explosive temper . . . but it was more than temper; there were flashes of a challenge that was absolute, a hint of total violence, powerfully controlled and dissimulated. Taggart suspected that there were things about him that Everett didn't know, and probably couldn't imagine. The youth shook hands almost passively, not gripping but allowing his own hand to be held. He winked at Everett.

They talked as they ate.

"There's no question here," said Lester Cohen. "I believe you, and I know these guys do. That doesn't matter—"

"That guy who planted that stuff, man, he's the biggest dealer down here. Ever'body knows it. Right, Everett?" Luis spoke in a soft, husky voice that without effort carried great conviction.

"That doesn't matter, kid," said Cohen. "You want to know what matters? Just one thing—they have to move the calendar along. I'm not being cynical, Luis, it's the way it is. If you insist on a trial over a little thing like this, they'll slaughter you, not to get back at you, but so the next guy will look at you and say, Unh-unh, don't go that way. So sure, we'll say it wasn't yours, but we'll try for a possession rap, and we'll make a case for your character, your studies, your social progress, your associates. Don't forget, they know you from before."

The youth bowed his head. "I do time?" he said softly.
"Yes."

"How much, you think?"

"A year, probably."

"Okay, that don't worry me."

But Taggart could see that he was gravely disturbed, and he guessed that what he feared was his own response to abuse.

Luis handed him a weighty brown envelope.

"You read Spanish?" he said.

Taggart shook his head. Luis looked at Everett.

"We'll get it translated," Everett said. "I'll do it myself. I'll dictate it. Sure. Marcia will type it up. It's no problem, Luis." Marcia was Morris Pasloff's secretary.

"You never write in English?" said Taggart.

"I never wrote *nothing* before. It's a play about the block. How could it be in English? Some of it's in English."

Luis and Taggart talked while the others ate.

Everett was contorting his face, struggling to get one molar above another to grind the stringy fibers of the boiled beef. With an angry sigh he gave it up and mashed it with his fork.

Luis complimented Taggart on his play.

"Everett took me," he said. "I seen it, man. It's nice, real nice."

He meant it . . . but he gazed at Taggart a long while silently, and Taggart quite abruptly understood that the furious outcasts he had written about, the baffled dropouts and salty existentialist comics, for all their misery and psychic stress, were privileged and enviable Americans, and he thought, Yes, the boy is right.

An hour after the interview with Luis Fontana, Taggart was weaving through traffic on his bike. Three books were strapped to the little shelf in back.

He was sinewy and tireless and ordinarily enjoyed these excursions, but he was breathing shallowly and his face was tense. How appalling it was to take a man out of the daylight and lock him in a cage! He remembered Fontana's bowed head and his grave, soft voice: "I do time?"

At the library he chained his bike to a lamppost near the entrance. Two black youths were inspecting it when he came out. They smiled at him appraisingly and sat on the wide marble bench a few feet away.

The fumes of midtown were dreadful. The faces in the crowds were exhausted and anxious. He made his way to Central Park. He was sweating enjoyably now and had begun to feel limber. And here were kites in the air, kids on bikes, Frisbees, dogs. Several ball games were in progress. It was, after all, a lovely day. Alternately hailing the beauty and vitality of life and lamenting the vanishing of everything good, he glided along, bending low over the handlebars, thrusting first with one leg and then with the other.

There were people who thought Taggart's situation enviable, and others who thought it a cul-de-sac. Taggart was of both opinions. He had inherited money, but it was held in trust and was so small an amount that one restaurant meal in the month could throw him into debt. Yet this money, together with discipline and simplicity, rendered him independent. It probably also curbed what small ambition he possessed. Often he wondered what he might accomplish under the pressure of need—except that he had come to believe that need itself was a creative act. Hadn't Dostoyevsky and Balzac enmeshed themselves in needs, debts, and obligations, those reliable, middle-class bulwarks against normal life?

Taggart augmented his income with book reviews and articles, a collection of which was being published in the fall. And he wrote poems and plays, but they earned him almost nothing. There were times when he yearned for a home, a bourgeois home, with a bourgeois wife and bourgeois children. But there were times when living just as he did, in his walkup flat, with his bike and his books, his freedom, his friends in all parts of the city, his "poet's uniform" of blue work shirt and khaki pants (summer) or gray sweatshirt and corduroy pants (winter, spring, and fall)—there were times when everything seemed absolutely right.

Gliding past buses like the shadow of a bird, dodging pedestrians like a ten-year-old boy, leaning on the handlebars like a poet deep in thought . . . he arrived at his corner in the Lower East Side.

His flat was five flights up. There weren't many like it in the city. The stairs were steep. Carrying up the bike was unendurable except as a spiritual exercise. He addressed himself to it. He stood with his feet together, closed his eyes, bowed to the Buddha. He gripped the bike lightly. He moved slowly, utterly relaxed, breathing for calm, for the taste of the air, for the felt emptiness of chest after every breath. He needed twenty minutes to reach the top, but he could almost always reach it feeling cheerful and refreshed.

In the next-to-the-last flight he heard footsteps down below, two sets of them. They overtook him as he began the last flight.

It was the young woman next door. She was nineteen. She had come from Iowa just three weeks ago. Taggart had rescued her mail when thieves had broken open the boxes and scattered letters over the grimy floor. She was wide and muscular, with long corn-silk hair. She wore thick glasses, behind which her light-gray eyes were as round as marbles. At her side was a stalwart black youth with long arms, wide cheekbones, shy, wide-set eyes. He wore steel-rimmed glasses and seemed like a country boy. A shy, wide smile was frozen on his face. They passed Taggart on their muscular legs, *step, step, step, step.* Taggart crept onward to the landing, breathing softly and deeply.

"Why, Taggart!"

Karla was sitting on the topmost step, reading the *Village Voice.*

"What in *thee* world have you been doing?" she cried.

"Karla! When did you get back?"

He left the bike and ran up and embraced her. The Iowa girl and the black youth were just stepping out of sight.

Holding him and leaning back, she said, "I heard the street door open half an hour ago—"

"That was me," he said.

"—and then I didn't hear *anything*. Just nothin'. And I thought, What in *thee* world!"

Taggart laughed. "You look great," he said. "Do you want some coffee? When did you get back? Tell me about your trip."

Taggart's kitchen table was one-half of a round table bolted to the wall. There wasn't room for the other half. Within reach of the table was the bathtub, waist-high on metal legs and covered with an enamel lid. In winter it served as a radiator, for if he filled it with hot water, which the landlord was obliged to supply, it somewhat warmed the room, which the landlord refused to insulate.

"I saw Duane three times," said Karla. "Just for lunch, but I think he still likes me."

They ate cheese and crackers and drank coffee out of large white cups with "USA" stamped on the bottom.

"Listen," said Taggart, smiling. His kitchen wall was the bedroom wall of the girl from Iowa. The creaking of the bed was audible, a strong, undeviating rhythm set in total silence. Nor were there voices when shortly later the creaking stopped. They heard the opening and closing of the door, and footsteps in the hall.

She spoke to him of her parents. A warm breeze came in at the open window. They could hear the passionate shouting of children, and the increasing-diminishing roar of traffic on Avenue A.

She told him of Dolores, who had been her classmate in high school. "She's not beautiful by any manner of means," she said, "but men pay a lot of money to go to bed with her. She can make a hundred dollars in an hour. You should see her clothes! I said, 'Dolores, don't you ever feel guilty or ashamed?' And she said, 'I'm not hurting anybody, Karla, and I'm not stealing anybody's money. As far as I can see I'm spreading happiness and good times.'

"What do you think, Taggart? I think she's right."

"Why are you telling me this?" he said. A sour, acidic sensation sped between his stomach and his lungs.

"Because I'm going to try it," said Karla.

"Don't be a fool!" he said. He spoke angrily and with a flash of contempt. She narrowed her eyes and thrust out her chin. "Now, will you please think real hard," she said, "and tell me why you said that?"

"You're a self-respecting person. You can't do that kind of thing."

"She is, too."

"Really?"

"Yes, Taggart."

"And is she self-deceived as well?"

"How would I know that? I can't see inside people the way you can."

"You *do* know."

"Taggart, I *don't!*"

She was getting angry. He looked away, lips compressed. But almost immediately he understood that his disapproval implied a relationship that didn't actually exist. She was not accountable to him.

They went to Chinatown, as they had agreed to do, and ate at a new Shanghai restaurant, but they scarcely talked. It was just as bad afterward, walking through Little Italy.

They went to the settlement house and saw the last twenty minutes of Taggart's play.

The little theater was crowded. There had been rave reviews in the *Village Voice* as well as in the *Post.* People were sitting in the aisle and standing in back.

Taggart's mood of hurt and bitter loneliness vanished utterly. He was elated.

A crew of young people cleared away the chairs and benches after the lights came on. Two young women served coffee from a big electric urn.

Morris Pasloff beckoned to Taggart and introduced him to a handsome middle-aged couple, Mr. and Mrs. a name like Oscar Hatcher.

"I've seen your play three times," said the man. "It holds up well."

"Thank you," said Taggart.

"I've done two of the settlement's plays," said the man. "I'd like to make yours the third."

"Oh! You must be Oscar Hatcher!"

"Yes."

It was all very simple. Taggart would sign a contract Monday. They would use the present cast and director. A Sheridan Square theater would be available in September.

Karla walked home with him. He was jabbering like a little boy. She smiled and took his arm, and he formed the comforting theory that she had abandoned the notion that had so upset him.

Praise, good luck, and her slender, luminous body in the twilight of the bed! He made love with her happily.

Afterward she said to him, "Taggart, if you had to put all your women on a scale, where would I be?"

"What do you mean?" he said. "To weigh them?"

"Taggart, you're giddy! You're giddy 'cause they're doin' your play. You know what I mean! In bed."

"Aw, Karla, what do you mean *scale?* Why do you ask me that, anyway?"

"Well, sometimes I feel like a dope. There must be all kinds of things to do, and I'm not doing them. You could teach me a lot, I bet."

He couldn't resist smiling; the flattery was irresistible— but why did she say "teach" when the normal course of love-making would accomplish exactly that, and more? Her saying it chilled him. Or was she asking for patience and special care?

Abruptly, he remembered their quarrel.

"Are you talking about business?" he said.

"Maybe," she answered swiftly.

"Do as you like."

He turned on his back and looked at the ceiling.

Their relationship had ended. He would never see her again. He hated her. He wanted to hurt her.

He felt abandoned.

He had heard of girls who had done this for a lark, and of others who had put themselves through school. . . .

She said, "I'm too tired to go home, Taggart. I'm going to sleep."

"I'm not mad," he said. But that was all he said.

The thought that he might never see her again was saddening . . . and the sadness of loss brought memories of Naomi. He could see her dark eyes and shyly parted lips as she stood in the doorway of the huge loft in which the wedding party of a mutual friend was underway. He had never forgotten that first glimpse of her. He had been a little drunk, bolder than usual, and had taken her hand and drawn her out among the dancing couples. She had protested, but soon was dancing with pleasure. She seemed to know where he would move before he knew himself. It was as if she had given up her will to him, was content to accept and respond, except that at times she seemed to be drawing him subtly after her and inspiring movements that melted excitingly into her own. They had met again the following night and had made love by lamplight.

His sadness opened out into older yearnings. On the landing of the stairway in his childhood home there had been a window seat under three panels of stained glass. He had loved to lie there as a boy and often had gone there when he wanted to be alone. His mother had been killed when he was four. His father had died when he was ten. He had grown up with extraordinary freedom in the too-large house, and had been cared for by his mother's unmarried sister, whom he had loved deeply. She too had died before he had met Naomi.

His marriage with Naomi had been doomed. She was too like him, had been lonely too much, and now consoled herself with love, undoing the sadness of the past with caresses. But the very completeness of their loving uncovered needs neither one could meet. Their quarreling had been bitter.

Taggart turned and looked at Karla, who was sleeping soundly. Sexuality and love, rivalry, egotism, jealousy—all the mysteries of self-and-others seemed to him utterly beyond comprehension—nor was he much persuaded by the ideologies that claimed to understand those things. He thought of the photographs he had studied once of the great temple of Konarak, the sides of which were covered with sculptured figures of orgiasts in acts of love, their spines curved and their shoulders lifted meltingly in erotic delight. That all those breasts, hips, and buttocks, gigantic phalluses, excited lips and eyes should be the meaning and adornment of a temple had made him wild with longing and with resentment of his own repressive traditions. What had moved him most had been the smiles. The smiles were childlike and unafraid, and expressed a lovely pride that was like the unconscious pride of animals.

Looking at Karla as she lay there sleeping, Taggart glimpsed a truth he hadn't seen before: the figures on the temple were not images of private bliss, but presupposed a community of trust, perhaps even a community of love. When had such a thing existed? The smiles were utopian. The orgy itself was a visionary hope of trust.

He didn't want to break with Karla. He would talk her out of her present plans. He would speak to her in the morning, and he would do it in a kindly way. He smiled and looked at her tousled hair, and fell asleep.

Something went wrong in the morning. His kindness faltered. Notes of pleading came into his voice, and then notes of anger and contempt. Karla's eyes flashed at him. She said that he was a moralist and had no right to pick on her. She said he didn't own her, and had better not try to control her. She left angrily while he was standing at the stove.

He opened the door she had slammed, and called, "Karla! I don't want to see you again!"

She turned in the hall, at the head of the stairs, and said fiercely, "Don't tell me what you want!"

It was Saturday morning. He ate the eggs he had cooked for Karla, wiped the kitchen table with a sponge, laid out some books and yellow second sheets, and sat down with a cup of coffee. But it was a long time before he could gather his thoughts.

The review he was writing was due Monday. The book was mean-spirited, full of pretense and false issues, but it was not without interest. Its authors were sociologists. They made a great show of having dispensed with scholarly machinery in order to talk the language of the layman, but it was clear that the machinery had never existed and could not exist: the book was a work of fashion, the more rarefied in that the Pop Art with which it dealt, and which presently flourished in the galleries, was itself indebted to the Pop sociology of the previous decade. To Taggart, the book was symptomatic of many things, among them the passing of the avant garde, though this was a term one heard more frequently than ever.

A more important book obtruded into his thoughts. He reduced his report on the first to a page and a half, and used it as an introduction to his comments on the other. The bound galleys had arrived several days ago. The author, a black lawyer and political journalist of Taggart's generation, called for total separation of the races; but more than that—and it seemed equally important—he displayed at every opportunity a programmatic yet stunning hatred of all things white.

The book was disturbing. What could come of separatism but a politics of dependence, however angry it might be?

Taggart distrusted both the platform and the rhetoric, whereas the civil-rights movement had stirred him deeply and seemed rich in courage and good sense. Yet that dreadful question still remained: How could the blacks pass from slavery and contempt to peer relations with the whites except by expressing their accumulated and well-founded hate?

He was obliged to abandon utterly the knowing conventions of book reviews. He wrote in perplexity and concern . . . and this ethical decision freed his intelligence and to some extent returned the abstractions of argument to the real world of open fate.

It was not until noon on Monday that the essay was finished. He delivered it himself and chatted with the editor. At a lawyer's office he signed a contract that already bore the signature of Oscar Hatcher, and on the way home deposited his check in the bank. That evening the editor telephoned to say that the piece was wonderful, they wanted to run it as an article.

He should have felt happy.

He wrote some dialogue based on words that had come of themselves the week before, but there was no life in it, and he put the pages into a folder.

He wrote a poem about the persistence of the past, the ghosts in bed, but it was bad, was not a poem, only a thought . . . and those pages too went into a folder.

How could Karla have experienced such ecstasy with Tilson, as she had told him, and yet have learned so little? Her ecstasy had been escape from self, not love. Or worse, intoxicated dream . . .

But no, the fault was his, as the fault had been his with Naomi . . . and he fell into a reverie of accusation and became depressed.

Karla called him unexpectedly several days later. She invited him to dinner. She said, "Be mah guest, Taggart." He had been sitting there smiling into the phone. "Yes," he said.

"With pleasure, Karla." And he sat there smiling for several minutes after their conversation had ended.

She was waiting for him at a table in the Chinese restaurant at the foot of the Bowery. Their eyes met, and he saw at once that she had forgiven him. But something was afoot. She wore an attractive new dress, and seemed both anxious and determined. As soon as they had ordered, she leaned across the table and said, "Taggart, I didn't tell you, but my girl friend Dolores was in town. She came with a buyer from Comfry's in Dallas. There was another buyer with him. . . ."

She looked into his eyes.

"I made two hundred dollars and three new dresses."

He wanted to strike her. But he saw that he was being tested. And he was baffled. She wanted his good opinion, wanted it as earnestly as she wanted her independence.

"I saw all that Times Square part of New York that I never see. Pretty stupid, if you ask me, but it's all a stranger has access to.

"Taggart," she said, "I don't see what's wrong with this work. It's a little bit like social work, only it really *does* something. He's got a daughter just got pregnant, and she's not married and doesn't know who the father is. And a teen-age boy on drugs. Taggart, he's got the identical, selfsame problems I used to hear from my welfare families, only here there's good food and they can afford a doctor. And would you believe, I *said* the same things to him, too, the very selfsame things . . . except I made love with him. Taggart, I cheered that man up. I performed a real honest-to-God service."

He nodded. There was a touching, and distressing, validity in everything she said. Nor was there any need to criticize her. The world was too harsh. She was too innocent and proud. She could not survive in this work for long.

"He said I was pretty good," she said.

"Yes," he said flatly, "you are."

She almost bounced on the chair with glee. He was astonished at the severity of the self-doubt implicit in this jubilation. She read the emotions on his face, and her own face grew dark and she stopped talking.

They walked through Little Italy after supper and stopped at a tiny bakery that still baked bread in brick ovens fired by wood. There was movement inside and a delicious aroma of fresh bread, but the door was locked and a green shade was pulled down. They went to Ferrara's and ordered pastry and coffee.

She told him that Marshall had come to see her. He had seemed anxious and confused, yet was happier than ever in his life.

"He's making love," she said. "He's got a boyfriend, an ex-minister. I think he's another patient. Marshall says he's brilliant, just a wonderful man. . . ." She saw that he wasn't interested.

Later, as they walked north, she said, "I don't understand you, Taggart. Sometimes I can't tell whether you even like me—"

"I like you," he said.

"—and sometimes it seems like you think you ought to love me, or I ought to love you. But we don't have to, Taggart. . . ."

He said, "No, we don't . . ."

"You never will love me," she added.

"I don't want to talk about these things," he said harshly.

They walked in hostile silence for several blocks and parted at the entranceway of Karla's building.

For five days Taggart scarcely left his apartment. When he wasn't depressed he was anxious. Twice, though he was agnostic and hadn't been to church since the age of ten, he dropped to his knees and prayed for an end to confusion.

The days were hot and pressing; there wasn't much air. Most of his friends had left the city. He stripped to his shorts, pulled down the shades, turned on the window fans, and spent an unusual lot of hours in sleep and waking dream.

Yet during this time, anxiously and without pleasure, but with urgency, relief, and preternatural clarity, he wrote poem after poem. There were fifteen in all. Five seemed good, one positively excellent.

He also roughed out two plays, and knew that the larger of the two was reliably alive. He paced about, sweating, or lay motionless, staring at the ceiling, speaking rapidly and audibly long speeches in voices that weren't his own.

The hours actually spent writing could not have exceeded three each day, but now weeks or months would be needed to finish what he had begun.

He felt strong again, and felt hopeful . . . and with hope came boredom, restlessness, and curiosity. He was hungry for the world.

It was while he was in this mood that, answering the ringing phone, he heard the voice of Everett Wilder.

"Taggart," said Everett, "they gave Luis three years."

Taggart gasped. He had forgotten all about that.

"No," said Everett, "don't worry. Lester says he'll be out in a year, for sure."

Everett's voice sounded weak. Taggart could hear an effort of will and a note of sadness that had nothing to do with what he was saying.

"We finished the play," Everett said. "It was mostly in English, actually. But that's not why I'm calling. Listen . . . Taggart . . . I have wonderful news. Morris got a grant from Lackland, a great big one. We're helping him spend it. . . ."

Twenty minutes later Taggart walked into Morris's office, where Everett, Morris, and several others were talking about a storefront school for neighborhood kids.

Karla was there. She was dressed in blue jeans and a red sweatshirt. She nodded sullenly to Taggart, but blushed deeply, with a look of shame, and turned again to Everett, who evidently had been speaking. Two Puerto Rican boys of fourteen or fifteen sat beside him.

Taggart looked often at Karla, wondering what had happened.

Morris turned to him and said, "Karla has agreed to run the place."

Taggart was aware that she was watching him while Morris spoke. She was still blushing, holding her head low.

". . . the salary's absurd," Morris was saying. "It's the best we can do. It's enough to live on . . ."

Taggart spoke to Karla after the meeting, but she didn't want to be questioned. Nor did she want to go out with him for a drink, or meet him for supper. He was touched by her hurt. And he was stirred in unexpected ways. In fantasy he pursued the one who had abused her, and punished him with such cruelty as he would have been loath to acknowledge even as fantasy. Yet he was angry with Karla, also. And, in spite of himself, there was a way in which, naggingly, he was pleased.

That night he read Fontana's play, which Everett had handed him in a small cardboard box. It was about a fatherless family, a beautiful sister, a brave younger brother, drugs, street fights, police. It was unplayable, was so out of control that one could not even say of it that it was badly written. Moreover, it was conceited and marred by ignorant, presumptuous pride. Taggart did not feel that it was salvageable for the stage, yet the enterprise as a whole took on a meaning that moved him greatly. For the fact was that this amorphous thing was alive with spirit, with a large, bold, dazzlingly energetic manifestation of self, in which intelligence and feeling supported each other, and in which, most surprising of all, there was compassion for the people who were apparently his neighbors. Taggart remembered Everett saying gravely, "He's worth it." It was true. And the thought of using art as the vehicle of an instruction that in reality would be spiritual and would intend growth and not mere expertise was exciting to

Taggart. He wrote Fontana a letter, and then sprawled on the bed and read parts of the play again.

He glanced at his books on their shelves. How mysterious it was that artistic form should absorb and recreate the spirit! And how wonderful that it should be so! For the other meaning of those books was death. The shelves were a graveyard. It would be horrifying if one could see those deaths nakedly, but one could not, except by ignoring the babble of life. The same persistent life was everywhere, scarcely altered from book to book. There was one human intelligence, one human pride, one human integrity and giving-forth.

How wonderful mankind was, that monster!

Tears were standing in his eyes, though he was filled with rejoicing.

II.

Of the six adolescents who had volunteered to help clean the little store that would become a school, only a girl and her brother ever came—and the boy sat on the shoeshine chair and read comics while the women worked. The place was musty and smelled of cats. Taggart came frequently and worked beside Karla, washing and painting. They were friendly again, were considerate of one another, a little guarded, all of which seemed more correct to him than being lovers. There was something he liked about it.

One day Hector, the boy, said that Everett was ill. That evening Taggart went with Karla to see him.

The three-day heat wave had broken. There were clouds in the sky and the air was mild. Taggart listened to Karla as they walked east. She was uncertain of her ability, uncertain of the real usefulness of such a school . . . but Taggart noticed that she spoke with animation and didn't want answers, and he walked beside her contentedly. They passed under the high windows of his apartment. There had been a killing on the street the week before. A minor accident, a mere scraping of fenders, had led to words, the words to blows, the blows to a stabbing.

The noise of traffic diminished as they walked east, and the sound of music grew loud. Radios and phonographs were everywhere, and it seemed that all the windows and doors were open. People were strolling on the sidewalks, were standing in groups and sitting on stoops and rickety chairs. Some were overhauling their cars at the curb. In several places restless teen-agers danced. Taggart and Karla passed a group of men in undershirts, cursing genially and slamming dominoes on a flimsy table. Beer-drinking friends hovered beside them. Wives and daughters leaned from nearby windows, pressing plump bosoms against plump arms.

Taggart heard a sound of metal wheels behind him, and something in that sound, the timbre of it, the scratchiness, aroused memories that were spacious and sweet. He turned and saw two boys come hurtling toward him, too engrossed to shout, one pushing the other on a skimming little cart made of two-by-fours and roller skates. It was steered by a clothes-line halter, and was adorned with bottle caps that had been hammered into the wood. . . .

Karla stayed with Taggart that night. He had invited her diffidently, not sure that she would accept or that he actually desired her, but she had no sooner shed her clothes and come walking on her knees across the bed than his mouth went dry and he began to pant. The familiar hollow of her waist, where it swelled to fullness, enflamed him more, and she, too, became aroused. Later, when they lay resting together, wet with perspiration and cooling comfortably in the warm air, they talked with an intimacy they hadn't experienced for weeks.

She told him of her childhood in Texas. She interrupted a description of her home and said passionately, "Oh, Taggart, why is it so hard to make a life in this country?"

Long after she had fallen asleep, Taggart lay there with open eyes. She had pulled up the bed sheet as far as her waist.

She lay on her stomach with her face turned toward him and her arms near her head. He could see the lateral softness of the small breast flattened by her weight. Her shoulders and arms were deeply relaxed, like the limbs of a child asleep, but there was a tension in her face that probably never left it.

He thought of Everett, and felt a terrible sadness for that impending death and the vanishing of all that experience. Everett had been twenty-nine at the time of the Russian Revolution, and had given himself utterly to the intoxication of hope. Hope for mankind! How exotic it seemed! And how bitter to have seen it destroyed and to have lived into this period of anxious dread for the planet Earth itself!

Everett had noticed his thoughtful, filial gaze that evening, and had smiled at him.

"What really ails you, Everett?"

"Age," he had said.

"Really?"

"Oh, I'll be around awhile, Taggart. I'll go all at once . . . like the wonderful one-hoss shay. Do you know that poem? Do kids read it anymore in school? 'Have you heard of the wonderful one-hoss shay, that was built in such a logical way . . .' Rosa . . . Rosa, honey, I'll do you a thousand favors when I get up . . ." He had asked her to bring a book from the apartment across the hall, where his study was, and in his throaty, weak, eager voice had read them the humorous lines of Holmes.

How diminished the world would be with the passing of that generation! Taggart had urged Everett to write of his life, and Everett had agreed, had apparently long wanted to, but nothing had come of it, only some marvelous all-night bouts of bourbon and reminiscence, dazzling occasions for Taggart, that had attached his love once and for all. Everett had told him of the Zapatista villages of Morelos, where he had lived for the ten years immediately after the Mexican Revolution, surveying the ever-changing boundaries of the common farmlands, and teaching mathematics and reading in the evenings.

He had discovered that the villagers had fought not to create a new world, but to return to a communal life that had been stable for centuries, a life permeated by custom and demanding to the point of narrowness, yet forbearing and generous. To see all that had humbled him. He had gone down a Communist and had come back, as he said, a Zapatista, to whom only anarchism was palatable. He had become a printer, and from the end of World War II had lived in the building he now occupied. Two generations of Puerto Rican immigrants had come to him for help. To see him in the street was to see something one would not imagine possible in the city of New York: he was at home as in a village; people waved to him, nodded, spoke. . . .

Karla's breathing was restful. The lids of her eyes were not entirely closed. Taggart sniffed her breath and lightly kissed her shoulder. He didn't want to sleep. It was past two in the morning, but faintly, through the wall beside him, came the strains of Fauré's *Requiem*. And there occurred to him an insight that he had had before, but that now, because he was falling asleep, seemed to expand with the combinatory openness of revelation: namely that between political theory and political action there had to be a middle term of character, an ombudsman, as it were, of civilization itself. And he thought how splendid it would be to write the story of Everett's life under the sign of this thought. . . .

One afternoon several days after his visit with Everett, Taggart answered the phone and heard a woman's voice he did not at first recognize. Her voice was tense and careful. She seemed to be fending off some shaking emotion.

It was Rosa, Everett's wife. She said, "Everett asked me to call you. . . ."

Taggart's heart began to race. Scarcely breathing, he said, "Is Everett all right?"

"Yes," she said, "but something bad has happened. Everett asked me to tell you. Well . . . you know, Taggart . . . this

is what happened . . . they killed Luis in the jail. You know
Luis, Taggart . . . the boy who wrote the play—"

He said, "Yes . . . yes—"

"Everett asked me to call you. He can't talk of it. You
know they were good friends."

"Yes, I know," he said. "When did this happen, Rosa?"

"Two days ago. We are just hearing of it now. They are
trying to say he killed himself. As if that boy would kill himself
. . . Oh, Taggart, I can't think of it. I have to go, Taggart."

He sat there dizzily. Nausea and faintness swept through
him. The face of the dead youth and the sound of his voice
came back to him vividly.

Karla called. She had heard of it from Hector and Helen.

"There's going to be a riot," she said.

That evening fifty or sixty youths rampaged at the pre-
cinct house and tried to make their way north to Gracie Man-
sion. Several were arrested.

It proved impossible to obtain the official autopsy, but the
youth's body was released to his family for burial, and a private
autopsy discovered internal hemorrhaging. The damage to his
throat had occurred after death. He could not have hanged
himself in his cell, as the guards were claiming.

Neighborhood leaders organized a protest demonstration at City Hall. WBAI devoted thirty minutes to it, and the
Times, the *Post,* and the *Daily News* quoted the mayor's
promise of an investigation.

And there it ended.

III.

In the northwest corner of Tompkins Square Park, in the
shade of gigantic elms, a foundation-financed theater company worked for two days assembling bleachers and sound
equipment. Taggart watched a crew of young laborers fit the
great wedges of the stage into place. He talked with them
while they rested. Several were aspiring actors.

The following day, late in the afternoon, he prepared a dinner for Karla and himself. He had finished the first draft of the new play. He had walked to Sixth Avenue for greens and pastries, to University Place for steaks, to Astor Place for wine, and now was listening to *The Magic Flute* and shelling peas. Beyond the open window the late August sun glowed like bronze on the western faces of the buildings. The Three Ladies of the Queen of Night were singing.

> *Du Jüngling, schön und liebevoll,*
> *Du trauter Jüngling, lebe wohl!*
> *Bis ich dich wieder seh!*

He sat in a white wooden chair, balancing a large blue bowl on his lap, over which his head was bowed like the head of a man at prayer. His hands—motionless for the moment—rested on the table in a clutter of pods. Through the golds and silvers of the music there came a sound that startled him. He looked up almost in alarm. The sound came again, and with it a wave of sadness and an image of his mother's face that he feared was only a remembered photograph. In it, she was younger than he, and young for her years, with straw-colored hair, straw-colored eyebrows, smiling at him. The sound he had heard was the sound of his name. "Taaaaagaart! Heyyyy, TAAA-gart!" He had never before been hailed like this in the vast city of New York. The small voice rang up confidently out of the vastness, and he began to smile and feel buoyant. In the few moments it took him to get to the window he remembered how his boyhood friends had called him mornings on the way to school, and weekends to play ball: "Oyyyyy, Taggart!" as he had called in the same style, "Oyyyyy, Fritzie!" He had never known where that *oy* had come from. It seemed to be *ahoy*, shortened—but there had been no mariners in the foothills of the Alleghenies. He leaned out the window. Once again his name proceeded upward, but the voice broke abruptly, and Karla, who was standing on the warm sidewalk far below, waved eagerly and shouted something he couldn't understand. He put on a shirt and went down. She took his hand and pulled him toward the avenue. She was grinning. "Taggart," she said, "there's an organ grinder with a *monkey*. I've never *seen* one! Come on!"

A crowd had gathered at the entrance to the park. And truly the lilting, gamboling music was irresistible. It was the music of merry-go-rounds and music boxes, cheerful and extroverted, yet actually sunless and mysterious, a tinkling, full-throated song, at the very heart of which one could hear the turning of the crank and the measured regularity of metallic pipes and valves. What a strange, beseeching charm! so heartfelt, and it never drew a breath! It was music played by a toy, a sorrowing toy.

The crowd was mostly black and Puerto Rican older children and teen-agers. Here and there young boys and girls held mothers and sisters by the hand. Shrill cries and laughter came from the center.

At close quarters the music seemed ragged and mechanical. Taggart and Karla pressed into the crowd until, over the heads of children and between the heads of adults, they could see the monkey and the organ grinder.

The odor of child sweat and dirty tennis shoes was strong. The children squealed and leaped back from the monkey. They called to him excitedly, holding out pennies, tiny stones, and bottle caps. The monkey's brow was wrinkled. He seemed confused and close to panic. He wore a dark red vest. A red fez was strapped to his head at a jaunty angle. He loped swiftly back and forth, his eyes darting this way and that.

Taggart remembered the organ grinder he had seen near Columbia after the war, an embittered, aging Italian, who had looked with cold contempt at everyone, had seemed to detest the wretched monkey and not to hear the ghostlike music he was cranking out. The youth in the circle now was similarly dressed, in a shapeless dark suit with a red bandana round his neck, but his face had the soft, blurred sweetness of suburban life. His smile was gentle, his eyes were gentle and took many things for granted. It was clear that he would go back to school in the fall, or perhaps he had begun a career in the theater . . . in any event, he belonged to the company that had set up the stage and that would perform *Coriolanus* a few hours from now. Smiling gently, he turned the crank, holding the monkey's leash with the other hand.

Taggart felt repugnance for it all; it was quaint, was a form of welfare, a cultural service sent back, as it were, to the colonies by those who had appropriated every resource to themselves. Yet he felt boorish in his discontent, for here, after all, were the music and the monkey, an entertainment for children, and the children were enjoying it.

The crowd grew larger. Taggart watched a teen-age Puerto Rican boy come running from the distance, apparently in the belief that some terrible violence had occurred. When he heard the music he slowed his pace, passing without a glance the exiled Ukrainian villagers who spent their days and evenings by the benches. A flock of pigeons rose in front of him.

The voices were becoming raucous. The loping monkey was like a child, the children wanted to pet him, but his long, resilient muscles were made for superhuman leaps in trees, and there was a frightening excess of force in all his movements. The older children began to taunt him. A bus opened its doors, and for a couple of minutes its powerful motor drowned the reedy music in blasts of hot air. Taggart watched a smiling black girl step cautiously out of the shadow of her huge, gravely vigilant mother and offer a penny on the flat of her hand. "That's right, that's right," her mother said. "He won't pinch you." The anxious monkey folded five fingers over the coin, and with awkward strong movements forced it into the pocket of his red vest.

Three tall black youths of fourteen or fifteen pushed to the inner circle. They carried long broom handles, which they posted before them with both hands, as samurai might rest on their swords.

One said, "Hey, man, dig this monkey"—and it was clear that he meant the youth who was cranking the organ.

"That all he do, take money?"

The organ grinder stared woodenly straight ahead.

Two youths like these had stepped out of the shadows of Taggart's entranceway one night and had pressed the points of knives on either side of his throat. "Holy cow!" he had gasped. "You could hurt somebody . . ." and one of the frozen-faced youths had cracked a smile. "That's right," he had said. "Turn around." The wallet had been plucked from his back pocket and the loose bills from the side, and one of the youths had struck him between the shoulder blades so powerfully that he had fallen to his knees gasping for breath.

A black woman took her two children by their hands and pushed away through the crowd. Others, too, moved away. The clear space grew larger. And now an odd thing happened. An attractive white woman—no more than eighteen or nineteen—wearing a flowery dress and a broad-brimmed romantic hat, stepped forward and said to the black youths, in a flat, throaty voice, "He can do real tricks if you give him a chance." One of the youths smiled at her hatefully and, with a glance at his friend, said, "Bet you can too." Taggart looked at her more closely. She was not young, was in her thirties, even her late thirties. She wore heavy makeup, and seemed to be a model rather than an actress. She rummaged with her finger-tips in a tiny purse, took out a fifty-cent piece, and knelt in front of the monkey. "Hup, Paddy, hup," she said, making a lifting motion with her hand, as if to throw the coin into the air. The soft voice of the organ grinder echoed her own— "Hup, Paddy, hup!"

But the monkey was confused. It skittered to the organ, dusting the ground with its knuckles, and pulled a chain that rang a little bell. The three youths laughed, and one said, "Yeah, Paddy . . . you doin' good."

Looking from face to face in the crowd, the monkey extracted some coins from its vest pocket and pushed them into a cup by the bell. The woman called to him again, "Here, Paddy. Come, Paddy," and again made the tossing motion with the coin. The monkey's brow was wrinkled. He jumped up and down, as if on springs, opened his mouth wide and screamed quietly. Then he went to her with spidery strides and reached for the coin. One of the black youths struck his hand aside with the tip of his long stick. The monkey shrieked with indignation, leaped away, righted itself, and sprang backward into the air. It turned in midair, as if on an axle, landed flatfooted, and sprang again. There was a burst of laughter from the crowd, but it was mixed in spirit, and in part was harsh. The youth nearest the organ bent down and cut the monkey's long leash. The appearance of the knife in his hand was startling. The music stopped. Karla took Taggart's arm, and he heard her voice, "Taggart, that boy has a knife!" As were many others, Taggart was scanning the block for police.

The organ grinder said faintly, "Come on, you guys . . ." but the woman in the hat shouted hammeringly, "How dare you attack a defenseless creature!" and the youth nearest her, glaring murderously, struck her on the shins with his stick, first with one end, then with the other. She was astonished and looked at him with terror. The crowd was scattering. The youth with the knife, who held the monkey's leash, was confused. He tugged the monkey this way and that, but he hadn't reckoned on the agility and strength of the creature, who outmaneuvered him and yet was panic-stricken. Its earsplitting shrieks rose above all the voices. A siren could be heard to the south. In less than a minute everything was over. The bewildered monkey sprang at the youth and clung to him, as if seeking protection. The youth gripped it to throw it off, and the monkey bit his hand. Within a moment the youth had dashed it against the pavement and cracked its head with his heel. Taggart heard screams and frantic sobbing behind him. The monkey crept into the shrubbery by the fence, holding its head with both hands.

The three samurai sped across the park. They looked back over their shoulders, bounding like gazelles, then veered, and vanished around the corner of Avenue B.

All through supper both Taggart and Karla were quiet. She saw that he was troubled far more than the event seemed to warrant, and she questioned him, but he couldn't explain himself.

At eight o'clock they left the apartment. They had gone down a flight and a half when Taggart heard the ringing of his telephone. "I'll never make it," he said. But the ringing proved irresistible; he ran—and sure enough, the phone stopped ringing as he entered the room.

The late-summer days were shortening. Already the evening light had softened. They went to the park and climbed to the topmost tier of the bleachers, so close to the overhanging trees that even sitting they could touch the leaves. The stands were half-filled.

Taggart revived as he studied the crowd.

Had Shakespeare ever had an audience like this? Some didn't speak English at all, many didn't speak it well. Here in the sloping stands, sitting sedately among the antic young, were elderly Italians from the old days of the neighborhood, elderly Ukrainians and Poles, and middle-aged Puerto Ricans. It was partly their lack of English that had made them cling for so many years to the old ways. How would they handle the complex, archaic language of the play? But the adolescents of all the races seemed no better equipped. The experience of listening was apparently unknown to them. Their speech was a babble of contending phrases. They shouted to one another from different sections of the bleachers, and stood talking, but not listening, in clusters between the stands and the low wooden stage. The girls especially talked almost frenziedly, glancing in all directions and chewing gum.

People kept arriving. Their entrances were more interesting to Taggart than those of actors. The moment of expo-
sure before the massed eyes in the bleachers seemed to affect
everyone, but especially the young men. The neighborhood
whites bulked their shoulders and moved with a brutish,
threatening gait, avoiding contact with other eyes. The blacks
took stances of elegance and disdain.

The sky was darkening. A voice of pleased surprise rose
from the crowd, a spontaneous, decidedly feminine *Ahhhhhh!*
accompanied by shrill whistling and several cheers. Strings of
yellow lights had been looped among the branches, and they
burst into color, bringing shades of green back to the trees,
and throwing a complex latticework of shadows over everything. A spirit of gaiety sped through the crowd.

The stands were almost filled now. Four or five transistor
radios could be heard. Here and there Taggart saw acquaintances, and saw also the familiar unknown faces he saw all the
time at concerts in Washington Square Park, or lectures at
Cooper Union, or simply in the streets. Sitting near the front,
studying the crowd with a fascination like his own, was a gray-
haired, attractive couple, friends of Everett's in their middle
sixties. They saw Taggart and waved. Both wore open sandals.
A magenta bandana framed the woman's handsome face. The
man wore blue jeans and a dark red shirt. They had never had
children. They were great listeners to music, readers of books,
spinners-out of night-long political-literary conversations.
Taggart had been to their tiny apartment once, and had seen
them several times at Everett's place. Near them, in strange
regalia, sat a group of the sweet, lost teen-age children who
had begun to appear in the neighborhood.

There was a light breeze, but Taggart could feel waves
of heat from the massed bodies below him. Several Puerto
Rican boys, thirteen or fourteen years old, walked noisily
across the wooden stage. One threw up his arm and shouted,
"Heil Hitler!" and there was an answering *"Heil* Hitler!" from
the stands that was immediately drowned in booing and im-

precations. A powerful male voice cried, "You ignorant little wretch! Don't you have any sense?"

The boys had no sooner left the dimly lit stage than a misshapen, terrible-looking Puerto Rican Negress with red hair and dully gleaming sores on her legs lurched to the edge of it and shook her fist at the audience. A large German shepherd dog with weak hind legs crept onto the stage beside her and moved in agitated patterns near her frayed canvas shoes, looking up at her continually. She spat at the audience and shouted, "You stink! You stink!" Voices roared at her to drop dead, to clear out, to shut up, to talk louder, to sing a song. She shook both fists in the air and shouted hoarsely, "I want bread!" and a youthful voice called back, "Bullshit! You want wine!" Another: "Show us your ass!" Two policemen who had been standing in the shadows drifted toward her. One took her arm and spoke to her, pointing to the dog with his club. Voices called, "Throw 'er out! Lock 'er up!" and others, "Leave her alone! She don' hurt nobody!" Three more policemen materialized out of the darkness and were met by a chorus of boos and calls of "Let 'er stay! Let 'er stay!" to which they didn't respond, but surrounded the woman and the dog, and without touching either, maneuvered them out of the gate. Four Puerto Rican youths ran into the stands. They stepped from tier to tier, balancing like acrobats, and passed out handbills. Taggart recognized them. They were friends of the dead youth Luis Fontana. The bills, in English and Spanish, announced that a public meeting would be held at the Luis Fontana Social Club. There would be talks on tenants' rights and on police brutality. Taggart didn't read his own, but that of a neighbor who had struck a match. As he was reading, a young voice called out quietly in Spanish, "Friends, don't forget Luis Fontana." A moment later the mellow, lovely sounds of an alto recorder drifted outward from a place not far from Taggart. He thought that the play had begun, but then he located the musician in the darkness, and it was a poet of his acquaintance. The melody was haunting and beautiful, and was expertly played. Many people were listening. Taggart looked upward. He wanted to see the stars, perhaps for the momentary illusion of solitude. And there were actually some to be seen, scattered in an opening in the overhanging leaves.

The yellow lights went out. The recorder stopped playing. Some latecomers with a transistor radio groped for seats at the end of the bleachers. Adolescent voices shrilled, *Ooooh! Ahhhh!* responding to the dark. There was a salvo of giggling. *"Maricón!"* More giggling. "Get y'hand away!" Giggling again. Now there was movement on the stage, a dim stirring of white garments and a rumbling of feet. A woman's voice, modulated carefully toward sweet reasonableness, called out pleadingly from the bleachers, "Won't you please turn that radio off?" The radio kept playing. A furious male voice shouted from somewhere else, "Shut that goddamn thing off or get the hell out!"—and a young voice, Spanish, answered, "Fuck you, man!" and the radio was turned up full blast. There was a flurry of movement around the youth, and a hubbub of voices. The radio was silenced. One of the policemen walked to the foot of the bleachers and stood there a moment, looking at the stars. The movement on the stage became a milling, and the sound of feet grew loud. Now strained, throaty voices called, "Down with him! Down with him! Kill him!" Abruptly there was light. A crowd of men in Roman garments milled on the stage. They carried clubs and poles. One said, "Hear me speak!" And the others: "Speak! Speak!" And the first: "You are resolved rather to die than to famish?" "Resolved! Resolved!"

After a few sallies of derision the audience was quiet. The elderly Ukrainians were leaning forward alertly. So were the old Italians.

But alas! the actors were not good. They seemed to be imitating actors. Some of the younger men, whose short tunics revealed richly curved buttocks and shapely legs, were clearly the lovers of doting offstage powers.

A truck hurtling down the avenue struck a pothole

with a *thump* that shook the bleachers.

Something was troubling Taggart, pressing toward awareness, something to be attended to. . . .

A few rows away, a black youth mumbled persistently and chuckled. The teen-age girl in front of him, also black, stood up, turned to him, and struck him hard on the forehead with the flat of her hand. "You just SHUT UP, Marvin!" she said, "and let me hear Shakespeare!"

The leading actor entered. For a moment it was not clear that this was Caius Marcius, soon to be called Coriolanus. The actor was a tall, wiry, fierce-looking black with sharp features and snapping eyes. He spoke his first speech at a bad angle before an offstage light that transformed the abundant spray from his lips into a shower of glimmering particles, a golden full-disk halo that enveloped the head of the actor opposite.

"He that will give good words to thee will flatter beneath abhorring," the black was saying. His words crackled like running fire. "What would you have, you curs, that like nor peace nor war? The one affrights you, the other makes you proud. He that trusts to you, where he should find you lions, finds you hares; where foxes, geese."

The audience was transformed. There wasn't a murmur now, or a movement of elbows or feet. The stage had become a core of energy. The tall actor inhabited and surrounded the words. They expressed him, and he appeared to be their source, both passionate and intellectual.

Taggart put his lips to Karla's ear. "My God," he whispered, "we're really seeing something." She nodded and smiled. He felt a rush of affection for her and kissed her cheek. She took his hand and pressed it, and didn't release it.

A moment later the unknown thing that was troubling him troubled him again, and he looked aside in baffled consternation. The figure of the shrieking monkey came before his eyes, leaping this way and that against the leash. Taggart had felt defeated because he had held back and let it happen—yet he knew that he would not do differently another time: the risks were incommensurate, the youths would have stabbed him. So much of life was like this! One survived in prudence and was grateful . . . and little cells of spirit melted away. . . .

No, there was something pleasant in that unknown thing —something close and special. Yet he felt at fault and was anxious.

He became engrossed in the play again. And, as always happened, the stimulus provoked thoughts and feelings of his own, which flourished briefly in his consciousness. Yes, it would be a splendid thing even to make an archive of Everett's recollections, to say nothing of a book. He saw the vivid colors of the small Rivera above the plywood slab that served Everett as a desk. It was a rendering in oil of a detail from the grand mural at Cuernavaca: Zapata himself, standing before his horse, holding it close by the bit, so that its neck arched upward in a great white curve. Behind him one saw the stern faces, the sombreros and upward-slanting rifles of the *agraristas*. The artist had inscribed it: "Por Everett con un abrazo fuerte."

The audience was becoming restive. Taggart too. The play was an odd choice for such an occasion.

A huge plane in a holding pattern, waiting to land at Idlewild, passed over their heads, and nothing could be heard but the roar of its engines. The actors' voices struggled upward.

> call him,
> with all the applause and clamor of the host,
> Caius Marcius Coriolanus.

The actors cheered the tall black, whose face was bloody and who glanced this way and that without pleasure.

"Oh, my God!" said Taggart aloud. He said it in such a voice that Karla turned to him with alarm and said, "What is it, Taggart?"

"My God!" he said again. "What time is it?"

He said, "What time is it?" three times, first to Karla, who he knew didn't have a watch; then to a stout woman on his left, and before she had even turned her head, he saw that she didn't have a watch; and finally to a balding man in front of him, an Italian, who said, "Eh? Oh . . ." and turning his eyes back to the stage, raised a hairy forearm so that Taggart could see for himself. It was ten after nine.

Ten after nine! Tonight was his poetry reading at the Eiffel! He was appalled. How could he have forgotten? There were posters in the bookstores, and in a couple of the restaurants, and in the tobacco shop, and in four of the bars. He had seen them all. It seemed suicidal. Was it suicidal? "My God," he said again. He had forgotten completely.

"I'm reading at the Eiffel tonight," he whispered. "Karla, come with me . . . please . . . My God, I should have been there forty minutes ago!"

She, too, was alarmed. "Why, sure, Taggart," she said.

He clambered down the back of the stands and supported her as she came after him. As they ran to his apartment he planned his repertory: the new poems, certainly, all of them. And maybe a scene from the new play, that would be nice . . .

Later, as they went side by side toward Second Avenue, she tried to calm him. He was carrying a large manila envelope under his arm. He kept breaking into a trot. She told him there was no need to run. The poets were surely reading to one another.

"Taggart," she said. "Don't worry."

"But I'm late," he said. "It's awful to be late like this."

"You could get there at one o'clock and they'd still be there."

"Oh, no . . ."

"Sure they would. And if they ran out of poems, they'd just write some more in those little notebooks."

"Aw, Karla . . ."

"Okay . . ."

She ran beside him. Halfway down the block he slowed to a walk and put his arm around her waist; but every ten steps or so he broke into a trot, and she would shrug and smile and run beside him.

SHAWNO

Finches and morning. Euphoria. Shawno.

We could hear our children's voices in the darkness on the
sweet-smelling hill by my friend's house, and could hear the
barking of Angus, his dog. At nine o'clock Patricia put our
three into the car and went home. My friend's wife and son
said goodnight shortly afterward. By then he and I had gone
back to the roomy, decrepit, smoke-discolored, homy, extremely pleasant farmhouse kitchen and were finishing the
wine we had had at dinner. It was late August. Our northern
New England nights would soon make frost, but the cool of the
night was still enjoyable. He opened a bottle of *mezcal* he had
brought from Mexico, and we talked of the writings of friends,
and of the friends themselves, and of our youthful days in New
York. He had written a paper on Mahler. We listened to the
eighth and ninth symphonies, and the unfinished tenth, which
moved him deeply. We talked again. When we parted, the
stars, still yellow and numerous in most of the sky, had paled
and grown fewer in the east. I set out to walk the four miles
home.

I was euphoric, as happens at times, even without *mezcal.* For a short distance, since there was no one to disturb (the
town road is a dead-end road and I was at the end of it) I
shouted and sang. But the echoes of my voice sobered me and
a dog began to bark. The night air was moist and cool. I be-

came aware that something was calling for my attention, calling insistently, and then I realized that it was the stream, and so I listened for a while to its noisy bubbling. The lower stars were blocked by densely wooded hills. A dozen or fifteen old houses lay ahead of me, still darkened for sleep.

Angus came with me. He is a pointy-nosed, black-and-white mongrel in whom border collie predominates, and therefore is bright-eyed and quick-footed, and is amazingly interested in human affairs. He pattered along beside me, turning his head every few seconds to look at me, and it was as if he were keeping up continually a companionable cheerful jabbering. I spoke to him at one point and he barked lightly and jumped toward my face, hoping to kiss me.

Abruptly he sat down. We had come to the edge of what he imagined to be his territory, though in fact we had crossed his line several paces back. He sat there and cocked his head, watching me as I walked away. I had taken only twenty steps when on my right, with jarring suddenness, came the explosive deep barking of the German shepherd tied before the one new house in the valley. Angus sprang up, braced his legs, and hurled his own challenge, which was high-pitched and somewhat frantic, and immediately there came a barking that seemed limitless. I could hear it speeding away into the far distance, dog after dog repeating the challenge. Certainly it passed beyond our village, very likely beyond our state. I was in a corridor of barking dogs.

A soft projectile of some sort spurted from the shadows to my right and came to rest not far from my feet, where it turned out to be a chubby little pug. It was bouncing with excitement, and was giving vent through its open mouth to a continuous siren of indignation. The cluttered porch it had been guarding flared with light. Two elderly spinsters lived here. They rose with the sun, or before it, as did many of the older folk. The clapboards of their house had been a mustard color, the trim of the windows white, but that had been thirty years ago. The barn beside the house had fallen down, the apple trees had decayed, the mound of sheep manure was grassed over. The pug stopped barking and began to wheeze excitedly. It reared up and tapped its tiny paws against my shin, and looked at me out of bulging eyes that seemed adoring and shy. I patted him and scratched his ears. Twenty paces on I was startled by a barking more savage than that of the shepherd, a murderous, demented screaming that aroused real fear and detestation. He was chained to a dying apple tree before a collapsing gray house on the left side of the road. The hard-packed yard was crowded with wheelless cars. The dog was a Doberman. He leaped at me fiercely, leaped again and again, and was jerked back violently by the chain, as by the hand of a violent master.

Overlapping these disturbing sounds there came the melodious deep tones of the long-legged black hound tied before his own little house in the strange compound farther on: a mobile home, half of a barn, some small sheds, a corral, all huddled before the large trees that bordered the stream. Nothing was finished. There was an air of disconsolate ambition everywhere, failure, and disconsolate endurance. The hound itself seemed disconsolate. He was not tugging at his chain. He had not even braced his feet. He followed me with his eyes, barking his bark that was almost a baying and was actually beautiful. His head was cocked and he seemed to be listening to the other dogs.

What a racket! What a strange, almost musical hullabaloo! I myself was the cause of it, but it wouldn't end when I passed. The sun would be up, the dogs would keep barking, the birds would twitter and chirp, and that wave of noise, of energy and intention, would follow the sun right across the land.

More lights came on. The sun hadn't risen yet, but the night was gone. It was the morning dusk, fresh and cool. Birds had been calling right along, but now there were more. At intervals I could hear roosters. There were only three. The valley had been noisy once with crowing, and the asphalt road had been an earthen road, packed by wagon wheels and shaded by many elms. The elms were stumps now, huge ones.

Even so, it was beautiful. There were maples and pines beside the road, a few cows were still milked, a few fields were still hayed, a few eggs were still gathered, a few pigs transformed to pork, a few sheep to mutton.

Swallows were darting about. They perched in long rows on the electric wires.

A car passed me from behind, the first.

And Brandy, the Kimbers' gray-and-ginger mutt, trotted up from the stream and joined me. His hair was bristly, his legs short. He was muscular, energetic, stunted, bearded and mustachioed, like some old campaigner out of the hills of Spain. He went beside me a little way, cheerfully but without affection. There was no affection in him, but gregarious good cheer and selfish, robust curiosity. He left me to consort with a fluffy collie, who wasn't chained but wouldn't leave its yard. I passed another German shepherd, a chained husky, an aged cocker spaniel who barked from the doorstep and wouldn't even rise to do it. I came to a small house set back from the road by a small yard. A huge maple overspread the yard. Beneath the maple there stood a blue tractor, a large orange skidder, a pickup truck, two cars, a rowboat, a child's wagon, several bikes. A large, lugubrious Saint Bernard, who all summer had suffered from the heat, was chained to the tree, and she barked at me perfunctorily in a voice not unlike the hound's, almost a baying, but it wasn't a challenge bark at all, or much of one. She wanted to be petted, she wanted to lie down and be scratched, she wanted anything but to hurl a challenge; nevertheless, she barked; it would be shameful not to. I came to a boxer, tied; a purebred border collie, tied; a rabbit hound, tied; several mongrels, not tied, but clustered and apparently waiting for their breakfasts. One, a black, squat hound, had a lame foot and a blind eye, mementos of a terrible midwinter fight with a fox in defense of newborn pups, who froze to death anyway. She barked vociferously, but then ambled out to apologize and be petted. How fabulous our hands must seem to these fingerless creatures! What pleased surprises we bring to their foreheads, their throats and backs and bellies, touching as no dog can touch another dog. . . .

At almost every house there was a dog. At absolutely every house with a garden there was a dog. One must have one to raise food, or the woodchucks take it all. A second car passed me.

The turn to my own road was close now. In the crook of the turn there was a trailer, a so-called mobile home, covered with a second roof of wood. There were three small sheds around it, and a large garden out back, handsome now with the dark greens of potato plants and the lighter greens of bush beans. Near the garden were stakes and boxes for horseshoe pitching. A few steps away, at the edge of the stream, there were chairs, benches, and a picnic table. Two battered cars and a battered truck crowded the dooryard, in which there was also a tripod, taller than the trailer, made of strong young maples from the nearby woods. From its apex dangled a block and chain. Bantam hens were scratching the dirt.

The house was silent. All had watched TV until late at night and were still asleep, among them my seven-year-old daughter's new-found friend. The uproar of dogs was considerable here. Six were in residence, more or less. The young German shepherd was chained. The handsome boxer was free; in fact all the others were free, and with one exception ran to upbraid me and greet me. The exception, the incredibly pretty, positively magnetizing exception was Princess, the malamute, who did not bark or move. She lay at her royal ease atop a grassy mound that once had been an elm, her handsome wolflike head erect and one paw crossed demurely and arrogantly over the other. Her slanted almond-shaped eyes were placed close together and gave her an almost human oriental-slavic air. It was as if she knew she were being admired. She followed me impassively with those provocative eyes, disdaining to respond. How strange she was! She knew me well. If I went near her she'd suddenly melt. She'd sit up and lift one

paw tremblingly as high as her head in a gesture of adulation
and entreaty. She'd lay her head to one side and let it fall
closer and closer to her shoulder in a surrender irresistible in
its abject charm—"I am yours, yours utterly"—as if pulling the
weight of a lover down on top of her. She ends on her back at
such times, belly exposed, hind legs opened wide, lips pulled
back voluptuously and front paws tucked under in the air.
Especially in the winter, when she alone of the six dogs is
allowed into the lamplight of the little home, she indulges in
such tricks. The place is overheated. There are times when
everyone seems glassy with contentment, and times when bad
humor, apparently passing over into bad character, seems
hopeless and destructive, and there are quarrels as fierce as
the fights of cats. But peace comes again, usually by the inter-
vention of Betsy, the mother, who is mild and benign. She has
lost her front teeth and can't afford dentures, yet never hesi-
tates to smile. The children drink soda pop and watch TV,
while Verne, who is deep-voiced and patriarchal, with the
broad back and muscular huge belly of a Sumo wrestler, sits
at the kitchen table sipping beer from a can, measuring gun-
powder on a little balance scale, loading and crimping shotgun
shells and glancing at the program on the tube. He is opin-
ionated, vain, and egotistical, to the point of foolish pomposity,
but he is good-natured and earnest and is easily carried away
into animation, and then the posturing vanishes. He issues an
order, directs a booming word to one of the kids or dogs, but
especially to Princess, who draws effusions one wouldn't think
were in him. "Well, Princess!" he roars, "ain't you the
charmer! Ain't you my baby! Ain't you now! Oh, you want your
belly scratched? Well, we all do, Princess! We all do! But you're
the one that gits it, ain't you! Oh, yes you are! oh, yes!"

This morning I didn't stop to caress the malamute. At the
turn in the road I heard a far-off barking that made me smile
and want to be home. I crossed the cement bridge and turned
into a small dirt road. There wouldn't be a house now for a
mile, and then there would be ours and the road would end.

Day had begun. There was color in the sky. The moisture in the air was thinning.

The land was flat and paralleled the stream, which was to my right now. Here and there along its banks, in May, after the flood has gone down and the soil has warmed, we gather the just-emerging coils of the ferns called fiddleheads. Occasionally I have fished here, not really hopefully (the trout are few), but because the stream is so exciting. Once, however, while I knelt on the bank baiting my hook, I glanced into the water, deep at that point, and saw gliding heavily downstream a fish that seemed too big to be a trout. What a passion of helplessness I felt! I would have jumped on it if I could have. I learned later that ice had broken the dam to a private fishpond in the hills and this prize and many others had escaped down tributaries to the main stream and the river.

To my left, beyond a miniature bog of alders and swale lay a handsome small pond. Its outlet joined the stream fifty yards on, flowing under a bridge of stout pine stringers and heavy planks. The game warden had been here several times with dynamite, but the beavers had rebuilt their dam across the outlet, and once again the pond was eighteen inches higher than the stream. It was not unusual to see them. They had cut their half-tunnels under all these banks, creating concave, overhanging edges. I had stood here with the children one night, downstream from the bridge, at the water's edge, looking for beavers, and two had passed under our feet. It was a windless mellow night of full moon. I saw the glint of moonlight on the beaver's fur as he emerged from his channel under the bank, and then I saw his head quietly break the water. The dark shape of a second beaver, following him, glided like a phantom among the wavering images of the moon and trees.

I couldn't hear the barking on the hill anymore. I was hungry now and felt sleepy, but here between the pond and the stream the morning air was endlessly refreshing and I entered that pleasant state of being wholly relaxed, utterly drained of muscular energy, yet suffused by awareness, interest, and approval—the mild, benign energies of momentary happiness.

Five or six bright yellow streamers—so they seemed to be—approached me and sped by, dipping and rising. They were finches. The pattern of their flight was of long smooth waves, in the troughs of which they would flutter their wings to ascend the coming slope, but fold them before the top and soar curvingly over the crest. Sleek as torpedoes or little fish, they would glide downward again into the next trough and there extend their wings and flutter them.

A glossy red-winged blackbird emerged from a clump of alders and glided to a large gray stump.

Beyond the bridge the road began to climb. On both sides vigorous ferns, green but no longer the vivid green of summer, crowded the sunny space before the trees. The coolness of night still poured from the woods, mingling with the warmer air of the road.

Abruptly I heard and saw him, and though no creature is more familiar to me, more likely to be taken for granted, I was thrilled to see him again, and gladdened, more than gladdened, filled for a moment with the complex happiness of our relationship, which is both less than human and utterly human. Certainly I was made happy by his show of love for me. But my admiration of him is undiminished, and I felt it again, as always. He is the handsomest of dogs, muscular and large, with tufted golden fur. The sound of his feet was audible on the hard-packed, pebble-strewn road. I leaned forward and called to him and clapped my hands, and he accelerated, arching his throat and running with more gusto. He ran with a powerful driving stride that was almost that of a greyhound, and as he neared me he drew back his lips, arched his throat still more and let out a volley of ecstatic little *yips*. This sound was so puppyish, and his ensuing behavior so utterly without dignity, so close to fawning slavishness, that one might have contemned him for it, except that it was extreme, so extreme that there was no hint of fawning, and certainly not of cringing, but the very opposite: great confidence and security, into which there rose up explosively an ecstasy he couldn't contain and couldn't express rapidly enough to diminish, so that for a while he seemed actually to be in pain. I had to help him, had to let him lick my face protractedly and press his paws into my shoulders. And, as sometimes happens in such early-morning solitudes, there came over me a sense of the briefness of life, and of my kinship with all these other creatures who would soon be dead, and I almost spoke aloud to my dog: how much it matters to be alive together! how marvelous and brief our lives are! and how good it is, dear one that you are, to have the wonderful strange passion of your spirit in my life!

As he wound around me and pressed his body against mine, I remembered another greeting when I had seen blood on his teeth and feet. He was three then, in his prime. I had been away for several weeks—our first parting—and he had been baffled. When I came back I had reached this very place in the road, in my car, also in summer, when I saw him hurtling toward me. His first sounds were pathetic, a mixed barking, whimpering, and gulping for breath. I had to get out of the car to prevent him from injuring himself. I had to kneel in the road and let him kiss me and wind around me. He was crying; I had to console him. And then he was laughing, and dancing on his hind legs, and I laughed too, except that it was then that I noticed the blood. He had been in the house, Patricia told me later, and had heard the car. He had torn open the screen door with his teeth and claws, had chewed away some protective slats and had driven his body through the opening.

He danced around me now on his hind legs, licking my face. I knew that I could terminate this ecstasy by throwing a stone for him, which I did, hard and low, so that he wouldn't overtake it and break his teeth. A few moments later he laid it at my feet and looked into my face excitedly.

Patricia and the children were still sleeping. I ate breakfast alone, or rather with Shawno, who waited by my chair.

I had hoped to spend the morning writing, but my eyes were closing irresistibly. I pulled up bush beans in the garden, and carried tall spikes of bolted lettuce to the compost pile. There is a rough rail fence around the garden to keep the ponies out. Shawno lay beneath it and watched me. I cleared a few weeds and from time to time got rid of stones by flinging them absently into the woods. I pulled out the brittle pea vines from their chicken-wire trellis, rolled up the wire, and took it to the barn. After two hours of this I went to bed. Shawno had gone in already and was enjoying a second breakfast with the children. I had forgotten about him, but as I left the garden I saw by the fence, where the grass had been flattened by his body, a little heap of stones. He had chased and brought back every one I had tried to get rid of.

His parents. Incidents in the park.

When Patricia was pregnant with Ida we were living on Riverside Drive in New York. One bright October day we saw a crowd of people at the low stone wall of the park. Many were murmuring in admiration and a few almost shouted with delight. Down below, on the grassy flat, two dogs were racing. The first belonged to an acquaintance in our building. She was tawny and short-haired with the lines of a greyhound, except for a larger head and more massive shoulders. She was in heat and was leading the other in fantastic, playful sprints, throwing her haunches against him gaily and changing direction at great speed. The male, a Belgian shepherd with golden fur, was young and in a state of transport. He ran stiff-legged, arching his neck over her body with an eagerness that seemed ruthless, except that his ears were laid back shyly. The dogs' speed was dazzling; both were beauties, and the exclamations continued as long as they remained in sight.

Shawno was the largest of the issue of those memorable

nuptials. He arrived in our apartment when Ida was twelve weeks old. She looked down from her perch in Patricia's arms and saw him wobbling this way and that, and with a chortle that was almost a scream reached for him with both hands. Soon she was bawling the astonished, gasping wails of extreme alarm (his needle-point bites), and he was yelping piteously in the monkeylike grip with which she had seized his ear and was holding him at arm's length, out of mind, while she turned her tearful face to her mother.

These new beginnings, and especially my marriage with Patricia (it was my third marriage), occurring late in my maturity, ended a period of severe unhappiness. And I found that loving the child, holding and dandling her, playing little games with her, watching her sleep, and above all watching her nurse at Patricia's breast, awakened memories of my childhood I would never have guessed were still intact. Something similar happened with the dog. I began a regimen of early-morning running, as if he were an athlete and I his trainer, and I had trotted behind him through the weathers of several months before I realized that my happiness at these times was composed in part of recovered memories of the daybreak runnings of my youth, times so full of hope and satisfaction as to seem to me, now, paradisaical.

The dog developed precociously. At eighteen months he was jumping seven-foot walls, chasing sticks I threw for him. He was a delight to watch, powerful and beautiful, with a quality of spirit that was like the nonchalant gaiety of human youth. He became a personage in the park and acquired a band of children, who left their games to play with him, and invented new games to include him. It was not only his prowess that attracted them, but the extraordinary love he showed them. The truth was, he was simply smitten with the human race. I was crossing upper Broadway with him once; he was leashed; the crossing was crowded. There came toward us an old gentleman holding a four-year-old boy by the hand. The boy's face and the dog's were on a level, and as they passed the two faces turned to each other in mutual delight, and Shawno bestowed a kiss that began at one ear, went all the way across and ended at the other. I glanced back. The boy, too, was glancing back, grinning widely. In fact, the boy and Shawno were looking back at each other. This incident is paired for all time with another that I witnessed in New York and that perhaps could not have occurred in any other city. It was in the subway at rush hour. The corridors were booming with the grinding roar of the trains and the pounding of thousands of almost running feet. Three corridors came together in a Y and two of them were streaming with people packed far tighter than soldiers in military formation. The columns were approaching each other rapidly. There was room to pass, but just barely, or not quite. The columns collided. That is, their inside corners did, and each of these was occupied by an apparently irascible man. Each hurled one, exactly one, furious round-house blow at the other, and both were swept away in their columns—a memorable fight.

I would never have known certain people in New York if it hadn't been for the dog; worse, it would never have occurred to me that knowing them was desirable, or possible, whereas in fact it was delightful. The people I mean were children. What could I have done without the dog? As it was, I changed my hours in order to meet them, and they—a group of eight or so—waited for us devotedly after school. Most were Puerto Rican. The youngest was only seven, the eldest eleven. They would spread themselves in a circle with the dog in the center and throw a ball back and forth, shouting as he leaped and tried to snatch it from the air. When he succeeded, which was often, one saw the merriest and most musical of chases, the boys arranged behind the dog according to speed of foot, the dog holding the ball high, displaying it provocatively, looking back over his shoulder and trotting stiff-legged just fast enough to elude the foremost boy, winding that laughing, shouting, almost singing line of children this way and that through the park. Invariably the boys asked me to make him leap, and I would throw the ball over fences and walls. Perhaps in emulation of the dog—and certainly because I myself wanted to do more than watch—we began a game of leaping, or rather of flying through the air, the boys diving headfirst from the steep stone wall by the stairs, holding out their arms like wings . . . and I would catch them at the armpits and set them on the ground. Most were too heavy to dive from very high, but one, a bold and wiry seven-year-old, launched himself from heights that made a few bystanders turn away in horror. He held out his arms like sparrows' wings, and lifted his head, his face shining with bliss. I would catch him and he would dart away to try it again, apparently unaware of the awe and the smiles of admiration on the faces of his friends. I discovered later that some of our audience came on purpose at this time to watch the children and the dog. One elderly white-haired man I have never forgotten. He was Jewish and spoke with a German accent, wore a felt hat and expensive coats. He came to the playground regularly and stood with his hands behind his back, his head dropped forward, nodding and chuckling, and smiling unweariedly. His face was wonderful. It was intelligent and kindly, was still strong, still handsome, and it possessed a quality I have come to associate with genius, an apparent unity of feeling, an alacrity and wholeness of response. Whatever he was feeling suffused his face; he didn't have attitudes toward his feelings, and counter-attitudes toward his attitudes. The dog delighted him. He deferred to the headlong, boisterous children, who when Shawno would appear would shout happily and in unison, and Shawno would go to them, bounding exuberantly, but it wouldn't be long before the old gentleman would call him, and Shawno would leave the children, not bounding now but sweeping his tail in such extreme motions that his hind legs performed a little dance from side to side independently of his front legs. The old gentleman would lean over him, speak to him, and pet him, and the dog would press against his legs and look into his face. We usually talked for a few minutes before

I went home. When I asked him about his work and life he waved away the questions with gestures that were humorous and pleading yet were impressive in their authority. One day I recognized his face in a photograph in the *Times,* alas, on the obituary page. He was an eminent refugee scholar, a sociologist. I discovered, reading the description of his career, that I had studied briefly with his son at Columbia. By this time we had moved to the remote farmhouse in the country and our second child had been born.

Past lives. Streams. Ferocity and family concern.

Our house had been occupied by Finns, as had many others near us. The hill, actually a ridge, sloped away on two sides, one forested and the other, to the south, open pasture with the remnants of an orchard. At the bottom of these fields was a stream, and in a bend of the stream, a sauna. It was here that the old Finn who had built the house had bathed his invalid wife, carrying her back and forth every day until her final illness. From this same small pool he had carried water in buckets to the garden a few strides away. The sauna was damaged beyond repair, but we let it stand; and we brought back the garden, which now was one of three. For the few years that country living sustained the glow of romance, this garden was my favorite, and I carried water to it in buckets, as had the old man. Just beyond the sauna a wooded slope rose steeply. Raccoons and deer entered our field here, and it was here that the ponies and dog all came to drink.

There were other relics of those vanished lives: handmade apple boxes with leather hinges cut from old boots; in all the sheds door handles made of sapling crotches; a split round apple ladder with flakes of spruce bark on the sides and rungs made of rock maple saplings; ten-foot Finnish skis that had been cut by hand and bent at the tips with steam from a kettle. There were hills wherever one looked, and there had been farms on all the hills. Some of the Finns had skied to market, and had cruised their woodlots on skis. Some of their children had skied to school.

The hills and ridges are so numerous that in the spring, while the snow is melting, the sound of water can be heard everywhere. It pours and tumbles; there is a continual roaring; and when the thaw is well advanced the large stream in the valley makes the frightening sounds of flood, hurling chunks of ice ahead of it, crowding violently into the curves, and hurtling over falls so deep in spume that the rocks are out of sight. Later, in the hot weather, one hears the braided sounds and folded sounds of quiet water. The orange gashes and abrasions on the trunks of trees are darkening. More trees are dead. The banks of the streams, however beautiful, and however teeming with new life, are strewn with debris in many stages of decay.

The streams have become presences in my life. For a while they were passions. There are few that I haven't fished and walked to their source. These have been solitary excursions, except for the single time that I took the dog. His innocent trotting at the water's edge disturbed the trout. Still worse was his drinking and wading in the stream. I called him out. He stood on the bank and braced his legs and shook himself. Rather, he was seized by a violent shaking, a shaking so swift and powerful as to seem like a vibration. It shook his head from side to side, then letting his head come to rest took his shoulders and shook them, then his ribs, and in a swift, continuous wave passed violently to his haunches, which it shook with especial vigor, and then entered his tail and shook the entire length of it, and at last, from the very tip, sprang free, leaving behind, at the center of the now-subsided aura of sparkling waterdrops, an invigorated and happy dog. It was at this moment of perfected well-being that one of those darting slim shadows caught his eye. He dove into the water headfirst, and thrust his snout to the very bottom, where he rooted this way and that. He emerged and looked in amazement from side to side. The trout had vanished without trace. The dog had no notion even of the direction of its flight. He thrust down his head again and turned over stones, then came up, smooth and muscular, with his streaming fur clinging to him, and stood there peering down, poised in the electric stillness of the hunter that seems to be a waiting but is actually a fascination. Years later, after my own passion for trout had cooled, I would see him poised like that in the shallows of the swimming hole, ignoring the splashing, shouting children, looking down, still mesmerized, still ready—so he thought— to pounce.

During most of the thaw there is little point in going into the woods. Long after the fields have cleared and their brown is touched with green, there'll be pools and streaks of granular snow, not only in the low-lying places in the woods, but on shadowed slopes and behind rocks. For a while the topmost foot of soil is too watery to be called mud. The road to our house becomes impassable, and for days, or one week, or two, or three, we park at the bottom of the road and walk home wearing rubber boots and carrying the groceries and perhaps the youngest children in knapsacks and our arms. This was once a corduroy road, and it never fails that some of the logs have risen again to the surface.

Spring in the north is almost violent: after the period of desolation, when the snow has gone and everything that once was growing seems to have been bleached and crushed, and the soil itself seems to have been killed by winter, there comes, accompanied by the roaring of the streams, a prickling of the tree buds that had formed in the cold, and a prickling of little stems on the forest floor, and a tentative, small stirring of bird life. This vitalizing process, once begun, becomes bolder, more lavish, and larger, and soon there is green everywhere, and the open fretwork of branches, limbs, and trunks, beyond which all winter we had seen sky, hills, and snow, has become an eye-stopping mass of green. The roaring of the streams diminishes, but the velocity of green increases until the inter-locking leaves can't claim another inch of sunlight except by slow adjustment and the killing of rival growth. Now the ani-mal presence is spread widely through the woods, and Shawno runs this way and that, nose to the ground, excited and dis-tracted by overlapping trails.

It was in this season of early summer that we came here. The woods were new to me. I was prepared for wonders. And there occurred a small but strange encounter that did indeed prove haunting. We had been walking a woods road, Shawno and I, or the ghost of a road, and came to a little dell, dense with ferns and the huge leaves of young striped maples. Shawno drew close to me and seemed disturbed. He stood still for a moment, sniffing the air instead of the ground, and then the fur rose on his neck and he began to growl. At that mo-ment there emerged from the semi-dark of a dense leaf bank, perhaps thirty steps away, two dogs, who stopped silently and came no further. The smaller dog was a beagle, the larger a German shepherd, black and gigantic. His jowls on both sides and his snout in front bristled with white-shafted porcupine quills. He didn't seem to be in pain, but seemed helpless and pathetic, a creature without fingers or tools, and therefore doomed. The uncanny thing about the dogs was their stillness. Shawno continued to growl and to stamp his feet uncertainly. Just as silently as they had appeared, the beagle and the shep-herd turned into the undergrowth and vanished.

I was to see these two dogs again. In the meantime, I learned that it was not uncommon for dogs to run wild, or to lead double lives; and that such pairings of scent and sight were frequent. The beagle could follow a trail. The shepherd had sharp eyes, was strong, and could kill.

In the city there had been but one threat to Shawno's life. Here there were several. He was large and tawny, and though he was lighter in color, he resembled a deer far more closely than had the cows, sheep, and horses that in the memory of my neighbors had been shot for deer—certainly more closely than had the goat that had been gutted in the field and brought to the village on the hood of the hunter's car. With such anecdotes in mind, I discovered one day, toward the end of hunting season, that Shawno had escaped from the house. At least eight hunters had gone up our road into the woods. I know now that his life was not at quite the risk that I imagined, but at that time I was disturbed. I ran into the woods calling to him and whistling, and wondering how I could find him if he'd already been shot. Several hours later, he emerged into our field loping and panting, and came into the house, and with a clatter of elbows and a thump of his torso dropped into his nook by the woodstove. He held his head erect and looked at me. The corners of his lips were lifted. His mouth was open to the full, and his extended tongue, red with exertion, vibrated with his panting in a long, highly arched curve that turned up again at its tip. He blinked as the warmth took hold of him, and with a grunt that was partly a sigh stretched his neck forward and dropped his chin on his paws.

In February of that winter I saw the beagle and German shepherd again. We were sharing a load of hay with a distant neighbor, an elderly man whose bachelor brother had died and who was living alone among the bleached and crumbling remains of what had been once a considerable farm. He still raised a few horses and trained them for harness, though there wasn't a living in it. I had backed the truck into the barn and was tossing up bales to him where he stood in the hayloft when a car drew up and a uniformed man got out. I recognized the game warden, though I had never met him. He was strikingly different from the police of the county seat ten miles away, who walked with waddling gaits and could be found at all hours consuming ice cream at the restaurant on the highway south. The warden was large but trim, was actually an imposing figure, as he needed to be—he had made enemies, and they had tried to kill him, once by shooting through the window, another time by throwing a gasoline bomb that had brought down the house in flames, at night, in winter. He and his wife and adolescent son had escaped. He was spoken of as a fanatic, but hunters praised his skill as a hunter. A man who had paid a fine for poaching said to me, "If he's after you in the woods he'll git you. No man can run through the woods like him." His large round eyes were a pale blue. Their gaze was unblinking, open, disturbingly strange.

He addressed the elderly man by his last name. The warden, too, was a scion of an old, old family here.

"We'd all be better off," he said, "if you'd kept him chained."

His voice was emphatic but not angry. He spoke with the unconscious energy and loudness that one hears in many of the rural voices. "He's been runnin' deer, and you know it. I caught him at the carcass. It was still kickin'." The warden handed him the piece of paper he had been carrying, which was obviously a summons. "I've done away with him," he said.

We had come out of the barn. The warden went to his car, opened the trunk, and came around to us with the small stiff body of the beagle. Its eyes and mouth were open, its tongue protruded between its teeth on one side, and its chest was matted with blood. The warden laid the body on the snowbank by the barn and said, "Come back to the car a minute."

The black German shepherd lay on a burlap sack, taking up the whole of the trunk.

"You know who owns that?"

The elderly man shook his head. No emotion had appeared on his face since the warden had arrived. The warden turned his blue, strangely unaggressive eyes on me and repeated the question. I too shook my head. The shepherd had been home since I had seen him in the woods: someone had pulled out the quills.

Shawno was barking from the cab of the truck. I had left the window open to give him air. It was his questioning, information-wanting bark. The smell of the dead dogs had reached him.

After the warden left, my neighbor went into the house and came back with money for the hay.

"Obliged to you for haulin' it," he said.

That night, on the phone, I told a friend, a hunter, about the dogs.

"The warden was right," he said. "Dogs like that can kill a deer a day, even more. Jake Wesley's dogs cornered a doe in my back field last year. She was pregnant with twins. They didn't bother killing her, they don't know how; they were eating her while she stood there. She was ripped to shreds. I shot them both."

There was a crust on the snow just then. Dogs could run on it, but the sharp hooves of the deer would break through and the ice cut their legs. They spent such winters herded in evergreen groves, or "yards," and if the bark and buds gave out many would starve. Occasionally the wardens took them hay, but this introduced another problem, for if the dogs found the snowmobile trails and followed them to the yards, the slaughter could be severe.

And what of Shawno? I realized that I regarded him habitually with the egocentricity of a doting master, as if he were a creature chiefly of his human relations, though certainly I knew better. I thought of the many cats his ferocious mother had killed. And I remembered how, the previous fall, while our children were playing with a neighbor's children in front of our house, Shawno had come into their midst with a freshly killed woodchuck. He held his head high and trotted proudly among us, displaying his kill. It was a beautiful chestnut color and it dangled flexibly full-length from his teeth, jouncing limply as he trotted. He placed it on the ground under the large maple, where he often lay, and stretched out above it, lionlike, the corpse between his paws. I was tying a shoelace for one of the children. I heard a rushing growl of savagery and out of the corner of my eye saw Shawno spring forward. I shouted and jumped in front of him. One of the visiting boys had come too close.

I doubt that Shawno would have bitten him. Nevertheless, in that frightening moment I had seen and heard the animal nervous system that is not like ours, but is capable of an explosive violence we never approximate, even in our most excessive rages.

He was with me in the pickup one day when I went for milk to a neighbor's dairy. There were usually dogs in front of the barn and Shawno was on friendly terms with them. This time, however, before I had shut off the motor, he leaped across me in the cab, growling and glaring, his snout wrinkled and his front teeth bared to the full. His body was tense, and instantaneously had been charged with an extraordinary energy. Down below, also growling, was a large black hound with yellow eyes. The window was open. Before I could close it or speak to him, Shawno put his head and shoulders through the opening, and with a push of his hind feet that gouged the seat cover, dove down on the hound.

There were no preliminaries. They crashed together with gnashing teeth and a savage, high-pitched screaming.

The fight was over in a moment. Shawno seized him by the neck, his upper teeth near the ear, his lower on the throat, and driving forward with his powerful hind legs twisted him violently to the ground.

The hound tried to right himself. Shawno responded with sirenlike growls of rage and a munching and tightening of teeth that must have been excruciating. The hound's yellow eyes flashed. He ceased struggling. Shawno growled again, and this time shook his head from side to side in the worrying motion with which small animals are killed. The hound lay still. Shawno let him up. The hound turned its head away. Shawno pressed against him, at right angles, extending his chin and entire neck over the hound's shoulder. The hound turned its head as far as it could in the other direction.

The fight was over. There was no battle for survival, as in the Jack London stories that had thrilled me in my youth. Survival lay precisely not in tooth and claw, but in the social signaling that tempered the dogs' savagery, as it tempers that of wolves. It was this that accounted for the fact that one never came upon the carcasses of belligerent dogs who had misconceived their powers, as had the hound.

The victory was exhilarating. What right had I, who had done nothing but watch, to feel exultation and pride? Yet I did feel these things. Shawno felt them too, I'm sure. He sat erect beside me going home, and there was still a charge of energy, an aura about his body. He held his head proudly, or so I thought. His mouth was open, his tongue lolled forward, and he was panting lightly. From time to time he glanced aside at me out of narrowed eyes. I kept looking at him, kept smiling, and couldn't stop. I reached across and stroked his head and spoke to him, and again he would glance at me. He was like the roughneck athlete heroes of my youth, who after great feats in the sandlot or high school football games, begrimed, bruised, and wet-haired, would walk to the locker rooms or the cars, heads high, helmets dangling from their fingertips or held in the crooks of their arms, riding sweet tides of exhaustion and praise. I remembered the glorious occasions, too, after I had come of an age to compete, when my brief inspirations on the field had been rewarded by teammates' arms around my shoulders.

But there was more to it than this. It was as if I had been made larger and stronger by his power; it was as if my very existence had been multiplied because he was my ally and loved me. These, so I take it, were the feelings of the boy who still lived in me and who looked with happy gratitude at this guardian with thick fur and fearsome teeth, who could leap nonchalantly over the truck we now rode in, and who had devoted his powers utterly to the boy's well-being.

Very little of this came into my voice when I said at home, "Shawno got into a fight!"

Ida and Patricia came close to me, asking, "What happened? What happened?"

Ida had never witnessed the animal temper I have

just described. What she wanted to know was, had he been bitten?

If anyone had said to Shawno what the little boy says in Ida's *Mother Goose,* "Bow wow wow, whose dog art thou?" he could not have answered except by linking Ida's name with my own. He often sat by her chair when she ate. Three of the five things he knew to search for and fetch belonged to Ida: her shoes, her boots, her doll. When I read to her in the evening she leaned against me on the sofa and Shawno lay on the other side with his head in her lap. Often she fell asleep while I read, and we would leave her there until we ourselves were ready for bed. When we came for her Shawno would be asleep beside her. On the nights when I carried her, still awake, to her bed, she would insist that both Shawno and Patricia come kiss her goodnight, and both would. Usually he would leap into the bed, curl up beside her, and spend part of the night. When she was five or six we bought two shaggy ponies from a neighbor and having fenced the garden let them roam as they would. The larger pony had been gelded, but was still mischievous and inclined to nip. Late one afternoon I glanced from an upstairs window and saw Ida leading Liza and Jacob across the yard, all three holding hands. Jacob had just learned to walk and they were going slowly. The ponies came behind them silently. Starbright, the gelding, drew close to Jacob and seemed about to nudge him, which he had done several times in recent weeks, toppling him over. Shawno was watching from across the yard. He sprang forward and came running in a crouch, close to the ground. I called Patricia to the window. His style was wonderful to see, so calm and masterful. There had been a time when he had harried the ponies gleefully, chasing them up and down the road without mercy, snapping at their feet, leaping at their shoulders, and dodging their kicks with what, to them, must have been exasperating ease. I had had to reprimand him several times before he would give it up. Now silently, and crouching menacingly, he moved in behind the children and turned to face the ponies. Star-bright knew that he would leap but didn't know when, and began to lift his feet apprehensively. Shawno waited . . . and waited . . . and the pony apparently breathed a sigh of relief, and abruptly Shawno leapt, darting like a snake at Starbright's feet. The pony pulled back in alarm, and wheeled, obliging the smaller pony to wheel too. Shawno let them come along then, but followed the children himself, glancing back to see that the ponies kept their distance. The children hadn't seen a bit of this. "What a darling!" said Patricia. "What a good dog!"

Down to Searles.

The owners of bitches, when their dogs were in heat, were often obliged to call the owners of males and request that they be taken home and chained. Four days went by once before we could locate Shawno. At last the call came. He had traveled several miles. When I went for him he wouldn't obey me, was glassy-eyed and frantic. The only way to get him home was to put the bitch in the car and lure him. It was pathetic. He hadn't slept for four days, was thin, had been fighting with other males, and had had no enjoyment at all: the bitch was a feisty little dachshund. For two days he lay chained on the porch, lost utterly in gloom. He didn't respond to anyone, not even to Ida, but kept his chin flat between his paws and averted his eyes. He had gone to bitches before, but I had been able to fetch him. He had suffered frustration before, but had recovered quickly. What was different this time? I never knew.

Apart from these vigils of instinct, his absences were on account of human loves, the first and most protracted of which was not a single person but a place and situation irresistible to his nature. This was the general store.

The one-story white clapboard building was near the

same broad stream that ran through the whole of the valley. The banks were steep here and the stream curved sharply, passing under a bridge and frothing noisily over a double ledge of rounded rocks. There had used to be horseshoe pits by the road and games before supper and at night under the single light at the corner of the store. Three roads converged here. One was steep and on winter Sundays and occasional evenings had been used for sledding. That was when the roads had been packed, not plowed, and the only traffic had been teams and sleds. Searles's father—the second of the three generations of C. W. Searles—though he was known to be a hard and somewhat grasping man, would open the store and perhaps bring up cider for the sledders. There would be a bonfire in the road, and as many as a hundred people in motion around it.

Searles was sixty years old when we arrived. The store was wonderfully well organized and good to look at, crowded but neat and logical, filled with implements of the local trades and pleasures. Searles had worked indoors for his father as a boy. Later, as a youth, he had gone with a cart and horse to the outlying farms, taking meat, hardware, clothing, and tools and bringing back not cash but eggs, butter, apples, pears, chickens, shingles. Now when he ordered the pâté called *creton,* he knew it would be consumed by the Dulacs, Dubords, and Pelletiers. The five sets of rubber children's boots were for the Barkers and were in the proper sizes. He displayed them temptingly, brought down the price, and finally said, "Why don't you take the lot, Charlie, and make me an offer?" He knew who hunted and who fished, and what state their boots, pants, and coats were in. A death in the town affected his business. He saw the price of bullets going sky-high, put in several shell- and bullet-making kits, and said, "Verne, what do you figure you spend a year on shells and bullets?" "Oh, it's horrible. I don't practice no more, that's what's come to . . ."

In the summer there were rakes, hoes, spades, cultivators, coils of garden hose, sections of low white fencing to put around flower beds, and perhaps a wheelbarrow arrayed on the loading apron in front of the store. In the fall, on the same apron, one found crated woodstoves, sections of black stovepipe, rolls of asphalt sheeting, rolls of plastic sheeting for window insulation, while inside, on racks, were checkered red-and-black hunting coats of thick wool, orange vests, orange caps, boxes of shells. When the getting-ready time was past and winter was really here, one saw stacks of broad shovels out front, and two or three of the large, flat-bottomed snow scoops that had to be pushed with both hands. Set up in rows on the window shelves were insulated rubber boots with felt liners, and two styles of snowshoes, glistening with varnish. Late in winter the sugaring supplies appeared: felt filters, wooden and metal spigots, zinc buckets with creased lids; and these were followed shortly by the racks of seeds to be started indoors, and the new fishing rods, new reels, the same old lures and hooks. At all times there were axes and axe handles, bucksaws, wooden wedges and iron wedges, birch hooks, a peavey or two, many chainsaw files and cans of oil. For years he kept a huge skillet that finally replaced, as he knew it would, the warped implement at the boys' camp. He carried kitchenware and electrical and plumbing supplies, and tools for carpentry, as well as drugstore items, including a great deal of Maalox. All this was in addition to the food, the candy rack, the newspapers, the greeting cards, and the school supplies.

People stopped to talk. Those he liked—some of whom he had sat beside in the little red schoolhouse up the road, long unused now—would stand near the counter for half an hour exchanging news or pleasantries. One day I heard Franklin Mason, who was five years older than Searles, say testily, "I seen 'em, I seen 'em." He was referring to the shingling brackets that had been propped up prominently at the end of the counter. Searles had known for two years that Mason wanted to replace his roofing; he had just learned that Mason had decided on asphalt shingles. "I might borrow Mark's brackets," said Mason, but he added, in a different tone, scratching his face, "these are nice, though. . . ."

People didn't say "Searles's place," but "down to Searles." "Oh, they'll have it down to Searles." "I stopped in down to Searles." "Let me just call down to Searles." He was C. W. the third, but had been called Bob all his life.

Of the men in the village he was certainly the least rural. He had grown up on a farm, loved to hunt and fish, play poker, drink whiskey, and swap yarns. But he had gone away to college, and then to business school, and had worked in Boston for three years. He was not just clever or smart but was extremely intelligent, with a meticulous, lively, retentive mind. He had come home not because he couldn't make a go of things in the city, but because he loved the village and the countryside and sorely missed the people. He subscribed to the *Wall Street Journal* and the *New York Times,* read many periodicals, was interested in politics and controversy and changing customs. When I met him his three children were away at college. We disagreed irreconcilably on politics. I was aware of his forbearance and was grateful for it. And I was impressed by his wit, and by his kindliness, as when, without reproach or impatience he would allow certain impoverished children to cluster for long, long minutes before the candy rack, blocking his narrow aisle; and as when he built a ramp for the wheelchair of a neighbor who could no longer walk but was still alert and lively. He was not a happy man. He drank too much to be healthy, and his powers of mind by and large went unused. Yet one could sense in him a bedrock of contentment, and a correct choice of place and work. He was tall and bony, carried far too large a stomach, and was lame in one leg. In damp weather he used a cane and moved with some difficulty about the store. I came to see that most of his friends were old friends and were devoted to him. I learned too that he had forgiven many debts and had signed over choice lots of land to the town, one for a ball field, another for picnics. His gregarious cocker spaniel, who possessed no territorial sense at all, lounged in the aisles and corners, and on sunny days could be found on the loading apron under the awning. And it was here, in front of the store, beside the caramel-colored spaniel, that one sunny day I encountered my own dog, who had vanished from the house.

He leaped up gaily, showing no guilt at all, and came beside me when I went into the store.

Searles, on the high stool, was leaning over the *Wall Street Journal* that was spread across the counter. The moment he raised his head, Shawno looked at him alertly.

Searles smiled at me. "I've got a new friend," he said; and to the dog, "Haven't I, Shawno? What'll you have, Shawno? Do you want a biscuit? Do you?" Shawno reared, put his front paws on the counter and barked.

"Oh, you do?" said Searles. "Well, I happen to have one."

He put his hand under the counter, where he kept the dog biscuits that had fattened the spaniel.

"Will you pay for it now?" he said. "Will you? Will you, Shawno?"

Shawno, whose paws were still on the counter, barked in a deep, almost indignant way. Searles was holding the biscuit, not offering it.

"Oh, you want it on credit?" he said. He held up the biscuit, and at the sight of it the dog barked in lighter, more eager tones. "What?" said Searles. "You want it free?" Again Shawno barked, the eagerness mixed now with impatience and demand. "All right," said Searles. "Here 'tis. On the house." He held it out and Shawno took it with a deft thrust of his head.

I had watched all this with a long-lasting uncomfortable smile.

I said that I hoped the dog wasn't a nuisance.

"Oh no," said Searles. "He's a good dog. He's a fine dog."

And I looked at Shawno, who was looking at Searles, and I thought, "You wretch, you unfaithful wretch! How easy it is to buy you!"

Yet I let him go back there again and again. He'd trot away in the morning as if he were going off to work, and then at suppertime would appear on the brow of the hill, muddied and wet, having jumped into the stream to drink.

I didn't have the heart to chain him. And I couldn't blame him. What better place for a gregarious dog than this one surviving social fragment of the bygone town? There were other dogs to run with, there was the store itself with its pleasant odors, there was Searles, my rival, with his biscuits, there were children to make much of him, and grownups by the score. Moreover, there were cars, trucks, and delivery vans, and all had been marked by the dogs of distant places. We would arrive for groceries or mail and find him stretched on the apron in front of the store, or playing in the road with other dogs, or standing in a cluster of kids with bikes, or stationed by the counter inside, looking up inquiringly at customers who were chatting with Searles.

My jealousy grew. I was disgruntled and seriously ill-at-ease. Somewhere within me I was saying, "Don't you love me anymore? Have you forgotten how I raised you and trained you? Have you forgotten those mornings in the park when I threw sticks for you and taught you to leap? Have you forgotten our walks here in the woods, and the thousand discoveries we've made together?"

Most serious of all was his absence while I worked. I had built a little cabin half a mile from the house. He had been a presence, almost a tutelary spirit, in the very building of it, and then he had walked beside me every day to and from it, and had lain near my feet while I wrote or read. Often when I turned to him he would already have seen the movement and I would find his eyes waiting for mine.

Those inactive hours were a poor substitute for the attractions of the store, and I knew it, in spite of our companionable lunches and afternoon walks. But what of me?

One day, several weeks after his first visit to the store, I jumped into the car and went down there rather speedily,

254   A TALE OF PIERROT

ordered him rather firmly into the back seat, and took him home. I did the same thing the following day. The day after that I chained him, and the day after that chained him again.

Life returned to normal. I took away the chain. He was grateful and stopped moping. I saw that he had renounced his friends at the store, and I was glad, forgetting that I had forced him to do it. Anyway, those diversions had never canceled his love for me—so I reminded myself, and began to see fidelity where I had established dependence. But that didn't matter. The undiminished, familiar love wiped out everything—at least for me.

Eddie Dubord. Sawyer's Labrador. Quills.

Just below us in the woods the stream was speeded by a short channel of granite blocks, though the mill wheel was gone that once had turned continuously during thaw, reducing small hills of cedar drums to stacks of shingles. There had been trout for a while in the millrace, but chubs, which eat the eggs of trout, had driven them away.

Upstream of this ghost of a mill, just beyond the second of two handsome waterfalls, one stringer of a rotted bridge still joined the banks. Snowmobilers had dropped a tree beside it and had nailed enough crossboards to make a narrow path. I had crossed it often on snowshoes, and then on skis, and the dog had trotted behind, but there came a day in spring, after the mud had dried, when Shawno drew back and stood there on the bank stamping his feet, moving from side to side indecisively, and barking. He had seen the turbulent water between the boards of the bridge. I picked him up and carried him across, and couldn't help laughing, he was so big, such a complicated bundle in my arms, and I remembered how he had nestled there snugly as a pup, lighter and softer than Ida.

Beyond the bridge a grassy road curved away into the

trees. In somewhat more than a mile it would join the tarred road, but halfway there, on the inside of its curve, a wagon trail branched off, now partly closed by saplings. It was here at the corner of this spur that my neighbor Eddie Dubord built a small cabin similar to my own.

It was summer. The dog had gone with the children to the swimming hole and I was walking alone carrying a small rod and a tin of worms. I saw two wedges of smoke ahead of me, expanding and thinning in the slight breeze, and then I saw a parked car and a man working at something. The smoke was blowing toward him and came from two small fires spaced twelve feet apart. The man was blocky and short. He wore a visored cap of bright orange and a chore jacket of dark blue denim. His movements were stiff and slow, yet there was something impressive and attractive about the way he worked. Every motion achieved something and led to the next without waste or repetition. He went to one of the fires carrying an axe, which he used only to lift some pine boughs from a pile. He threw several on each of the fires. I walked closer, but stopped again and watched him. We had never met, but I knew that it was Dubord. He was seventy-four years old. He had driven the corner stakes to mark the floor of a cabin, had tied a cord on one of them and had carried it around the others. Evidently he had already leveled the cord. I watched him as he picked up a five-foot iron bar and went away dragging a stoneboat that was simply the hood of an ancient car turned upside down and fitted with a rope that could be used as a yoke. He stopped at a pile of stones, and with his bar levered a large flat stone onto the car hood. With the same bar he lifted the yoke to where he could reach it. He stepped into the yoke, placed it across his chest and under his armpits, and angling his substantial weight sharply forward, using the heavy bar now as a staff, set the skid in motion and dragged it easily to one of the corner stakes. When I walked by he was on his hands and knees firming the stone and didn't see me.

Several days later I went that way again, and again

stopped to watch him. He had finished the floor and had built a low platform the length of it, and had equipped the platform with steps. He would be able to work on the rafters and roof without resorting to a ladder.

He had assembled several units of studs, rafters, and cross braces, and now as I watched he pushed one erect with a stick, and caught it in the fork of a long pole that held it while he adjusted it for plumb. He nailed bracing boards at the sides, and drove in permanent nails at the base. His concentration was remarkable. It was as total and self-forgetful as a child's. Later, after I had come to know him well, I marveled more, not less, at this quality. I had seen him at work on all kinds of things: radios and TVs, pop-up toasters, lawn mowers, snow-blowers, Rototillers, outboard motors, locks, shotguns, clocks. On several occasions I had come close to him and had stood beside him wondering how to announce my presence . . . but it had never mattered how—he had looked up always with a start of panic, and then had blushed. It was not merely as if his concentration had been disturbed, but as if some deep, continuous melody had been shattered. Then he would smile shyly and greet me in his unassuming, yet gracious, almost courtly way.

He had already roofed the cabin and was boarding the sides—on the diagonal, as the old farmhouses were boarded—when we finally met. And, as has often happened, it was the dog who introduced us, ignoring utterly the foolish shyness on both sides.

The smudge fires were going again to drive away the bugs. A small stack of rough-cut boards lay on a pallet of logs. Dubord had just hung the saw on a prong of the sawhorse and was carrying a board to the wall when Shawno trotted up to him and barked. He was startled and backed away defensively, ready to use the board as a weapon. But Shawno was wagging his tail in the extreme sweeps of great enthusiasm, and he did something he had almost abandoned since our coming to the country: he reared up, put his paws on Dubord's broad chest, and tried to lick his weathered, leathery face with its smoke-haze of white stubble beard. By the time I reached them Shawno had conquered him utterly. Dubord was patting the dog, bending over him, and talking to him in that slurred, attractive baritone voice that seemed to have knurls in it, a grain and dark hue as of polished walnut, and that he seemed to savor in his throat and on his tongue, just as he savored tobacco, black coffee, and whiskey. And of course he knew the dog's name, as he knew my name, and as I knew his. It was the simplest thing in the world to shake hands and be friends.

To hold Dubord's hand was like holding a leather sack filled with chunks of wood. His fingers seemed three times the size of ordinary fingers. He scarcely gripped my hand, but politely allowed me to hold his. Gravely he said, "Pleased to meet you," and then his small blue eyes grew lively behind the round, steel-framed spectacles. "I'd ask you in," he said, "but there ain't much difference yet between out and in. You got time for a drink?" I said I did, and he opened the toolbox and handed me a pint of Four Roses.

His skull was shaped like a cannonball. His jaw was broad and gristly. Everything about him suggested strength and endurance, yet his dominant trait, I soon came to see, was thoughtfulness. He listened, noticed, reflected, though it was apparent, even now, that these deliberations must often have been overwhelmed in his youth by passions of one kind or another. He had come from Quebec at the age of twenty, and for almost two decades had worked in lumber camps as a woodcutter and cook. He had farmed here in this valley, both as a hired hand and on his own—had dug wells, built houses, barns, and sheds, had installed his own electric lines and his own plumbing, had raised animals and crops of all kinds. In middle age he had married a diminutive, high-tempered, rotund, childishly silly, childishly gracious woman. They had never had children. They had never even established a lasting peace. Her crippled mother lived with them in the small house he had built, knitting in an armchair near the TV while her daughter dusted the china knickknacks and photographs of relatives, straightened the paper flowers in their vases, and flattened the paper doilies they had placed under everything. Dubord liked all this, or rather approved it, but felt ill at ease with his heavy boots and oil-stained pants, and spent his days in a shed beside the house. There, surrounded by his hundreds of small tools, he tinkered at the workbench or table saw, repairing things or building them, listening to cassettes of French Canadian fiddle music, and occasionally putting aside the tools to play his own fiddle. The camp in the woods served the same purposes as the shed, but promised longer interludes of peace.

I got to know him that summer and fall, but it was not until winter—our family's third in the little town—that Dubord and I realized that we were friends.

The deep snow of our first winter had made me giddy with excitement. The silence in the woods, the hilly terrain with its many streams, most of them frozen and white, but a few audible with a muted, far-off gurgling under their covering of ice and snow, occasional sightings of the large white snowshoe hares, animal tracks—all this had been a kind of enchantment and had recalled boyhood enjoyments that once had been dear to me. I went through the woods on snowshoes, and Shawno came behind. The following year I discovered the lightweight, highly arched, cross-country skis, my speed was doubled, and our outings became strenuous affairs for the dog. Often he sank to his shoulders and had to bound like a porpoise. Except in the driest, coldest snow, he stopped frequently, and pulling back his lips in a silent snarl, bit away the snow impacted between his toes. His tawny, snow-cleaned, winter-thickened fur looked handsome against the whiteness. When we came to downhill stretches I would speed ahead, and he would rally and follow at a run.

We had taken a turn like this through the woods in our third year, on a sunny, blue-skyed day in March, when I decided to visit Dubord.

I could smell the smoke of his tin chimney before I could see it. Then the cabin came in view. His intricately webbed, gracefully curved snowshoes leaned against the depleted stack of firewood that early in the winter had filled the overhang of the entranceway.

I could hear music. It was the almost martial, furiously rhythmic music of the old country dances—but there seemed to be two fiddles.

Shawno barked and raced ahead . . . and Dubord's pet red squirrel bounded up the woodpile. When I reached the camp, Shawno was dancing on his hind legs barking angrily and complainingly, and the healthy, bright-eyed squirrel was crouching in a phoebe's nest under the roof, looking down with maddening calm. The music stopped, the door opened, and Dubord greeted us cheerfully—actually with a *merry* look on his face.

"You won't get that old squirrel, Shawno," he said. "He's too fast for you. You'll never get 'im. Might's well bark . . .

"Come in," he said. "I just made coffee. Haven't seen those for a while. Where'd you get 'em?"

He meant the skis. He had never seen a manufactured pair, though he had seen many of the eight- and nine-foot handmade skis the Finns had used. He didn't know why (he said later) only the Finns had used them. Everyone else had stayed with snowshoes, which were an Indian invention.

"Nilo Ansden used to take his eggs down to Searles on skis," he said. The Searles he meant was Bob Searles's father. "He took a shortcut one day down that hill 'cross from your place. We had a two-foot storm all night and the day before. He got halfway down and remembered Esther Barden's chicken coop was in the way, but he thought, *There's enough snow to get up on the roof* . . . and there was. Once he was up there there was nothin' to do but jump, so he jumped. Had a packbasket of eggs on's back. Didn't break a one."

In the whole of any winter there are never more than a

few such sunny days, gloriously sunny and blue. One becomes starved for the sun.

He left the door open and we turned our chairs to face the snow and blue sky and the vast expanse of evergreen and hardwood forest. He stirred the coals in the woodstove, opened the draft, and threw in some split chunks of rock maple. There was a delicious swirling all around us of hot, dry currents from the stove and cool, moist currents from the snow and woods. Occasionally a tang of wood smoke came in with the cold air.

As for the fiddle music—"Oh, I was scratchin' away," he said. "I have a lot of fiddle music on the cassettes. I put it on and play along."

His cassette recorder stood on the broad worktable by the window. The violin lay beside it amidst a clutter of tools and TV parts.

"If I hear somebody's got somethin' special or new, I go over an' put it on the recorder. Take a good while to play the ones I got now. You like that fiddle music, Shawno?"—and to me: "That was a schottische you heard comin' in."

He was fond of the dog. He looked at him again and again, and there began a friendship between them that pleased me and that I never cared to interrupt.

Shawno lay on the floor twisting his head this way and that and snapping at a large glossy fly that buzzed around him. He caught it, cracked it with his teeth, and ejected it with a wrinkling of the nose. Eddie laughed and said, "That's right, Shawno, you catch that old bastard fly." The dog got up and went to him and Eddie gave him a piece of the "rat cheese" we had been eating with our coffee. For a long time Shawno sat beside him, resting his head on Eddie's knee.

We laced our coffee with Four Roses whiskey and had second cups. The squirrel looked in at the window, crouching eagerly, its forepaws lifted and tucked in at the wrists, and its feathery long tail arched forward like a canopy over its head.

"I built that platform to feed the birds, but he took over, so I let him have it. That's where the birds eat now."

He pointed to a wooden contraption hanging by a wire from a tree out front. Several chickadees fluttered around it angrily. It was rocking from the weight of the blue jay perched on its edge, a brilliant, unbelievable blue in the sunlight.

Eddie had hinged a tiny window in one of the panels of the side window. He opened it now and laid his hand on the feeding platform, a few peanuts and sunflower seeds on the palm. The squirrel shied away, but came back immediately and proceeded to eat from Eddie's hand, picking up one seed at a time. Shawno went over and barked, and the squirrel snatched up one last morsel and leaped into the eaves. Dubord closed the window, chuckling, and again the dog sat with him, this time stretched at his feet with his chin extended over one wide rubber boot.

I saw his packbasket in the corner. He used it daily to bring in water and whiskey and a few tools. The handle of his axe protruded from the basket.

The basket was of ash strips, such as the Indians make. I had bought several two towns away. Dubord had made this one himself.

"The Indians can take brown ash wherever they find it," he said. "Did you know that? They used to camp every summer on the Folsom place. Diamond National owns it now. There's brown ash down there, downhill goin' toward the pond. I used to trap beaver with one o' the men, and he showed me."

The basket was thirty years old.

He sipped his coffee.

"Have you met Mister Mouse?" he said.

"Who?"

"Don't know if he'll come while Shawno's here."

Smiling like a little boy, he said, "Keep your eyes open, but don't move. Don't even blink. He can see it."

He put a peanut on the two-by-four at the upper edge of

the far wall, stepped back from it and stood there making a strange little whimpering sound. Shawno perked up his ears and became excited, but I whispered to him, *no, no . . . stay.*

Again Dubord made the squeaking sound, sucking air through his lips. Presently, quite soundlessly, a round-eared gray mouse appeared on the ledge, sniffing. It crept forward a few inches and froze, sniffing alertly and angling the delicate long antennae of its whiskers this way and that. It nibbled the peanut rapidly, listening while it ate, its bulging black eyes glinting with light from the windows and the door.

Shawno got to his feet . . . and that huge movement and the sound of his claws on the floor put an end to the performance.

Dubord came back chuckling, and stroked the dog's head.

We stayed for two hours. He talked of his early days in the States, and his years in the woods. I could hear the French Canadian and the Yankee accents alternating in his speech, the one stressing the final syllables, the other drawling them. Shawno sat close to him, sometimes upright with his chin on his knee, sometimes lying flat with his nose near the broad booted foot. Until now all his friendships had been friendships of play. This was a friendship of peace. It was one of those rare occasions on which, perhaps only momentarily, a little family of the spirit is formed.

It was good sapping weather. The days were sunny, the snow melting, the nights cold. When we saw Dubord several days later he was gathering sap from the huge maples near his camp.

A rapidly moving cloud of light-gray smoke rolled over and over in the lower branches of the trees. I skied closer and saw that it was not coming from the cabin, as I had feared, nor was it smoke, but steam from a large tray of bubbling maple sap.

He had shoveled away some snow and had built a fireplace of fieldstones he had gathered in the fall. The sides were lined with scraps of metal. The back had been cut from a sheetmetal stove and was equipped with a metal chimney five feet high. A shallow tray, two feet by four, rested on top of the fieldstone walls. It was from this tray that the clouds of steam were rising.

While I was examining all this Dubord came in sight, plodding blockily on snowshoes, pulling a toboggan that I recognized, since I had helped at all stages in the making of it, first splitting out boards from a squared-off log of ash, then boiling the tips, and finally nailing them around a log to cool and set. On the toboggan were two five-gallon white plastic jugs, each half-filled with sap. A tin funnel bounced against one of them, secured by a wire to its handle.

He glanced at me in a furious and bitter way. I didn't inquire what the trouble was, but took it for granted that he had been quarreling with Nellie. His teeth were clamped and his mouth was pulled down. How long he would have maintained this furious silence I don't know, but it was more than he could do to hold out against the dog. A deep blush suffused his weathered round face. He dropped the toboggan rope, and smiling helplessly bowed his head to the uprearing dog, petting him with both hands and allowing his face to be licked.

He took off the snowshoes and put more wood on the fire. The four-foot strips of white birch—edgings from the turning mill—had been stacked in the fall and covered with boards and scraps of asphalt roofing. Papery white bark still clung to them. The wood was well dried and burned hot—the "biscuit wood" of the old farmhouse kitchens.

The tray was slanted toward one of its forward corners, and there, with his brazing torch, Dubord had attached a little spigot. He drained some syrup into a large spoon, blew on it, and tested it with his finger.

I poured one of the jugs of new sap into the noisily bubbling syrup. The steam was sweet and had a pleasant odor.

Several galvanized buckets stood by the fire and Eddie divided the rest of the sap between two of them. I noticed that just as he had not filled the plastic jugs he did not fill the buckets—an old man's foresight, avoiding loads that might injure him.

I went with him back to the maple trees, and at last he broke his silence.

" 'Twas a damn good farm fifty years ago," he said. "I wanted to buy it but I couldn't meet the price."

The huge, slowly dying maples lined the road. There were smaller trees around them, some in the road itself, but the maples, in season, were leafy, and were well exposed to the sun, and their sap was far richer than that of forest maples. The boiling ratio would be forty to one, or even better.

Buckets, four to a tree, clung to the stout, coarse-barked trunks waist high, as if suspended from a single belt. They hung from short spouts of galvanized metal that had been driven into the tree, and were covered with metal lids that were creased in the middle and looked like roofs.

Since I was helping, we filled the jugs, and soon had sledded sixty gallons to the fire.

Nellie's canary had been killed that morning. The quarrel had followed its death.

She had been cleaning its cage and had let it out to stretch its wings.

"She could've put it in the other cage," he said.

He was stirring the boiling sap with a stick of wood, and in his anger he splashed it again and again.

" 'Twas right there under the bed," he said. "Damn thing shittin' all over the place! If I come in with one speck o' mud on my boots she raises hell! I wanted to go out. 'Don't open the door!' 'Well, put 'im in the cage!' "

He thumped the tray as if he meant to drive holes through it.

"Freddie Latham was outside fillin' the oil tank," he said. "Nellie's mother'd knitted some mittens for the new baby, so Nellie says to me over her shoulder, 'Git Buddy,' and she comes right past me and opens the door. 'Yoo hoo, Freddie.' "

He ground his teeth awhile.

"Git the bird!" he muttered explosively. "What'd she expect me t'do, fly up an' catch it? Damn thing flew out the door right behind her and she didn't even notice. She opened the porch door and it flew out that one too. Damn! If I had a stick o' wood in my hand I'd heaved it at 'er! You could o' heard her down t'village. 'Save Buddy! Here, Buddy! Git Buddy!'"

Dubord glared at me. "Damn thing perched on the roof o' the shed," he said, "I got some birdseed in my hand and got the ladder and started up. Freddie hauled out my smeltin' net and tried t'hand it to me. Fat lot o' good that did! Soon as Buddy saw me gittin' close he flew over an' perched on the ridgepole o' the house. Then he flew up to the antenna, and Nellie's whistlin' to him an' suckin' her lips. 'Eddie, git that canary record, maybe if we play it Buddy'll come down.' Now ain't that a goddamn smart idea! If he could hear it up there what'd he want t'come down for?

"By the time I come off the ladder the bird'd flew up to the electric wire. He was just gittin' settled . . . wham! Some damn ol' red-tail hawk been watchin' the whole thing. I never seen 'im. Where he come from I don't know. Couple o' yella feathers come down like snowflakes. I thought, here's your canary, Nellie. An' I thought, enjoy your dinner, mister hawk. You just saved me two hund'd dolluhs."

Eddie faced me and stood absolutely still. "Yessuh!" he said. "That's what I said! Two hund'd dolluhs! That's what I spent for birdseed! I'm tellin' the truth, I ain't makin' it up! And I ain't sayin' Buddy et that much, I'm saying we BOUGHT that much! You seen him do that Christly trick! You and the Missus seen that trick the first time you come down. Sure you did! You had the girl with you. . . ."

The trick he was referring to was something Nellie had taught the bird, or had discovered, namely, that when she put his cage up to the feeding platform at the window, he would pick up a seed from the floor and hold it between the bars, and the chickadees outside would jostle one another until one had plucked the seed from his beak, and then Buddy would get another. Nellie had loved to show this off.

Eddie was glaring at me. "WHERE DID YOU THINK THEM BIRDS COME FROM?" he shouted. "We had t'have them birds ON HAND! We was feedin' a whole damn flock right through the year so Buddy could do his Christly trick two or three times a month!"

He paced back and forth by the evaporating tray grinding his teeth and glaring. "I guess I warn't upset 'nough t'suit 'er," he said. "God damn! Hasn't she got a tongue!"

One last wave of anger struck him and he howled louder than before, but there was a plaintive note in his voice and he almost addressed it to the sky.

"IT WAS NELLIE HER OWN GODDAMN RATTLE-BRAIN SELF OPENED THE DOOR!" he cried.

And then he calmed down. That is to say, he walked around the steaming tray panting and lurching and thumping the sides and bottom with the little stick.

He had brought some blankets in his packbasket and was planning to spend the night.

He drained off some thick syrup into a small creamery pail and set it aside to cool. He drained a little more into an old enamel frying pan and with a grunt bent down and thrust it under the evaporator tray right among the flames and coals. After it had bubbled and frothed awhile, he knelt again and patted the snow, and scattered the hot syrup over it. When Shawno and I went home I had a jar of syrup for Patricia and a bag of maple taffy for the kids.

At around two o'clock the next afternoon I answered the phone and heard the voice of Nellie Dubord, whose salutation, calling or receiving, is always *Yeh-isss,* as if she were emphatically agreeing with some previous remark.

Eddie had not come home. She knew that he had taken blankets to the camp, but she was worried.

"I just don't feel right," she said. "I can't see any smoke

up there. I should be able to see the chimney smoke, though maybe not. Ain't he boilin' sap? I should see that smoke too. Can you see it up there? Take a look. I guess I'm bein' foolish, but I don't know . . . I just don't feel right."

I went upstairs and looked from the west windows. There wasn't any smoke. I skied across.

There was no activity at the cabin, no smoke or shimmering waves of heat, no fire out front. Shawno sniffed at the threshold. He chuffed and snorted, sniffed again, then drew back and barked. He went forward again and lowered his head and sniffed.

The door was locked. I went around and looked in the window. Dubord lay on the floor on his back beside the little platform bed. He was dressed except for his boots. The blankets had come away from the bed, as if he had clutched them at the moment of falling. I battered the door with a piece of stovewood and went to him. He was breathing faintly, but his weathered face was as bloodless as putty.

He was astonishingly heavy. I got him onto the bed, covered him with the blankets and our two coats, and skied to the road. I saw his car there and cursed myself for not having searched him for the key: the nearest house was three-quarters of a mile away. I telephoned there for an ambulance, and made two other calls besides, then went back and put him on the toboggan and set out pulling him over the packed but melting trail, dreadfully slowly.

I hadn't gone twenty paces before the men I had called appeared. The two elder were carpenters, the young man was their helper. They were running toward us vigorously, and I felt a surge of hope.

But it was more than hope that I felt at that moment. Something priceless was visible in their faces, and I have been moved by the recollection of it again and again. It was the purified, electric look of whole-hearted response. The men came running toward us vigorously, lifting their knees in the snow and swinging their arms, and that unforgettable look was on their faces.

Ten days later Patricia, the children, and I went with Nellie to the hospital. The children weren't allowed to go up, and Nellie sat with them in the lobby.

Dubord was propped up by pillows and was wearing a hospital smock that left his arms bare. I was used to the leathery skin of his hands and face; the skin of his upper arms, which were still brawny, was soft and white, one would say *shockingly* white.

"Sicker cats than this have got well and et another meal," he said. And then, gravely, "Nellie told me you went in for me. I'm much obliged to you."

"Did the girls like their candy?" he asked Patricia. She answered him promptly, but it took me a moment to realize that he was referring to the maple taffy, the last thing he had made before the heart attack. A few moments later he said to me, "How's my dog?" and I told him how the dog had known at once that something was wrong. A rapt, shy look came over his face.

A neighbor leaned in at the doorway, Earl Sawyer. He joined us, and after chatting briefly, said to Eddie, "Well, you won't be seein' Blackie no more."

Dubord asked him what had happened.

"I did away with him," said Sawyer. "I had to. He went after porcupines three times in the last two weeks. Three times I took him to the vet, eighteen dollars each time. I can't be doin' that. Then he went and did it again, so I took him out and shot 'im, quills and all."

Sawyer was upset.

"If he can't learn," he said. ". . . I can't be doin' that. Damn near sixty dollars in two weeks, and there's a leak in the goddamn cellar. He was a nice dog, though. He was a good dog otherwise."

Sawyer was thirty-three or -four, but his face was worn and tense. He worked ten hours a day as a mechanic, belonged to the fire department, and was serving his second term as road commissioner. He had built his own house and was raising two children.

"I don't blame you," said Dubord. "You'd be after 'im every day."

"He went out an' did it again," said Sawyer.

There was silence for a while.

"I can't see chainin' a dog," Sawyer said. "I'd rather not have one."

"A chained dog ain't worth much," Eddie said.

Months went by before Eddie recovered his spirits. But in truth he never did entirely recover them. I could see a sadness in him that hadn't been there before, and a tendency to sigh where once he had raged.

The change in his life was severe. He sold the new cabin he had liked so much, and spent more time in the little shed beside the house. I drove down to see him frequently, but it wasn't the same as stopping by on skis or walking through the woods. Nor was he allowed to drink whiskey anymore. Nor did I always remember to bring the dog.

A walk with Ida. Wandering dogs.

Most of the snow was gone by the end of that April. One night Shawno failed to appear for supper, and there was no response when I called from the porch. I called again an hour later, and this time I saw movement in the shadows just beyond the cars. Why wasn't he running toward me? I went out, calling to him. He crept forward a few paces on his belly, silently, and then lay still. When I stood over him, he turned his head away. His jowls and nose were packed with quills. He couldn't close his mouth. There were quills in his tongue and hanging down from his palate. The porcupine had been a small one, the worst kind for a dog.

He seemed to be suffering more from shame than from the pain of the quills. He wouldn't meet my eyes, and the once or twice that he did he lowered his head and looked up woefully, the whites showing beneath the irises.

I was afraid that he might run off, and so I picked him up and carried him into the house. This too was mortifying. His eyes skittered from side to side. What an abject entrance for this golden creature, who was used to bounding in proudly!

The black tips of the quills are barbed with multiple, hair-fine points. The quills are shaped like torpedoes and are hollow-shafted, so that the pressure of the flesh around them draws them deeper into the victim's body. They are capable of migrating then to heart, eyes, liver . . .

He wanted to obey me. He lay flat under the floor lamp. But every time I touched a quill with the pliers, a helpless *tic* of survival jerked away his head.

Ida was shocked. He was the very image of The Wounded, The Victimized. It was as if some malevolent tiny troll had shot him full of arrows. She knelt beside him and threw her arms around his neck, and in her high, passionate voice of childgoodness repeated the words both Patricia and I had already said: "Don't worry, Shawno, we'll get them out for you!"—but with this difference: that he drew back the corners of his open mouth, panted slightly, glanced at her, and thumped his tail.

I took him to the vet the next day, and brought him back unconscious in the car.

I thought of Sawyer and his black Labrador, and saw from still another point of view the luxury of our lives. I didn't go to bed exhausted every night, I wasn't worried about a job, a mortgage, a repair bill, a doctor's bill, unpaid loans at the bank. And here was another of the homely luxuries our modest security brought us: he lay on the back seat with his eyes closed, his mouth open, his tongue out, panting unconsciously.

Great quantities of saliva came from his mouth, and the seat was wet when we moved him.

Spring comes slowly and in many stages. The fields go through their piebald phase again and again, in which the browns and blacks of grass and wet earth are mingled with streaks of white —and then everything is covered again with the moist, characteristically dimpled snow of spring. But soon the sun comes back, a warm wind blows, and in half a day the paths in the woods and the ruts in our long dirt road are streaming with water.

Black wasps made their appearance on a warm day in March, then vanished. This was the day that a neighbor left his shovel upright in the snow in the morning and in the evening found it on bare ground. It was the day that a man in his seventies, with whom I had stopped to talk while he picked up twigs and shreds of bark from his south-facing yard, turned away abruptly and pointed with his finger, saying, "Look! Is that a bee? Yes, by gurry! It's a bee! The first one!"

But there was more rain and more snow, and then came the flooding we had hoped to be spared, as the stream jumped its banks and poured down our lower road, to a depth, this time, of two feet. For several days we came home through the woods with our groceries in packbaskets, but again the snow shriveled and sank into the ground, and high winds dried the mud. I saw a crowd of black starlings foraging in a brown field, and heard the first cawing of crows. The leaves of the gray birches uncurled. There were snow flurries, sun again, and the ponies followed the sun all day, lolling on the dormant grass or in the mud. Shawno, too, basked in the sun, like a tourist on a cruise ship. He lay blinking on a snowbank with his tongue extended, baking above and cooling below. I pulled last year's leaves out of culverts, and opened channels in the dooryard mud so that the standing water could reach the ditch. Early one morning six Canada geese flew over my head, due north, silently, flying low; and then just before dusk I heard a partridge drumming in the woods.

Several days after Easter, when the garden was clear of snow and the chives were three inches high, Ida came striding into my room, striking her feet noisily on the floor and grinning.

"Wake up, dad!" she called. "It's forty-forty!"

She was seven. I had told her the night before how when she was four years old and could not count or tell time she had invented that urgent hour, forty-forty, and had awakened me one morning proclaiming it.

When she saw that I was awake, she said eagerly, "Look out the window, daddy! Look!"

I did, and saw a world of astonishing whiteness. Clinging, heavy snow had come down copiously in the night and had stopped before dawn. There was no wind at all. Our white garden was bounded by a white rail fence, every post of which was capped by a mound of white. The pines and firs at the wood's edge were almost entirely white, and the heavy snow had weighted down their upward-sweeping branches, giving the trees a sharp triangular outline and a wonderfully festive look.

The whiteness was everywhere. Even the sky was white, and the just-risen sun was not visible as a disk at all but as a lovely haze of orange between whitenesses I knew to be hills.

An hour later Ida, Shawno, and I were walking through the silent, utterly motionless woods. We took the old county road, which for decades now had been a mere trail, rocky and overgrown. It went directly up the wooded high ridge of Folsom Hill and then emerged into broad, shaggy fields that every year became smaller as the trees moved in. We gathered blueberries there in the summer, and in the fall apples and grapes, but for almost two years now we had been going to the old farm for more sociable reasons.

After breakfast Ida had wanted to hear stories of her earlier childhood, and now as we walked through the woods she asked for them again, taking my bare hand with her small gloved one, and saying, "Daddy, tell me about when I was a kid."

"You mean like the time you disappeared in the snow?"

This was a story I had told her before, and that she delighted in hearing.

"Yes!" she said.

"Well . . . that was it—you disappeared. You were two years old. You were sitting on my lap on the toboggan and we went down the hill beside the house. We were going really fast, and the toboggan turned over and you flew into a snowbank and disappeared."

She laughed and said, "You couldn't even see me?"

"Nope. The snow was light and fluffy and very deep."

"Not even my head?"

"Not even the tassel on your hat."

"How did you find me?"

"I just reached down and there you were, and I pulled you out."

She laughed triumphantly and said, "Tell me some more."

While we talked in this fashion the dog trotted to and fro among the snow-heavy close-set trees, knocking white cascades from bushes and small pines. Often he would range out of sight, leaping over deadfalls and crouching under gray birches that had been pressed almost flat by the snows of previous years, and then he would come back to us, sniffing at the six-inch layer of wet snow, and chuffing and snorting to clear his nose. Occasionally, snorting still more vigorously, he would thrust his snout deep into the snow, and then step back and busily pull away snow and matted leaves with his paws.

Watching all this, I understood once again that the world of his experience was unimaginably different from the world of mine. What were the actual sensations of his sense of smell? How could I possibly know them? And how were those olfactory shapes and meanings structured in his memory? Snout, eyes, tongue, ears, belly—all were close to the ground; his entire life was close to it, and mine was not. I knew that in recent weeks complex odors had sprung up in the woods, stirring him and drawing him excitedly this way and that. And I could see that last night's snowfall had suppressed the odors and was thwarting him, and that was all, really, that I could know.

After three-quarters of a mile the trail grew steep. We couldn't walk side by side; I let Ida go in front, and our conversation now consisted of the smiles we exchanged when she looked back at me over her shoulder. I watched her graceful, well-proportioned little body in its blue one-piece snowsuit, and felt a wonderful happiness and peace.

Milky sky appeared between the snowy tops of the trees. A few moments later there was nothing behind the trees but the unmarked white of a broad field—at which moment there occurred one of those surprises of country life that are dazzling in much the way that works of art are dazzling, but that occur on a scale no artwork can imitate. I called to Ida, and she too cried aloud. The dog turned to us and came closer, lifting his head eagerly.

The sight that so astonished us was this: several hundred starlings, perhaps as many as five hundred, plump and black, were scattered throughout the branches of one of the maples at the wood's edge. The branches themselves were spectacular enough, thickened by snow and traced elegantly underneath by thin black lines of wet bark, but the surprising numbers of the birds and their glossy blackness against the white of the field were breathtaking.

I threw a stick at them. I couldn't resist. The entire tree seemed to shimmer and crumble, then it burst, and black sparks fluttered upward almost in the shape of a plume of smoke. The plume thinned and tilted, then massed together again with a wheeling motion, from which a fluttering ribbon emerged, and the entire flock streamed away in good order down the field to another tree.

Shawno, who had remained baffled and excluded, resumed his foraging. He stopped and raised his head alertly, then leaped forward in a bounding, enthusiastic gallop, and in a moment was out of sight. When Ida and I came to that very place, she too brightened, and with no more ceremony than had been shown me by the dog, let go of my hand and ran.

And if I had been a child, I would have followed, since it was here, at this very point, that due to the lay of the land, that is, the acoustics of the field, the playful gaiety of two voices could be heard quite clearly, a girl's voice shouting, "I *did*, Leo! I *did!*" and the voice of her brother, who was eight, replying, "Ha, ha, ha!" and then both shouting, "Shawno! Shawno!" I stood there and watched Ida's diminutive figure as she ran by herself across the snowy field toward the house that had not yet come in sight.

I looked back for a moment down the long slope of the field, toward the woods, the way we had come. I had intended to look for the birds, but our three sets of footprints caught my eye, and I couldn't help but smile at the tale they told. They were like diagrams of our three different ways of being in the world. Mine seemed logical, or responsible, or preoccupied: they kept on going straight ahead. Ida's footprints, in contrast to mine, went out to the sides here and there; they performed a few curlicues and turns, and were even supplanted at one place by a star-shaped bodyprint where she had thrown herself laughing onto the snow.

But the footprints of the dog! . . . this was a trail that was wonderful to see! One might take it as erratic wandering, or as continual inspiration, or as continual attraction, which may come to the same thing. It consisted of meandering huge loops, doublings, zigzags, festoons. . . . The whole was traveling as a system in the direction I had chosen, yet it remained a system and was entirely his own.

The voices of the children grew louder. I saw the dark gray flank of the made-over barn that was now their home, and then saw the children themselves, running with the dog among the whitened trees of the orchard.

These two, Gretl and Leo Carpenter, together with Ida and me and Eddie Dubord, complete the quintet of Shawno's five great loves.

Gretl is Ida's age, Leo a year older. They are the children of Waldo and Aldona Carpenter, whom Patricia and I have known for years. But I have known Waldo since the end of World War II, when we both arrived in New York City from small towns to the west.

Aldona was evidently waiting for me. She was standing in the doorway, and when she saw me she beckoned. I hadn't planned to stop, except to leave Ida and the dog, since in all likelihood Waldo would be working, but Aldona had no sooner waved to me than the broad window right above her swung open and Waldo, too, beckoned to me, cupping his hands and shouting. Aldona stepped out and looked up at him, and they smiled at one another, though his expression wasn't happy.

Aldona was fifteen years younger than Waldo. By the time I came into the kitchen she was standing at the stove turning thick strips of bacon with a fork.

"Waldo was up all night," she said to me. "I hope you're hungry enough to eat." The large round table was set for three.

She looked rested and fresh—it was one of the days, in fact, that her entirely handsome and appealing person seemed actually to be beautiful. She wore a dark blue skirt, a light sweater-blouse of gray wool, and loose-fitting boots from L. L. Bean. Her long brown hair, which was remarkably thick and glossy, was covered with a kerchief of deep blue.

She said to me, in a lower voice, "We *are* going back."

She meant back to New York.

I had known that they wanted to. Waldo's excitement, coming here, had had nothing to do with country life. He had been fleeing New York and an art world that had become meaningless to him. His own painting, moreover, after two periods of great success, was in a crisis of spirit, and he had begun to mistrust his virtuosity. Country life had relieved him, but something was lacking, and he had said to me several times in the last two months, "We won't be staying forever."

I wasn't surprised, then, by Aldona's remark. Nevertheless, it was saddening, and I knew that the loss for Ida would be severe.

I said as much to Aldona.

"We'll certainly miss you," she said. "All of you. All of us. But we'll be back every summer."

"When are you going?"

"Soon. I don't know."

"How do the children feel about it?"

"We haven't told them yet," she said. "They've been happy here . . . but there's so much to do in New York . . ."

I could hear Waldo walking on the floor above our heads, and moving something. I asked him, shouting, if he needed a hand. "I'll be right down," he called back.

Aldona looked into the oven. She closed it quickly, but warm air and the delicious fragrance of yeast rolls reached me.

The kitchen had been the stalls of the old barn. The ceiling was low and was heavily beamed. Narrow horizontal windows ran the length of two sides and gave fine views of our mountains, though today nothing could be seen but snowy woods and a misty white sky. Intricate leaves of plants, overlapping this way and that from suspended pots, were silhouetted against the whiteness. By the kitchen door stood a battered upright piano, on which Waldo, with his large hands, played Scott Joplin. At the far end of the room, beyond the open stairs that led to Waldo's studio, a large window was fitted with a window seat, on which were a cushion and many pillows. There were plants hanging in front of the window. A stool was drawn up to a small, neatly arranged table, on which there were some books and some sheets of paper, jars of ink, tubes of paint, and an earthenware crock holding a cluster of small brushes. For two years, in this pleasant nook, Aldona, who was fluent in Lithuanian, had been translating a cycle of folktales for a children's book. She had done a great many gouache illustrations, and I knew that the project was nearly finished.

I heard Waldo on the stairs. He stopped part way down, and leaning forward called across to me, "Do you want to see something?"

After the whites and blacks and evergreen greens of the woods the colors of his work were dazzling.

Small abstract paintings on paper were pinned to the white work wall, as were clippings from magazines and some color wheels he had made recently. Larger paintings on canvas, still in progress, leaned here and there, and two were positioned on the wall for work. A stack of finished paintings, all of which I had seen, leaned against the wall in the corner.

Waldo had placed the new painting on the seat of a chair, and we stood side by side studying it. The paint was still wet and gave off a pleasant odor of oil and turpentine.

Waldo's manner was that of an engineer. Physically he was imposing. He was large but trim, with a stern, black-browed, bristly-mustached face that was actually a forbidding face, or would have been except that an underlying good humor was never entirely out of sight. When he was alight with that humor, which after all was fairly often, one saw an astonishing sweetness and charm. Aldona, at such times, would rest her hand on his shoulder, or stroke the back of his head; and the children, if they were near, would come closer, and perhaps climb into his lap.

The studio windows were sheeted with a plastic that gave the effect of frosted glass, shutting off the outside and filling the space with a shadowless white light. Beyond one of those milky oblongs we heard a sudden shouting and loud barking. Ida and Gretl were shouting together, "Help, Shawno! Help!" in tones that were almost but not quite urgent, and the dog was barking notes of indignation, disapproval, and complaint, a medley that occurred nowhere else but in this game, for I knew without seeing it that Leo was pretending to beat the girls with his fist, and was looking back at the dog, who in a moment would spring forward and carefully yet quite excitedly seize Leo's wrist with his teeth.

"It's a total dud," Waldo said dispassionately, "but it's interesting, isn't it? Kerosene light does such weird things to the colors. It's like working under a filter. Look how sour and acidic it is. It's overcontrolled, too, and at the same time there are accidents everywhere. That's what gives it that moronic look. I should have known better—I've done it before. *When you rob the eye you rob the mind.*"

Abruptly he turned to me and lowered his voice.

"We're going back to the city," he said. "I'm going down in a couple of days and see what has to be done. . . ."

I knew that he had not sublet his studio, which he didn't rent but owned—a floor-through in a large loft building.

"We haven't told the kids yet," he said, "but I think they'll take it pretty well. There's so much to do there. . . ."

Aldona's voice came up from below. We cut short our conversation and went down into the warm kitchen, the very air of which was delicious now with the smells of bacon, rolls, just-brewed coffee, and fried eggs.

The rosy, bright-faced children stormed in just as we sat down. Leo and Gretl clamored for juice, while Ida looked at them joyfully. Shawno came with them. He trotted to Aldona, and to Waldo, and to me, greeting us eagerly but without arresting his motion or taking his eyes from the children. "Hi. Hi," they said to me. "Hi, daddy," said Ida. All three tilted their heads, took on fuel, and with the dog bounding among them rushed out again as noisily as they had entered.

The sky was beginning to clear when I left half an hour later, and it was blue now, but a pale, wintry blue. A light, raw breeze was blowing.

I crossed the dooryard without calling to the children. They were throwing snowballs at Shawno, except for Ida, who was tagging along. Gretl hit him and shouted, "Bull's eye!" and witty Leo, throwing quickly but missing widely, shouted, "Dog's eye!" They dodged among the budded but leafless apple trees, while the dog, who didn't understand that he was their target, kept leaping and twisting, biting the snowballs with swift snaps that reduced them to fragments.

I went alone down the snowy road to the right, toward the river. Little clumps of snow were falling wetly from the roadside trees.

I had been cheerful coming through the woods with Ida and the dog, and cheerful talking with Waldo and Aldona, though their imminent departure was troubling, but now as I walked away alone, I passed into a mood of sadness-without-a-present-cause, a twilight mood I knew to be somewhat obsessional, and that I had learned not to take so very seriously, yet often I had to pass through it to reach the solitude of my work.

My footprints were the only markings between Waldo's house and the larger road, but as soon as I made the turn I found myself walking between the muddy tracks of a car. In ten minutes I stood on the high ledge that overlooked the river.

The river was broad in this stretch, and was flowing heavily. The water was dark. Huge pieces of ice were strewn in a continuous line on the steep bank across from me. The ice had been dirty and interspersed with debris a week ago, but now the entire bank was white.

Two miles downriver lay the town, on which all such villages as ours were dependent. There were its hundreds of houses, its red roofs and black roofs, snow-covered now, its white clapboard sidings, its large, bare-limbed shade trees, all following the slopes of the hills. I could see the gleaming bell towers and white spires of the four churches, the plump wooden cupola of the town hall, also white, and several red-brick business buildings. It was a lovely sight from this height above the river, but it no longer stirred me. The town was spiritless and dull, without a public life of any kind, or much character of its own, but the usual brand names in the stores and the usual cars on the streets.

Just this side of the town, the timbered latticework of a railroad trestle crossed the river high in the air, emerging from evergreens on one bank and plunging into evergreens on the other.

I had grown up in a town of hills like these. At the top of one, in the branches of a large maple, my friends and I had built a platform. I was then just twelve. I used to lie there alone at times, looking out through the leaves, dreaming of the future, except that there weren't any dreams, or rather the dreams consisted entirely of the marvelous town that I could see in the distance: white houses in a sea of trees, rising up in terraces on both sides of a valley. The town was larger than ours, more various, and more attractive. A white, winding highway led to it through a vista of wooded hills, large pastures, and cultivated fields. To see all this was tantamount, really, to dreaming awake. If there were events in those reveries I have forgotten them, but I remember the almost painful yet joyful yearning stirred by that sight.

Halfway to the trestle before me now the hills gave way to lowland for a short distance. There must have been oxbow bends here at one time, but the river had jumped them and simplified its course, and now a sweeping arc of water bounded a large flat field. Black-and-white cows, a good-sized herd, moved almost motionlessly across their white pasture toward the river.

There came a loud metallic scraping and banging from the gravel pit below me. A bucket loader was scooping up gravel. It swiveled and showered the stones heavily into a waiting truck, which crouched and shuddered under the impact. Another truck, as I watched, drove down the long incline to the riverbank.

I went home by the same route, thinking now chiefly of the work that I had in hand.

Shawno and the children were still playing, but they were no longer running. Ida and Gretl were holding the two sides of a flattened cardboard box, quite large, and Leo, wielding a hammer, was nailing it to the rails of the broken hay wain by the house, apparently to be the roof of a hut. The dog sat near them, more or less watching. I didn't call or wave, but Shawno saw me. He responded with a start . . . and then he did something I had seen him do before and had found so touching I couldn't resent it. He pretended that he hadn't seen me. He turned his head and yawned, stood up and stretched, dropped abruptly to the ground with his chin on his paws, and then just as abruptly stood up again and moved out of sight around the house. What a display of doggy craftiness! It makes me smile to remember it—even though I must now say that this was the last that I saw him in the fullness of his life. I did see him again, but by our bedtime that night he was dead.

I went back alone through the woods, walking on the footprints we had made that morning. In a scant three hours the snow had shriveled and become wetter. It was no deeper than three inches now, and was falling noisily from the trees, leaving the branches wet and glistening.

At the bottom of the first hill, where I had to jump a little stream, and where that morning I had lifted Ida, I noticed a complicated track: the footprints of a deer and of two dogs. The deer had gone somewhere along the stream and then had come back, running, evidently pursued by the dogs.

Instead of going home, I turned in to the little field at the far end of which my cabin studio was situated. Everything was quiet, the fresh snow untouched. I was halfway across the field when I caught a movement in the sky. High up, drawing a broad white line behind it, a military jet drifted soundlessly. A moment later the thunderclap of the sonic boom startled me . . . and as if it had brought them into being, two dogs stepped out of the woods behind my cabin. Or rather, one stepped out, a brown-and white collie, and came toward me. The other, a solemn-looking rabbit hound, stood motionless among the trees.

I thought I recognized the collie and called to it. It came a few steps, and then a few steps more. It stood still when it heard my voice, then it turned and went back to the other dog, and both vanished into the woods.

I built a fire in the cabin, in the cast-iron stove, and spent the rest of the day at my work.

Before the house.

As was my custom, whether I had done the cooking or not, I mixed some scraps and pan rinsings with dry food and went to the door to call Shawno, who ate when we did and in the same room. Ida had come home that afternoon with Patricia, but Shawno had not.

Half an hour later, after we had finished eating, and while the water was heating for coffee, I went outside again and called him, but this time I went across the road and stood before the barn. The lay of the land was such that in this position, and with the help of that huge sounding board, my voice would carry to Waldo's fields, at least to the sharp ears of the dog. I shouted repeatedly. As I went back to the house I thought I saw movement on the woods road we had traveled that morning. I was expecting to see him come leaping toward me, but nothing happened and I went into the house.

We finished our coffee and dessert. Liza was staying overnight with the twins who had become her friends. Patricia sat on the sofa with Jacob and Ida and read first a picture book and then a story of Ernest Thompson Seton's, which enchanted Ida and put Jacob to sleep.

I telephoned Aldona. She said that the dog had left them shortly after Patricia had come in the car for Ida. He had stayed like that often with Leo and Gretl and had come home through the woods at suppertime.

I put the porch light on and went across to the barn again. I was preparing to shout when I saw him in the shadows of the road. A turbulence of alarm, a controlled panic raced through me, and I ran to him calling.

He lay on his belly. His head was erect, but just barely, and was not far above the ground. He pulled himself forward with his front paws, or tried to, but no motion resulted. His hind legs were spread limply behind him. His backbone seemed inert.

I knelt beside him and took his head on my knees. He was breathing so faintly that I doubted if any air was reaching his lungs. I heard my own voice saying in high-pitched, grievously astonished tones, "Oh dog, dog . . ."

I ran my hand down his body. Near his lower ribcage, even in the shadows, I could see a dark mass that here and there glistened dully. It was smooth and soft, and there jutted out of it numerous fine points sharper than a saw. I was touching the exit wound of a large-caliber bullet.

I put my face close to his and stroked his cheek. He was looking straight ahead with a serious, soft, dim gaze. He gave a breath that sounded like a sigh because it wasn't followed by another breath, and instantaneously he was heavy to the touch.

I stayed there a long while with his head on my knees, from time to time crying like a child.

I heard the front door open and heard Patricia calling me. A moment later she was kneeling in the mud beside me saying, "Oh, oh, oh . . ." in a voice of compassion and surprise.

We conferred briefly, and I went into the house.

Ida sat on the sofa, in the light of the floor lamp, looking at the pictures in the Seton book. Jacob lay asleep at the other end of the sofa.

I said to her, "Ida, something has happened . . ." and knelt in front of her. She saw that I had been crying, and her face became grave.

I said, "Shawno has been hurt very badly." I did not want to say to her that he was dead. "He's out front," I said. "Come."

She said, "Okay" quickly, never taking her eyes from mine. She gave me her hand and we went outside, into the road, where Patricia still knelt beside him just beyond the light from the porch. She was bowed above him and was stroking him. She looked up as we approached, and held out one hand for Ida, but with the other kept stroking his head, neck, and shoulders.

In the morning, though she had cried herself to sleep the night before, Ida asked Patricia, "Is Shawno dead?" and hearing her say, "Yes, honey, he's dead," threw herself on the sofa, sobbing. We explained to her that Shawno had been killed because he was chasing deer. She understood very little of that, but didn't question us until weeks later. She thought about it probably for years.

I went out after we had eaten and tested the ground with a spade. I could dig down only six or seven inches; after that the ground was frozen.

All three children came outside. Ida had hugged him the night before, and had cried at breakfast, but now she only stared. I too looked without much feeling at the wet and muddy corpse, though when I glanced uphill toward the barn my expectation of seeing Shawno come running into sight was so complete that the fact of his death was more real in my thoughts than in the motionless body on the ground, which in some way seemed to be an impostor.

I had dug a temporary grave under an apple tree near the sauna. We wrapped him in some old blankets and plastic sheets and laid him in the damp depression. I had thought of performing some sort of ceremony, but I decided against it. We said goodbye to him, covered his wrapped body with soil and rocks, and went back to the house.

Two months later we got a golden retriever, and I made

a point of saying to Ida, "He's not Shawno, honey, he can't be —but he's a real nice pup."

Her acceptance of the new dog was similar to mine: she simply didn't invest it with so much love, didn't draw it so ardently into relation as in her great love she had drawn Shawno.